ZOMBIE
APOCALYPSE!
HORROR HOSPITAL

Lewisham and Greenwich **NHS**
NHS Trust

University Hospital
Lewisham

ZOMBIE APOCALYPSE!
HORROR HOSPITAL

MARK MORRIS
CREATED BY STEPHEN JONES

ROBINSON

RUNNING PRESS
PHILADELPHIA · LONDON

Constable & Robinson Ltd
55–56 Russell Square
London WC1B 4HP
www.constablerobinson.com

First published in the UK by Robinson,
An imprint of Constable & Robinson Ltd, 2014

Zombie Apocalypse! Horror Hospital
© Stephen Jones and Mark Morris 2014

Photographic memento mori copyright © Smith & Jones 2014

"Zombie Apocalypse!" and "ZA!"
© Stephen Jones. All rights reserved.

A copy of the British Library Cataloguing in
Publication Data is available from the British Library

ISBN 978-1-47211-066-4 (paperback)
ISBN 978-1-47211-079-4 (ebook)

1 3 5 7 9 10 8 6 4 2

First published in the United States in 2014 by Running Press Book Publishers,
A Member of the Perseus Books Group

Books published by Running Press are available at special discounts for bulk purchases in the
United States by corporations, institutions, and other organizations. For more information,
please contact the Special Markets Department at the Perseus Books Group, 2300 Chestnut
Street, Suite 200, Philadelphia, PA 19103, or call (800) 810-4145, ext. 5000, or email special.
Markets@perseusbooks.com.

US ISBN: 978-0-7624-5232-3
US Library of Congress Control Number: 2014931618

10 9 8 7 6 5 4 3 2 1
Digit on the right indicates the number of this printing

Running Press Book Publishers
2300 Chestnut Street
Philadelphia, PA 19130-4371

Visit us on the web!
www.runningpress.com

Printed and bound in the UK

11:26 pm

CAT HARRIS WAS thinking about bridesmaids' dresses when the woman ran out in front of her car.

More specifically, she was wondering whether the dresses should have bows or not and, if so, what size those bows should be. She didn't want the girls to look cutesy, but neither did she want them to look too plain. She was already wondering whether she'd made a mistake in choosing the peach over the maroon, but the girls themselves – especially little Emily – had favoured the lighter colour, as had Cat's mother, who'd declared with horror that the maroon made the girls "look like blood clots".

Cat still wasn't sure, though. She'd thought the maroon dramatic, whereas wasn't the peach a bit wishy-washy, not to mention predictable? She didn't want to look back on her wedding photos in years to come, only to regretfully conclude that she and her friends had resembled giant meringues.

Six weeks on Saturday. She couldn't believe that the wedding was so close. After months of planning, it suddenly seemed to have rushed up on her. The framework was in place, of course, but her head was buzzing with the decisions that still had to

I

be made. In the next few days she would be finalizing details with the caterers, the DJ, the photographer, the car hire firm and the hotel in Venice where she and Ed were spending their honeymoon.

It didn't help that the economy was so uncertain, the country riven by strikes and cutbacks. There were times when Cat felt it would be a miracle if everything went according to plan. She kept expecting to be told that one of the companies supplying some vital component of her celebrations had gone bust, or that the hotel where the reception was due to be held had been forced, like many others, to close down.

It was bad enough at work. NHS funding had always been tight, but this current government didn't even *pretend* to give a shit about the health of the nation. There was no denying that the country was going to the dogs; her Dad had said it was becoming a "totalitarian regime", like Nazi Germany or Stalin's Russia. And despite the suppression of media coverage, everyone knew what was *really* going on. You couldn't hide something like the Trafalgar Square massacre, no matter how many people said they couldn't believe such a thing could happen in dear old Blighty.

In the present climate Cat was nervous about working nights, but she knew that everyone had to take their turn, plus she needed the money. And in some ways the night shifts *were* easier, because the curfew meant that the roads were quieter, less congested. Not that she considered that much of a bonus. Maybe she was being silly, but she found the silent streets eerie, as if the country had a kind of "calm-before-the-storm" atmosphere about it. It was like that weird stillness you get before the thunder rumbles and the rains batter down.

Cat wished that everything could just get back to normal, to how it used to be. But she couldn't imagine how it ever would.

At least she didn't live far from work. Ten minutes' drive at the most. And it was an easy route. From Greenwich it was pretty much straight down Lewisham Road, which then became Lewisham High Street. The only dodgy bit was the area near that church, All Hallows, which was due to be pulled down to make way for one of those Festival of Britain sites. There'd been quite a few protests around there lately, some of which had turned violent. Twice this week Cat had been stopped on her way to work by armed police – that SO22 mob – asking for ID. They'd been civil enough, especially when they found out she was a nurse at the hospital, but she still found their presence intimidating.

She wasn't sure what she thought about this New Festival of Britain thing. She'd been so preoccupied with her wedding plans that she hadn't given it much thought. She felt it was a shame that the Olympics had been cancelled – especially for all those poor athletes who'd been training so hard – and she supposed, with the country the way it was, the Festival, which had been brought in to replace it, was nothing but a poor substitute, not to mention a waste of money that could have been diverted more effectively elsewhere – like to the National Health Service, for example.

Ed and her Dad were angrier about it than she was, though. Ed called it a national disgrace and said it was like trying to disguise the stench of a cesspit with a quick blast of air freshener. Most of the people who Cat had spoken to thought pretty much the same thing. She certainly hadn't met many that were in favour of it, which is probably why it wasn't surprising that most of the posters she saw advertising the Festival had been defaced. On the one she passed on her way to work, the words had been amended to NEW FUCK-UP OF BRITAIN.

She was at the junction at the bottom of Greenwich South Street, about to cross over to Lewisham Road, when the woman appeared, lurching out from the direction of Blackheath Hill. She seemed to come from nowhere, a dark shape, a sudden flash of movement.

Cat's heart leaped and her body went rigid, her hands tightening on the steering wheel. Her foot stamped instinctively on the brake pedal and the car stalled, jerking her forward in her seat, her seatbelt locking across her chest. For a moment her mind spun as she tried to orient herself. Then she looked up.

The woman was drunk. That was Cat's first thought. She had stumbled into the road, directly in front of the car, with no thought for her own safety. She was well dressed, trim and looked to be somewhere in her thirties, but there was clearly something wrong with her. Her smart jacket and suit were dirty and dishevelled, her auburn hair was matted with what looked like dust or cobwebs, and somewhere along the way she had lost a shoe and was now tottering lopsidedly on one heel.

Despite the screeching sound that the tyres had made, the woman seemed oblivious to Cat's presence. She was half-turned away from the car, her movements uncoordinated. Cat began to wonder whether she wasn't drunk, after all, but had, in fact, been attacked. It was hard to tell under the streetlights, but was it possible that the dark stains on the collar and sleeve of the woman's jacket was not dirt but blood?

She wound down the window and stuck her head out. "Excuse me, are you okay?"

The woman froze, hunching up her shoulders. Cat wondered whether she had startled her by shouting out, though oddly the woman's stance reminded her of a big cat tensing its muscles in readiness to leap upon its prey.

"Sorry," Cat said. "I didn't mean to—"

And then the words dried in her throat as, with a guttural snarl, the woman spun around.

She wasn't just drunk, and she hadn't just been attacked; there was something seriously *wrong* with her. She looked bestial – her lips curled back over teeth that were caked with blood and what appeared, grotesquely, to be fur. There was more blood on her chin, mixing with the drool that spilled

4

from her bottom lip. When she raised her hands, Cat saw that they were red and wet, and that her well-manicured fingernails were clogged with what looked like meat.

With a sound somewhere between a howl and a roar the woman leaped at the car. Her hands slammed on the bonnet, and for a moment she was crouched there on all fours, her skirt riding up over her thighs, her face glaring in at Cat through the windscreen.

Cat was chilled to see that there was no humanity in that face. It wore an expression of utter rage, and yet the pale eyes were strangely dead, the pupils contracted to pin pricks, so that it looked almost as though a pale, grey, cataract-like film had formed across them. Cat and the woman were eye to eye for no more than three seconds, but it was long enough for Cat to understand that the woman meant her nothing but harm.

Then, unable to maintain her grip on the smooth metal, the woman began to slide backwards. She crumpled to the ground in front of the car like a slow-motion hit-and-run victim.

Before she could recover, Cat rammed the car into reverse and stamped on the accelerator. The engine screamed and the car shot backwards, slewing into a half-curve as she wrenched on the wheel. The woman was on her knees in the middle of the road, but as Cat tugged at the gear stick again she saw that she was already scrambling to her feet.

Putting the car into first, Cat veered around the woman, who made a reckless lunge as the car accelerated past her. Shaking with fear, Cat sped away, glancing into her rear-view mirror, as if afraid the woman would come bounding after her.

Trying to concentrate on the road ahead, she saw only the woman's smeary red handprints on her car bonnet. She was still shaking when she arrived at work.

11:41 pm

IF HE HADN'T been distracted by the approaching sirens, it might never have happened. Carlton wasn't even supposed to be on the streets; he was seventeen, and so subject to curfew. But there was no way he was gonna stay home and let the Deptford Road Crew take over Greenwich. Those fuckers had been bold lately, scrawling their tags all over the 'hood, muscling in on the payroll, intimidating the growers and the suppliers. They'd even torched Elijah's A3, which was unforgivable. They had it coming big time.

Elijah had called Carlton that afternoon. "It's happenin' tonight," he had said. "I'm bringin' all my soljas in. Every last one of those motherfuckers gonna get merked."

The party in Catherine Street was supposed to be secret, but one of the dealers had let slip to Fitch's sister that that was where the Deptford crew were gonna be. Word was that all three wanted guys would even be there, which was fucking disrespectful. The three top boys of any crew should *never* be together at the same time. The fact that they were gonna be meant they thought they were untouchable, and that was the biggest insult of all.

6

Elijah's soljas converged on the house like shadows, trailing darkness as they came. They wore black hoodies, black jeans, black boots, black scarves around their faces. The only parts of them that caught the light were their eyes and the glint of bottles protruding from pockets and clutched in hands. The five-oh was out on the street in force tonight, as they were every night, but the boys evaded them easily, slipping between the strands of their web like invisible flies.

Like Carlton, many of the crew was defying the curfew, risking arrest and worse. Latest word was that the five-oh were capping tinies just for eyeballing them after lights out. Carlton didn't know anyone it had happened to personally, but Fitch swore that his cousin's top boy in Wandsworth had been merked just for leaving the flat to get bread for his Mum after dark. Black van came and took the body away, he told Carlton, and nothing more was said about it.

Carlton moved through the crowd on the pavement, nodding and bumping fists. There must have been thirty soljas here tonight, but no one was saying anything. There was no joking, no chatter. The houses either side were sealed up tight, no one wanting to get involved. But all it took was one anonymous phone call to the five-oh from a shook neighbour and this place would be swarming in minutes.

Even if you didn't know the address, the party house would not have been hard to find. It was like the Deptford crew *wanted* a battle, like they were *inviting* it. The place was pumping like a heart, lights and music throbbing from the windows. Time was, the yard and street in front of the house would have been overflowing with bodies, but the curfew meant that these days, if everyone stayed inside, then the five-oh left them alone.

Following up complaints from killjoys was something the police never bothered with no more. It was such small fry compared to the real shit that was going down that it no longer even registered as an offence – not since the five-oh stopped caring about "community relations" anyhow. For them, everyone was now just a problem that had to be contained.

If you stayed where you was supposed to be and kept your opinions to yourself, then chances were you'd be okay. But if you stepped out of line and made a fuss, you'd be gone like Fitch's cousin's boy, taken away in a black van never to be seen again, nothing left behind but a smear on the pavement.

Carlton spotted his best boy Fitch hanging with Jermaine. Jermaine was cool, a nineteen-year-old Tonk, hubz to Fitch's older sister, Letitia. Jermaine nodded at him, his eyes so hooded he looked on the verge of falling asleep. Carlton nodded back, then turned to Fitch. Though he could only see Fitch's eyes, the younger boy looked shook.

"You tooled?" Carlton whispered.

Fitch jerked his right elbow, the hand forming a bulge in his hoodie pocket. "I got a rock."

Carlton was incredulous. "A rock?"

"I couldn't get nothin' else," Fitch muttered defensively. "What about you?"

"Shank," said Carlton.

"Jermaine's carryin' a nine," Fitch whispered.

"Safe," said Carlton respectfully.

"Believe it."

There was a low whistle and the boys clammed up, moved into position. Those with bottles slipped through to the front, lining up along the wall, facing the house. Lighters were produced, and next moment a series of tulip flames danced in the night. The bottles in the boys' other hands were full of petrol, fuses made of rags trailing out of the necks. The rags were lit, arms drawn back. Next moment a dozen flaming glass projectiles were arcing towards the house.

A few hit the wall of the house itself, smashing against the brick, erupting in a spatter of flame, which quickly went out. Most, though, found their target, smashing in through the big front window in a din of shattering glass, hot white comets drooling liquid fire.

The closed curtains on the other side of the glass (*not even metal shutters*, thought Carlton. *Fucking amateurs*) went up in a sheet. Instantly there were screams and angry shouts from inside the house, the thump of running feet, clatters and bangs as furniture and maybe even people were knocked aside. The Greenwich crew was already diving for cover as the front door opened. Then the gunfire started.

It came from both sides, cracks and pops and bangs depending on the calibre and efficiency of the weapons. The first motherfucker out the door, who was wearing a white vest like he was *asking* to be merked, fell back, though Carlton didn't know whether that was coz he got shot, coz he threw himself backwards or coz he was dragged back inside. The door was slammed shut and the gunfire continued, back and forth, everyone hiding behind walls, bullets hitting brick and concrete, wood and metal.

Carlton lay on his belly on the pavement while the bullets whizzed above him, his ears singing with the din, wondering how long it would be before the five-oh showed with their AK-47s or whatever and joined in.

Fitch was there too, still clutching his rock, his eyes so wide that Carlton thought they might fall out of his head and splat right there on the pavement. Jermaine was slumped against the wall, poking his gun up every now and again, and pulling the trigger without even looking where he was firing.

Carlton didn't know whether the house was still burning, whether people were still screaming inside; his whole world at that moment consisted of the ringing in his ears and the cold pavement against which he was pressing his body. Then someone shouted something and, although Carlton couldn't make out the words, he knew that the shout was some kind of warning.

He sensed movement and looked up, saw members of his crew looking beyond where he was lying, some of them starting to run for the cover of walls and parked cars, doubled over to make themselves smaller targets, raising their gats.

A small chunk of pavement next to Carlton's face exploded, showering him with shards of stone. For a second he thought something was going to burst from under the ground, then he realized the damage had been caused by a bullet. He'd been six inches away from getting his face blown off.

He scrambled to his feet, suddenly aware of how big a target his back was, of how easily a bullet would rip through his flesh, shatter his bones. He turned, his feet clumsy, his hand scrabbling for the knife in his pocket, to see a skinny kid, no more than a tinie, pointing a gat at his head.

The kid, and others with him, must have come out of the back of the house and round the side, hoping to spring an ambush. But now they'd been spotted, so it was open fucking warfare, with Carlton and Fitch caught in the middle.

Carlton knew there was nothing he could do, nothing he could say. The kid was little but he was all rage, teeth clenched, eyes on another planet. In a second he would pull the trigger and Carlton would be dead. He didn't have time to prepare for that, or even to be scared. All he could do was stare at the kid and wait for it to happen.

But then the kid's shoulder turned to meat and his arm flew back like it was nothing but a long sock full of sand. The kid's face went blank with shock and he dropped like a dead weight, the gun spilling from his hand. Carlton half-turned to see that Jermaine, face wild, was no longer pressed against the wall of the house, but had moved across to take shelter behind a Renault spanged with bullet holes. He had capped the kid and now he was firing at others who were coming up the street behind him.

Carlton had no time to thank him. Looking round he

spotted Fitch, still cowering on the pavement, too scared to move. Bending low, Carlton ran over, grabbed the back of Fitch's hoodie and yanked him upright, half-strangling him. Fitch gave a yelp and swung his left arm in a half-hearted attempt to fight back.

"Chill," Carlton yelled in his ear. "It's me, blud. You need to be up and wettin'. Mashmen comin'. You get merked if you stay. You good?"

Fitch nodded, and this time when Carlton dragged him to his feet he didn't resist. Crouching low, sticking to the shadows, the boys ran towards the car sheltering Jermaine and dived behind it.

It was chaos on the street now, everyone spread all over. Looking round, it was hard to tell which of the shapes were bodies and which were trees or bushes or clumps of darkness. There was no discipline, no strategy, and despite the amount of shooting, no casualties that Carlton could see, apart from the tinie that Jermaine had shot, who was now writhing on the ground, feet pedalling, making breathless little screaming noises.

The shooting was still going on, but it was intermittent, more hopeful than full of any real intent. It didn't help that thick, black smoke from the house was now drifting across the road, making it even harder to see.

There were a few more shots, then things went quiet. For a while the three of them sat tight, waiting for someone to make a move. Though the fire seemed to be out, the smoke was getting thicker, swirling around them. It stung their eyes and throats, and soon all three boys were trying to stifle coughs, fearful of giving their position away. Jermaine shook his head.

"This is crump, man. We should fucking bail. The five-oh be all over this in a minute."

"Where should we go?" Fitch asked nervously.

Jermaine nodded towards the wounded tinie, who was now

barely visible through the smoke. He was still pedalling his legs as if he wanted to detach himself from his pain, walk away from it. The Deptford crew who had been coming up behind him was nowhere to be seen. If they were still around they were taking refuge in the smoke and darkness, sitting it out like Carlton, Fitch and Jermaine.

"Not that way," he said and jerked a thumb over his shoulder. "So let's go this."

Peeling away from the car the boys began to slip along the pavement, heads darting back and forth as they tried to scope every direction at once. It was eerie how quiet the street had suddenly become. It was as if everyone had melted away, as if they were the only ones left.

The boys froze, their heads snapping up as they heard a siren in the distance, faint but getting closer. Jermaine stepped forward and dropped his gun over a low garden wall, concealing it in the narrow gap between the wall and a wheelie bin. Carlton pulled his knife from his pocket and did the same.

"Where now?" Fitch said, panic creeping into his voice.

"Chill," said Jermaine. "We fine. The five-oh see us, we just out strollin'. Ain't no law 'gainst that."

"I'm sixteen," said Fitch.

"And I'm seventeen," said Carlton. "We curfew bait, man."

Jermaine narrowed his eyes, and Carlton wondered whether he was about to bail on them. Then he said, "The five-oh comin' from High Road, so we cut across the park. Easy. You babies be tucked up in bed by midnight."

Carlton and Fitch scowled at him, but this was no time for banter. Scurrying across the road, Carlton felt like a fox, moving silently through the cracks and crevices of the city.

The opposite pavement was lined with cars, the gleam of their bodywork under the streetlights dulled by smoke. The sirens were getting closer. Jermaine reached the pavement first, followed by Fitch, with Carlton bringing up the rear. Carlton was so distracted by the approaching sirens that he didn't see the kid until it was too late.

The kid stepped out of the shadows and the smoke behind him and punched him in the hip. It didn't hurt at first, and so Carlton had no idea he'd been shanked until he turned to see the kid running away, disappearing into the darkness.

He was about to yell out, maybe give chase, when his hip, where the kid had punched him, started to go hot and cold, and then to really *hurt*. He looked down and saw the hole in his jacket and the blood pouring out of it, black under the bleached-out glare of the streetlights.

Then his head started to spin and the world greyed out and suddenly his legs seemed to disappear. Next thing Carlton knew he was on the ground and he couldn't move and the sirens were almost upon him. They were screeching at him, right in his ear, like a pack of wild animals moving in for the kill.

11:56 pm

"I'VE GOT THIS strange bulge in my trousers, nurse. Fancy taking me round the back for a thorough examination?"

Lisa rolled her eyes. She was starting to regret suggesting this whole "sexy nurse" theme for Chris' hen night. It had been a laugh at first but, after hearing the same predictable chat-up lines over and over again, it was now starting to wear a bit thin. If it wasn't a variation on what the testosterone-fuelled knob-head with the alcohol-pink eyes had just said to her, it was: *"I'm getting a bit hot, nurse, I think you need to loosen my clothing"*, or: *"Why don't you take me home and show me your bedside manner?"* or: *"Want to come back to mine for a game of doctors and nurses?"* One guy earlier in the evening had said, "I think I've got a temperature, nurse. Where do you want to stick your thermometer?"

Lisa had sighed and muttered, "Through your eye and into your brain would be a good start."

Maybe, on reflection, the four of them should have come as nuns – *"Got any dirty habits?"*; *"I've always fancied p-p-picking up a Penguin"*; *"Are you a Catholic or a prostitute?"* – but then again, maybe not.

14

What about top hat and tails then? Or boiler suits? No doubt the former would have led to comments about ringmasters and whips, and the latter to jokes about lesbians and how to "cure" them.

It wasn't that Lisa was averse to a bit of flattery and attention, it was just that she wished what had passed for it this evening hadn't been so depressingly predictable. Maybe she was getting uptight in her old age. Maybe, since turning twenty-five, marrying Robbie and giving birth to Jake, she didn't have it in her to have *fun* any more.

But no, she couldn't believe that. She *wouldn't* believe that. Before meeting Robbie she'd always been the wild one, the adventurous one, the life and soul. And she'd organized tonight's little shindig, hadn't she? And it wasn't as if (despite the endless comments) they weren't having a good time.

Okay, so Elevation wasn't exactly the most salubrious club in south London (it wasn't even the most salubrious club in Catford), but it was cheap and cheerful, and most importantly it was *open*. So many clubs weren't these days. They'd closed down partly because people didn't have the money to socialize any more, and partly because a lot of former pubbers and clubbers didn't like being out on the streets after dark.

Maybe that's why the clientele in Elevation seemed a bit more . . . well, *full on* than the kind of mid-week crowds that Lisa had been used to in her young, free and single days. Maybe the hardcore element that *did* still venture out were just that little bit more determined to throw caution to the wind, more intent on forgetting about the drudgery of life in the recession-hit slagheap that was modern Britain and simply enjoying themselves.

The boys who'd been chatting them up tonight – all hard pecs and hard drinking and streaky blonde highlights in forty-quid haircuts – had certainly been wanting to enjoy themselves

15

a bit more than the girls were prepared to let them. They'd been like flies around sugar, mesmerized by the girls' little white nurses' caps and white micro-dresses which failed to hide the stocking tops of their white fishnets.

Some of them had looked so hot and bothered that Lisa had half-expected them to erupt like lustful volcanoes, or perhaps melt like steroid-flavoured ice cream. She felt sorry for them, even if, at the same time, she found their transparent and competitive fawning embarrassing and pathetic.

Turning to the leering stud-muffin who had made the comment about his bulging trousers, she said, "You'd regret it, mate. In cases like yours I'm generally in favour of amputation."

Then she picked up the tray containing the four Stoned Smurfs and strutted away on her six-inch heels.

As the crowd parted before her, guys looking her up and down with the same lust and admiration they would no doubt bestow on a passing Porsche or Ferrari, Lisa's attention was snagged by a strange figure standing on the street beyond the glass box that formed Elevation's main entrance.

She noticed him because of the way he was dressed and because his burning eyes seemed to be fixed on her. He was tall and skinny, with long, dark, matted hair and a straggly beard that cascaded over his chest. He wore a coarse, loose-sleeved robe, once white but now stained and filthy, that reached to his ankles, beneath which his bony bare feet were filthy too, the toenails almost black.

When Lisa caught his eye his mouth stretched into a wide grin, although it seemed to her less an expression of friendliness and more like that of a butcher exposing his collection of knives.

She shuddered and wrenched her gaze away. Suddenly, dressed as she was, she had the absurd notion that she was being *judged*. If the man was an apostle, though, he was a raddled and dissolute one – one who looked as if he had succumbed to all kinds of temptations.

16

Lisa slipped deeper into the crowd, seeking refuge in the humid crush of her many suddenly harmless-seeming admirers. Even so, in spite of whether he could still see her or not, she couldn't help feeling the man's gaze crawling over her all the way back to her table.

Only when she was in the company of her friends – or at least in the company of Sam and Christine – did she begin to relax. The fourth member of their group, Fay, whose delicate and exotic beauty came from having a Ghanaian father and a French mother, was on the dance floor, having finally relented to dance with the cute, love-struck guy who'd been unable to tear his gaze away from her all evening.

Chris, the bride to be, and by far the drunkest of them, let out a shrill cheer when the drinks appeared on the table and made a grab for her Stoned Smurf. She'd downed half the blue liquid before Lisa and Sam had even picked up their cocktail glasses. Surfacing with a gasp, she belched and giggled. Lisa and Sam laughed.

"Oh my God. You're gonna feel *so* ill tomorrow," Sam said.

Chris grinned and fluttered her false eyelashes. "I couldn't give a monkey's cock. Tomorrow's fucking ages away. Right now, I feel *great!*"

To demonstrate, she finished her drink and slammed her glass down on the table. "*More booze!*"

Sam laughed. "Go easy, girl."

"Go easy yourself," retorted Chris. "I don't wan' go easy. I wan' get pissed."

"You *are* pissed," laughed Lisa.

"I wan' get pisseder."

As the girls shrieked with laughter, a craggy-faced guy in a mustard-coloured polo shirt leaned over the table. "Sorry, ladies, I couldn't help overhearing. Please allow me to get this next round for you."

Chris peered at him, squinting as if she couldn't get him in focus. "Who're you?"

"My name's Gavin."

"I'm not fucking you, if that's what you're after."

Gavin laughed a little forcedly. "I'm just offering to buy you a drink."

"I'm gettin' married," Chris said. "I'm gonna be a married woman in two weeks."

"Well, congratulations. So come on, what are you drinking?"

"I'm fine," said Lisa quickly.

Chris looked outraged. "Bollocks you are. This is *my* hen night, so *I* make the rules." She wafted a queenly hand. "We'll have the same again, my good man."

Lisa and Sam exchanged a resigned glance. As Gavin turned to head towards the bar, there was a ripple in the crowd behind him. Lisa tensed as the man she had seen standing outside – the raddled Jesus clone – suddenly stepped out of the parting sea of bodies.

"Oi," Gavin said as the bearded man all but shoved him out of the way. The man ignored him. He squirmed his way up to the girls' table and leaned over. Lisa recoiled.

The man's breath stank like he hadn't brushed his teeth in years. But it wasn't *just* his breath. A rank, cheesy odour wafted from him in waves so thick and putrid that she instantly felt sick. Above the music his voice was a rasp, low but audible.

"Beltane is come. Tread softly, for lo, the Beast Himself is nigh."

The girls stared at him for a moment, then Chris nodded. "Right, thanks for that, mate," she said. "Now please fuck off. You stink of shit."

Sam giggled nervously. Though Lisa was loath to antagonize the man, she was unable to resist pressing a hand to her mouth and nose. She expected him to react angrily to Chris' rebuttal, but although he pointed a long, grimy finger at her, his face remained placid.

"Anarchon, the Master of Fleas is upon us," he rasped. "All will succumb to His judgement."

"You'll succumb to *my* fucking judgement in a minute," Chris muttered.

Gavin, who had been glaring at the man throughout the exchange, stepped forward and placed a hand on his bony shoulder. "Look, mate, you're upsetting the ladies. I think you should leave before you get your arse kicked."

The man turned and glanced at Gavin as if he was nothing but a minor distraction. "I have come amongst you to share His gift."

"Yeah, well, no one wants anything you've got, so why don't—"

Before he could finish his sentence, the man's head darted forward and he bit Gavin on the cheek.

The movement seemed almost innocuous, oddly without aggression, as if he was merely testing the resistance of Gavin's flesh. Lisa screamed and jumped to her feet as she saw the man's dirty yellow teeth sink into Gavin's face and blood spurt from the wound.

Before Gavin had time to respond, the man whipped around like a snake, grabbed Sam's arm, and bit into that too. Sam shrieked in pain as blood oozed up around the man's teeth.

Lisa did the only thing she could think of. She picked up her cocktail glass and hurled its contents into the man's face.

Whether it was this that encouraged him to release Sam she wasn't sure. He certainly seemed calm enough as, with blue liquid dripping down his face and on to his grubby white robe, he opened his mouth and stepped back.

Lisa's stomach turned over as she saw the crescent of teeth marks on Sam's forearm, from which blood was dripping on to the glass table. For a moment Lisa was stunned with shock – and then she was suddenly overcome by a surge of white-hot rage.

"What's your fucking problem, you freak!" she screeched. *"Why don't you just fuck off?"*

As she yelled she was aware of heads turning, of shocked, outraged, angry expressions appearing on the faces of many of the people around her. She was aware of them looking at Gavin, who was standing shell-shocked and pale with his hand pressed to his bleeding cheek; at the stinking, bearded prophet with blood around his mouth; and at Sam's mangled arm.

What happened next was perhaps inevitable. Fuelled by a sense of drunken chivalry, many of the guys who had been buzzing around their table all evening suddenly surged towards the stinking outsider who had dared to violate their world.

All at once hands were grabbing him, yanking him this way and that, dragging and punching him to the ground. Lisa felt a wild surge of both exhilaration and horror as his white-robed form was suddenly engulfed within a frenzy of writhing bodies, of whirling arms and legs.

Loath to watch any further, she turned away, to see Sam clutching her bleeding arm and weeping, and Chris, who appeared to have sobered up in an instant, comforting her. Bewildered and sickened at how quickly the evening had turned from one of joy and celebration to one of violence and trauma, Lisa started to shake, to feel sick. All at once she felt stifled by the heat and the noise and the press of bodies.

Slumping forward, fists supporting her weight on the table, she yelled, "I'll find a cab. We need to get Sam to a hospital."

Chris glanced up and nodded, but she looked so shell-shocked that Lisa doubted her friend had registered a word she'd said.

Even so, she muttered, "Won't be long," and pushed herself away from the table. Skirting the heaving circle of still-punching, kicking boys, she plunged towards the main entrance, feeling like a deep-sea diver trying to make it to the surface before the air runs out.

12:02 am

"YOU ALL RIGHT, Cat? You're shaking like a leaf."

Cat was standing at the sink in the Staff Room, filling the kettle, when her friend and fellow staff nurse Susan Jenkins spoke to her. She had been going through the motions of making tea while replaying the incident with the crazy woman over and over in her mind.

She kept wondering if she had misread the situation, if she could have handled it differently. Perhaps the woman *was* the victim of an assault, and had been so deeply traumatized that she had simply lashed out without thinking. In which case, shouldn't Cat have stopped to help her instead of driving away?

It all seemed so simple when she thought it through reasonably, but that didn't help her shake the memory of how *ferocious* the woman had been, of how crazy she had looked.

In seven years of nursing, most of which had been spent in Lewisham A&E, where Cat had had to deal with her fair share of nutters, she had never encountered anyone quite like that before. Although well dressed, the woman had resembled a rabid animal, utterly beyond reason.

Cat was so engrossed in her thoughts, and so jumpy after what had happened, that Susan's voice made her leap out of her skin. Her hand sprang open, releasing the kettle. It clattered into the sink, causing everyone in the room – mostly colleagues of Cat's waiting to go on shift – to jerk their heads up from their magazines and newspapers and conversations.

Susan, standing just behind her, jumped too, then laughed and placed one hand on Cat's arm, the other on her own chest.

"My God," she said with a breathless laugh. "I'm so sorry."

Cat looked at her, eyes wide and startled, and then her face relaxed into a wavery smile. "Not your fault," she said. "I was miles away." She glanced over her shoulder to address the room. "Sorry, everyone."

Susan leaned in closer. "*Are* you all right?"

Cat nodded tersely. "I'm fine."

"It's not Ed, is it?"

"Ed?"

"The wedding, I mean. Nothing's wrong? It's not getting too stressful?"

Cat shook her head almost irritably. "No, everything's fine." She paused. "Something happened on the way to work, that's all. It shook me up a bit."

"Want to talk about it?"

Cat shrugged.

"Look, go and sit down and I'll make us a cuppa. We've still got ten minutes."

Susan, who at thirty was six years older than Cat, had always been dependable, unflappable, the voice of reason. She listened intently to Cat's account of what had happened to her on her way in to work, but at the end of it she shrugged airily and said, "It sounds horrible, but I wouldn't worry about it. Sounds to me like she was just drunk or on drugs."

"No, it was more than that," Cat said, frowning. "You weren't there, Sue. You didn't see her. She was like an animal."

23

"There are all kinds of drugs that can cause psychosis," Susan said. "Amphetamines, coke, alcohol, marijuana, even sedatives and inhalants . . ."

Cat stopped her with a raised hand. "I know all that, but this was different."

Any further discussion was curtailed by the door opening to reveal Sister Parkhurst's stocky frame and flushed, plump features. "Come along boys and girls," she called, her gaze sweeping the room. "It's time to break out those wands and work more of our magic."

The comment elicited a ripple of slightly bitter laughter. Sister Parkhurst had qualified as a nurse in the early 1970s and over the past forty years had seen the NHS deteriorate from a once shining beacon of communal care and welfare to the under-funded, under-valued, under-staffed and under-resourced shambles it was today.

She often said that it was like watching the slow decline of a much-loved relative and that if she had a decent pension she'd retire from her job like a shot. She said, too, that if she ever got to the point where she was reliant on the NHS for long-term care she'd fill her pockets with rocks and jump in the Thames.

It wasn't the NHS itself (which she invariably referred to as the No Hope Situation or the National Horror Show) that she vilified, of course, but the Coalition Government, which was running it into the ground.

Another of Sister Parkhurst's favourite comments was that the NHS, once a proud thoroughbred, was now a whipped and whimpering dog, abused on a daily basis by "that bunch of thugs in Parliament". She often talked of modern nursing being like "pushing custard uphill" or of trying to "make a silk purse out of a sow's ear". Needless to say, she was fiercely supportive of the senior and regular staff nurses, student nurses and care assistants who scurried around her like chicks around a mother hen, and they loved her to bits in return.

At the staff hand-over on the A&E ward, Cat tried to concentrate as details of admissions and discharges, and of the care and medication requirements of specific patients, were relayed by those staff who were coming off shift. But it was difficult; in her mind's eye she was still seeing the bestial, blood- (and fur? Had it *really* been fur?) smeared face and meat-clogged fingernails of the woman who had leaped on to her car bonnet.

Where was that woman now, she wondered. Had the police responded to the phone call she had made as soon as she had arrived at work? Had they picked her up? If so, was it possible that she might be brought here, that Cat might encounter her again? She shivered inwardly at the prospect.

"Cat! Catherine!" It wasn't until she heard her full name being called that she snapped from her reverie. Instantly she tried to appear alert.

"Yes, Sister?"

Sister Parkhurst scowled, and Cat became suddenly aware that everyone was looking at her, their expressions ranging from amusement to sympathy.

"Did you hear a single word that I just said? Or are you far too busy picturing how pretty you'll look in that wedding dress of yours?"

Cat blushed. She wondered whether she should bluff it, but then decided to come clean. "Sorry, Sister, I drifted off for a minute there. I . . . haven't been sleeping too well."

Sister Parkhurst rolled her eyes. "God help the ill and needy," she muttered. Then her expression softened. "We've got a stab wound and a gunshot wound coming in within the next few minutes. Same gang fight, separate admissions. Do you think you can assist on the stab wound without nodding off?"

"Yes, Sister. Of course."

"Splendid." Abruptly Sister Parkhurst clapped her hands, startling a dozing patient in a nearby bed. "Right then, gang, action stations. Stay focused, have fun, and may the god of swabs and sutures grant us all a peaceful night."

12:13 am

AS SOON AS Vince Garvey checked his phone, Shirley knew from the look on his face who the message was from.

"Diane?" she said.

Sitting behind the steering wheel of the ambulance that had just delivered Carlton Tyler to University Hospital, Vince nodded.

"She'd better not be ringing up to cancel," he muttered.

Shirley pursed her lips in sympathy. "She can't do that, can she?"

He shrugged, his square, goateed face compressed in a scowl. "I wouldn't put it past her. You know what a vindictive bitch she is."

Shirley didn't know, not really. She had never met Vince's ex-wife. All she had to go on was what he had said about her and, much as she liked Vince, she couldn't help but think that his opinion was perhaps a bit one-sided.

She knew that he had had drink and gambling problems a few years back, and even though he had said that he'd only sought solace in the bottle because Diane had "done his

27

head in", Shirley suspected that if she were to talk to Diane she would get an entirely different view.

She didn't know *exactly* what had gone on within the marriage, but she did know that the divorce proceedings had been messy, vicious and prolonged, and that it had taken over two years for Vince to finally get access to his eight-year-old son, Luke.

Now, though, it was all sorted, and tomorrow Vince would get to take Luke out on his own for the first time. He was almost childishly excited by the prospect, but Shirley knew that he was apprehensive too – not that he would ever say as much. He was a bluff and beefy Yorkshireman who had never been one to wear his heart on his sleeve. Whenever he was upset, it manifested itself not as sorrow or anxiety or self-pity, but as anger.

"I bet that bitch has poisoned his mind, told him all sorts o' shit about me," he had snarled earlier that evening. "What if he doesn't want to know me, Shirl? What if he's scared o' me because o' the lies she's told him?"

"Well, then, I guess you'll just have to win him over with your natural wit and charm, won't you?" Shirley had said.

Vince had paused before grinning wryly and shaking his head. "Sorry, love," he had muttered. "I'm going off on one again, aren't I?"

Shirley, a plain-speaking Cardiff girl, who at thirty-three was ten years younger than Vince and probably weighed about half as much as her hefty companion, said to him now, "Shall I make myself scarce while you ring her back?"

Vince looked grateful. "Would you mind, love? That'd be smashing."

"No problem. I could do with a fag anyway."

She slid from the cab of the ambulance and went to stand against one of the brick pillars by the entrance to A&E. She was close enough to scurry straight back if they got a call out,

28

but far enough away to give her colleague a bit of privacy.

As she smoked she stood with her back to the ambulance and stared out across the car park towards the line of trees that bordered the inner wall of the hospital grounds. She tried to make it look as though she was lost in thought, though in truth she could hear every word that Vince was saying to his ex-wife. She willed him to stay calm, to stay reasonable, so as not to give Diane ammunition to use against him.

"Hi," she heard him say, trying hard to keep his voice casual, "I got your message. What's up?"

There were a few moments of silence and then, his voice slightly *less* casual, he said, "What do you mean? What's wrong with him?"

More silence, then Vince blurted a laugh. "Is that all? I'm sure he'll be fine. Haven't you got any antihistamine you can give him?"

Shirley tried to fill in the silences, to imagine what Diane was saying. From Vince's responses she suspected that his ex-wife had told him that their son was suffering from hay fever.

Sure enough, a moment later Vince said, "Of course I'm not making light of it. I know hay fever can be miserable. But I also know that it's easily treatable. I'm sure he'll be fine."

Diane's reply, whatever it was, caused him to sound defensive. "Well, the plan was to go to Epping Forest for the day. I thought we could hire bikes, take a picnic." When he next spoke, after a prolonged pause, there was a growl in his voice. "I don't *want* to take him to the cinema. What's the point of us sitting in darkness and silence? I haven't seen him for two years, not properly anyway. I want to *talk* to him. I want the chance for us to get to know each other."

Shirley glanced briefly over her shoulder. Vince had a scowl on his face and was gripping his phone like he was trying to squeeze blood out of it. *Stay calm*, she urged, *stay calm*.

"Of course I'm not just bloody thinking about myself," he blurted. "With the schools closed and this damn curfew, I thought he'd jump at the chance to get away from the city for a bit. He must be bored stiff being cooped up all the time." The briefest of pauses, and then, "Oh, for God's sake, of course it's not a criticism of you. It may surprise you to learn that not everything's about you, you know."

There was such a long silence this time that Shirley wondered whether Diane had hung up. Then eventually, in a voice that he was clearly taking great pains to control, he said, "Look, let's just play it by ear, shall we? If he's bad, then obviously I won't take him somewhere where there's gonna be loads of pollen . . . Yes, ten o'clock . . . Yes, I knock off at four . . . No, I'll be fine . . . I won't get much sleep, but I'll be fine. I'm used to it."

At that moment there was a crackle from the radio in the cab, followed by a tinny voice, which Shirley instantly recognized as Asif, one of the emergency medical dispatchers they communicated with on a regular basis. As she dropped her cigarette and stamped on it, she heard Vince say, "Sorry, Diane, gotta go," and then he was shouting her name.

"Already here," she said, climbing into the cab and dragging the door closed behind her. By the time she had clipped her seatbelt into place, Asif had sent through the details of the 999 call he had just received – sixty-six-year-old man, cardiac arrest, Foxberry Road.

"Hi ho, Silver," Vince said, as he often did, and in a swirl of lights and a wail of sirens they were away.

12:22 am

"PLEASE HELP. OUR friend's really ill. Some guy bit her and I think he's infected her with something."

Tottering across the A&E Admissions area in their tiny white nurses' uniforms, Lisa was all too aware of how she and her friends must look. But the lascivious glances, filthy comments and wolf whistles that trailed them as they headed towards the main desk – not least from a couple of cocky-looking black kids in hoodies and baggy jeans, who were sprawled across several of the interlocking metal seats – were the least of their worries.

Even on the short cab journey from Catford to Lewisham, Sam's condition had deteriorated rapidly. Lisa had initially thought her friend would have to put up with nothing more than a few stitches and maybe some tests to check that the guy who'd bitten her didn't have AIDS or something, but whatever the guy *did* have (and he clearly had something), it was far more aggressive and fast-moving than any virus or infection Lisa had ever come across.

Sam's arm was now horribly inflamed, and the teeth marks were leaking a disgusting white pus. The flesh around the wound was almost black, and the infection seemed to be

31

spreading both up and down her arm on a tracery of dark veins, which gave the skin an almost marble-like appearance. Furthermore, Sam was sweaty, feverish, her body limp and her eyes rolling as she slipped in and out of consciousness.

Chris, Lisa and Fay had had to drag her from the cab, and Lisa and Chris were now all but carrying her between them, while Fay, shorter and slighter than her friends, fluttered anxiously in the background, hands half-raised as if to catch Sam should she fall.

The beaded dreadlocks of the plump, middle-aged woman behind the Admissions desk chattered as she raised her head from the paperwork in front of her. At the sight of the girls her eyes widened, first with amusement and then with shock when she saw Sam's wound.

"Take a seat," she said curtly. "I'll get someone to see to you right away."

As Lisa and Chris manoeuvred Sam towards the only batch of four free seats that Lisa could see – which happened to be directly opposite the two black kids – the receptionist was already lifting a phone and speaking urgently into it.

Lisa helped lower Sam into a seat, then sat down herself, taking care to keep her knees together. Even so, she was uncomfortably aware of the eyes of the kids opposite – especially the older and taller of the two – crawling all over her. She tried to ignore them, even when the older kid muttered something to his friend which made them both snigger; even when the older kid made kissy sounds with his lips.

However, when he said something that she didn't quite catch but had the words "fucking" and "bitches" in it, she glared at him and said, "What's your problem?"

The younger kid looked startled, even a little ashamed, but the older one appraised her with hooded eyes. She thought he wasn't going to answer at first, but eventually, in a lazy drawl, he said, "I ain't got no problem, lady."

32

"No? Well I do. My problem is the offensive comments that you and your friend are making. Frankly, we've had enough shit tonight without you two adding to it."

Lisa could feel the sudden tension in the room, not only from Chris and Fay, who she sensed were willing her to shut the fuck up, but from people nearby who were casting nervous glances in her direction.

The eyes of the older kid became even more hooded. He sucked his teeth as though troubled by a sliver of food that had become stuck between them. "Seems to me," he said, "that if you dress like a ho then you gwan be treated like one."

Lisa reddened. She felt rage boiling inside her. "Oh yeah?" she barked. "And what have you come as? A pathetic little gangsta rapper who thinks he's a tough guy? You people make me sick."

She was aware of Fay, sitting to her right, flinching as if slapped, and instantly felt ashamed. She hadn't meant that phrase – *You people* – to sound how it had evidently come across.

The older of the two kids leaped on it instantly. "That some kind of fascist shit, lady? You a fucking racist or what?"

"Of course not," she said. "I was referring to your life choices, not your ethnic background."

"Life choices," the older kid said and leaned back, cackling. Any further comment he might have been about to make was curtailed by the arrival of a nurse, who said, "Who has the infected wound?"

Lisa's head snapped round. She glanced at the white name badge on the nurse's blue uniform, which identified her as STAFF NURSE CAT HARRIS.

"It's our friend," Chris said, who was on Sam's left. She took Sam's limp hand and lifted it gently so that Cat could see the wound. The nurse sucked in a sharp breath. Her hands sheathed in disposable gloves, she examined the bite tentatively.

33

"That looks very nasty. When did this happen?"

"About . . . half an hour ago?" Chris said, looking to Lisa for confirmation. Lisa nodded.

Cat raised her eyebrows. "Only half an hour? Are you sure?"

The three girls nodded. Sam herself was slumped forward, apparently unconscious, her reddish-blonde hair hanging over her face like a curtain.

"And it was a human bite?"

"Yeah," said Lisa. "But the guy was filthy. He was one of those mad religious types. You know, beard and white robes, like something out of the Bible?"

"He stank," added Chris.

"And where is he now?" asked Cat.

Lisa thought of the circle of punching, kicking, stamping bodies. "No idea. We were more worried about Sam."

Cat straightened. "Okay, well, we'll get your friend seen to straight away. What's her name?"

"Sam," said Chris. "Sam Mellor."

"Have any of you filled out an admissions form?"

They shook their heads.

"Right, well, if one of you could do that while I take Sam through to get some treatment—"

"I'll do it," Fay said, jumping to her feet and tottering towards the Admissions desk, pausing en route to exasperatedly remove her white high heels.

Cat kneeled in front of Sam and tried to peer under her overhanging fringe of hair.

"Sam?" she said, touching her gently on the knee. "Sam, can you hear me? Are you able to walk?"

Receiving no response, she continued, "I'll get her a wheelchair. I'll just be—"

And then, like a puppet whose head had been jerked by a string, Sam looked up.

Cat gasped and instinctively recoiled, which, because she was crouching, caused her to overbalance and plump unceremoniously on to her backside. Lisa caught only a glimpse of Sam's deathly-white face, the most startling feature of which were her pale, staring eyes, the pupils having shrunk to the size of pinpricks, and then Sam's head jerked away from her as Chris said uncertainly, "Sam, love, are you all right?"

Sam responded by growling like a dog and lurching lop-sidedly towards Chris. Alarmed, Chris jumped to her feet – but not before Sam had lashed out, raking long red fingernails across the back of her friend's forearm and drawing four thin strips of blood. Chris cried out in surprise and pain, stumbling backwards on her high heels as Sam sprang to her feet.

A curly-haired and bespectacled student nurse, who had been speaking to the dreadlocked woman on the Admissions desk, came hurrying over, grabbing Cat under her armpits and hauling her upright.

Across from the girls, the older of the two black kids laughed at the drama unfolding before him, attracting Sam's attention. Her head snapped around like a dog's. As he laughed at her, she raised her hands, her fingers rigid and hooked like talons and then, to everyone's astonishment, she leaped at him.

Still sprawled in his seat, the kid was as surprised as everyone else by the attack. By the time he realized what was happening, Sam was already clawing at his face. He reared back to put himself out of her reach and instinctively raised a hand to fend her off. Quick as a snake, she twisted her head, her lips curling back over teeth which Lisa knew she had recently paid a great deal of money to have straightened and whitened, and bit right through the fleshy part of the kid's hand, tearing a chunk of flesh out of it.

"*Fuck!*" he screamed as blood spurted over Sam's chin, dripped on to her ample cleavage and speckled the front of her white uniform. He wrenched his hand away from her and leaped scramblingly to his feet. "Fucking get off me, you mad bitch!"

Mangled hand dripping with blood, he kicked out at Sam as she lunged at him again. His foot connected with the side of her head, drawing screams from Lisa and Chris, but it barely even slowed her down. She took a staggering step sideways, but quickly recovered and sprang again.

By now the younger of the two kids was also on his feet and a couple of security guards, at a shout from Cat, were running through the crowd towards them.

As Sam leaped at him, the older kid caught her in mid-air with both hands, half-twisted and slammed her down on to the floor. Before she could rise, he jumped on to her back, then brought the sole of his foot down hard on the back of her head, mashing her face into the vinyl tiles.

"Stay down, bitch!" he yelled, as she thrashed like a beached fish.

Chris screamed again, her elbows tight against her body and her bunched fists pressed against her chest as if protecting herself from attack. Appalled by the violence, Lisa ran forward and shoved the older kid, causing him to stumble from his perch. "*Leave her alone, you cunt!*" she screamed. "*Leave her fucking alone!*"

Then the student nurse was screaming. Freed of the kid's weight, Sam had leaped instantly on to all fours and attacked her, sinking her teeth into the girl's leg just above the ankle.

The security guards had arrived now. The taller and burlier of the two slammed into Sam from behind, pinning her arms to her sides as he used his weight to force her back to the ground. He must have been twice as heavy, twice as wide and about a foot taller than she was, but even so he clearly found it incredibly difficult to subdue her.

She bucked and thrashed beneath him, her head twisting and her bloodied teeth snapping at air. The second security guard jumped on her legs, smothering her kicking feet and enabling the first guard to concentrate on the upper half of her body.

The bigger man manoeuvred himself into a position whereby he was kneeling on Sam's shoulder blades, crushing her against the floor. Red-faced and sweating, perched atop her body like a rodeo rider on a bucking bronco, he turned to Cat, who was trying both to tend to the wounded and console a weeping Chris.

"Fetch ropes, sedatives, anything that'll keep her down," he gasped, raising his voice above the rising clamour of the watching crowd.

When Cat hesitated, torn between caring for the injured and fulfilling his request, a flicker of panic appeared in his eyes. "For God's sake," he barked, "do it now and do it quickly." As Sam bucked again, almost throwing him off, he added desperately, "I don't think we can hold her much longer."

12:37 am

ALL THE WAY to the hospital, Cliff, who was driving, had had the oddest urge to rub the back of his neck, as if he had an itch there or a cold spot. He was not a fanciful man – he had been a paramedic too long to view life as anything more than a short, brutal interlude between one stretch of oblivion and the next – but there was something about their current patient that disturbed him.

He couldn't put his finger on what it was, though. It wasn't as if he had spoken to the man or even seen him conscious. In fact, the guy was currently clinging to life by nothing but the thinnest of threads, his body a sickening catalogue of broken bones, cuts and contusions.

By the time he and Matt had arrived on the scene, armed police had already had the building in lockdown and were questioning witnesses and potential suspects. There had been plenty of guys with blood on their hands (literally) and plenty of others, both girls *and* guys, sitting around crying or trembling with shock.

From what he and Matt had been told, the patient had walked into the club and bitten a couple of people before being set upon by a frenzied mob of between twenty and thirty onlookers. The attackers – all men – had not apparently encountered their victim before, and had had no particular affiliation to those that the man had attacked.

Evidently alcohol had played a large part in the escalation of the violence, though even Cliff had been shocked at the extent of the man's injuries. The pool of blood in which he had been lying was so extensive that it had been impossible to attend to him without walking in it. His face had been so battered and misshapen that it looked as though it had been whacked repeatedly with a hammer.

The man's jaw had been shattered and was hanging loose, his teeth had been splintered into fragments, one of his eyeballs had been split and dislodged, and his left ear was hanging by a thread. Additionally, his limbs had looked like a collection of broken sticks barely contained within tubes of skin, jagged edges of bone having torn through in several places. The man's robe was so saturated with blood that only a few pale patches here and there showed that it had once been white, and one of his feet had been stamped on so brutally and repeatedly that it had been mashed to a pulp.

What was left of the guy was in the back now, hooked up to pretty much everything they'd got. Matt was attending to him, and although Cliff knew he'd do everything within his power to keep the guy alive, he had known from the look on Matt's face that the thoughts of his colleague reflected his own – that it would be more of a kindness to put the poor bloke out of his misery than to haul him back from the brink of extinction.

Poor bloke? he thought. Yes, the guy was undoubtedly that. And Cliff's overriding emotions since his first sight of the man's injuries had been – and still were – pity and horror. Yet, for all that, he couldn't deny the fact that the guy elicited in him a sense of unease, even of revulsion. It was an instinctual thing, something that was buried deep, almost like a race memory. It had no basis in rationality whatsoever, and yet Cliff knew not only that it was there, but that Matt felt it too.

They hadn't spoken about it, but he had seen his own feelings reflected in his friend's face, in his body language, in the way that he had had to overcome his reluctance to touch the man, to attend to him. Cliff prided himself on remaining cool and professional whatever the situation, but he couldn't deny that his stomach was currently crawling with nerves, or that cold sweat was even now trickling down his back and chest and soaking the armpits of his uniform. Never before had he been so eager to get a patient to hospital.

He knew that once he and Matt relinquished responsibility for the guy, they would both feel an inexplicable but overwhelming sense of relief.

Pulling off Lewisham High Street and in through the main entrance of the tree- and railing-bordered hospital grounds, Cliff noticed a number of dark-windowed military-looking vehicles parked nose-to-tail on the other side of the road. Though they were some distance away and partly shaded by trees, which made it hard to make out what colour they were, they looked to him like the armoured vehicles that the new "Heavy Weapons" police mob, SO22, drove about in – the kind that looked like Black Marias crossed with tanks.

Although there was no sign of activity from the vehicles, Cliff wondered why they were here. Was something kicking off, or about to? Their brooding presence added to his sense of unease, and he put his foot down as he skirted the car park in front of the hospital and headed towards the large, open turning area that fronted the entrance to A&E.

Sliding into a gap between two ambulances, he brought the QRV to a halt and jumped out. By the time he had raised the rear hatch and pulled down the ramp, Matt was already sliding the wheeled stretcher towards him.

"How is he?" Cliff asked.

Matt's face was deadpan. "Doubt he'll regain consciousness."

Both of them were startled, therefore, when, as they manoeuvred the stretcher down the ramp and on to the ground, the man's remaining eye suddenly popped open.

At first Cliff thought it was a muscular spasm – the guy had enough drugs in him to stun a rhinoceros – but then the eye swivelled to look at him. It was bloodshot, glaring, and it sent a cold, almost metallic shiver scuttling through Cliff's body. He wondered how aware of his surroundings and situation the man was, and whether he felt any pain.

He heard a hideous liquid-like sound that was somewhere between a gurgling and a hissing, and saw something moving within the gaping ruin of the man's shattered jaw.

My God, Cliff thought, *surely he's not trying to speak?*

Horrified though he was, he leaned in closer, half-raising a hand to quieten the man, placate him. Yes, there was definitely something moving in the glistening cavern of the man's mouth, but what? His tongue? A foreign body? Clots of matter that were choking him and that he needed to expel?

All at once the man began to shudder, to spasm, his single eye rolling back into his head. From deep within his throat came a *surge* of twitching, frantic movement, and then, as his body began to buck in its final death-throes, he made a terrible retching sound and suddenly thousands of tiny red *things* were erupting from his mouth.

With a cry of revulsion, Cliff sprang back, feeling a cloud of the things engulfing him, feeling them pattering against his face like seaspray. At first he assumed that the man had simply regurgitated a final gout of lifeblood, but then, to his astonishment, he saw that the cloud of what he had thought were blood droplets were still airborne and, not only that, but they were darting, moving, spreading upwards and outwards.

41

"They're insects." Matt's voice was choked, incredulous. "The guy was full of *fucking insects!*"

Cliff watched in astonishment as the insects dissipated into the air. Already he could feel the skin on his face itching where they had bitten him.

12:46 am

"I'M NOT SURE this is a good idea, Tim," said Gill Eaves, peering nervously at the ceiling of the steel lift as it clanked and creaked its way upwards.

Dr Tim Marshall, senior in rank but junior by almost ten years to the forty-year-old charge nurse, frowned in irritation.

"On the contrary, it's perfect. No one will think to look for us here. We can take as long as we like."

"But what if we're missed?"

"With everyone running around like blue-arsed flies? Do *you* have time to keep tabs on what your colleagues are doing?"

"Well, no, not all of them, but—"

"Exactly. If anyone asks, we'll just say we've been busy – which we will have been." He grinned wolfishly.

"What if there's an emergency?"

"Then they'll page me." He raised his eyebrows condescendingly. "Relax, Gill. Everything will be fine."

The main entrance to the Lewisham Medical Museum was on Albacore Crescent, off Lewisham High Street; though because the Museum shared maintenance staff with the cluster of buildings that comprised University Hospital, the two institutions were linked via a service tunnel in the hospital basement, at either end of which a steel lift provided access from one building to the other.

It was rare for anyone other than cleaners, electricians and the occasional contractor to pass from one building to the next, and almost unheard of for members of the hospital's medical staff to use this route to visit the Museum. Those who *did* occasionally wander in at the end of their shift to view the various displays of medical paraphernalia from bygone days did so during the Museum's official opening hours between 10:00 am and 06:00 pm, and not in the dead of night when the Museum was locked and deserted.

The "thing", as Gill referred to it, between herself and Dr Marshall had been stuttering along for almost three months now. It was not exactly a great love affair, it wasn't even particularly impassioned, but it was nevertheless a habit she seemed both unable and unwilling to break.

It had started, as such things often do, with shared glances, brief touches and flirtatious comments. The reason Gill had allowed it to develop at all was because she had started to feel lonely, taken for granted at home. She did not feel unloved by Gerry as such, but undesired, and so Dr Marshall's interest had come as both a boost to her confidence and a much-needed reminder that she could still turn heads.

Though the past three months had been deliciously exciting ones, they had been terrifying and frustrating too. Despite the fact that Tim wasn't married or even had a steady girlfriend, so far as Gill was aware, he had been reluctant to see her outside of work. Their trysts, therefore, had mostly been quick, fumbling affairs within the hospital – hasty fucks in toilets, store cupboards and empty offices. Gill had been anxious on more than one occasion that someone might walk in on them, but she couldn't deny that the prospect had also provided her with a frisson of reckless excitement.

There were times when she had felt used, and other times – when Gerry was being nice to her, or when it struck her how much she adored her two kids, and how innocently and completely they believed in her flawlessness – that she had felt guilt-ridden, and subsequently determined to draw a line under the affair.

But she hadn't – at least, not yet. For now, the temporary highs of their encounters, the euphoria of knowing that she was still alluring enough to attract a handsome doctor almost a decade younger than herself, was enough to keep the guilt at bay. She knew it wouldn't go on forever; there was even a part of her that hoped Tim would end it soon. But for now she would take what she could get and live with the consequences. She would have her cake and eat it.

She wasn't entirely sure about this latest idea of Tim's, though. She liked the fact that he had thought about it, that he had shown a desire to prolong the amount of time they could spend together . . . but what she didn't like was the choice of venue itself.

The building that housed the Medical Museum was considerably older than those it was attached to. Indeed, it had once been the oldest part of the hospital, but had eventually been shut down and put to another use – so the rumour went – because of its unsavoury reputation.

Gill's knowledge of the building came mainly from Reg Pulis, the oldest porter by some years, who had worked at the hospital for as long as anyone could remember. Gill had no idea how old Reg actually was, but he *seemed* ancient – certainly well past retirement age. He was tall and stooped with snow-white hair, fingers stained yellow with nicotine, and a face that had the texture of a brown paper bag that had been screwed into a tight ball and then slowly uncrumpled. For all that, he was a sprightly old man, more than capable of pushing patients – some of whom, though decrepit, were younger than he was

– up and down hospital corridors all day. He was a Lewisham man, born and bred, and claimed that his family connection went so far back that they had first started living here when the area was just fields and marshes.

Reg was full of stories of the old days, and particularly of local folklore. He loved to gossip, and Gill had spent many a happy fag break round the back of the canteen in his company, listening to him nattering away. Always one for a bit of sensationalism, he had told her that the old Underground line to Hobbs End had run right under the building, and that, even though the line had been abandoned for years, patients and staff had often complained not only of hearing bangs and bumps from beneath the floor, but had claimed to see small, shadowy figures appearing and disappearing through the walls.

All nonsense, of course, though Gill knew that even now the staff who ran the Museum were reluctant to be there alone, especially after dark. It was common knowledge that the place had not only an unsettling reputation, but also a genuinely strange atmosphere. One student who had worked there a few summers ago had had what amounted to a nervous breakdown after only a few weeks into the job. She had said that she had felt constantly watched, even while alone, and eventually she had claimed that something – a hunched shape she could see out of the corner of her eye, but which disappeared whenever she turned to focus on it – had followed her home.

Even without the stories, the Museum was not the sort of place you would ordinarily wish to visit at night. Fascinating and informative though the displays and exhibits were, the majority of them – separated by partition walls, and often built on a number of levels to give visitors a sense of authenticity – did tend towards the lurid and the grotesque.

They included a lovingly detailed Victorian slum dwelling, complete with appropriate sounds and smells (the intention being to show how rife with disease such places were); a reconstruction of a 19th-century operating theatre, enlivened by wax effigies of a bloodied surgeon and a screaming patient having his leg sawn off; and a padded cell containing another waxen, wild-eyed patient, this one wearing a straitjacket and foaming at the mouth.

As well as these macabre delights, there were display cases full of surgical instruments and post-mortem equipment, several racks of bulbous specimen jars in which malformed foetuses and various bodily organs floated in urine-coloured preserving solution, and a selection of paintings of the diseased, the disfigured and the insane by a renowned Victorian artist who had taken inspiration from the many patients who had passed through the hospital's doors during the latter half of the 19th century.

As soon as the lift clanked to a halt and the doors juddered open, Tim strode out, leading the way along a short, nondescript corridor to a door at the far end. Trailing in his wake, Gill glanced up. The ceiling was composed of polystyrene panels, many of which were crumbling or missing entirely. Through the gaps she could see metal pipes and straggling lengths of multi-coloured wire, some of which were cinched together with metal clips. The sight put her uncomfortably in mind of a body, the flesh peeled back to expose the tendons and veins.

Tim paused only briefly at the door to punch the four-digit code into the entry panel on the stained wall beside it. There was a faint, complicit *whirr* as locks disengaged and he pushed the door open. Instinctively Gill stepped up close to his back, as if to shield herself from whatever might come lurching out of the darkness. But there was nothing except a tentative breath of chilly air, which carried a fleeting plasticky – or was it waxy? – odour.

"It's a bit dark," she said nervously, peering over his shoulder. Though a little light from the street lamps outside seeped in through the mostly glass entrance at the far end of the room, it

47

was not enough to do more than give the faintest definition to the many angles and surfaces before them.

"I've thought of that," Tim said smugly and produced a quartet of candles and a box of matches from the pockets of his long white coat.

"How are you going to stand them up?" Gill asked.

"I've thought of that too," he said. "Wait here."

Before she could protest he had darted away from her, into the shadows, turning right somewhere ahead so that she quickly lost sight of him. She stood, almost rigid, flanked by a waist-high display case on her left and a partition wall on her right. She was suddenly and acutely aware of the darkness and silence surrounding her, and of the vague sound of Tim's movements, which, rather than reassuring her, reminded her only of the murky distance between them.

Now that she was here, she felt nothing but sympathy for the student who had felt constantly under surveillance.

A prickling in her shoulders quickly ballooned into a certainty that someone was standing behind her. With a small, shrill gasp, she spun around – and saw eyes gleaming wildly in the darkness. But although they were the eyes of a madman, he was trapped in a portrait on the wall.

He was sitting bolt upright on a wooden bed with his mouth agape and his hands clutching the coarse blanket at his waist. Thankfully the gleam that animated his eyes was not that of life, but of the meagre light from outside captured and reflected by the twin daubs of white oil paint that gave him such a wild and vacant expression.

Though Gill was relieved, she didn't feel secure enough to smile at her foolishness – especially not when she heard the chink of chains somewhere beyond her left shoulder.

She spun again, to see a shape looming out of the darkness, hunched with the weight of the chains it was dragging behind it. Then she realized her mistake. The shape wasn't hunched;

it was merely concentrating on where it was putting its feet. And it wasn't chains she could hear, but the chink of ceramic mugs, two of which it was carrying in each hand. It was Tim, back from what she guessed must have been the staff kitchen.

He held up the mugs triumphantly. "Here we go," he said. "We can put the candles in these." He jerked his head behind him. "There's a display over here with a bed in it. And before you say anything, it's only been made to *look* filthy. It isn't really."

He turned and led the way, the shrill chink of the mugs making her think of the chattering teeth of a cartoon character in a haunted house. As soon as they stepped through the non-existent fourth wall of the display he had mentioned, he set about placing the mugs strategically around the room, like a dinner host attempting to create ambience. But the flickering light of the candles was no comfort – it only emphasized the room's squalid cheerlessness.

Gill looked with distaste at the sagging, stained bed, the motionless rat nibbling at the plate of bones on the table, the silent onlooker perched on a stool in the corner: a woman dressed in rags and clutching a swaddled baby, her waxen face disfigured by weeping pustules.

When she looked back at Tim, he was already yanking off his tie, his eyes made avid by candlelight.

"Well, come on," he almost snapped, tossing his tie on the table beside the rat and plumping down on to the bed, which creaked beneath his weight, to drag off his shoes, "we haven't got all night."

Gill sighed inwardly. "So romantic," she muttered.

Dutifully but unenthusiastically she began to unbutton her uniform.

01:00 am

CAT HOPED SHE didn't look as pale and shaken as she felt. She paused for a moment in the corridor to take a long, shuddering breath, and then she adopted what she trusted was a composed expression and stepped through the arch into the main Admissions area.

After the commotion half-an-hour earlier things seemed to have settled down. There was perhaps a thrum of tension in the air, illustrated by the nervous glances she received from waiting patients, but on the whole the majority of people had reacted to what had happened by becoming subdued rather than agitated. Even those who had been involved in the brawl seemed to have now retreated into their shells.

The three "nurses" were sitting quietly, not speaking, two of them staring into space and the third – the bride-to-be, whose friend had scratched her arm – slumped to one side with a blanket around her shoulders, apparently asleep.

The two black kids sitting opposite the girls – who she supposed were waiting to see their friends, unless the police who had brought them in had ordered them to sit tight until they finished questioning the kid with the gunshot wound

– were quiet too. The younger, smaller one had drawn his knees up to his chin so that his heels rested on the edge of his seat and was doing his best not to look as anxious as he clearly felt, whereas his taller, rangier friend had pulled his hood up and was now slumped with his legs stretched out, his arms crossed and his head bowed so far forward that the only part of his face that wasn't in shadow was the chin resting on his chest.

As she approached the group, Cat noted that the thick bandage around the older kid's injured hand was spotted with blood, as though the wound was still seeping. She hoped that he wouldn't resist her suggestion of more intensive treatment. In light of how quickly the infection had already spread in the two girls currently under care – one of them her colleague – she couldn't help feeling that she was racing against time.

The tall, pretty, hazelnut-haired girl with the matching eyes – what was her name? Lucy? Lisa? – looked up at her approach and stirred, her back stiffening as though she was bracing herself for bad news. Her voice, whose harshness Cat guessed was due to anxiety rather than hostility, roused her friend, the willowy, dark-skinned girl with features so delicate they seemed overpowered by her almost-black eyes and raven-glossy hair.

"How is she, nurse? How's Sam?"

Cat saved her reply until she was standing directly in front of the girls, until she was bending her knees to crouch at their level. Murmuring so that her voice wouldn't carry, she said, "She's not so good, I'm afraid."

The dark-skinned girl's eyes widened and her hand flew to her mouth as if Cat had told her worse news than that.

With enough presence of mind to realize that Cat was trying to thwart eavesdroppers, the tall girl (Lisa/Lucy) asked quietly, "Why? What's wrong with her?"

Cat sighed. "That's part of the problem. We don't know yet. We haven't identified the infection."

"What about the man who bit her?" the dark-skinned girl blurted, and then responded to both Cat's and the tall girl's wincing looks by instantly lowering her voice. "Can't you find him?"

Cat paused before saying, "He's already on the premises. Or at least his body is."

Lisa/Lucy's glossy lips parted in shock. "His body? You mean he's dead?"

"I'm afraid so."

"What of?" asked the dark-skinned girl. "The infection?"

"No. I'm afraid he was murdered."

This time Lisa/Lucy's shock was pronounced enough to pluck her upright so abruptly that her cleavage quivered. "You mean at the club? When he was attacked?"

"So I'm led to believe."

Lisa/Lucy's mouth formed an O before the words emerged as a hushed exclamation. "*Holy shit.*"

"Can they find out from his . . . from his body what he's got? Passed on, I mean?" asked the other girl.

"That's one possibility certainly," Cat said. "For now, though, our main concern is to treat the infection as best we can, which means, in the case of those who've come into contact with it recently, like your friend here, nipping it in the bud."

She turned towards the still-sleeping bride-to-be, whose name, Cat suddenly remembered, was Chris, but Lisa/Lucy wasn't about to be fobbed off so easily.

"You still haven't told us how Sam is. Really is, I mean. How bad is she?"

Cat paused. "We've had to restrain and sedate her—"

"Restrain?" interrupted the dark-skinned girl, too loudly, and immediately lowered her voice to a hiss again as heads turned. "You mean tie her up?"

"Her *and* my colleague, Nurse Ollerenshaw, who your friend bit. The infection seems to affect the brain, to make its victims aggressive."

"Like rabies?" suggested Lisa/Lucy.

"Well, we're trying not to jump to conclusions just yet."

"*Could* it be rabies?" the dark-skinned girl persisted.

Cat hesitated, though only because her immediate thought was that, based on what she had seen, the infection might yet be *worse* than rabies. "I don't see how."

"So what are you doing?" Lisa/Lucy said. "How is Sam being treated? How long will she have to stay in hospital?"

Cat thought of how quickly the girl's condition had deteriorated, how the wound had seemed to spread and devour her arm, her flesh turning dark yellow, her veins almost black. She pictured the look of alarm on the face of Dr Blackstock, the on-call senior house officer, as he had observed the phenomenon taking place almost before his eyes, and recalled the phrases he had spoken in a voice breathless with disbelief: *ischaemia* and *necrotizing fasciitis*.

Almost in desperation they had pumped broad-spectrum antibiotics into the girl in a bid to reverse the infection: co-amoxiclav, metronidazole, gentamicin. But so far she had failed to respond, as had Tammy Ollerenshaw, who now seemed to be going the same way. As Cat had said, both girls had had to be restrained and sedated due to the fact that as the infection had spread it had not only attacked their flesh but had subsumed their personalities too, replacing conscious thought with hostility, and the ability to communicate with raw animal aggression.

Forcing a smile, Cat said, "We're doing all we can for her, believe me. Pumping her full of antibiotics. There's little more I can tell you at the moment – besides which, I really ought to be seeing to Christine. Can't have her being ill on her wedding day, can we?"

She wasn't sure whether the scowl she received from Lisa/Lucy was because the girl thought she was being condescending or because she was simply anxious about her friends.

Taking the sleeping girl's hand, Cat squeezed it gently and said, "Christine, can you hear me?"

It was only as she realized how clammy Christine's hand was that it occurred to Cat that the girl's sleeping face was the same. It was her heavy make-up that had disguised the fact that the skin beneath was pale and damp-looking, the beads of sweat glinting beneath her feathery blonde fringe suggestive of fever.

"Christine," Cat said again, and then, more familiarly though sharply, "*Chris.*"

The girl stirred, her eyes opening as if fingers were forcing them. Her unmeshing eyelashes reminded Cat of the yawning jaws of Venus Fly Traps, albeit clumped stickily with mascara. When Chris parted her lips along with her eyes, Cat tried not to recoil from a gust of breath that stank of stale alcohol.

Chris looked blearily at her and then at her surroundings. "Wha? Wherrami?"

"You're in the hospital, Chris," Cat said gently.

"Hospital? Whahappen?"

Lisa/Lucy leaned in. "Sam got bit, Chris. Remember? By that bloke?"

Chris seemed not to register this. Instead she grimaced in pain. "Arm hurts," she muttered.

"Mind if I take a look?" asked Cat.

Without waiting for an answer she lifted the blanket carefully away from the scratches on Chris' arm, her heart sinking at what was revealed. The wounds were inflamed and leaking pus, the flesh around them already showing signs of the necrosis she had observed in both Sam and Tammy.

"*Jesus Christ!*" said Lisa/Lucy.

"Oh my God," muttered the dark-skinned girl.

"Come on, sweetheart," Cat said, rising to her feet and taking the hand of Chris' uninjured arm in both of hers, gently coaxing the bride-to-be on to her feet. "Let's get you seen to."

She was half-afraid that Chris might suddenly turn aggressive, as both Sam and Tammy had done, but for the moment she appeared compliant enough, if confused. With the help of her two friends she rose unsteadily to her feet, swaying on her white heels.

"I'll take you through to the back where it's quieter and we can compare wedding plans," said Cat. Partly to Chris' friends she added, "I'm getting married soon too."

She led Chris away, the woozy girl moving as slowly as a pensioner. They had taken no more than half-a-dozen steps when from behind them Cat heard a groan and a thump, followed immediately by a shriek of surprise.

Turning her head she saw that the older of the two kids, who she had planned on coming back to once she had got Chris settled, was no longer sprawled on his seat opposite the girls, but lying full-length on the floor between the two rows of chairs. He was on his front, twitching and groaning, and as Cat looked at him she saw that the bandage around his hand was now stained not only with blood but with a greenish-black discharge.

The younger kid was looking at his friend as if he had been shot, but as his eyes flickered to meet Cat's his expression of almost boyish alarm became a scowl.

"Why you standing there?" he said. "Can't you see Jermaine's collapsed?" He gestured disdainfully at Chris, whose hand Cat was still holding. "Never mind 'bout that bitch. Was her friend what did this. So go get help for Jermaine *right now*."

01:05 am

"WHAT WAS THAT?"

Tim Marshall paused in the act of pulling on his trousers. "What was what?"

"I thought I heard something."

The candlelight dragged at his features, exaggerating the scepticism on his face. "*I* didn't hear anything," he said as if that was an end to it.

"Well *I* did." Gill took her irritation out on her uniform, snapping the press-studs together as though squashing bugs beneath her thumbs, vigorously smoothing the blue material over her only slightly drooping boobs and still relatively flat stomach. "Two or three thumps. Like someone knocking on a door."

Now he looked petulant, and seemed to be doing nothing but mocking her as he became motionless while making a point of tilting his head. After a couple of seconds he said decisively, "Nope. Silent as the proverbial grave."

"Well, yes, it is *now*," she said. "But that doesn't mean it was a minute ago."

He shrugged. "Pipes. Or a noise from outside. I wouldn't worry about it."

They continued dressing, or at least he did. Gill had dressed as quickly as she could once their coupling was over and was now waiting with her arms crossed, eager to return to work. From her point of view the sex tonight, for the first time since she had started seeing him, had been purely functional, all biology and no passion. How much that had to do with their surroundings and how much with the simple fact that the magic for her was on the wane, that she was finally coming to her senses, she had no idea.

As she watched him leaning forward from his seated position on the grubby bed to pick up his tie from the floor, she wondered seriously about ending it there and then. She even started to rehearse what she would say, what approach she would take.

Should she be blunt or compassionate? Should she flatter him by emphasizing what a heart-breaking decision it was for her, or make him realize that she was the one with everything to lose, the one who was taking all the risks?

But what if he responded by telling her that he couldn't bear to let her go, that he was prepared to commit himself to her, to make their relationship public? Would that prompt her to discover that she wanted him, after all? Would it be enough for her to consider turning her back on everything she had with Gerry and the kids?

Her train of thought was derailed when he suddenly shouted, "*Bugger!*" and slapped the back of his neck.

Her first instinct was to hunch her shoulders and clench her teeth for fear that his outburst would draw attention to them – though attention from whom or what she couldn't say.

"What's wrong?" she asked.

"Something bit me." He removed his hand from his neck and showed it to her. His palm was smeared with something dark. "Look at that. Little fucker."

She pushed herself up from the table she'd been leaning against and stepped towards him, candle flames flapping as she displaced the air. The ragged, pustule-faced woman, who had been a silent though distracting presence throughout their love-making, seemed to shift slightly, to crane forwards on her stool, her animation so momentarily pronounced that Gill had to glance at her in order to ensure that the movement was nothing but an illusion of wavering light and shadow.

Leaning forwards she saw something squashed and not quite dead in Tim's palm, something whose hair-thin legs were still twitching feebly.

Grimacing she said, "What is it? A mosquito?"

He raised his hand to his face as if to check the creature's identity by tasting it. "It's fatter and rounder than a mosquito. Looks more like a flea."

"A flea? But it's huge. And bright red."

"Probably with my blood. Vampiric little bastard."

With the pugnacity of a victor he made a show of wiping his hand on the bed. It was as he was aggressively knotting his tie, as if challenging anything else to mess with him, that the two of them heard three distinct, sharp raps from elsewhere in the room.

Gill jumped so violently that it was enough to set the candle flames flapping again. For a moment the reconstructed Victorian hovel seemed to tilt like the deck of a ship, the walls warping around them. Tim went rigid, apart from his head, which jerked up, shadows sliding in and out of his eye sockets like black tidal water.

"What the fuck was that?" he muttered.

Gill's left knee popped as she dropped into a crouch, clutching the edge of the table to anchor herself. Her voice was a dry rasp. "There's something in here with us."

For a few seconds Tim's toffee-like features tried a number of different expressions before settling on defiance. Rising to his feet he barked, "Who's there?"

Appalled by his brazenness, Gill glared at him, but he

seemed emboldened enough by the silence that greeted his challenge to add, "Whoever you are, we're not scared of you."

Speak for yourself, Gill didn't say. Instead she opted for, "Don't encourage it, whatever it is. Let's just get out of here."

Tim appeared not to have heard her. "Where did it come from, do you think?"

"I don't know. Who cares? Let's just go."

He swivelled in a half-circle as if trying to tune in to a signal. "I think it came from over near the main doors. Maybe somewhere to the right of them."

"So let's go the opposite way," she hissed, fear harshening her words. "That's where we need to go anyway."

He stooped to pluck a candle from the nearest of the four mugs that they had placed around the room. "I think we should check it out."

"What?" she breathed incredulously. "No. No way. Don't be an idiot, Tim."

His jaw tightened. "If we're being spied on, I want to know who by."

"We're not being spied on." She paused and her voice dropped to even less than a hiss. "You know the stories people tell about this place."

His snort made her cringe. It felt too much like a challenge to the unknown. "You stay here if you like. But I'm going to take a look."

She was too angry with him – with his pig-headedness, with his lack of consideration for her feelings – to do anything but mutter, "Go on then." Seething, she remained crouched beside the table as his sketchy form accompanied the quivering flame from the three-walled, ceilingless room. The instant he was out of sight, however, she felt an urge to snatch up a candle and hurry after him. But the desire not to be alone was not quite strong enough to overcome the desire to remain where she was. She felt . . . not exactly *safe* here, but at least inconspicuous.

59

She would be less conspicuous, of course, if she blew out the three remaining candles, but she couldn't bear the thought of being in darkness. For the next few minutes she remained where she was, hardly daring to move, hardly daring even to breathe, her hand gripping the table she was crouched beside and her eyes fixed on the patch of darkness beyond the invisible fourth wall of the reconstructed hovel, the darkness that Tim had disappeared into.

Her face was set in concentration as she strained to listen for sounds of his progress, but she heard only silence, as if she was suddenly alone in the room. She wondered what she would do if he didn't come back, how long she would leave it before venturing out on her own. She wondered if she had been missed, if her colleagues were starting to wonder where she was. She felt as if she had been gone for hours.

Eventually her thighs and knees started to ache. If she crouched here any longer she'd get cramp. Perhaps now was the time, she thought. Perhaps she ought to take a candle and hurry to the door at the back of the building. It was a straightforward enough route. She could be there in a couple of dozen steps. And it would serve Tim right if he got back to find her gone; it would send him the message that she wasn't reliant on him and didn't appreciate the way he disregarded her feelings and opinions.

Gripping the table tighter, she rose slowly to her feet, wincing as her knees creaked. She pictured the route she had to take. Twenty-four steps. Fifteen seconds. If she counted the steps it would take her mind off her surroundings, of what might be lurking in the darkness. She half-turned to pick up the nearest candle, lolling lopsidedly in its mug. As she did so the pustule-faced woman sidled into her peripheral vision. But it wasn't the waxen model that made her freeze. It was the small, dark figure standing beside it.

For a moment she saw it quite clearly, a squat, dwarfish biped, with bowed legs and over-long arms. Despite the candlelight she couldn't see its face. Clots of shadow were obscuring its features, unless they were matted clumps of hair.

A sense of terror so acute it was like the onset of unconsciousness rippled through her. She felt her muscles lock, her vision blur, her mouth drain instantly of moisture. There was a second, perhaps less, when the figure was not only as motionless as she was, but when Gill felt certain that it was staring at her, *marking* her. Then it turned and ambled away, walking – as far as she could tell – directly through the wall.

Its disappearance unlocked the full brunt of her terror. Staggering away from the spot where the figure had stood, she opened her mouth and gave vent to a ragged but full-throated scream. Head pounding, she blundered out of the makeshift hovel and into the darkness, oblivious now to the fact that she was drawing attention to herself.

She could hear her heart drumming, getting louder and faster, and then she realized that it wasn't her heart, it was footsteps, rapidly approaching. A flame bloomed in the darkness, veering wildly as it hurtled towards her, and behind the flame was a chalk-white face with charred holes for eyes and a gaping black pit for a mouth.

01:14 am

"YOU AND YOUR corned beef," said Shirley. "Who eats corned beef these days?"

"I do," said Vince, demonstrating the fact by devouring half of his sandwich in one bite. Chewing, he added, "Corned beef and brown sauce on white bread wi' proper butter. Food o' champions."

She shook her head pityingly. "Corned beef, luncheon meat, potted crab paste, spam . . . you're like a throwback to the '70s."

"Nowt wrong wi' that. All the best things came out of the '70s."

"Oh yeah? Like what?"

He finished the last of his sandwich, dusted his hands together to rid them of crumbs and began to reel off a list, counting each item off on his sausage-like fingers. "*Jaws, Star Wars, The Sweeney*, punk rock, best Leeds United team that ever walked the planet . . ."

She held up a clenched fist and raised a considerably slimmer finger for each of her own examples. "IRA bombings, Idi Amin, the Three-Day Week, the Bay City Rollers . . ." her voice rose, became an exclamation of triumph ". . . *Margaret Thatcher!*"

Vince slumped in his seat and held up his hands in surrender. "Aye, well, you've got me there. There's no coming back from that." He gave a sudden, sly grin. "Still reckon my sandwich is better than yours, though."

"Bollocks!" she retorted, her Cardiff accent raging to the fore.

"You can try and sweet-talk me all you like, lass, but you know I'm right. What the bloody hell is that anyway?"

Haughtily she said, "It's a proper sandwich, this. Sophisticated. You wouldn't understand."

"Aye, but what is it?"

"What does it look like, numpty? It's prawn salad on granary, isn't it? And it's bloody delicious."

She took a bite and made an exaggerated "*Mmmm*" sound, half-closing her eyes in ecstasy.

Vince shuddered. "Prawns."

"What's wrong with prawns?"

"What's right with 'em? They're like little pink foetuses. And the texture when you bite into 'em . . . like lumps o' soft gristle."

Shirley slapped his arm. "Shut up, you bugger. You're putting me off."

He laughed. "Call yourself Welsh? I didn't think anything could put you lot off your food."

"Yeah, well, you're wrong about that, aren't you? Delicate soul, me. Like a little flower."

He laughed again, a real guffaw this time, and Shirley grinned along with him. She was glad to see him looking more relaxed. That call from his ex-wife earlier had wound him right up. At least the cardiac arrest on Foxberry Road had stopped him brooding about it, especially as it looked as if their patient was going to be all right. In fact, he'd been quite a card,

63

chatting and joking despite the chest pains that occasionally caused his grey, sweaty face to clench in pain.

They had managed to get him stabilized fairly quickly, and in fact it had been his wife, a voluminous woman with jowls so pronounced it looked as though her skin was several sizes too large for her, who had given them the most problems, her distress becoming so acute that she had had to be sedated. Shirley could sympathize with her agitation, though. The heart attack had been her husband's fourth, and apparently after suffering his third nine months ago his doctor had warned him that if he didn't cut down on his smoking he'd be dead within a year.

"But did he listen?" his wife said, her red face quivering. "No, he bloody well didn't."

"What are you talking about, woman?" her husband had rasped from his stretcher, giving Shirley an exaggerated wink. "You know I used to smoke sixty a day and now I only smoke fifty-nine."

Having delivered him *and* his wife to the hospital, Vince and Shirley were now sitting in their ambulance in one of the parking bays, having a well-earned break and indulging in their usual banter. As Vince unscrewed the flask of tea he always brought with him and poured them both a plastic cupful, he said, "Right weird do they're havin' in there tonight."

Shirley accepted a cup from him, wincing at the taste as she always did. "All that biting, you mean?"

"Aye. That nurse wi' the dark hair – what's her name?"

"Susan Jenkins?"

"That's the one. She said folk were going crazy, gettin' bitten then bitin' other folk. She said it was some infection."

"What sort of infection makes you want to bite people?" said Shirley.

"Buggered if I know. Rabies?"

She shivered and locked the door.

"What you doin'?" asked Vince.

64

Lewisham and Greenwich
NHS Trust
AMBULANCE
Main Entrance
University Hospital
Lewisham
Emergency Department and Urgent Care

She shrugged, embarrassed. "Just taking precautions. You can't be too careful."

His laugh seemed to produce an answering crackle from the radio, and then a voice. Shirley put her cup on the dashboard and grabbed the receiver. "We're here, Asif. Go ahead."

"Where are you at the moment?" Asif asked.

"Still at the hospital. Grabbing a quick sandwich."

"Okay, well you're needed at All Hallows Church. There's a report of a man with a severe bite wound. Details are a bit sketchy, but I'm sending them through now."

The details sheet oozed from the in-cab printer with an insect-like whine. "Thanks, Asif, got it," Shirley said, then looked across at Vince with still-widening eyes. "Bite wound?"

He looked just as bewildered. "What the fuck is goin' on?"

She tore her gaze away from him and nodded towards the window. "Guess we'll find out soon enough. Drive."

01:39am

PERHAPS, THOUGHT PIOTR, he ought to give up on the whole speed-dating thing and just let things happen naturally, or not at all. Perhaps he ought to concentrate on finding someone who worked within the medical profession, and so wouldn't be put off when they found out what he did. Because however he dressed it up, however long he avoided the question, the truth always managed to squirm out in the end. And when it did, the fact that he'd been trying to cover it up always made it seem worse somehow.

He'd try to laugh it off, of course, but he'd see the girls looking at him with distaste, as if he was some kind of ghoul. He'd see them stealing glances at his hands and wondering where those hands had been. And he'd know there and then that there was no way they would ever allow those hands anywhere near them.

"*I wash them all the time,*" he often wanted to say. "*Hygiene is paramount in my job. I'm cleaner than nearly all the other guys you're likely to meet tonight.*"

But he'd know that if he said that it would just make him sound even more creepy, not to mention desperate and lecherous, and so most of the time he just shrugged and mumbled apologetically that it really wasn't as gross as it sounded, that most of it was just paperwork.

Anatomical Pathology Technologist. That was his official title. He'd muttered those three words – albeit reluctantly, and only when it got to the point in the conversation where he couldn't avoid it any longer – several times last night. But whichever girl he had spoken to, no matter how different they had been, the conversation had ended up going down pretty much the same route.

"Ooh, that sounds impressive. So are you a doctor?"

"Kind of."

"Kind of? What does that mean?"

"It means I'm a member of the healthcare science staff, based at University Hospital in Lewisham."

"Riiight. So . . . er, what do you actually do?"

"I assist pathologists. I keep records of sample analysis and that kind of thing. There's a lot of administration involved. It's actually quite boring."

"So you deal with patients?"

"Well . . . not patients as such."

"What then?"

"It's . . . awkward."

"Why is it awkward?"

"Because I never know how people are going to react."

"Why? What do you mean? React to what?"

"Well, you see, the thing is . . . I deal not with live patients, but with dead ones. I work in the Mortuary."

He sighed and took a swig of coffee. Perhaps he should start by telling the girls that he was an electrician or a plumber, and only reveal his true profession once they had got to know and like him. He found it ironic that his family back in Poland was so incredibly proud of what he had achieved. Working in a hospital in London! For his grandparents and parents and aunts and uncles such a thing seemed beyond their wildest dreams. He knew that his grandparents in particular couldn't even *begin* to imagine what mighty steps he must have taken to reach his goal, and what an incredible lifestyle he must now be living in one of the most vibrant and glamorous cities in the world.

The truth, however, though he would never burst their bubble by revealing it, was very different. Piotr was lonely. And although he earned more money than he could ever earn in his native country, London was such an expensive place to live that in real terms he was no better off. His home here consisted of a bedsit above a Chinese takeaway that was only half the size of his bedroom back at the farm. London was a vibrant city, yes, but it was also smelly and dirty and horribly overcrowded.

Often Piotr found himself yearning for the fields and forests and open spaces of his homeland; often he wished he had stayed home to grow rye and potatoes and tend to livestock. The irony was, if he had told the girls that he was a Polish farmer they would probably have found that interesting and romantic. They would have been left with an impression of him as some rugged outdoor type, strong and practical, rather than some skulking fiend who dabbled with corpses in a hospital basement.

He took another gulp of coffee – black and bitter, like his mood – and tried to concentrate on the matter in hand. He was sitting in front of a computer screen in his cramped office, collating data from tonight's input. After that he would put another call through to the police to check whether they had discovered the identity of the unidentified murder victim who had been brought in an hour ago.

The guy had been in such a state that at first Piotr had thought he'd jumped from a tall building or been hit by a car. The fact that other human beings had inflicted the damage that had killed him was sickening, though Piotr had become hardened to the more brutal aspects of human nature in his four years in the job. Not that that was any sort of consolation. Although it was necessary, he hated the fact that he could compartmentalize his shock and disgust and compassion, that he had reached the stage where he often viewed corpses as pathological puzzles to be solved rather than as individuals who had once had lives of their own.

Hearing the sound of someone jabbing in the four-digit door code and then of the main Mortuary door at the end of the corridor beyond his office sighing weightily open, Piotr briefly looked up. He didn't bother rising from his seat to greet the newcomer, however; it was probably the pathologist, Hathaway, who Piotr had helped perform the post-mortem on the elderly pulmonary embolism case earlier in the evening. No doubt he was after the records that Piotr hadn't finished collating yet for his pathology report.

Hathaway was all right, but like most pathologists he didn't appreciate that once his job was done and he had toddled off back to his tea and biscuits, Piotr was left with a mountain of work still to do. He had to reconstruct and store the deceased after examination, record and store the deceased's property, clean and sterilise the lab, record and store samples and specimens, dispose of waste matter, speak to the nursing staff, the bereaved and sometimes the police, and just generally make sure that everything was running smoothly and the paperwork was up to date.

He sighed as he heard footsteps halt outside his office, followed almost immediately by three sharp and (in his opinion) impatient raps on his door. Knowing it was petty, he counted slowly to three – one second for each rap – before distractedly calling, "Come in."

The door jerked open and a tall, loose-limbed figure stepped into the room. He had tightly-curled black hair that glistened with oil and a stern, swarthy, hook-nosed face that made Piotr think of Holy Roman emperors or Spanish pirates.

Piotr was taken aback. This wasn't Dr Hathaway.

"Professor Déesharné," he said. "What brings you here?"

Déesharné, who Piotr had never spoken to before – whose role in the hospital, in fact, was a mystery to many, and therefore a topic of some debate – glared at Piotr as if the APT was responsible for some personal slight or misdemeanour.

"Where is the body of the murder victim who was brought in earlier?"

Déesharné's voice was clipped, and bore the hint of an accent which Piotr couldn't place. Taken aback both by the abruptness of the man's manner and by his question, he felt himself becoming unaccountably defensive.

"It's in cold storage, where it should be."

"It is to be delivered to me for immediate post-mortem. I have the necessary authorization."

Piotr felt himself bridling. "I'm sorry, Professor Déesharné, but I'm afraid that's not possible. The deceased has yet to be identified."

Déesharné scowled, rolling his eyes dismissively. "What has that got to do with anything?"

"Until identification of the deceased is established and relatives have been contacted," Piotr said, matching Déesharné's scowl with one of his own, "we can't seek consent for a post-mortem examination. And until consent is granted we can't release the remains, at least not until—"

Déesharné wafted Piotr's protestations away. "Never mind all of that. This is a matter of urgency. I have special dispensation."

"Dispensation from whom?"

"From the highest possible authority." Déesharné reached into his jacket and with a flourish produced an ivory-coloured envelope, which he handed to Piotr. "In there you will find a

71

Government edict granting me authority under the Planning Special Powers Act to procure whichever organic materials I deem necessary for the progression of my research."

Piotr took the envelope, but didn't open it. Bewildered, he said, "Powers Planing Special Act? I don't understand. Since when did the death of an unidentified murder victim come under that?"

Déesharné leaned forward, his hook-nosed face putting Piotr in mind of an eagle closing in on its prey. "I don't have to explain myself to you, Mr Bajorek, but what I will say is this: I do not expect my authority to be questioned. So I suggest that you accede to my request without delay, or face disciplinary action which I guarantee will almost certainly result in the direst of consequences." He straightened up, folded his arms, and for the first time a razor-thin smile appeared on his face. "The choice is yours, Mr Bajorek."

01:58 am

"NOW WHAT?" SAID Shirley.

The ambulance was parked outside the grounds of All Hallows Church, its engine idling. There was no sign of the wounded man they had been dispatched to pick up, who – according to the anonymous member of the public who had called in the incident – had been wandering around in a dazed state with blood pouring from what appeared to be a severe bite wound to his neck. Why the caller hadn't stayed with the wounded man they had no idea. Neither could the blonde, well-dressed man who had jumped out of the Audi A4 Saloon as soon as they had pulled into the space behind it enlighten them. The man had been hostile at first. Scowling, he had slammed the door of the Audi and marched round to the passenger side of the ambulance, indicating with a swirling motion of his finger that Shirley should lower her window. She had glanced at Vince, non-plussed.

"Who the hell's this guy?"

Vince had dipped his head to peer at the blonde man, who was all but bouncing impatiently on his heels. "Dunno, but he looks as though he thinks he's important."

73

With a sigh Shirley had pressed the button to lower her window, stopping it halfway. "Hello, sir, can I help you?"

The blonde man glared at her. "You can tell me why you're here."

Before Shirley could speak, Vince said in a voice that was both jovial and hard-edged, "I'm not sure that's any business of yours, old pal."

The man's hand darted towards the inside breast pocket of his jacket, and for one alarming moment Shirley thought he was reaching for a weapon. Then he produced a leather wallet, which he opened and pressed to the window.

"I'm Special Security Agent Viner. I have jurisdiction here. I assume you're on a call-out?"

Shirley nodded. "Yes."

"Care to give me the details?"

Raising his eyebrows and sighing deeply, Vince handed the details sheet to Shirley, who fed it through the half-open window. Pocketing his wallet, the blonde man, Viner, snatched the sheet from her and scanned it briefly.

"Looks like you're here on a wild-goose chase," he said.

"I think we'll be the judges o' that, if you don't mind," Vince replied.

Viner fixed him with a penetrating stare. There might have been something a bit public schoolboy about him, Shirley thought, but she sensed a dangerous vibe emanating from the man all the same.

"My colleague and I have been here all night and we haven't seen anything," he said bluntly.

Was he lying? Shirley couldn't tell. Her bullshit detector was usually pretty well-tuned (considering the hairy situations she and Vince sometimes found themselves in, it was important to be able to read people); but this guy, aside from his hostility, was a tightly-closed book.

Vince peered through his windscreen at the car in front,

hunching down behind the steering wheel to get a better look through the Audi's back window.

"Your colleague, you say? Far as I can tell, you're on your own, old pal."

Was it concern that flickered across Viner's face? It was too fleeting to be sure.

"My colleague is on his rounds," Viner said.

"You know that for a fact, do you? You don't look so sure."

Viner's expression remained fixed, though this time when he looked in at Vince there was fury in his eyes. "Just do what you have to and get out of here," he said brusquely, thrusting the details sheet back in through the window and walking away.

Vince and Shirley watched the blonde man march back to his car, yank the door open and fold himself into the driver's seat.

"Touchy bugger," Vince muttered.

Shirley suppressed a shudder. "There's something lizard-like about him. He gives me the creeps."

"He's just a jumped-up little posh kid with more power than he knows what to do with," Vince said dismissively.

"So what now?"

Vince paused for no more than a second, then popped open the glove compartment, reached in and took out a torch. He clicked it on and off to check it was working, then handed it to Shirley. Taking out a second torch, he said, "We do our job. We look around for this fella with the bite wound. If we can't find him we call it in."

Vince grabbed the equipment bag and looped it over his shoulder, and then the two of them got out of the cab. It was too dark to tell whether the blonde-haired man was watching them, though Shirley couldn't imagine that he wouldn't be. Deliberately averting her gaze from the Audi, she peered at the crumbling spire jutting into the night sky beyond the temporary fencing erected by the construction company who were carrying out excavations on the church grounds.

Despite the lack of news coverage, she knew via the community grapevine that a great deal of bad feeling had been centred around All Hallows in recent weeks. Ever since the Coalition Government had announced that the nearly 250-year-old church – which had apparently been designed by an apprentice of the famous architect Nicholas Hawksmoor – was being demolished and its grounds dug up to accommodate a tram-link for the so-called New Festival of Britain, protestors had been out in force.

Never mind that the run-down church had previously been considered an eyesore or that the local kids considered it "haunted". Now that its existence was under threat, it had magically transformed itself into a much-loved example of London's architectural heritage.

Not that Shirley could see that there was much here worth preserving. Although she agreed with what seemed to be overwhelming public opinion that the New Festival of Britain was nothing but a political distraction and a scandalous money-pit, she couldn't deny the truth of the Government's argument that All Hallows had in recent years become a blight on the landscape. The church was a squat, ugly, moss-covered building that perched like a toad in a sea of mud and tangled vegetation, from which broken, slanted gravestones jutted like old teeth. Desolate enough in the daylight, at night it resembled a set from a horror movie, the image consolidated by the fact that a creeping mist seemed to rise from the ground and hang in the air, whatever the weather.

As Vince's torchlight probed through the fence and alighted on a headless stone angel looming from the murk, Shirley shivered.

"Do we really have to go in there?"

Vince looked at her in amusement. "What's up? Think a ghost'll jump out from behind a gravestone and grab you?"

"More like a homicidal maniac," she said. "Remember

what Nurse Jenkins told us? That those who get bitten become aggressive and attack other people. What if this bloke's got a knife or a machete or something?"

Vince shook his head. "This has got nowt to do with that lot at the hospital. Whatever infection it was that sent *them* doolally, it all came from some nutter in a nightclub. It'd be a bit of a coincidence if our fella's wandered down here from Catford. It's more likely he got into a scrap or was attacked by a stray dog or summat."

Shirley looked unconvinced, but she set her face determinedly. "Okay. But we stick together, right? We don't split up."

"Course not," said Vince. "This isn't *Scooby-Doo*."

He pushed open the gate and they stepped through, their torch beams exploring the ground ahead, bouncing back with a flare of white whenever they hit a particularly thick clump of mist. As they moved forward, Shirley was unnerved by the way tombstones and bushes and the trunks of stunted trees seemed to fidget and shift around them, though she knew it was only the sidling of crisp-edged shadows which the objects cast under scrutiny of torchlight that lent them the illusion of life.

Raising his torch to direct its beam further afield, Vince picked out the excavation site surrounding the church. It resembled a dinosaurs' battlefield – skeletal, long-necked digging machines, silhouetted against the night sky, towering above a cluster of Portakabins. Sheets of rain-soaked tarpaulin, humped and ridged by the mounds of equipment they protected, were reminiscent of the glistening flanks of fallen prey.

"Hello?" Vince bellowed suddenly. "Anyone around?"

"For God's sake," said Shirley, slapping him on his brawny arm, "I wish you'd warn me before doing that. Nearly gave me a heart attack, you did."

He grinned at her, his teeth in the darkness seeming preternaturally white as they sprang from the bristly dark mass of his goatee. "Sorry, love."

77

Shirley was about to reply when, out of the corner of her eye, she glimpsed a flash of movement. Turning quickly, she directed her torch beam across the path ahead.

"Did you see that?"

"What?"

"Something moved."

"Some*thing* or some*one*?"

"I don't know. It was too quick to tell."

Vince added his torchlight to hers, their conjoined beams dancing across twitching vegetation and swelling, fungus-like tombstones.

"Hello?" he called again. "Is anyone there? My colleague and I are paramedics. We're here to help."

They paused to listen, but the churchyard seemed enclosed within a bubble of silence. Vince moved his arm in a slow sweep to the right, his torch beam scampering over the uneven ground before leaping to slither across the pock-marked surface of the church itself. Exposed by the light, they saw that the drainpipes and window sills of the old building were putrescent with moss, the windows themselves boarded up with sheets of water-stained wood or corrugated iron, across which had been plastered warning notices: NO UNAUTHORIZED ENTRY TO THESE PREMISES. TRESPASSERS WILL BE PROSECUTED UNDER THE PLANNING SPECIAL POWERS ACT.

"Creepy place," muttered Shirley.

Though his words were teasing, Vince's voice was sombre. "Is there owt you don't find creepy tonight?"

Shirley gave him a withering look. "Come on, Vince, you can't deny that it hasn't got an atmosphere about it."

He shrugged. "Atmospheres are created by imagination, nowt else."

"I'm not so sure about that," Shirley muttered, but Vince was already moving away from her. He drifted closer to the church, the long wet grass and bedraggled clusters of weeds which sprawled across the path brushing against his legs, darkening the thick green material with moisture.

"Perhaps our fella's gone inside," he suggested, the light from his torch jittering restlessly across the stonework and picking at the dead vegetation hanging like dripping hair from the gutters.

"The place is boarded up," Shirley said, hoping it was true. She wasn't easily spooked, but the prospect of setting foot inside the grim building was not an appealing one. In fact, although she wasn't entirely sure why, the thought of it filled her with dread.

"You can always find a way in if you want to," Vince said.

I don't want to, Shirley thought. But she kept quiet, knowing that he would only make fun of her.

She followed mutely, reluctantly, as Vince led the way up to the church. As they approached the edifice, the span of their torchlight became narrower and more condensed, which gave the impression that it was being driven back by a darkness that was seeping from the very stones of the building, and that at any moment it might fall over them like a net.

Vince called out again, but this time his voice sounded flat and muffled, as if the ancient stonework were absorbing it. Shirley winced, half-expecting something to peel away from the hovering darkness and come flapping towards them.

As before, however, his words were greeted with a stillness that seemed almost calculated. Redirecting his torch beam on to the path ahead that curved around the church, he said, "If this bugger's still here he's not half playing hard to get." He glanced back at Shirley, eyes glinting. "What do you say, Shirl? Once round the block and then we'll give it up as a bad job?"

She nodded eagerly. Much as she hated the thought of abandoning a potentially injured man, she knew how relieved

79

she would feel once they were back in what all at once seemed the homely and familiar surroundings of their cab.

Moving in a clockwise direction, keeping the building on their right, they resumed their dogged plod. Although she would have preferred to fix her gaze on her partner's reassuringly broad back, Shirley swept her torch back and forth across the grounds to their left, the beam leaping from tombstone to tombstone.

They had entered the churchyard via the south gate, which meant that the main door of All Hallows was on the opposite side of the building. It took several minutes of tramping through wet vegetation, during which time they rounded two corners, before the shadow-clotted vestibule came into sight, like a gaping, dark maw halfway along the wall. The long, arched windows above it that resembled eyes were blinded here too, and the wide path that lolled from it like a grey tongue was splotched with lichen and weeds.

"If there's any way in, it'll most likely be here," Vince muttered.

Shirley nodded, hoping secretly that they would find the door into the church firmly sealed.

They edged forwards, more cautiously now, and had perhaps covered half the space to the door when the darkness within the vestibule seemed to shift.

Shirley halted abruptly. "Did you see that?"

Vince, who had moved a couple of steps ahead of her, glanced back, his face unreadable. "I saw summat. I thought it were my eyes."

He directed his torch at the mass of shadows, but at the angle he was standing the light made little impression.

"Anyone there?" he called. "If there is, don't be scared. My name's Vince, I'm a paramedic. I'm here with my partner, Shirley. We got a call to say there was a man here with a neck wound who needed help. Is that you?"

Receiving no response, he and Shirley exchanged a look and then he started forwards again, albeit more cautiously this time. Shirley knew there was no real need to tell him to be careful, but she was unable to resist saying the words anyway.

When he was maybe half-a-dozen yards from the vestibule, his torch beam still trained on the shadows packed densely within, Vince stepped to his left, moving off the path and into the thicker patches of vegetation between the graves, his intention being to put himself out of the range of anyone who might suddenly lurch from the shadows. Side-stepping carefully through the knee-high foliage, he moved round in a wide semi-circle, his torchlight slicing through more of the blackness within the vestibule as the angle at which he was facing it became less acute.

Three-quarters of the space had been revealed when what remained of the darkness seemed to heave and a hunched, long-limbed creature sprang out into the full glare of Vince's torch.

That was Shirley's first impression anyway – that what emerged was not human but somewhere between ape and grasshopper. It seemed to be possessed of a tensile energy and strength, and she took an involuntary step back, her heart lurching.

Then her perception shifted, and she realized that what she had taken for intent was in fact a reeling lack of coordination. And although the figure was hunched, it was not, as she had thought, ape-like, but was merely a man, doubled over in obvious pain.

The man, his face a white, anguished glare and his throat a collar of blood, was in his early- to mid-thirties, his dark hair shaved close to his scalp, his clothes – dark jacket and jeans over a black or navy polo shirt – sombre but conventional.

Less conventional, however, was the expression on his face. He stared wildly around, as if skewered like an insect on a pin by the shaft of light that had prised him from the darkness. His gaze flickered to his left and fixed on Shirley. He stared at her a moment, and then opened his mouth, as if to speak. Instead of words, however, what emerged from between his lips was a thick, yellowish drool, which spilled down the front of his shirt. Almost tripping over his own feet, he re-adjusted his position, then took a couple of stumbling steps in her direction.

Nervously she said, "It's okay, we're here to help. My name's Shirley. What's yours?"

As if agitated, or perhaps excited, by the sound of her voice, the man gave a low groan and broke into a shambling run.

For a moment Shirley thought that the man was going to attack her. He looked crazed enough, murderous even. But then, as he was lurching towards her, he stumbled and fell, his arms out before him.

Shirley's training kicked in immediately. Instead of holding back, she ran up to the guy and crouched beside him to check on his condition. As he'd fallen he'd rolled so that he was on his back with his arms above his head. Although seconds earlier he'd shown signs of aggression, he now looked done in, his eyes half-closed to reveal only a sliver of white, his chest heaving as if his lungs were struggling to take in air, and she leaned over him without hesitation. But then all at once she flinched back, an expression of disgust on her face, her hand flapping at the air.

Vince, who was squatting beside her now, already unhooking the equipment bag from his shoulder and dumping it on the ground, looked at her curiously as she rubbed at her tightly-pursed lips with the tips of her fingers.

"What's up?" he asked. "Just had a meeting with your old friend, Hally Tosis?"

Her brows twitched in a warning frown and she glanced meaningfully at the injured man. Although she didn't say anything, she could see that Vince understood the gesture instantly: *Shh, he might hear you.*

"It was insects," she said.

"Insects?"

"Yeah, a whole cloud of them. Like . . . flies or gnats or something. They seemed to . . ." she lowered her voice, at the same time glancing meaningfully at their patient once more ". . . come out of him."

Vince looked sceptical. "Come out of him? What do you mean?"

"I don't know. They just seemed to rise up into my face when I bent down. I'm sure I swallowed one of them."

"There was an old woman who swallowed a fly," Vince said.

She gave him a look. "Hey, you, I'm not *old*."

While they were talking Vince was unzipping the bag, sorting through its contents, expertly assessing what they would need. He took out gauze, bandage, tape and scissors, all of which he handed to Shirley. Slipping on latex gloves, he turned the man's head gently, examining his wound. The man groaned a little, but his eyes had now drifted fully closed and his body was limp.

Vince carefully cleaned the bite on the man's neck with antiseptic wipes and then, while Shirley dressed the wound, he gave the guy a shot of antibiotics, then unpacked the emergency stretcher, which was attached to the outside of the equipment bag in an orange nylon carry bag of its own.

Lying the stretcher on the ground, he and Shirley manoeuvred the man on to it, then carried it between them back to the ambulance. As they opened the back doors and lifted their patient inside, Shirley sensed Special Security Agent Viner watching their every move through his rear-view mirror. Climbing into the cab a couple of minutes later Vince gave the Audi a cheerful wave.

Viner didn't wave back.

02:04 am

"STEVE, WAKE UP, it's starting."

The voice seemed to break through from another place, as if the sky above him had fractured and he was about to be plucked to safety. Certainly he could see no other way out of his predicament, which involved being forced to lie down at the edge of the incoming tide while his mother-in-law crouched behind him, poking a gun into his back.

"Why are you making me do this?" he asked. "Why don't you just shoot me?"

"I want it to look like an accident."

Somehow, though he was facing the incoming waves, he knew that there were people on the beach, kids playing, dogs running and barking.

"But they can see you," he said. "They can all see you."

His mother-in-law was behind him, but he knew she was smiling. "Nobody cares."

"*Steve!*" The voice cracked through again, more urgently this time. "*Please wake up!*"

A wave rushed in, and he took a deep breath, bracing himself for it, as mortal fear, the fear of drowning, spiralled within him.

Then his eyes opened and he was in another place, some-where dark but so weighty and solid and *real* that he knew, immediately and instinctively that, vivid though it had been, the beach and the sea and his mother-in-law had been nowhere but inside his own head, a jumble of his fears and anxieties formed into the narrative of a dream.

But he was still wet. Why was he wet? Had part of the dream leaked through into the waking world? Then a more shameful explanation occurred to him. He had pissed himself. Oh Jesus. Lying in the water in his dream had made him piss the bed for the first time since he was . . . what? Seven? Eight? Nine?

Bracing an arm underneath his body, he pushed himself up, grimacing as his wet T-shirt unpeeled from the saturated sheet beneath him. He swung his legs over the side of the bed, the cold air making him shiver as it hit the wet patch all down his left side and brought his flesh out in goose bumps. Rubbing his sleep-heavy face with one hand, he reached out with the other and switched on the bedside lamp.

Immediately the room was filled with a soothing, mauve light. And as though the light had sharpened his senses, all at once he became aware of a sound he'd been hearing since he had opened his eyes, but had been registering only subconsciously – the rapid, soft panting of his wife.

Even as he twisted to look at her, he realized what was happening, what *had* happened, what the soaking wet bed sheets really indicated.

Melinda, her belly so swollen that it looked almost cartoonish, as if her real body had been flattened by a huge round rock from which only her limbs and head protruded, was going into labour.

Or at least, her waters had broken, which he knew was the start of it. He mustn't panic, though. Despite appearances – despite her bulging, panicked eyes, the strands of her rust-red hair, darkened by sweat, which were glued to her forehead, the way her ruddy, freckled cheeks were rapidly inflating and deflating as she practised her breathing exercises – he knew that it could be hours yet, that it might not necessarily even be today.

Pulling his wet T-shirt over his head in one fluid movement and dumping it on the already soaked mattress, he said, "How quickly are the contractions coming?"

"About every three minutes." Her amazing pale-green eyes, the first thing he had ever noticed about her, suddenly shone with tears. "Oh God, Steve, I'm scared."

Steve reached across and took his wife's hand, trying not to wince as she gripped it hard. "It's okay," he said soothingly, "everything's going to be fine." In response to her fear he felt his own mind clearing, calming down. He knew that Melinda was already anticipating the pain ahead and would be relying on him to be her rock through all of this. "Do you think you can get out of the bed and get changed if I help you? I don't want to take you to hospital in your soaking-wet nightie. You'll be freezing."

He could see that her instinctive response was to shake her head – *no, I'm in too much pain, I can't move* – but then, as if drawing on his aura of calm, gaining strength from it, she swallowed and nodded.

"I'll try."

"Good girl." Gently he released her hand. "You just lie there for a minute and prepare yourself while I get dressed. No point having you sitting waiting any longer than you have to."

They'd had it planned for weeks – their clothes, in case it happened early or in the middle of the night, folded neatly on the blanket box at the bottom of their bed; Melinda's bag containing all the essentials she would need in hospital for both herself and their baby perched under the telephone table beside the front door like a faithful pet.

Steve stripped off his wet boxer shorts, dried himself rapidly with a towel from their en suite bathroom (a proper shower would

86

have to come later, when it was all over) and dressed quickly in fresh underwear and socks, sweatshirt, jeans and trainers.

That done, he held Melinda's hands to take her weight and encouraged her to slide out of bed, to sit up, to lift her bum so that he could peel off her wet nightie. As he dried her and dressed her, he couldn't help but think that his actions, albeit for entirely different reasons, paralleled what his Dad now did every day for his Mum, who was not yet sixty, but who had been diagnosed with early-onset Alzheimer's at the age of fifty-four and was now utterly incapable of looking after herself.

All at once, made vulnerable by the sudden shock of waking and by the sheer momentousness of the fact that by this time tomorrow he would more than likely be a father (*Christ, where did the time go? He could still recall with utter clarity the sense of pride he felt pulling on his long trousers for his first day at Big School*), his composure faltered and he was overcome with a rush of melancholic bitterness. His Mum – his *proper* Mum, not the drooling, mindless thing she had become – would have *loved* to have been a grandma. And she'd have been great at it too. Like all good grandmas she would have spoiled her grandchild rotten.

"Steve?" Melinda's voice was concerned. "Are you okay?"

Sniffing back the tears he could feel prickling behind his eyes, he forced a smile. "Course I am. Better than okay. I've never been happier."

"You were thinking about your Mum, weren't you?" she said, her eyes growing tender in response to the guiltily startled look he was unable to suppress. "You can't hide your thoughts from me, you know, Steve Fuller. I know you inside out. That's why I love you so much."

He helped her to her feet, stretched his arms around her, leaned forward over her bump and kissed her. "I love you too, Melinda Fuller," he said. "Now let's go and have a baby."

Three minutes later, having stretched the seatbelt carefully over her belly and snapped it into place, Steve was backing the car out of the garage. They lived just west of Greenwich Park, no more than a couple of miles from the hospital. As he reversed into the road and swung the car round, Melinda winced, then began to breathe hard and fast once again.

"Another contraction?" Steve said. "Don't worry, we'll be there in five minutes."

Their route took them down the side of Greenwich Park, across Shooter's Hill Road and along Wat Tyler Road on the western edge of Blackheath. Despite his eagerness to get his wife to hospital, Steve drove carefully, even though the amount of traffic moving on the roads was all but negligible at this time in the morning.

"Soon be there," he said encouragingly as the railings caging the dense woodland that bordered Eliot Park whipped by on their left. Although his eyes were fixed on the road, Steve was momentarily distracted when what he had thought was a bag of rubbish slumped against the railings suddenly shifted.

He looked again, and saw that the mound was in fact a person, who was now unbending his knees, stretching his legs across the pavement. He had no doubt that it was a *he*. Though he couldn't see the person clearly – it was no more than a black shape – it looked too . . . well too *manly* to be a woman.

A tramp, he thought. Or a drunk having a little rest on the way home.

But as he got close enough to the figure for the edge of his headlights to sweep across it, he saw that it was neither a tramp nor a drunk.

It was a police officer.

Instinctively Steve slowed the car, glancing at Melinda. She was sitting with her eyes closed, hands clutching her thighs, still doing her breathing exercises. But as the car slowed, she opened her eyes and looked around, frowning in confusion when she realized that they hadn't yet reached the hospital.

"What's going on?"

Steve nodded across her, towards the window on her left. "There's a policeman on the ground."

She looked at the slumped figure, then back at him. "What are you going to do?"

Steve brought the car to a halt beside the recumbent figure. "I can't just leave him. What if he's been attacked? He might be injured."

Melinda's green eyes flashed with alarm. "Steve, we need to get to the hospital."

"We'll only be a minute. We can't just drive away without seeing if he's all right."

"Can't we just tell them when we get to the hospital? They can send an ambulance for him or something."

His brow furrowed in disapproval. "You don't mean that, Mel. We can at least ask him if he's okay. Wind down your window."

"What if he's not a real policeman?" she said.

"He looks like a real policeman. Now will you please wind down your window or am I going to have to do it?"

All at once, as though plucked upright by strings, the man rose to his feet.

"Look, he's fine," said Melinda. "He's standing up."

"I don't know," murmured Steve. "He doesn't look too steady on his feet. Perhaps he's got concu—"

Before he could finish his sentence, the man released a guttural snarl that they could hear even inside the car, and hurled himself across the pavement in a loose-limbed leap. He slammed against the vehicle with a meaty thud, causing it to rock on its suspension.

As his hands scrabbled at the still-closed passenger window, no more than a few inches from Melinda's face, leaving greasy marks on the glass, she screamed and jerked back in her seat. The unexpected movement clearly did her no good at all; almost immediately her scream choked off and her face clamped with pain as though something had been wrenched inside her.

"Fuck!" yelled Steve, his shock turning instantly to anger – *how dare some drunken moron frighten his wife like that!* He floored the accelerator and the car lurched forward, slewing from side to side before smoothing out as he slammed up through the gears. He had no idea whether he'd dealt the policeman (if he'd even *been* a policeman) a glancing blow as he roared off, but frankly he didn't care. He was not a violent man, but as far as he was concerned, anyone who was prepared to attack a pregnant woman, especially when that woman happened to be his wife, *deserved* to be run over.

"You all right, Mel?" he asked, gripping the wheel hard to stop not only his hands but his whole body from shaking.

Melinda didn't reply. She was sitting holding her belly, her face pastry white and her mouth and eyes still screwed up with pain.

"We won't stop for anyone else," he promised her, "no matter what state they look to be in." He leaned forward, glaring at the road ahead as if daring it to defy him. "From now on, the only thing that matters is you, me and our baby."

02:11 am

"NURSE HARRIS, COULD I borrow you for a moment?"

Cat looked up. Sister Parkhurst's plump face was poking through a gap in the curtains surrounding the treatment bay. There were around a couple of dozen such bays in A&E, each one little more than a curtained-off alcove, which contained a bed and little else. Patients would be assessed and often treated here, before being either sent on their way or, if their condition merited it, transferred to a ward for further treatment and observation.

The occupant of the bed in this particular bay was bride-to-be Christine McGough, who was still wearing her sexy nurse's uniform, albeit minus the shoes now, but who looked nothing like the embodiment of male desire that she had been when she had set out for fun and frolics with her three best friends earlier that evening.

She was currently unconscious, breathing stertorously, her face deathly pale, her hair dark and stringy with sweat. Despite the cocktail of antibiotics that had been pumped into her system, the infection in her arm was continuing to spread. The flesh around the scratches was now purplish-black and seeping an evil-smelling discharge, and the skin almost up to her shoulder was turning yellow like old parchment. Her hand too was yellow, though the tips of the fingers were dark and wet-looking, as if her life-juices were oozing out of her.

Cat was standing on her "good" side – though even the skin of Christine's left arm was now pale and blotchy – with a white surgical mask covering her nose and mouth and her hands encased in disposable gloves. She was holding Chris' limp wrist and frowning as she consulted the watch attached to her breast pocket, but as she looked up at Sister Parkhurst her brow unfurrowed and she blinked.

"Yes, of course," she said distractedly.

Sister Parkhurst glanced at Christine. "How's the patient?"

"I'm struggling to find a pulse even in her left wrist," Cat admitted.

The older woman's grimace was part sympathy, part concern and part puzzlement. "Are you happy leaving her alone for a couple of minutes?"

"I can ask the student nurses to keep an eye on her. Why, what's the occasion?"

"Quick conflab. Need to work out a plan of attack."

Cat smiled wearily. "Who are we attacking?"

Sister Parkhurst's answering smile was grim. "Poor choice of words. Perhaps I should have said a plan to *prevent* attack."

Cat placed Christine's arm gently back down on the bed, then peeled off her gloves and dropped them into a waste disposal unit before quickly washing her hands and pulling down her mask. "Lead the way."

By the time they reached the Staff Room Susan Jenkins had made coffee for everybody. The fourth member of the group was Marcus Blackstock, the on-call senior house officer, who was leaning against the sink with his arms folded and a troubled expression on his face. Everyone liked Dr Blackstock. He was easy going and friendly, not to mention lithe and

92

good-looking. He was always running marathons and half-marathons to raise money for research into cancer or SIDS, or to save various specialist hospital units around the country that were being threatened with closure.

"Thanks," Cat said, accepting a mug of coffee from Susan and adding half a spoonful of sugar.

"Right," said Dr Blackstock, his own steaming mug sitting ignored on the counter behind him. Pushing himself upright, he unfolded his arms and tucked his hands into the pockets of his white coat like a university don about to deliver a lecture. "Sister Parkhurst and I thought we ought to get together for a little chat to discuss the current situation – namely, this bloody infection that's currently flummoxing the lot of us."

In different circumstances his use of the word "flummoxing" might have prompted some light teasing, but all three women remained silent.

"As you know," he continued, "the first to be infected was twenty-two-year-old Samantha Mellor, after being bitten in a nightclub by an unidentified man, now deceased, whose body is currently in the hospital Mortuary awaiting post-mortem. Samantha has subsequently infected her friend Christine McGough, a nineteen-year-old man called Jermaine Paterson and one of our own staff members, Tammy Ollerenshaw.

"As you also know, we've tried to treat the infection with broad-spectrum antibiotics, without success. We're now fast reaching the stage where we're going to have to decide whether to employ more drastic methods. But of course the physical effects of the infection are not our only consideration, which is why Sister Parkhurst and I thought we ought to open this discussion out to the on-site nursing staff – the front-line troops, as it were – of which you two have been selected as representatives.

"As both of you have witnessed at first-hand, the infection

93

doesn't only have a physical effect on the patient, but a psychological one. To put it bluntly, it makes them extremely aggressive, psychotic even. Whether this works in a similar way to rabies, which causes encephalitis, we've yet to establish. But while we wait for test results, our overriding priority is to prevent the infected from passing on the infection to others, which it seems it is their instinct to do. To that end, we've been forced to sedate and restrain both Samantha Mellor and Tammy Ollerenshaw while we administer treatment.

"Of course now we're faced with an ethical question: do we also sedate and restrain those who we know to be infected but are not yet showing signs of aggression – namely Christine McGough and Jermaine Paterson – purely as a preventative measure?" He paused. "I see you're nodding, Susan."

Cat, whose attention had been fixed on Marcus Blackstock, now glanced at Susan Jenkins. She *was* nodding.

"Yes," she said in her usual calm and thoughtful way, "I think we *should* restrain them. I know it seems . . . well, a bit barbaric, but the safety of the staff and the rest of the patients must be paramount. There's no point waiting until the infected patients turn aggressive and *then* start grappling with them. As we've seen, even a scratch could be . . ." she broke off and Cat knew she'd been about to say "fatal". Instead, after a moment's hesitation, she said, ". . . extremely dangerous."

Sister Parkhurst was nodding too. "Much as it goes against my abhorrence of the violation of human rights, I have to say that I agree with Nurse Jenkins. This infection is frighteningly aggressive. We need to nip it in the bud before it gets out of hand, and if that means restraining those infected until we find a cure, so be it."

Marcus Blackstock pursed his lips and looked at Cat. "What do you think, Nurse Harris?"

Cat, who was cradling her mug against her belly as though it was a frightened animal, said, "I agree with everyone else.

I also think that until we find out more about the infection, those already infected should be isolated from the rest of the hospital. I also think the number of staff treating the infected patients should be kept to a minimum, and that they should wear masks and gloves at all times."

Marcus Blackstock looked at her in approval. "Excellent suggestions. In light of which I'll arrange for a ward to be cleared immediately. I think there's one on the fourth floor we can use. In the meantime, if the three of you can deal with Mr Paterson and Miss McGough?"

Nodding, they put down their mugs, Cat first pouring the remainder of her coffee down the sink. As Marcus Blackstock went off in one direction to make arrangements to create a temporary isolation ward, Cat, Susan and Sister Parkhurst hurried back to the treatment area. Cat had never had to restrain a patient before, and hated the thought of having to do so now, even though she accepted that it was necessary.

"I'll fetch the restraints," Sister Parkhurst said. "Could you two kit yourselves out with masks and gloves and watch over the patients for a few minutes?"

She bustled away, and Cat and Susan headed towards the store cupboard. A few minutes later, suitably protected, Cat was standing outside the curtained-off treatment bay where she had left Christine McGough. Despite the fact that nothing appeared to have changed in the ten minutes since she had last been here, she felt nervous.

Part of it was because Marcus Blackstock's summing up of the situation, even though he hadn't said anything that she didn't already know, had served to sharpen and clarify her fears, and part of it was because ten minutes ago she had *known* that Chris was unconscious and therefore of little immediate threat, whereas now she *didn't*; for all Cat was aware, the bride-to-be might well be crouched on the other side of the curtain, waiting to leap out at her.

One scratch. That was all it would take for her flesh to turn gangrenous and for madness to blot out her mind. One little scratch.

Standing on the other side of the curtain and trying to keep the waver out of her voice, she said, "Christine? Christine, are you awake?"

No response. Not even a groan, or a rustle of movement.

"Christine?" she said again. "Answer me if you can hear me."

She thought of Ed, of her wedding in six weeks' time. She thought of how Christine McGough, the girl whose arm was so badly infected that it might have to be amputated, was supposed to be getting married the weekend after next.

Oh fuck, she thought, *oh fuck*. Gripping the curtain she yanked it back, rising on to the balls of her feet, preparing to run.

But there was no need. The bed inside the treatment bay was empty. And a quick glance was enough to assure her that there was no one crouching beside it.

Christine McGough was gone.

02:16 am

TO STEVE'S RELIEF, they reached the hospital without further mishap. As he slowed the car gently to turn in to the main entrance, he noticed that on the other side of the road, parked nose-to-tail in the shadows beneath a clump of overhanging trees, were at least three, and possibly more, armoured TSG wagons.

What they were doing here he had no idea, but – although he didn't mention it to Melinda – they made him uneasy. He had been a Met Police Volunteer before the introduction of the Special Powers Act had prompted him to resign his post in protest, and like many citizens was concerned that the law enforcement service he had formerly held in high esteem was now turning into little more than a private army of jack-booted Government thugs. Although the Trafalgar Square atrocity had caused widespread outrage, it had ultimately resulted in surprisingly little change to the status quo. If that wasn't an indication that the Government stranglehold on the country was becoming ever tighter, while "democracy" – which the Prime Minister constantly claimed to be trying to preserve – became an increasingly distant and meaningless concept, Steve didn't know what was.

Tearing his eyes from the silent line of sinister black vehicles, he glanced at Melinda. "How you doing, honey?"

Since the incident with the crazed policeman, she had been sitting silently, her eyes closed, trying to breathe through her pain. Now she looked at him and gave him a weary smile. "I'll be glad when we're there."

"That'll be in less than a minute. Look, there's the sign for the Maternity Unit."

He pointed at a blue metal plaque perched on a couple of tall poles at the entrance to the car park. In white letters was listed a variety of hospital departments and services with arrows pointing every which way: MAIN REGISTRATION, ACCIDENT AND EMERGENCY, RADIOLOGY/ULTR-ASOUND, ENDOSCOPY UNIT, INTENSIVE CARE, HAEMATOLOGY. Pointing to the right was the arrow for the Maternity Unit, whose entrance (they had already previously established; they were nothing if not prepared) could best be reached by circling a small roundabout and following the road leading around the eastern edge of the car park. At this time of night the main car park at the front of the hospital was only half-full, but Steve ignored it. He knew that the Maternity Unit had a small parking area of its own.

He took the mini-roundabout slowly, trying not to jerk through the gear changes. Despite the lack of traffic, he was indicating to peel off between a pair of box hedges when he caught a glimpse of movement to his left. His first impression was that a chunk of hedge had somehow detached itself and tumbled across his path. Then, as he braced himself to swerve around the obstacle, it lurched on to the roadway and stepped into the full glare of his headlights.

Astonished, Steve saw that the object was not a chunk of vegetation at all, but a woman – a nurse, in fact. However, it was a nurse wearing what appeared to be the skimpiest uniform imaginable. Her cleavage was spilling out of the front of her low-cut, tightly buttoned tunic and her skirt was so short that he could see the stocking-tops of the white fishnets clinging to her long, shapely legs.

In the split-second before he was able to react to her appearance, several emotions raced through Steve's mind. He was alarmed by the fact that she had stepped in front of the car, confused by her uniform (*had the hospital really discarded the practical blue nursing tunics he'd seen on previous visits in favour of ones that made their employees look like porn stars?*) and concerned for Melinda and how this latest shock would affect her. Then he stamped on the brake and wrenched the steering wheel to the right.

His effort was in vain, however, because instead of trying to avoid the car that was bearing down on her, the "nurse", astonishingly, seemed to deliberately throw herself in front of it. Steve's stomach flipped as he heard the thud of impact and felt a jolt as the wheels passed over her body. At his side, Melinda jerked forward in her seat and let out an almost indignant scream, before the seatbelt locked across her chest and turned the scream into a grunt. By the time the car jolted to a stop, Steve was pressing himself back against his seat, his hands gripping the steering wheel and cold sweat springing out over his body.

"Oh, fuck," he groaned, "oh, fuck. Please tell me this isn't happening."

Melinda's voice was small and full of what sounded like dreamy disbelief. "Are you okay?"

For a moment Steve's body was so rigid that he couldn't move his head. Then, with a creak that was almost certainly in his mind, he looked in her direction.

"Never mind me. Are *you* okay?"

Her face was all eyes, her skin bloodless as marble. Instead of answering him, she asked, "Did we kill her?"

Despite the situation and the stew of conflicting emotions inside him, there was a tiny part of Steve that noted that "we", that suggestion that this was a shared responsibility – not *his* fault, but *both* their faults – and he loved her for that.

"I don't know," he said. "I don't think so. I hope not."

"Maybe you should take a look," Melinda said.

She sounded eerily calm. Steve wondered whether she was in shock. Hesitating, he said, "But what about you? The baby?"

She blinked at him, and a note of admonishment crept into her voice. "We can't just leave her, Steve. You're not suggesting we leave her lying in the road?"

"Course not," he said quickly – though a part of him *had* been thinking precisely that. Melinda was his priority, and in the back of his mind had been a vague notion that he could drive to Maternity, deliver his wife safely into the hands of the staff there, and then mention that they'd run over a nurse on their way in and perhaps someone ought to take a look?

"Course not," he said again, a little appalled at himself. To consolidate his words he shoved the car door open.

Immediately a cool night breeze rushed over him, freezing the sweat on his body. He shuddered, partly with cold, partly with reaction, but at least the air cleared his head. He stepped out of the car, already turning to look back along its length to where a dark shape lay in the roadway. He gripped the door firmly as the shuddering in his body increased – it was definitely reaction, albeit coupled with apprehension at what he might find. He closed the car door, afraid that his response might upset Melinda. He felt incredibly protective of his wife, and angry too; neither of them deserved this. Melinda already had a tough enough night in prospect without this added hassle.

"Hello?" he called as he moved towards the shape in the roadway. "Are you okay?"

There was no reply, but he saw the shape twitch like a beached fish.

Not dead then, he thought with relief, but wondered whether the woman's silence was a good sign or a bad one. Could it be that she was so badly injured that she was beyond speech, or even sound? Or perhaps she was unconscious and the movement he had seen was nothing but a muscular reaction. What was the phrase – the twitch of the death nerve?

"Are you hurt?" he asked, edging closer. "Can you speak?"

The woman's uniform was soaked in red – but only by the brake lights of the idling car. Steve saw her move again, saw her trying to push herself up using her left arm, which, although encouraging, also sent a wave of horror bristling through him. Because it was only as she attempted to rise using her left arm that Steve was able to get a good look at her right. It was hanging from her shoulder at a weird angle, as crooked and limp as a broken branch. That must have been what he had driven over, what had caused the car to judder.

The sight of it made him queasy and faint, so much so that the car park lights, like flat, glowing dinosaur heads perched on long, stiff necks, seemed to pulse and blur for a moment, blotting out his vision. He rested his weight against the rear end of the car, blinking and breathing hard. He surely wasn't going to swoon like a teenage girl, for goodness sake. He had a badly injured woman to attend to, and a heavily pregnant wife who was relying on him.

Come on, he thought; he might even have muttered it under his breath. *Come on.*

A streak of white suddenly rose into his still-blurred field of vision. He blinked, and gradually his vision cleared, his eyes focused. He was surprised to find that the streak of white was the nurse. Despite the terrible injury to her right arm, she had succeeded in rising to her feet and was now standing with her head bowed, her mouth hanging open and much of the rest of her face hidden beneath a shaggy, tangled mass of dirty blonde hair.

"Are you okay?" he asked again. He could see that she wasn't – in fact, he didn't know how she was managing to ignore the terrible pain she must be in. When she didn't reply, he babbled, "I'm sorry I hit you with the car. I couldn't help it. You ran right out in front—"

Then she looked up and the words dried in his throat.

In fact, she didn't just *look* up; her head *snapped* up, like a predator catching the scent of prey on the breeze. But it wasn't this that silenced Steve. It was the expression on her face. He had seen it once before tonight. Only a glimpse, but the way she was looking at him was the way the policeman who had attacked their car had looked at Melinda. There had been something avid in his expression, avid and also ferocious. It was as if his mind had been scooped out and replaced by nothing but hunger.

Instantly Steve knew that there would be no reasoning with this woman. He knew too that whatever was making her look at him like she wanted to kill him was also why she appeared to feel no pain from her broken arm. Thinking only of Melinda and their unborn baby, he headed back towards the driver's door, moving in a kind of rapid sideways scuttle as he attempted to keep the woman in view.

Like a lion responding to the sudden flight of a panicked deer, the woman came after him. It was a ludicrous situation, being chased across a hospital car park in the middle of the night by a sexy nurse with a shattered arm, but Steve wasn't laughing. He reached the car door, wrapped his fingers around the handle and yanked it open. Throwing himself into the driver's seat, he tried to pull the door shut behind him – but the woman hurled herself recklessly into the gap, preventing him from doing so.

She might have been all legs and chest, but the only thing

Steve could focus upon was her mouth. It was snarling and drooling, frothy spittle trickling from it and running down her chin, her lips curled back over gnashing, lipstick-smeared teeth. For a moment she glared into his eyes, and he saw with gut-chilling horror not only that her pupils had shrunk to the size of pinpricks, but that there was no trace of humanity in them whatsoever. What was *wrong* with people tonight? Had *everyone* gone crazy? Then she grabbed his outstretched arm with her left hand, the overlong fingernails painted a deep ruby red, and dipped her head, clearly intending to bite him.

Steve tried to wrench his arm out of her grasp, but her strength, despite the terrible state of her other arm, was prodigious. In desperation he leaned back so far he was almost resting his head in Melinda's lap – who was screaming again, though he barely registered it – and pistoned out his legs. He kicked the nurse hard in the midriff, both feet making contact with such an impact that he felt sure he heard at least one of her ribs snap. Yet although she was knocked back momentarily, she failed to relinquish her grip – in fact, her fingers only tightened further, exerting a bone-crushing force. He howled with pain, certain she was about to pull his arm out of its socket.

In desperation he began to kick and flail at her, but although he managed to fend her off she kept coming at him, as fearful and tenacious as a terrier. His ears were ringing with Melinda's screams and the woman's snarls and his own panicked, wordless yells. Beneath these sounds was another too – a rumbling, perhaps a roaring. Although by this time he was barely capable of coherent thought, on some instinctual level he wondered what it was.

Then, just as he was beginning to contemplate the terrible possibility that this was a battle he might actually lose, and in so doing lose Melinda and his baby too, something incredible happened. Not only incredible, but awful and shocking. He was desperately trying to hold the woman at bay, his arm, still in the grip of her left hand, no more than a few inches from her snapping, spitting maw, when the top of her head, from her eyes upwards, simply disappeared.

It happened as abruptly as that. One second it was there and the next it erupted up and away from her in a burst of red wetness so sudden it was more an impression than something he felt he had actually witnessed. There was a moment of stillness, of almost comical astonishment, and then the woman fell to the floor like a sack of sand, her hand loosening around Steve's arm, sliding away. The next moment he was sitting up, gasping and shaking, his arm throbbing with pain, unable to believe what had happened.

Before he could speak, however, before he could comfort Melinda, who seemed to be hyperventilating, sucking in shrill, panicked, whooping breaths, black shapes were swarming around the car. They looked like big beetles, their heads black and smooth and round, their bodies bulky, encased in ribbed, cockroach-like shells. They were holding weapons as black as their armour, all of which were pointing at him – maybe even at Melinda too.

"Out of the car!" one of them screamed at him, his voice raw with fury. Steve opened his mouth to stutter something conciliatory, but before he could find his voice the same man was yelling at him again. "Out! Now! And keep your hands where we can see them!"

Shaking so much he wasn't even sure whether he would be able to stand upright, Steve did as he was ordered. Both clumsily and delicately he stepped over the body of the nurse, who was sprawled on the ground beside the car like some grotesquely broken sex toy, her shattered head leaking darkness.

"Turn round!" bellowed the spokesman of the black-armoured group. "Up against the car! Hands on the roof!"

Steve did so. He tried to speak again. His voice was a croak. "I'm not armed. Please . . . my wife's pregnant, about to have a baby."

"Shut up!" the man screamed at him. Then Steve was aware of the bulky presence of someone behind him. He felt the sleeves of his sweatshirt being pulled up past his elbows, his jeans being yanked up roughly to his knees.

"Were you bitten?" the man barked.

"What?"

The voice was angry, impatient. "Did she bite you?"

"No, she tried to, but . . . no. I didn't let her."

"You're certain?"

"Yes."

"What about scratches? Did she scratch you?"

"No."

He was examined again, a couple of the black shapes turning his hands and arms over, crouching down to inspect his legs, their gloved hands probing at his skin.

"He's clean, sir," one of them said.

"You're sure."

"Yes, sir."

Steve sensed rather than saw the men relaxing a little around him. From the car he could hear Melinda still wheezing, sobbing.

"Please," he said, "I need to get my wife to Maternity. She's in labour. We were on our way there when the woman attacked us."

There was silence for a moment, a shuffling, the squeaky scrape of Kevlar. Then the man who had screamed at him, interrogated him, spoke again, and his voice, though gruff, was quieter now.

"All right. You can go."

02:32 am

WITH THEIR PATIENT safely delivered, Vince and Shirley were ensconced in the staff canteen at University Hospital, a grim little place of vinyl-topped tables and dusty, bedraggled pot plants beneath bluish-white strip lighting that made everyone look deathly. They were sitting at a window table that looked out over a dark corner of the car park, drinking sludgy coffee that Shirley took black, but that Vince thought was only palatable if you drowned out the bitterness with plenty of milk and sugar. Despite the corned-beef sandwiches he had devoured earlier, Vince had ordered a cheese toastie and an orange Kit Kat to go with his coffee.

Shirley eyed the food he was shovelling down his gullet with distaste. "You're like a human dustbin."

"Got to keep me strength up, I'm a growin' lad," he said and grinned widely, showing her a mashed-up mouthful of bread and cheese.

"You're disgusting, you are," she said, rolling her eyes.

"So why are you smilin'?"

"I'm not smiling, I'm grimacing."

"Looks like a smile to me."

"Yeah, well, that's where you're wrong."

She closed her eyes and rubbed a hand slowly back and forth across her forehead.

"You all right?" Vince asked.

"I'm fine," she said unconvincingly.

"You don't look fine. You look like shit."

"Oh, thanks. Remind me again which charm school you went to. I'd like to send my kids there one day."

Vince swallowed the last of his cheese toastie and licked his greasy fingers. Frowning, he said, "No, seriously, though, Shirl, you don't look too good."

"It's these lights," she said.

He shook his head. "No, it's more than that. You're sweatin' and your eyes look sort of . . . heavy. Like you're comin' down wi' summat."

She sighed. "Actually, I don't feel too clever."

"Perhaps *you* ought to eat summat. Want me to get you a Kit Kat?"

She considered it, then shook her head. "Don't think I could face it, to be honest with you."

"Cup o' tea then? Or some hot chocolate? Give you a bit of energy?"

She looked as if she was about to answer, then her eyes glazed over and she jerked in her seat, like someone fighting a losing battle to stay awake.

"Shirl?" Vince said again. "You sure you don't—"

But he got no further. Abruptly Shirley's eyes closed, her head slumped forward, and the next second she slid almost gracefully out of the plastic chair in which she was sitting and on to the floor.

02:38 am

"SO HOW OLD are you anyway?"

Though Cat raised her eyebrows, there was a half-smile on her face. The kid was cocky, impudent, and despite his denials he had almost certainly been involved in the gang fight over in Greenwich earlier tonight, which meant that he was not averse to violence. For all that, though, she couldn't help but like him. He might have attitude, but at least he wasn't sullen with it.

"Too old for you," she said.

"Dat right?" He gave her a withering look. "I reckon I could teach you plenty."

"Really?" she said lightly.

"Believe. You look like you had a pretty sheltered upbringing."

"Appearances can be deceptive."

"Yeah?"

"Oh yes."

He looked at her shrewdly, "So go on, girl, tell me how old. I'm guessing twenny-one, twenny-two?"

"Flatterer."

"Twenny-three?"

She sighed. "All right, if you must know, I'm twenty-four."

"Aw, man, that's nuthin'. We's practically the same age."

"You're seventeen," Cat pointed out.

"Yeah, in years. But up here . . ." he tapped the side of his head with one finger ". . . and down here . . ." he pointed at the crotch of his black jeans ". . . I'm full-grown, girl." He grinned.

In other circumstances, and with another patient, Cat might have been wary, but she prided herself on being able to read people well and she was as sure as she could be that the kid was only having fun with her. And not in a malicious or threatening way, but simply because he was enjoying the banter between them and understood how far he could take the joke without offending her.

Cocking an eyebrow she said, "Are you trying to shock me, Carlton?"

His own expression was equally exaggerated – he pretended to be startled by the accusation. "I's just pointing out a fact." Suddenly he winced. "Ow! Go easy, girl."

"Sorry."

Now that the bleeding had stopped, Cat was removing the old dressing from Carlton's wound in order to check it over and apply a new one, and the last piece of tape had snagged on his skin, pulling it. Even though the wound had nothing to do with the infection that had originated with the bite to Sam Mellor's arm from the now-dead and still unidentified man in the nightclub, she was nevertheless half-afraid that as she peeled off the dressing she would see the now-familiar sight of necrotizing tissue.

They still had no idea what the infection was; all they knew was that it was extremely aggressive. Who was to say, therefore, that it couldn't be passed on not only via bites and scratches but also by airborne bacteria? However, she was relieved to see that the stab wound – although the flesh was swollen and discoloured by bruising – looked as healthy as she would have expected under the circumstances.

"I gonna have a scar?" Carlton asked, peering down at himself.

"Afraid so," said Cat. "I don't think it'll be a bad one, though."

He shrugged. "Don't bother me. Scars is pretty cool."

"Something to show your friends? To prove how tough you are?"

She meant the comment as a joke, but all at once the playful expression on Carlton's face was replaced with wariness. His eyes narrowed and his jaw tightened. Almost sulkily he said, "Dunno what that suppose to mean."

Cat immediately realized that, unintentional though it had been, she might have overstepped the mark. She hadn't meant to sound as though she was judging him or accusing him of anything, but that might have been how it had come across. Trying to laugh it off, she said, "Come on, Carlton, don't all boys like to be thought of as tough? They certainly did at my school."

"Oh yeah, and what school was that? You have little straw hats and satchels and picnics on the lawn?"

His eyes were still narrowed, but his voice was now so neutral that it was hard to tell whether he was teasing her or being vindictive.

Still smiling, she said, "Hardly. We didn't have a lawn at Finchley Comp."

His eyes flickered. "That where you from, yeah?"

"Born and bred. What about you? Greenwich boy?"

He shrugged, nodded. "Yeah, man."

She re-dressed his wound quickly, expertly. When she had finished she said, "There you go. Good as new. You'd better pull your top down now before you drive me mad with desire."

That brought a smile out of him, albeit a reluctant one.

Plucking at the hospital smock that he was wearing over his jeans, a shapeless monstrosity in pale-blue nylon, he said, "How long I have to wear this for? It's shameful."

"Well, I suppose until someone brings you in an alternative. Your own top was covered in blood." She paused and said, "Are your family coming to see you, Carlton? Do you want me to call them?"

He shook his head. "They all be asleep, innit? S'okay, I got my crew with me. They sort me out."

Cat hesitated. "You know the police will want to talk to you further, don't you? *All* of you, I mean. About that boy that got shot?"

Carlton's face was deadpan. "I already tole them, I don't know nuffin 'bout that."

"Be that as it may, they're not going to let your friend leave the building until that boy comes round from his operation. They're going to want to talk to him, and then, depending on what he tells them, they're going to want to talk to you. Which means they'll want you all to stay here for the time being."

"They can't do that," Carlton said stubbornly. "They ain't my boss."

Cat shrugged. "Unfortunately there's a lot the police *can* do these days that they couldn't before."

Carlton looked at her shrewdly. "What you mean, 'friend'?"

She blinked. "Pardon?"

"You said the five-oh wouldn't let my *friend* go out. Why not *friends*? Why just *friend*?"

Flustered, Cat averted her eyes as she cleared up the paraphernalia around Carlton's bed. Wadding up his old dressing and putting it into a tie-up bag for disposal, she said, "I meant friends. It was just a slip of the tongue."

"Wassup with Jermaine? He serious?"

She looked startled. "I don't know what you mean."

"Yeah you do. My boy Fitch tole me Jermaine got bit by some mad bitch and collapsed and got taken away, and now no one tellin' him what's happenin'."

"When did he tell you this?" Cat asked.

Carlton patted his hip. "I got a phone, innit? He texted me."

"You're not supposed to use that in here," she said quickly. "You're supposed to switch that off."

"Yeah, whatever. So where's Jermaine at? What's the big secret?"

"There's no secret," said Cat.

"So if I text my boy Fitch and tell him it's okay to see Jermaine, that be fine, yeah?"

Cat sighed, looking thoughtful. Finally she said, "As far as I know, your friend, Jermaine, is having treatment for a wound on his hand. As soon as he's either discharged from care or moved to a public ward, your other friend will be able to visit him. Until then, you and he will have to be patient."

Carlton stared at her. "So what you not tellin' me?"

"Nothing."

"Yeah, right. So why you gone red?"

"I haven't."

"Yeah you have. Somethin's up, I know it."

"Nothing's up," Cat said. "We're just very busy, that's all."

Hurriedly she gathered everything together and took a step back towards the curtains surrounding the bed. "Now, hard though it is for me to tear myself away, I have other patients to attend to. You just rest here, and if the pain in your hip gets too bad or the wound starts leaking again, press the call button and someone will come and see you. Okay?"

Without waiting for a reply she stepped back through the curtain and was gone. Carlton listened to her receding footsteps for a moment, then reached into his pocket and pulled out his phone. Speed-dialling Fitch's number, he waited. After a moment a surly voice said, "Yo."

"It's me," Carlton said.

Immediately Fitch's voice rose, became more animated and boyish. "Hey, wassup, Carlton. Where you at, man?"

"Never mind that," Carlton said. "Just listen up. There's somethin' you need to do."

02:50 am

WALKING DOWN THE hospital corridor, Staff Nurse Susan Jenkins tried taking deep breaths to stop her stomach contracting with fear. As if the infection alone wasn't terrifying enough, it now seemed likely – no, more than likely, highly probable – that it was not merely confined to the dead man in the Mortuary and the small group of patients who had been infected as a result of his attack on Samantha Mellor.

Around three-quarters of an hour ago another man had been found wandering around the grounds of All Hallows Church with a bite wound – a *human* bite wound – on his neck. Although he had been unconscious upon arrival at the hospital and had remained so ever since, he had been taken straight to the makeshift isolation ward on the fourth floor, where, due to the fact that he had been exhibiting similar symptoms to those of the other infected patients, he had been restrained.

Although Susan knew it was a necessary precaution, it didn't make it any easier to tie an unconscious and evidently sick man to a hospital bed. It was like adding insult to injury, and it made the whole medical team feel wretched – so much so that one of the student nurses, Andrea Dempsey, a pretty, red-haired Irish girl, had stumbled from the ward in tears, tearing off her face mask as she went.

Although Susan and her colleagues had begun to work immediately and intensively on the new arrival, he had, like all the others, failed to respond to treatment. The wound on his neck had continued to deteriorate, quickly turning gangrenous and exuding a foul-smelling discharge, while the flesh around it had started to take on the all-too-familiar yellowish-grey hue common to cell death.

Dr Blackstock had been particularly concerned that the bite was so close to the patient's head, but try as they might they had been unable to stop the necrosis from creeping across his face. They knew from the wallet they had found in his jacket that his name was Martin Balfour and that he was a thirty-three-year-old computer salesman, who lived with his widowed mother on the edge of Nonsuch Park in Cheam.

When Susan had left the makeshift isolation ward a few minutes ago, Martin Balfour had no longer looked thirty-three. He had looked more like a dying seventy year old, and the thought of his mother, who was on her way from Cheam in a taxi, seeing her son restrained and desperately ill, filled Susan with horror.

She had a son of her own, eight-year-old Connor, who was currently obsessed with building robots and dinosaurs out of Lego, and a daughter, too, four-year-old Mollie, who mostly just enjoyed breaking her brother's creations while cackling like a comic book super-villain. Susan didn't often think of her children when she was at work, not directly anyway, but she was thinking of them tonight – thinking of them and wishing she was with them.

Because something was going down here. Something bad. She was not prone to panic or sensationalism, but she *was* a realist and she knew that an infection as contagious and as virulent as this needed to be contained quickly or the effects could be catastrophic.

How had Martin Balfour come by his bite wound? Was it too much to hope that he was one of the dead man's victims too? Yes, in all reality it probably was. Which meant that there were more "biters" out there, more people spreading the infection. How long before the trickle of admissions to the hospital became a flood? How long before they were overwhelmed?

Although she had a duty of care, and a responsibility both to her patients and her work colleagues, Susan had already decided what she would do if things started to get seriously out of hand. Her priorities lay with her family, with Connor and Mollie and her husband, Ben. So if the worst came to the worst she would simply abandon ship. And not only that, but once she got home, she would impress upon them the need to pack their bags and get the hell out of London before it was too late.

Despite the isolation ward, and the restraints, and the other precautions they were taking, she had a horrible feeling that things were already spiralling out of control. Even though four of the infected patients – Samantha Mellor, Jermaine Paterson, poor Tammy Ollerenshaw and now Martin Balfour – were safely contained, another, the bride-to-be Christine McGough, seemed to have disappeared. Whether she was lying low, roaming the hospital or had slipped out through one of the building's many exits and was now wandering the streets dressed in her sexy nurse's uniform, no one seemed to have any idea. The security guys had promised to check CCTV footage to see if they could spot her, but as yet they had been too busy to do so.

And as if all that wasn't bad enough, it now seemed possible that someone else had turned up at the hospital with the infection. Susan had been sitting at the nurse's station in the isolation ward – a large desk in the centre of the room – and trying to cope with the hopelessness she felt at being able to do little for the patients in her care, when Sister Parkhurst had drifted across and crouched beside her.

"I don't want to panic anyone," she had murmured, "so let's keep this strictly between ourselves for now, but we may have another one."

She didn't need to elaborate for Susan to immediately grasp her meaning. Feeling the muscles in her back and shoulders stiffen with tension, she said, "Oh, surely not. Who?"

Appalled though she was by her own thought processes, she half-hoped Sister Parkhurst would tell her that it was another of the hen night girls, or Jermaine Paterson's little friend, or even one of the security guys. At least then they could cling to the belief that the infection was still small-scale, containable.

But Sister Parkhurst said, "It's a twenty-six-year-old female called Anna Carstairs. She's a known drug user, so it could just be that she's taken an overdose, which is what her boyfriend claims."

"But . . .?" said Susan in response to the grimace of doubt that appeared immediately on the older woman's flushed face.

"But she's being aggressive and abusive and is showing signs of confusion and disorientation."

Susan swallowed. "What's she supposed to have taken?"

Spreading her hands, Sister Parkhurst said, "Your guess is as good as mine. Apparently her boyfriend Peter James found her in an agitated state when he got home. He says the medicine cabinet and drinks cabinet were empty and that Anna barely recognized him."

"Well, that's understandable if she's taken a cocktail of stuff. It could just be a botched suicide attempt."

Sister Parkhurst raised an eyebrow. "*Just?*"

"You know what I mean," said Susan, flushing. A hand fluttered up to her cheek as if to cover her embarrassment.

Regarding her shrewdly, and not a little sympathetically, Sister Parkhurst said, "I *do* know what you mean. And I know that we're all thinking what we dare not say – those of us with the foresight to think it at all, that is."

Already half-rising from her seat, Susan said, "So I'm guessing you want me to assess the Carstairs girl, see what I think?"

Sister Parkhurst nodded. "If you wouldn't mind, dear. Just run the routine checks on her. Chances are we're all just getting a little paranoid, but you never know. It's better to be safe than sorry."

Heading towards A&E Admissions, Susan consoled herself with the thought that Sister Parkhurst was probably right – they *were* all getting paranoid. It was highly unlikely that the girl would be infected, and if she was . . . well, the thing would be to get her contained as quickly as possible. Of course, it would take the nature of what they were dealing with here to a whole new level, and push Susan closer towards the decision she was dreading, but it was best not to think about that just now. Best just to take one thing at a time.

Even so, by the time she arrived in Admissions, Susan's stomach was cramping with tension despite the deep breathing. The waiting area was large, and even though it was almost 3:00 am it was still around half-full.

It didn't take a genius to work out who Anna Carstairs was, though. She just had to be the stringy haired, pale-complexioned woman in the ripped jeans and shabby combat jacket who was flailing her arms about and moaning. And the tall, skinny guy with the scrappy beard, acned cheeks and filthy Ramones T-shirt – who was trying in his long-limbed, lollopy way to restrain her while, in his husky voice, simultaneously exhorting her to calm down – had to be her boyfriend, Peter James.

They were putting on quite a floorshow, one that had drawn the attention of everyone in the room. Some were viewing their antics with amusement, others with expressions of sneery irritation, whereas the rest – including the two hen-night girls who *hadn't* been infected – looked wary, even a little fearful, as if nervous of being attacked.

Susan was grateful to see Jim and Duncan, two of the hospital's fitter and bulkier security guys, hovering on the periphery of the action, ready to move in if things got out of hand. Jim was an ex-policeman with a round, shaven head and a body so solid it looked as if it was padded with tyre rubber. When she nodded to him he nodded back, and they moved forwards as one, she approaching the couple from the front, Jim and Duncan from the rear.

Coming to a halt out of range of the woman's flailing arms, Susan cleared her throat and said, "Anna Carstairs?"

Still dancing around his girlfriend, reminding Susan of a scrawny sheepdog trying to contain a particularly lively ewe, Peter James squinted at her.

"She is, I'm not."

"You surprise me," said Susan. "I'm guessing you're Peter?"

He nodded.

"I understand that Anna has swallowed various substances, Peter?"

"Yeah. Least, I think so. I didn't see her do it." He ducked back as Anna lashed out at him. "Whoa there. What you playing at, you mad bitch? It's me, it's Pete."

Susan looked at Anna. The woman's eyes were unfocused, her face slack, her mouth hanging open. She looked completely unaware of what she was doing. It was almost as if she was being animated by an outside force.

"*Anna*," Susan said sharply. "Anna, can you hear me?"

Anna paused for a moment, as if her own name might have penetrated the fuzz in her mind, but then she continued her wheeling, staggering, arm-swinging perambulations.

Wary though she was of distracting Peter from containing

his girlfriend, Susan asked, "Has she vomited at all, Peter? Or had any fits or convulsions?"

He shook his head. "Nah, she's just been like this."

"And she hasn't scratched you or bitten you?"

"She's fucking tried, but I'm like that old boxer, me – whatsisname. Float like a butterfly, sting like a bee."

"Muhammad Ali," muttered Duncan.

Peter wagged a finger, which Anna tried to grab. "That's the geezer."

"Okay, well we'd better take her through and examine her straight away," Susan said.

"Is she gonna be all right?" Peter asked.

"We won't know that until we know what she's taken." Turning again to Anna, Susan said, "Anna, my name's Susan. I'm a nurse. I need to run some tests on you. I want to make you better, but I can't do that unless you calm down and come through to the treatment area with me. Will you do that?"

Anna paused, her head swinging round as if homing in on Susan's voice. Susan tried not to shudder as the woman's pale, unfocused eyes, her pupils no more than tiny black dots, seemed to fasten on her face. For a moment Anna remained still, her body hunched over and swaying slightly, her head cocked to one side. Then she made a guttural sound deep in her throat and lurched towards Susan, one arm outstretched.

Susan jumped nimbly back, and Jim and Duncan moved in on Anna, flanking her like bodyguards. They clamped her arms to her sides and half-carried, half-frog-marched her out of the waiting area and along a corridor towards the treatment area. Anna's head weaved from side to side and a frown wrinkled her pale, pimply forehead. In a gruff, slurred voice, she muttered, "Gerroffmeyafuckazzzz . . ."

Though the words were hostile, Susan was oddly heartened by them. At least they meant that the real Anna was still in there and still functioning, however inadequately, as a human being. She marched behind Jim, Duncan and their wriggling captive, while Peter buzzed around them like a mosquito, hands fluttering, alternating between scolding Anna for "behaving like a twat" and urging the security guys not to hurt her.

Entering the treatment area, Susan spotted Andrea Dempsey, her eyes still pink from her recent outburst, at the nurse's station – a cubbyhole containing a desk, a wall-mounted intercom and a row of shelves bearing far too few basic supplies. The student nurse was hunched over the desk, jotting notes on a form attached to a clipboard, but she looked up as Susan and her group appeared, her eyes widening in apprehension as she spotted Anna.

Hurrying forward to plant herself at the head of the group, Susan asked, "Is bay 16 free, Andrea?"

The student nurse blinked and nodded. "Er . . . yes, I think so."

"Good. Then perhaps you'll assist me? I need you to call Dr Blackstock and tell him we have a twenty-six-year-old female, admitted due to possible ingestion of unknown narcotic substances, in need of urgent medical assessment. Tell him the patient is conscious, but confused and disorientated. And when you've done that, get Mr James here to fill in a patient admissions form. Oh, and stick around if you're not too busy. I may need your help."

"Okay," murmured Andrea.

As she picked up the phone, Susan turned back to Jim and Duncan and said, "Would you bring Anna this way, please, guys? Peter, take a seat over there and Andrea will bring you a form to fill in."

"But I wanna go with Anna," Peter protested.

Susan smiled. "I'll take good care of her, don't worry."

Peter pushed out his bottom lip and began to whine about how Anna needed him, but before Susan could tactfully explain that the bays were not big enough to accommodate non-essential personnel, Jim said curtly, "You'd only get in the way, son. So why don't you sit yourself down and let Nurse Jenkins do her job, eh?"

High spots of colour blossomed on Peter's cheeks, but he meekly did as he was told. Jim glanced at Susan and winked, and Susan smiled back before leading them along the line to bay 16.

Once Jim and Duncan had manoeuvred Anna inside, Susan stepped in after them, turning to tug closed the flimsy sea-green privacy curtain. The metal hooks looped through the curtain rings slithered and clattered as the curtain swung across.

On the short journey between the Admissions area and the treatment bay Anna had become more agitated. Clamped between the two burly security guards she wriggled like a fish on a hook and her head thrashed from side to side, causing Jim and Duncan to incline their own heads away from her so as not to get their faces lashed by her stringy hair.

At Susan's request the two security guards lifted the woman effortlessly and, each taking a different side of the bed, laid her down on the mattress between them. To prevent her from getting straight back up again, they then clamped their hands around her wrists and ankles. Jim's face was red with the effort of holding her down and Duncan was sweating.

"I'm guessing you want us to stick around?" Jim gasped.

Susan nodded. "If you wouldn't mind?"

"Not at all," Jim said, clenching his teeth in an effortful grin. "It's not like we've got anything better to do."

Grimacing in apology, Susan said, "I'd give Anna a sedative to calm her down, but we don't know what she's already taken, so I can't risk it. Can you keep hold of her while I take her pulse, temperature and blood pressure?"

"No problem," grunted Jim.

Andrea stuck her head through the curtain, and all but recoiled at the sight of Anna writhing on the bed. Stepping up close to her, Susan said quietly, "Andrea, would you fetch the restraints? If you can't find them, ask Sister Parkhurst where they are."

A look of horror flickered across Andrea's face, and for a split-second Susan thought the girl might burst into tears again. But then she swallowed, gave a brief nod and withdrew. Turning back to the bed, Susan said, "Right, Jim, if you can move your hand a little higher so that I can get access to the patient's wrist I'll try taking her pulse."

Slipping on a pair of disposable gloves, Susan regarded Anna's hand as though it was a poisonous spider. She was glad at least that the woman's fingernails were bitten down to the quick, which meant that she couldn't use them to scratch and claw. After a moment's hesitation Susan grabbed Anna's wrist and attempted to find a pulse. But it was illusory. One minute there – fluttering, almost buzzing, like a hummingbird – and the next undetectable.

Anxiously Susan looked at Anna's bucking body, at her clenched teeth and pin-prick eyes, and wondered if it was the drugs she had taken that was causing the strange arrhythmia. Though she hated herself for doing so, though she knew that it was an *appalling* way to think, she hoped that it was, if only because the alternative was far worse. Weak and inconsistent vital signs were a symptom of the infection.

Licking her dry lips and trying to ignore another painful stabbing cramp in her stomach, she took a disposable thermometer from the breast pocket of her tunic and stripped it from its cellophane wrapper with trembling fingers. Looking at Duncan she said, "Okay, I'm going to take Anna's temperature. So if you could—"

It happened so quickly that no one had time to react until it was over. Afterwards Duncan was not even sure how it *had* happened. The only explanation he could offer was that he must have been momentarily distracted when Susan spoke to him, must for a split-second have loosened his grip on the patient's wrist.

All he really knew was that one moment Susan was talking to him, and the next Anna Carstairs had wrenched herself free of his grip, reared up and bitten Susan on the forearm. The bite was swift, but deep enough to leave two semi-circular bite marks. The instant it happened Susan screamed and staggered back from the bed, dropping the thermometer.

As Duncan, also yelling, tried to regain control over Anna's now wildly flailing arm, Susan stared down at the bite wound with utter horror. When she reached the curtain surrounding the treatment bay, she pushed her way through it and out into the corridor. And that was when her legs crumpled from under her, the shock of what had happened, and more specifically of what it might mean, simply robbing her body of strength.

Sitting in the middle of the hospital corridor, her body hunched forward, Susan continued to stare at her arm as though it was the most appalling sight she had ever seen in her life.

When Andrea Dempsey came running up a few seconds later, tears were streaming down Susan's face and she was whispering, "No, no, no, no," over and over again.

02:58 am

GILL STILL HADN'T forgiven Tim Marshall. Not only had he frightened her half-to-death, looming out of the darkness like that, his face uplit by candlelight, but then, even though she was clearly terrified, he had asked her what the fuck she was playing at, screaming like an idiot. Even when she told him what she had seen, he had refused to believe it.

"Fuck's sake," he had muttered, his face twisting into a sneer, "I can't leave you alone for five minutes, can I, without you getting hysterical over a few shadows?"

He had insisted on marching her back to the Victorian hovel display just so that he could belittle her. "See," he had said smugly, sweeping his arm in an arc like a landlord showing off a flat to a prospective tenant, "there's nothing here."

"Well, of course there isn't *now*," she had responded acidly. "But there was. I saw it."

"A dwarf that walked into the wall?" he had said, looking at her so condescendingly that she had wanted to punch him in the face.

In that moment she had wondered how she could ever have found him attractive. And she was still wondering it as she found herself knocking on the door of his office two hours later. She worked on the Women's Surgical ward and his office was on the corridor leading to Men's Surgical on the floor above. But she was still nervous that one of her colleagues might spot her and report back; despite their attempts to keep their affair a secret, there were enough rumours buzzing around about her and Tim as it was.

"Come on," she muttered when he didn't respond to her knock, and knocked again harder. Concluding that he must be attending to a patient or out and about on his rounds, she was about to slip away when she heard – *thought* she heard – a groan from behind the door.

"Tim", she almost said, and immediately looked around guiltily as though she *had* said it. "Dr Marshall?" she murmured. "Are you there?"

Without waiting for a reply she tried the handle. She was almost surprised when the door opened.

There was nothing actually *wrong* with a nurse walking into a doctor's office – it happened all the time, nurses and doctors exchanging information, consulting one another about this and that. Even so, she felt suddenly exposed, found out even, and she stepped into the office and closed the door smartly behind her almost before registering that the room was dark.

Not *completely* dark, though. There was a lamp on the desk, which had been turned on, but the flexible neck had been bent over so that the bulbous head was almost touching the surface. Light spilled from it like luminous liquid from an overturned cup, illuminating the desk and, to a lesser extent, the area immediately around the desk, but leaving the rest of the room blanketed in grainy, soft-edged shadow.

Despite his silence, Tim was here, after all, but Gill's first shocked thought was that he was dead. He was sitting on the leather chair behind his desk, but had slumped forwards and was now sprawled face-down across the polished surface, one arm stretched out as though reaching for her, the other tucked beneath his head.

For a moment Gill did nothing but stare at him, too startled to speak. Then, recovering, she said tentatively, "Tim? Are you all right?"

He stirred, his outstretched arm slowly bending as he drew it in, his head rising with a faint groan. He stared at her groggily, but didn't say anything.

"Sorry," she said. "Were you having forty winks?"

She hated the diffidence in her voice, the inference that she was a subordinate deferring to a superior. Determined to say nothing else until he responded to her question, she simply stared at him as he stared back at her.

Then, finally, he blinked, raised a hand and scratched at his neck.

"What do you want?"

"I need your help."

He frowned and continued to scratch at his neck. The sound was dry, rough, like fingernails on sandpaper: *scritch-scritch-scritch*.

"What? What help? What do you mean?"

"I've lost my mobile phone."

He scowled as though she was annoying him with trivialities. "So? What has that got to do with me?"

She took a step closer to the desk. "I can't find it anywhere. It's not in my locker or my jacket, which means I must have been carrying it around with me. I do that sometimes, in case the kids want to get hold of me."

She paused, took a deep breath. He continued to stare at her. Continued to scratch too: *scritch-scritch-scritch*.

"I think I must have left it in the Museum. It must have dropped out of my pocket. When I was getting undressed. Or dressed."

"Or when you were running around, shrieking like a hysterical child," he said spitefully.

She clenched her teeth, tried not to rise to the bait. She needed his help. She didn't want this to turn into a slanging match.

"Anyway," she said, "I wondered if you'd come with me to look for it."

His reply was not just spiteful this time, it was scornful. "Come with you?"

"Yes. I don't want to go on my own. It'll only take five minutes."

He snorted, as if he had never heard anything so ridiculous. "No. I won't go with you. I haven't got time. Besides, I'm not feeling well."

"Why?" she said accusingly. "What's wrong with you?"

"I feel sick, dizzy. No energy. And my neck is . . . *fucking . . . itching!*" He punctuated the words with a renewed bout of scratching.

"Where that insect bit you, you mean?"

His confirmation was little more than a groan.

"Maybe you've got malaria."

"Don't be stupid," he said dismissively and laid his head back down on the desk.

She felt a surge of panic. She couldn't leave her phone in the Museum. If someone found it they'd know it was hers and they'd wonder how it had got there. Perhaps she could say it had been stolen, that someone had taken it from her jacket pocket. But what if the staff who worked in the Museum read her texts? Weren't there some from Tim? Intimate ones? *Explicit* ones? Or had she deleted those? She couldn't remember.

"Please, Tim," she said. "Please come with me. I'm scared to go on my own. That place gives me the creeps." Only half-jokingly she added, "I need a big, strong man by my side."

He groaned again. "Fuck's sake. I've told you once. I'm ill. Leave me alone."

"I will if you do this one thing for me. I promise. Please, Tim. I don't even know the combination for the door."

"One eight zero three," he said. "Same as it is for every other fucking door in the hospital – 1803."

She felt desperate, at her wit's end. She could hear the wheedling quality in her own voice. "But you're not *really* going to let me go on my own, are you, Tim? I can't believe you'd be that mean. There are texts on that phone. Texts from you. What if someone were to read them?"

His head was still resting on the desk, but he hunched his shoulders in a shrug. "What if they were?"

"Well . . . they'd *know* about us. They'd know what was going on."

He was silent for a moment, then he said. "You think I care? I couldn't give a shit. You're just a shag to me. One of many."

Despite her earlier decision to end the affair, she felt tears spring to her eyes, her throat close up. She tried to speak and couldn't. Then she tried again, and this time she managed it, though her voice was a rasp. "You don't mean that."

"Yes, I fucking do. And not only are you just a shag, but you're not even a very good one. Now fuck off and leave me alone. You're getting on my nerves."

She wanted to rage at him. She wanted to tell him what a vicious little shit he was. She wanted to tell him that she hoped he *did* have malaria, and that it was a particularly rare and lethal strain, and that he died in agony from it.

But she didn't. She couldn't. She was reeling; she couldn't breathe; she thought she might pass out.

All at once the darkness in the room felt oppressive. She felt it stifling her, trying to force its way inside her.

She staggered to the door, reached for the handle. She knew that if there was someone outside when she opened it they would only have to take one look at her and they would *know*, they would know everything.

But she didn't care. She couldn't stay here. She opened the door.

Behind her she could still hear him scratching, the sound like rat's teeth gnawing through wood.

Scritch-scritch-scritch.

03:04 am

SHE FINDS HERSELF back in the churchyard. She has no idea how she got here, but here she is.

It's dark like before, and almost preternaturally quiet. Nothing stirs, not even the mist hanging like thick swathes of cobweb between the tombstones. And yet she senses that she is expected, that they – whoever *they* are – know she is here.

Although she has no torch she realizes that she can see perfectly well. She looks up at the moon, expecting it to be glaring down at her like a giant white eyeball, light spilling from it, but it is concealed within layers of cloud, which are themselves wrapped in darkness. Perhaps she has boosted one sense in exchange for another, because when she begins walking it dawns on her that it's not just quiet, but utterly silent. She can't even hear her feet on the pitted gravel or the long grass swishing against her legs.

As she walks she forms the impression that the path is a spiral from which there is no escape. It will lead her in ever-tightening circles to the centre, the Pit, in which the church of All Hallows squats like some ancient and loathsome god, drawing its acolytes to it, reeling them in.

This ought to bother her, but she feels oddly fatalistic about it. Although she is not being coerced in any way, she somehow knows that she is committed to seeing this through, that stepping off the path or turning back is not an option.

As she gets closer to the church she feels its pull, like cold, dark tentacles curling not only around her but pushing their way through her skin, infiltrating her mind. The church is a vast, black, motionless presence and yet it seems to rise in front of her, a behemoth awakening after centuries of sleep, rumbling its way to the surface.

Like flotsam around a sinkhole she circles the church. She can feel the weight of its dark and terrible history bearing down upon her. Its walls ooze with it; it fills her head with terrible images: sickness, rot, almost unendurable pain. She feels stinking, decaying bodies crushing down upon her. She feels grave dirt pattering on her skin, falling into her open eyes.

The main entrance to the church is a wound, an aperture; an absence of light, of hope. The pull is stronger here. She cannot resist it. She is carried along on the flow, feels herself rushing towards the blackness. And then the blackness envelops her, absorbs her, she becomes part of it, and all at once she is inside the church. She waits at the back of the aisle, like a bride about to make her entrance. She is staring up at the man.

He stands at the pulpit and seems to draw the energy of the place towards him, or perhaps he radiates it. He is stout, dressed in old-fashioned clothes – a white shirt with a lace collar, a heavy red velvet coat brocaded with gold trim – and a powdered wig. He has piercing eyes that transfix her where she stands, and when he smiles his wide, red smile she feels a shudder of fear run through her.

"Welcome, my dear," he says, raising his hands. "Won't you join the congregation? You're one of *us* now."

She becomes aware that the pews in front of her, to the right and the left, are full of people. She sees them stir, and she realizes she can hear them too – the dry rustle of dead skin, the click and scrape of bone. As they turn to regard her with their eyeless sockets, to reach for her with their fleshless fingers, she hears a high buzzing whine. She realizes it is coming from the man, and when she tears her gaze from the undead hordes now shuffling and rustling and slithering towards her, she sees that he is enveloped in a cloud of insects that jitter and crawl across his face, and in and out of his grinning mouth.

"Who are you?" she whispers.

His grin widens. "I am your Master. I am the King of the Dead."

A hand that is more bone than flesh closes around her arm. She jerks away – and her eyes open.

A new face is looming over her. A face that is chubby and bearded and full of concern. The mouth widens in a smile, but it is nothing like that terrible smile of the demon in the pulpit.

"Back with us, lass, are you?" the face says, and as it does so she remembers its owner's name – Vince. "How are you feelin'?"

Shirley reaches out from her hospital bed and clutches his hand. "Oh, Vince," she says, "oh, Vince."

"It's all right, love," he says, "you're safe now."

She shakes her head vigorously. "No," she says, "I'm not. None of us are." She clutches his hand tighter, so tightly that he winces.

"Something's coming, Vince," she says, almost choking on the need to tell him, warn him. "Something terrible."

And in her mind a name slithers to the surface. A name that she has no memory of having heard before, except perhaps within a dream. Or a nightmare.

Thomas Moreby.

03:09 am

"OH NO!"

Cat stepped back in shock, as if she could distance herself from the news. Her action was so sudden that the receiver of the wall-mounted phone, its dangling cord a twisted red knot, jerked from her hand and clattered against the floor. For a moment the bustle in the isolation ward stopped and heads, their faces mostly obscured by white protective masks, turned in her direction. Then Marcus Blackstock, at the far end of the ward, broke from the tableau and hurried towards her.

"Nurse Harris, what's wrong?"

Cat looked at him, stricken, bunching her hands into fists. "It's Susan. She's been bitten."

Despite the bleeps and burbles of the many and various monitors clustered around the beds of the tethered but still unconscious patients, her voice was loud enough to create a stir of disquiet among her colleagues. Sister Parkhurst, who had been speaking to one of the student nurses at the foot of Jermaine Paterson's bed, jerked as if slapped.

"Oh no! Not by Anna Carstairs?"

"Is this the suspected overdose?" Marcus Blackstock asked.

Sister Parkhurst nodded miserably. "Yes. It was me who sent Susan over to assess her."

"I was literally just on my way over there myself." Dr Blackstock nodded at the internal phone, which was still swinging gently on its cord. "Who were you speaking to?"

"Er . . . Andrea Dempsey."

"Is she still there?"

"I don't know."

Stepping past her, Marcus lifted the phone by its cord and swung it neatly into his other hand. Pulling down his protective mask, he said, "Hello? Nurse Dempsey?" After the briefest of pauses he continued, "This is Dr Blackstock. How *is* Nurse Jenkins?" As he listened, a slight frown on his face, the room seemed to hold its collective breath. Eventually he said, "I see. And what about the patient who attacked her?"

He listened some more. Then he said, "All right, try not to panic. Help is on its way. Just do your best until it arrives."

Replacing the receiver he turned to Sister Parkhurst. Despite the situation he seemed composed, in control. "Sister, would you mind heading down to the treatment area and giving Nurse Dempsey a hand? I'm afraid the poor girl is a little out of her depth."

Sister Parkhurst nodded. "Certainly. But aren't you coming too?"

"In a moment. But I think it's time we got to the bottom of this infection, and sooner rather than later."

"What are you going to do?" asked Cat, making an effort to pull herself together.

"I'm going to see if I can get Patient Zero's PM conducted immediately."

Patient Zero was how they had started referring to the dead man in the Mortuary. Sister Parkhurst, halfway to the door, paused and turned. "Won't that involve cutting through rather a lot of red tape?"

"Yes. But I think this poor chap—" he indicated Martin Balfour, who was lying in the bed behind him, unconscious and breathing stertorously "—and Anna Carstairs provide justifiable cause for concern that the infection has spread beyond acceptable grounds. I'll just have to persuade the powers-that-be that extreme circumstances call for extreme solutions."

"So you think Anna Carstairs definitely has the infection then?" Cat Harris asked, still trying to mask her distress.

Although Marcus' face and voice were sympathetic, his words were honest. "We won't know for certain until we've assessed her condition and analysed her stomach contents, but Nurse Dempsey has just told me that she's becoming increasingly aggressive and that it's taken the combined efforts of herself and two security guards to get restraints on to her wrists and ankles. Given the evidence I would say it's a reasonable assumption, wouldn't you?"

Cat drew a long, shuddering breath and nodded.

From the doorway, Sister Parkhurst asked, "Did Nurse Dempsey say whether she'd given the Carstairs girl a sedative?"

"She did, and she hasn't, which is entirely the correct procedure. Until we know what, if anything, she's taken, it would be inadvisable to give the patient any medication."

The scowl that accompanied Sister Parkhurst's abrupt nod was all that Marcus needed to raise his hand in apology.

"Sorry, I'm teaching my grandmother how to suck eggs. I didn't mean to be insulting."

"If you're suggesting that I'm old enough to be your grandmother then it's even more of an insult," Sister Parkhurst said fiercely, but there was a twinkle in her eye. More softly she said, "Sometimes it's useful to spell things out. It helps to clear the mind. Especially under pressure."

She exited the room, the double doors swinging back into place behind her.

Like a hypnotist rousing his subjects from a stupor, Marcus brought his hands together in a decisive, almost teacherly clap. "Right, let's keep focused everyone. Keep doing what you're doing, but remember to be careful."

Flashing Cat a brief but encouraging smile, he picked up the phone and punched in the extension number for the Mortuary. Although he kept his voice low, Cat, who was attending to Martin Balfour — which in truth involved little more than monitoring his seemingly unstoppable deterioration — heard him say in surprise, "Really? When was this?"

As soon as the young doctor put the phone down, she turned to him. "What's wrong?"

He curled his lips in a wry expression too troubled to be termed a smile. "Were you eavesdropping on my conversation, Nurse Harris?"

Boldly she said, "I didn't realize it was private."

He wafted a vague hand. "It wasn't really. What do you know of Professor Déesharné?"

She shrugged. "Not much. I've seen him around, but never spoken to him. Isn't he here doing research?"

"Yes, for a pharmaceuticals company, NWP."

She nodded. NWP supplied the hospital with most of its drugs. "What of him?"

"Well, it looks as though he's beaten us to it where Patient Zero is concerned."

"What do you mean?"

"He's requisitioned the remains in order to conduct his own post-mortem examination. Patient Zero's body is no longer in the Mortuary."

Cat gaped at him. "Is he allowed to do that?"

"It seems so. Piotr Bajorek, the Mortuary attendant, said Professor Déesharné was carrying government papers, granting him ultimate authority."

Cat felt a blend of anger, despair and spiralling disorientation.

She thought of her friend, Susan Jenkins, who might even now be afflicted with the infection that seemed to be devouring every single one of the patients around her.

"So where's the body now? And is Professor Déesharné going to reveal his findings to us?"

"I don't know," said Marcus, "but I bloody well intend to find out."

03:16 am

PIOTR PUT DOWN the phone, feeling guilty in spite of himself. He knew there was nothing he could have done to prevent Professor Déesharné taking the body, but that didn't stop him from wishing that he had offered more resistance.

The Professor's actions – in spite of his credentials – had been highly irregular, and at the very least Piotr should have made a couple of phone calls to confirm that the requisition was above board as far as the hospital was concerned.

Déesharné would no doubt have griped about it, might even have threatened Piotr with disciplinary action, or worse, but at the end of the day he couldn't have denied that Piotr was merely doing his job – behaving with admirable diligence and dedication, in fact. There was no *way* that Piotr could have been punished for that. Even if Déesharné had made trouble for him, Piotr felt sure he would have had the full support of his colleagues and employers, and that, government dispensation or not, Déesharné would ultimately have been the one left squirming like a fish on a hook.

But hindsight was all very well. The simple fact was, Piotr *had* allowed the Professor to browbeat and bully him. And not only that, but the incident had left such a bad taste in his mouth that he had subsequently done nothing to rectify the situation. He should have contacted the site manager to query Déesharné's actions or report them, but he hadn't done so. Instead he had simply brushed the incident under the carpet in the hope that it would go away.

But it hadn't gone away. And now it was coming back to – what was the phrase? – bite him on the arse. Dr Blackstock, who Piotr liked and respected, had sounded surprised and angry when Piotr had told him what had happened. Not at Piotr necessarily, but still . . .

He wondered what was going on. Of what possible importance was this murdered tramp? The story Piotr had heard was that the man had been killed in a nightclub, but perhaps it was more than that? Perhaps it was a cover-up of some kind, something involving the Government or the police? Could it be that the police had brutalized and ultimately killed the man?

But no, that didn't ring true. Five years ago the death of a man – even a homeless man – at the hands of British officers would have led to front-page newspaper headlines and a national inquiry, but not now. After what had happened in Trafalgar Square, this country that Piotr had always considered so affluent and civilized was now a far different place – a place of fear and danger.

So what then? Why all this fuss over a corpse? Piotr couldn't even begin to guess, but that didn't prevent him from having a very bad feeling about the situation. There was a crawling sensation in the pit of his stomach, and he didn't know why. All he knew was that something was very wrong, and that, if at all possible, he wanted no further part in it.

He felt so unsettled that he couldn't even drum up much enthusiasm for the web page currently open on his computer. BuiltForSpeed.com, which sounded like a meeting place for car racing enthusiasts, was in fact a listings page for speed-dating events, and in spite of the dismal outcome of last night's various encounters, Piotr had been toying with the idea of giving it another try and attending that evening's event at The Fox in Bexley. Now, though, after speaking to Dr Blackstock, he wasn't sure he felt up to it. He doubted he'd be able to give a good account of himself to potential . . . what was the word? Suitors? Or were suitors always men? Even after nearly five years in the country his language was not always perfect.

With a sigh he closed down BuiltForSpeed.com and maximized the tabulated page of specimen data awaiting his attention. He stared at the screen for a moment, then groaned and leaned back. He would make himself another coffee and then get stuck into the input figures and forget all about Professor Déesharné and the mystery of the requisitioned corpse.

He was reaching for his coffee mug – which bore a picture of Bart Simpson proclaiming DON'T HAVE A COW, MAN! – when he heard a noise.

He froze, listening hard, his forehead creasing in a puzzled frown. Beyond his little office, which was one of four similar, currently unmanned offices, was a corridor leading to the main doors – the same doors through which Professor Déesharné had entered and exited the unit earlier.

But the sound hadn't come from that direction. Unless his ears were deceiving him, it had come from deeper within the Mortuary – from the area housing the dissection tables and pathology lab and cold storage unit. He couldn't pinpoint exactly what the noise had been. It had been too vague and brief to identify. If pushed, he'd have said it was a kind of scratching. Or scrabbling. Definitely not the sound of something breaking or falling over, but perhaps of movement, of something alive.

Rats. That was his first thought. He had never seen one down here, and the unit was kept scrupulously clean, but this *was* an old building, and he supposed it wasn't beyond the realms of possibility that there might be rats in the walls or under the floors, perhaps burrowing up from the tunnels and passages that, according to various stories he had heard, were supposed to run below the building.

It wasn't until he had put his mug back down on his desk and stood up that he had his second thought. Ghosts. He paused for a moment, then smiled. He had heard the rumours, of course. He had even spoken to people who claimed to have heard strange noises or seen things down here – small, shadowy figures glimpsed out of the corner of the eye and gone when you turned to look.

Like everyone, Piotr liked a good ghost story, but he didn't believe in spooks. He believed only in science, in that which was quantifiable. Which meant that to make a sound like the one he had heard required form and substance. And as he was almost certain that he was the only person down here – the only living one, at least – that left him with only one option. Unlikely though it seemed, the perpetrator, in Piotr's opinion, was either an insect or an animal. There was no other explanation.

A little nervously – and not because he still harboured a secret fear of phantoms, but because rats were filthy, feral creatures and could be vicious if cornered – he moved into the corridor and turned right.

The floor was grey vinyl, the walls painted a shiny cream gloss that reflected the overhead strip lights. People not used to the environment often wondered how Piotr could work here without getting a headache, but his eyes had learned to adapt, to absorb more light than perhaps the average person was comfortable with. As a consequence it was shadows and darkness that he struggled with. Bars and pubs that his colleagues thought were cosy he often regarded as dingy and unwelcoming.

At the end of the corridor was another metal door, to the

left of which was a short flight of steps up to a viewing gallery. This was where students or pathologists or police officers stood if they wanted to witness post-mortems. This was also where the "ghost" had most often been seen.

In fact, Dr Hathaway had once told Piotr that his mentor and former colleague, the now-retired and much-revered Dr John Searle, had once looked up from doing a PM to see a small, dark shape flitting past the window of the viewing gallery. When Searle had asked who was up there, he had been told that the gallery was empty. A subsequent investigation had proven that to be the case.

Piotr barely gave the staircase a second glance now, however, but tapped in the four-digit code to open the door. The door gave a click and a sigh and he pushed it open. Stepping into the well-lit and spotless laboratory area, he looked carefully around, even though he knew there was barely anywhere an intruder could hide. The place was large, open plan, adorned with half-a-dozen metal dissection tables, a laboratory bench running the length of one wall, various equipment cupboards, some of which were affixed to the walls and others free-standing, and a trio of large, stainless-steel sinks.

After pausing for a moment, he walked slowly between the tables, glancing left and right, and over to the free-standing cupboards, which contained sets of freshly-laundered operating scrubs in vacuum-packed plastic bags and various other items of equipment. Bracing himself, he opened one after the other, but all were empty. On the far wall, to the right of the sinks, was another metal door, this one leading to the cold-storage unit, where the dead were stored both before and immediately after their PM examinations. Piotr was closing the last of the equipment cupboard and turning his head to look at this door when he heard the sound again.

He started. This time he was certain. The sound had come from behind it! Instantly he pictured rats, perhaps driven mad by hunger, gnawing their way into the room and feasting on the corpses. The idea horrified him. He imagined opening the door to see a pack of over-sized rats, all of them turning to regard him, hissing and snarling, their snouts caked in gore.

He wondered whether he should call for back-up before going in, but then he thought of how, if there *were* rats down here, it would reflect badly on him. It was his job to keep the place clean, after all. And besides, what if it wasn't rats, but mice – or even a single mouse? He'd feel an idiot if he dragged security down here only to discover that what he was asking them to face was nothing more than a cute and harmless rodent.

Pressing his ear to the door – cautiously, as though afraid that whatever was on the other side might hear him and smash its way through the metal in a superhuman frenzy – he listened. He could hear nothing now. The room beyond this one sounded as silent as . . . well, as the grave.

Even so, his heart was thumping hard as he straightened up and tapped in the four-digit security code. He winced, feeling suddenly vulnerable, as the locks disengaged with a click. Then, deciding that it was better to surprise a potential enemy than to forewarn one, he shoved the door open.

The room beyond again had a pale-grey vinyl floor, white walls and a white ceiling, inset into which were strip lights, which came on automatically and immediately when the door was opened. Although there was a small sink on the left-hand wall, the room's main focus was the stainless-steel storage unit, like a vast refrigerator with eight square doors in two rows of four, that stretched from wall-to-wall and floor-to-ceiling, directly opposite him.

Even though Piotr's eyes darted left and right as he stepped inside, it was immediately evident that the room was empty. There was no scuttling pack of bloodthirsty rats, no holes gnawed in the walls or floor, not even a spider web in the corner of the ceiling. There was nothing, in fact, which could explain the sound he had heard, and although he gave a vast exhalation of relief he had to admit that he was puzzled. Because the fact was, he *had* heard something. And it couldn't be a sound that had carried from another part of the building, because he had been here long enough to know that that simply didn't happen.

He stood in the doorway of the cold-storage room, as though, despite the austere surroundings, he half-believed he might have missed something obvious. Finally, however, he shrugged and took a step back, intending to pull the door closed behind him, go back to his office, and dismiss the incident as imagination, or one of life's great unsolved mysteries.

That was when he heard the sound again, much louder and closer this time. Loud enough and close enough, in fact, for him to pinpoint its source: the second door from the left on the bottom row of the storage unit – the one, coincidentally, next to that which had contained the body of the murdered tramp, which Professor Déesharné had appropriated. Piotr's head snapped in that direction, and a cold snake of fear, which had nothing to do with the temperature in the room, slithered from the hairs on the base of his neck all the way down his back.

There was a part of him that wanted to speak, to ask whether anyone was there, and a part of him that wanted to make no sound whatsoever, that wanted to get out of the room as quickly and silently as he could.

Second door from the left, bottom row. Piotr knew all too well who was in there – or rather, what, because the mortal remains of George Wheatley, the eighty-five-year-old man who had died of a pulmonary embolism four days ago, were now merely dead flesh, and could no longer be referred to as a person.

Logic told him – *science* told him – that Mr Wheatley couldn't possibly be making the sounds that Piotr had heard. Which meant that something else was, that there was something in there with him.

Piotr covered his mouth with a trembling hand and rubbed reflectively back and forth, hearing the scrape of his stubble. He thought again about the sound he had heard coming from the drawer containing George Wheatley's remains – a sort of shifting, rustling, like an animal trying to make itself comfortable. He thought again about calling someone, and then, with sudden decisiveness, he marched across the room to the storage unit. He halted in front of George Wheatley's drawer, staring down at it for a moment. And then he pulled it open.

He saw it immediately. The old man's corpse, wrapped in a loose, white mortuary shroud, was moving. His torso under the material was jerking, as though tics were breaking out under his stitched-up skin, and his left arm, the hand scrawny and claw-like, was twitching, the fingers stretching then relaxing, as though subject to a series of muscular spasms.

Piotr stared down at these tiny but impossible movements, fascinated and repulsed, and then he diverted his attention to the old man's face. It was sunken and waxy and utterly without life, the mouth and eyes half-open.

But even as Piotr watched, the mouth opened wider, and then wider still, and now Piotr could see that there was movement in there. Writhing, frantic movement, the movement of a thousand tiny creatures desperate to emerge into the light. For a moment it seemed as though the old man's face was cracking open, splitting like old clay around the lips, and then Piotr realized that what he had taken for cracks were, in fact, emerging, hair-thin legs. And suddenly creatures began to spill out of the corpse's mouth, tumbling over one another, and then out of its nostrils, and finally, horribly, they began to hatch from its eyes.

Sickened, Piotr stumbled back, a thin, high sound of distress coming from him. He was no expert, but he could see that the things pouring out of the old man were fleas, fat and red as though engorged on meat and blood.

As if responding to the sound that Piotr was making they suddenly took to the air in a rustling crimson cloud, erupting from the corpse and swirling towards Piotr, engulfing him, blinding him, landing on his skin and biting him.

He screamed and thrashed at them, slapping at his own skin, but it didn't deter them; in fact, it only seemed to encourage them to increase the ferocity of their attack. Through a buzzing red curtain of insects, Piotr saw George Wheatley's corpse, now disgorged of fleas, continue to twitch and jerk.

Then it sat up.

03:24 am

"IS THAT PROFESSOR Déesharné?"

"It is."

"Good evening, Professor Déesharné. This is Dr Blackstock. I'm the on-call senior house officer at the hospital."

"What of it?"

"Um . . . I understand that you requisitioned the corpse of an unidentified murder victim from the Mortuary a couple of hours ago for the purposes of an immediate post-mortem?"

"I did. But I don't see what concern that is of yours."

"It's actually a great concern of mine, Professor. May I ask *why* you requisitioned this corpse?"

"No. You may not."

"I beg your pardon?"

"You may not ask. My research here is confidential."

"Are you aware, Professor Déesharné, that several patients, including two members of the hospital medical staff, are currently suffering from the effects of an extremely aggressive and as-yet unidentified infection? An infection which was passed on by the very man whose corpse you requisitioned?"

"I'm sorry. I'm not at liberty to discuss the matter."

"You're not at *liberty*? What the hell is that supposed to mean?"

"I would have thought that the meaning was perfectly clear."

"Professor Déesharné, let me explain this situation in the simplest possible terms. The post-mortem results of the man who passed on this aggressive and very possibly lethal infection to the majority of the infected patients here at the hospital could be *vital* in identifying the infection and treating the afflicted patients. It is imperative, therefore, that if the post-mortem has been carried out, which I believe to be the case, you share your findings with me."

"With all due respect, Dr Blackstock, I'm afraid that won't be possible. I am not answerable to the hospital *or* its staff, and I'm afraid that any results that I may have obtained constitute part of my research, and are therefore confidential."

"I don't believe I'm hearing this. Don't you realize that human lives are at stake?"

"Whether they are or not is of no concern of mine."

"No concern? For God's sake, man, don't you *care*?"

"My personal feelings are irrelevant."

"All right . . . all right. Who can I speak to about this?"

"You are speaking to me."

"Don't be obtuse, man. Who are you doing the research for?"

"I'm not at liberty to say."

"It's NWP, isn't it? New World Pharmaceuticals. They're your paymasters."

"No comment."

"Everyone knows that they've set up their own little research enclave on the top floor, but what nobody seems to know is why. So what do NWP know that we don't, Professor Déesharné? Why were you so keen to carry out such a hasty post-mortem on the murdered man's corpse?"

"No comment."

"I can only conclude that you had prior knowledge of this infection, that you knew it was coming. But how? *How* did you know?"

"No comment."

"All right, listen. I don't care *how* you know. All I care about is saving the lives of my patients – and in some cases my friends and colleagues. So strictly between us, can't you give me *something*? Some clue? Some way of *dealing* with this?"

"I can't believe you're a dispassionate man, Professor Déesharné. I can't believe that you'd stand by and do nothing while people are suffering, *dying*. Especially now that the indications are that this is more widespread than we previously thought.

"I don't know if you're aware, but we've had two further admissions in the past hour or so, patients who we've now confirmed are suffering from the infection. If this turns into an epidemic, then . . . well, frankly I'm terrified of what the consequences might be. So I'm begging you, Professor Déesharné, I'm *pleading* with you. Help me out. Please."

"Look after your patients, Dr Blackstock. Take very good care of them."

"I would if I knew how. What would *you* suggest would be the best way to do that?"

Click.

"Professor Déesharné? . . . Are you there? . . . Professor Déesharné? . . . Professor Déesharné . . .?"

03:28 am

WHEN THE DOOR to the ward opened, Fitch hunched in his seat and turned his face away. He counted to three, then turned back, to see that skinny doctor guy with the gay hair striding away down the corridor, his white coat flapping behind him. The door to the ward was flapping too, though not wide enough for Fitch to see inside. Fitch wondered why the doctor was in such a hurry, and why he looked so mad.

Last time he'd seen him he'd been pushing a trolley with a woman strapped to it. The woman had been snarling like a dog, spit flying out her mouth and running down her face. With the doctor and the woman had been one other guy and two nurses. The nurses had been walking by the doctor's side, one helping the other. The one being helped had a bandaged arm and her eyes were wet and red like she'd been crying.

The other guy had been skinny with scarecrow hair and a shit beard and clothes that looked like he'd found them in a skip. He'd been flapping round the woman on the trolley like a chicken, calling her Anna, even though she wasn't paying him no attention, and telling the doctor to treat her good. One time he'd reached down like he wanted to undo the strap round her wrist and the doctor had jumped forward and pushed him away and asked him what the hell he was doing. The skinny guy had said he was trying to hold his girlfriend's hand, just to let her know he was there, but the doctor had leaned towards the skinny guy and said something quiet, like he didn't want no one to hear, something about a scratch and ending up like her.

The doctor with the woman on the trolley and the two nurses went through the doors into the ward, but when the skinny guy tried to follow the doctor wouldn't let him. The guy was vexed, but the doctor said, "You can argue all you like, Mr James, but this is an isolation ward, and as such the danger of infection is too great to allow access to anyone but essential medical personnel." The skinny guy tried to argue, but Fitch saw straight up he was wasting his time. In the end he gave up and walked across and sat in a seat two down from Fitch.

He fell into the seat and went all floppy like he didn't have no bones, his head falling forward and his scarecrow hair dangling in his face like a bird's nest that was coming apart. Fitch felt nothing. Guy who looked like that, no respect for himself, didn't deserve respect from anyone else either. Normally Fitch would've blanked him – the guy was so low he was off the radar – but he was on a mission and Carlton had tole him to find out what he could.

So he leaned over and said, "Hey, wha'gwan?"

The guy looked up, piggy little eyes blinking away. "What?"

"I said wha'gwan? Like wass happenin'? Dat your girl they took in there?"

"Oh, er . . . yeah."

"Wass wrong with her?"

The guy hunched his skinny shoulders. "Overdose."

"For real? What she took?"

"Everything. Pills, booze . . ." Then he frowned. "At least I *thought* that's what was wrong with her."

"What you mean? Docs and that think different, yeah?"

He nodded almost eagerly. "They think she's got some sort of infection."

Fitch narrowed his eyes. "She bit?"

"What?"

"She bit? Someone bit her?"

The skinny guy looked at Fitch in bewilderment for a moment, and then his face cleared. "Oh. No. At least I don't think so. Unless it was the cat." He sniggered. Then he said, "*She* bit someone, though. That nurse with the bandage on her arm."

"Brutal," said Fitch quietly.

The guy looked indignant. "She didn't *mean* it. She wasn't herself. She was just upset and did it without thinking."

Fitch shrugged and silence fell between them. The corridor was quiet. In the last half-hour or so only the occasional nurse or doctor had passed by (aside from those going in or out of the isolation ward with the blacked-out windows), but none of them had stopped to ask Fitch what he was doing there.

"What about you?" the skinny guy said at last.

"Huh?"

"Who are you waiting for?"

"My man, Jermaine. He in there." He jerked his head at the double doors of the isolation ward "Least I think so. He got bit."

"Oh," said the skinny guy, as if he didn't understand. "Have they told you how he's doing?"

"Nah. They ain't tole me nothing."

"Doctors, eh?" said the skinny guy, half-smiling like he wanted Fitch to agree with him, like he wanted to be his friend.

Fitch stared at him, blank-faced, until the guy looked away. Then the guy leaned forward and rubbed his hands together. "Think I'll go and get a coffee," he said. "You want one?"

"Nah," Fitch said.

The man nodded, half-smiled again, then stood up and wandered away. When he was out of sight, Fitch reached into his jeans pocket and took out his phone. He called Carlton on speed dial.

"Yo, wass happenin'?"

"Yo, Carlton, it's me, Fitch."

"I know it, you dumbass. Where you at?"

"I followed that nurse like you tole me. She is *chung*, man."

"So where you *at*?" repeated Carlton, exasperated.

"Fourth floor. There's this room, innit? With the windows all blacked out, like you can't see in, yeah? I heard this doctor guy talking about it with this other guy. He called it the isolation ward."

"So that where they got Jermaine, yeah?"

"I tink."

"You *tink*? How come you don't know?"

"Like I say, windows is all blacked out and they ain't lettin' no one in. But that's where they's taking all the psychos. I seen this one bitch strapped on a trolley, growling and foaming at the mouth. For real."

"Jermaine ain't no psycho," Carlton said.

"Nah, but he got bit, man. I heard this doctor talking about an *infection*. And there was this other nurse. She got bit too by the mad bitch, and she was cryin' like she knew it was bad." He hunched over, glancing up the corridor and lowering his voice. "I tell you, blud, somethin's goin' down. I seen people comin' out of that room, and they's mad or cryin' or scared, and nearly all of them's movin' fast, like they's runnin' out of time."

There was silence on the other end of the line.

"You still there, Carlton?"

"Shut up, dickwad, I'm thinkin'."

Cowed, Fitch said, "What you want me to do?"

"Nothin'. Sit tight. I'm comin' up there."

"You *comin'*? But what about your guts, man? Ain't you all stitched up? Ain't you bleedin' and shit?"

"Fuck that. I'm comin' up there and ain't no one gonna stop me."

"Okay, blud, see you soon."

The line went dead.

03:30 am

SHE ALMOST DIDN'T go back. She almost decided that losing her phone and living with the possibility of having her affair with Tim Marshall discovered was the lesser of two evils.

But then she started playing over and over in her mind what that would mean. She thought of her children, Louise and Ethan, and how much they relied on her and trusted her and believed in her. At seven, Ethan, although a typical rough-and-tumble little boy, was still her baby. Louise was three years older, and yet in many ways that made her even more vulnerable.

She would be starting secondary school – Big School – in September (if the bloody Government hadn't closed them all down by then, of course), and she was incredibly nervous about that, needing constant reassurance that everything would be all right. Also she was now old enough and aware enough to pick up on any frictions between her parents, although what she *wasn't* yet mature enough to do was to put those frictions into perspective. As far as Louise was concerned, every argument was the prelude to a divorce, and therefore something to be feared and fretted over.

More than once, after a bickering session with Gerry, Gill had found her daughter sobbing and had had to reassure her that no, of *course* she and Daddy weren't about to split up, like Amy's parents, or Bethany's, or Louise's former best friend Martha's, whose Mum had ended up moving back to Tewkesbury and taking Martha with her.

Although it was three decades ago now, Gill remembered all too clearly how it felt to be Louise's age. The prelude to puberty and baffling hormonal changes was a giddily exciting time of life, when the highs were euphoric, friendships seemed lifelong and unbreakable, and the most minor of anxieties could overwhelm you like a crushing black wave. It was a time when the world was full of promise and also terrifyingly inexplicable. It was a time when you were often in such turmoil that it was imperative to be assured of the stability of those things on which you had always relied, like home and family.

Of course, Gill knew that not every child could be assured of that stability. Some were brought up in the most appalling circumstances and were often tainted by it, sometimes permanently. But she herself had had a *good* childhood, a happy childhood, and she had always been determined that her own children would have the same.

In the past three months she had somehow lost sight of that, had had her head turned, her focus deflected. She had been tempted by the forbidden fruit, but having tasted it she had found it to be not only disappointingly sour, but ultimately full of poison. After the awful encounter with what she now thought of as the *real* Tim Marshall, she was more than ready to pick up her old life again, or rather sink comfortably back into it. Her only hope was that she would be able to do it without any repercussions.

Which was why it was so important that she find her phone. Despite her fear of what might happen if someone were to come across the phone before she did, she put off returning to the Museum for as long as possible. Even though she had already looked in all the obvious places within the hospital, she spent the half-hour after her bruising encounter with Tim searching those places again. She re-checked the Staff Room, the Canteen, the toilets, the nurse's station both in the ward and outside it, and she even looked around and under the patients' beds. After debating with herself for a while, she finally decided to ask her colleagues if *they'd* seen her phone, but none of them had.

All of which, inevitably and unavoidably, left her with only one alternative: she had to face her fears and go back to the Museum. And she had to do it alone.

Which was how, at 03:30 am, she found herself standing outside the door at the end of the shabby service corridor, her skin prickling with apprehension. Reaching out to punch in the security code, she saw and felt the hairs on her forearm standing up as though there was electricity in the air. Even after committing herself to coming back here, she had half-hoped she might be spared this, that she might come across her lost phone in the lift or the corridor. But it was not to be, and now here she was.

Perhaps, she thought, this was her punishment for the way she had been carrying on these past few months. Perhaps once she'd got through this ordeal she'd be exonerated, allowed to reclaim her former life. She knew that real life wasn't *really* this neat, but it was comforting to imagine that there might be a balance to everything, a way of tipping the cosmic scales of justice back in her favour simply by confronting her fears.

It was as she was punching in the second digit of the four-digit entry code that it struck her she hadn't brought a light. For a moment she considered giving up, or at least going back to look for one – but then she thought again of her kids, and of the fact that, having already gathered her courage to come this far, it would be so much harder to retrace her steps and do it all again.

Besides, it wasn't as if the Museum was in total darkness. There was a big glass entrance at the front of the building, through which filtered at least a little grainy orange light from outside. Although it wasn't much, it was better than nothing; it would enable her to make out vague shapes, at any rate. And it might even be to her advantage in a way, because if she *was* carrying a light she would only feel as if she was drawing attention to herself.

Before she could change her mind she punched in the last two digits and opened the door. She told herself that the sudden displacement of air didn't *really* sound like an anticipatory inhalation made by something in the room, or even the room itself.

Squinting as if that could improve her vision, she peered into the murk. Shapes in various gradations of shadow populated the space in front of her, but they were lumpen, ill-defined, bleeding one into the other. As her heart pumped harder, the overlapping chunks of darkness seemed to pulse in time with it, but that was only an illusion too.

Twenty-four steps, she thought. Thirty at the most. If she didn't hang about she could be in and out of here in three minutes.

She shuffled forwards, barely lifting her feet from the floor, like someone walking on ice. She left the door ajar (*not* because she might need to make a quick getaway, she told herself), but almost jumped out of her skin when she heard a bump behind her. Whirling round, she was relieved to discover that it was only the weight of the door swinging back against its frame.

As she turned to face the room again, the darkness seemed to shift in front of her, bringing to mind the image of the squat figure she had seen standing beside the waxen effigy of the woman in the hovel, the one whose face had been made of clots of darkness, and who had melted into the wall.

She shuddered and tried not to think about how exposed

she was, how vulnerable. Fighting an urge to seek something solid to hide behind, she continued edging into the darkness.

Ten steps . . . fifteen . . . twenty . . . She reached the hovel after twenty-seven steps and paused on the threshold. Her eyes were drawn to the spot where she had seen the dwarfish figure, but if there was anything there now it was simply one shadow among many. The wax figure on the chair was nothing more than a patch of darkness a little more dense than its surroundings. Gill was glad she couldn't see its pustule-raddled face and glassy-eyed stare.

She waited until her eyes had adjusted to the darkness and then she crept forward. First she went to the bed and ran her hands over it. Finding nothing, she dropped to her knees and, taking a deep breath, reached into the blackness underneath. On all fours, with her face almost touching the floor, she felt horribly vulnerable. She kept imagining that someone was creeping up behind her, or that something under the bed might grab her hand. It took all her willpower to stick to her task, but stick to it she did.

However, although her roving hands covered every inch of floor space, she failed to find her phone.

As soon as she was done looking, she jumped to her feet and spun around. She was so relieved to find no one behind her that she almost laughed out loud. She crossed to the table and stretched her hands towards it, then leaped back when her right hand encountered coarse, bristly fur.

Instinctively she crossed her arms defensively in front of her, half-expecting something small and savage to leap at her face. Then she remembered the stuffed rat gnawing on the plate of bones, and this time she *did* laugh, though the sound she made was more like a stifled sob.

More cautiously this time she felt around on the table and then, bracing herselfs, on the floor around the chair occupied by the wax figure. Finding nothing, she moved towards the back wall, in case the phone had skidded or been kicked across the floor.

So much for being in and out in three minutes, she thought, struggling to her feet, dishevelled and frustrated, some six or seven minutes later. She had been so sure her phone would be here, but clearly it wasn't. So where was it? Had someone found it and handed it in? Perhaps she ought to enquire at the Admissions desk.

Then a cold ripple of dread went through her as it suddenly occurred to her that she might not have brought it in to work at all. What if she had left it at home? She had been using it as an alarm, so was it possible that she had forgotten to grab it from the bedside table? If she had, then in all likelihood it would still be there when she got home.

All the same, the possibility gave her a sick feeling in the pit of her stomach. She couldn't help thinking that it was like leaving behind a ticking time bomb. Perhaps she ought to throw a sickie and head home? Her colleagues must already be wondering why she kept disappearing this evening, which could fit in with her story. She could claim that she had to keep rushing off to throw up.

Picking her way through the darkness, she moved back to the hovel's entrance. Stepping into the corridor, she turned in the direction of the door through which she had entered – and froze.

Was there someone there? A dark figure standing in front of the door? She stared so hard that the edges of her eyes began to smart, but even so she couldn't be sure. Perhaps she was imagining it, conjuring a shape out of nothing simply because she half-expected to see one. In which case, should she walk towards it? But what if it *was* a figure? On the other hand, she couldn't stay here all night.

Fighting the urge to pant in time with her racing heart, she crept forwards. If it *was* a figure, would it be able to see her or was she as vague to *it* as *it* was to her? She had covered about a third of the distance back to the door when the figure moved –

or seemed to. Once again she froze, like a child playing statues, and tried to make out whether the shifting she could see was actual movement or simply the result of her own restless vision.

If it *was* movement, then the figure seemed to be swaying or writhing; she was put in mind of a cobra weaving to and fro in response to a snake-charmer's pipe. She licked her lips, wondering whether to go on – though what was the alternative? She took a cautious step forward . . . and the figure responded by swaying and rippling towards her.

Instinctively she turned and headed back in the direction she had come. It was too dark to run, but she nevertheless moved as fast as she could, her hands wafting the air in front of her in anticipation of unexpected obstacles. At the entrance to the hovel she hesitated, wondering whether she should duck inside and hide under the table or bed. But what if the thing came after her? She'd be trapped. And so she pressed on, moving deeper into the Museum, further away from her only means of escape.

Feeling her way around a corner, she heard, not too far away, something fall and smash. The something was clearly made of glass, and judging by the noise it was something that was both heavy and filled with liquid. Unable to stifle a scream, Gill dropped to her haunches and shuffled backwards until she felt a solid surface behind her. Hunching her shoulders and tucking her clenched fists under her chin, she squatted there, all too aware that she was doing what any animal under threat would do – making herself as small a target as possible.

After the din of breaking glass, however, the silence closed in again. Awkward though it would be to explain why she was here, Gill half-hoped the noise would attract someone. Crouching in utter terror she squeezed her eyes shut, and remembered how, as a child, she had believed that if you shut your eyes then the monsters couldn't see you. There was still a modicum of comfort to be gleaned from that idea. Perhaps the ten-year-old girl of three decades ago was closer to the surface than she had thought.

At first, when she heard the wettish shuffling noise, she thought it was the susurration of blood inside her head. It was only when she slowly raised her clenched fists and pressed them over her ears that she realized she hadn't trapped the sound but blocked it, which meant that it was outside of her.

Opening her eyes, she saw something moving on the floor to her left, something that was slithering slug-like towards her. Although she couldn't make it out, she gained the impression that it was small and wet and so nightmarishly misshapen that she was unable to stifle a cry of fear and repugnance.

She scrambled to her feet, turning away from the thing – only to find that the swaying shape that had been pursuing her was in the centre of the corridor, no more than four or five metres away. It seemed to be composed of something like black electricity. Up close she realized that it wasn't silent at all, but was making a faint, dry, somehow frantic crackling sound. It was in the shape of a wide column rather than a man, though it seemed fluid around the edges, as though black sparks were constantly disconnecting from, and then re-joining, the main mass.

Then it hit her like a revelation. The swaying thing wasn't a figure at all, nor even a phantom – it was a cloud of insects! She recalled the insect that had bitten Tim earlier, like a big, red flea.

Distracted by the insects, she jumped as the slow slithering behind her culminated in a sudden flurry of movement – the sound of something which had been creeping up on its prey launching its attack. Even as she turned, she felt something cold and wet wrap itself around her stockinged ankle, followed instantly by the sting of something biting her leg.

With a shriek of revulsion she kicked out, at the same moment getting her first proper look at the thing that had bitten her. Her world tilted, horror and disbelief slamming through her with such force that it wrenched not just a shriek from her this time, but a full-blooded scream.

At her feet was a two-headed baby, its flesh white as tripe and still slick with preserving fluid. Its body was punctured and glittering with shards of glass from the specimen jar that Gill had heard smash on to the floor a few minutes earlier. The baby, an exhibit in the Museum, should have been dead – it *was* dead – and yet it was moving, its tiny body even now crawling back towards her.

As Gill stared down at it, the creature seemed to sense her scrutiny and raised its twin heads. With a horror so dream-like it felt as if it was the prelude to unconsciousness, she saw that one of the eyeless, puckered faces had blood – *her* blood – on its twisted lips. The other, as though bemoaning its own lack of sustenance, opened its mouth, expelling a gout of treacly preserving fluid, and *mewled* at her.

03:37 am

"COME ON, DEAR, stay with us."

As Sister Parkhurst reached out to touch Susan Jenkins' cheek, Marcus Blackstock said quietly, "I wouldn't do that if I were you."

Sister Parkhurst frowned, but her hand dropped to her side. "I don't think she's quite at the biting stage yet," she said a little tersely. "She's been perfectly coherent up to now."

"Up to now, yes. But you've seen how unpredictable the infection can be. With some the deterioration is gradual, whereas others can turn in almost an instant. It's best not to take any chances. I'm sure Nurse Jenkins herself would agree."

They both looked at Susan Jenkins, though for the moment she did not look in any state to agree with anything. A few minutes ago she had been sitting up in bed talking, but then she had started to drift a little, to claim that she was feeling woozy. She had closed her eyes and within a minute had fallen into what appeared to be a deep sleep. Her head was now tilted on to her shoulder and she was taking long, relaxed, though slightly rasping breaths.

Although, at her own suggestion, Susan was now a patient in the isolation ward, the curtains had been pulled around her bed so that she didn't have to look at her fellow sufferers and thus be reminded of what she might become.

In spite of being understandably distressed at what had happened to her, and furious with herself for having allowed her guard to drop, she had not lost her professionalism. It was she who had insisted that her wrists and ankles be restrained – "just in case I lose it and hurt someone" – and she who, through every stage of the infection, had kept her colleagues informed as to how she was feeling.

Even at the beginning, when she had been gasping and writhing in agony, she had had the presence of mind to describe the pain of the wound, which she had claimed felt "like having a thousand red ants biting you all at once". A little later, presumably as a result of the painkillers kicking in (although Marcus had suggested that it might also be because the nerves and cells in her arm were starting to die), she had told them that the wound was no longer hurting, that her arm was becoming numb.

At the same time she had admitted that she was starting to think differently, that she was undergoing what she could only describe as a psychological transformation. She told them she was feeling increasingly detached from what was happening to her – even that she was beginning to feel oddly optimistic, bordering on euphoric.

When Marcus suggested that her mood was affected by the drugs being pumped into her body through the cannula in her left arm (the severity of the infection was already such that her right arm was no longer viable), she shook her head.

"No, it's more than that. It's like I can hear a voice calling to me. Welcoming me. Telling me that everything will be all right." Her face pale and damp with sweat, she had offered Marcus a beatific smile. "It's a good feeling, Dr Blackstock. A calm feeling. Everyone should feel like this. Everyone should join us."

It was not long after this that she had started to feel woozy. And minutes later, her wrists and ankles restrained and her back propped by pillows, she had fallen asleep.

"I'm worried that if we don't keep her awake she'll slip into a coma like the others," Sister Parkhurst said now, peering anxiously at the dark rings that had already formed around Susan's eyes.

Marcus flashed her a sympathetic look. "Do you honestly think that keeping her awake will slow the progress of the infection?"

Sister Parkhurst's answering scowl was so fierce that it made her look like a pugnacious bulldog. "It might. If we can convince her to fight. The human mind is a remarkable thing, Dr Blackstock. We both know that cancer patients who maintain a positive outlook often have a better chance of survival."

"True," Marcus agreed, "but few cancers are *this* aggressive. In such cases the patient usually has time to adapt to his or her circumstances." Perhaps in response to the expression on Sister Parkhurst's face, he raised his hands. "But look, if you think it'll make a difference, go ahead, wake her up if you can. If Nurse Jenkins was in pain I'd be opposed to it, but she seems quite comfortable, so I can't see that it'll have a detrimental effect on her either way."

Sister Parkhurst poured water from a jug on the bedside table into the tumbler beside it and produced a straw in a sealed plastic packet from the storage cabinet beneath. She was cautiously feeding the straw between Susan's dry lips when the curtains at the bottom of the bed parted and Cat Harris poked her head through.

The night's events had clearly taken their toll on the young staff nurse. Usually so radiant and cheery, she currently looked sallow with anxiety.

Glancing at Susan, she asked, "How's she doing?"

"She's hanging in there," said Sister Parkhurst, which they all knew meant that there had been no improvement.

Cat nodded, albeit distractedly. "Dr Blackstock, do you have a moment?"

"Of course. What's the problem?"

"We're not sure . . . but we think one of the patients might have died. That is . . . we can't get any vital signs."

"Which patient?" Sister Parkhurst asked. "Martin Balfour?"

Cat shook her head. "No," she said, "not him. I'm afraid it's the boy. Jermaine Paterson."

03:47 am

"WHERE JERMAINE AT?"

The question, which followed the thumping clatter of the ward doors, was not a polite enquiry but an aggressive demand. Cat, who at that moment was standing beside Jermaine's bed, recognized the voice immediately. It belonged to Carlton Tyler, Jermaine's friend.

The reason he couldn't see Jermaine's body was because, as a matter of both procedure and decorum, the privacy curtains had been pulled around the bed five minutes earlier to allow Dr Blackstock to carry out his examination. Now Dr Blackstock, having confirmed Jermaine's death, was making the necessary arrangements to have his body transferred to the Mortuary. He had left Cat to remove the drip from Jermaine's arm and the oxygen mask from his face in preparation, both of which Cat had done.

As Cat turned she heard Sister Parkhurst say, "I'm sorry, young man, but you can't come in here. This is an isolation ward. Only authorized personnel are allowed."

"Never mind dat," Carlton retorted. "What you done to Jermaine? Why you hidin' him away?"

Peeling off her disposable gloves and dropping them into the medical waste bin, one of which had been set up beside the bed of each of the infected patients, Cat lifted aside an edge of green curtain and stepped through into the ward. She saw Carlton and a smaller boy (the name *Fitch* popped into her mind) standing a metre or two inside the double doors, shoulders back and legs apart, as if preparing to fight their way through the crowd of masked and gloved medical personnel who had turned to confront them – and who, in a few cases, were drifting towards them with the obvious intention of expelling them from the room.

Although the boys looked like archetypal examples of what the Coalition Government (in an attempt to justify its recent heavy-handed tactics) had claimed were the "feral and predatory agitators threatening to overwhelm our society", all Cat could think about was how vulnerable Carlton was. Even though the wound in his side wasn't all that serious, he *had* lost quite a bit of blood and she knew that any amount of manhandling might burst his stitches open again.

At the moment it was Sister Parkhurst – *of course* – who was leading the charge to rebuff the intruders, but behind her and closing in fast were the beefy forms of Mark Hardy, who played rugby twice a week, and the slimmer but impressively ripped Nareed Ghazali, who, when he wasn't in the gym, was doing press-ups in the Staff Room or pull-ups on the nearest doorframe.

Tugging down her face mask so that Carlton would recognize her, Cat darted forwards, slipping between Mark and Nareed like a pilot fish between killer sharks.

"Hey, Carlton," she said brightly. "How's the hip?"

Caught off-guard, he blinked at her, then tried to re-establish his hard-man act, but only ended up looking sulky.

"S'all right."

"You should be resting it, giving it time to heal. You shouldn't be wandering around the hospital."

Cat was aware of Mark and Nareed behind her, itching for a fight. Was aware too of Sister Parkhurst, a couple of paces ahead of her, glancing back at her over her shoulder with a half-raised eyebrow, as if assessing her performance.

"Wanna know where Jermaine is," Carlton said.

"Yeah," piped up Fitch. "How we know you ain't doin' weird experiments on him or whatever?"

Cat saw Carlton wince. She guessed that his instinct was to round on the younger boy, tell him to shut up, and that the only reason he wasn't doing that was because he felt it important that he and Fitch present a united front.

A wave of sarcastic, slightly bitter laughter rippled around the room. Sister Parkhurst rolled her eyes. "Oh, for goodness sake!"

Cat, though, raised a hand and said calmly, "We've been looking after Jermaine, not experimenting on him. We've been trying to save his life."

"Save it from what?" Carlton said.

Cat glanced at Sister Parkhurst, who shrugged resignedly, as if to concede that they couldn't keep it a secret forever.

"If you step into the corridor, I'll explain everything."

"Why not tell us right here?" Fitch retorted. "What you hidin'?"

This time Carlton looked as though he *was* about to tell Fitch to shut up, but before he could Sister Parkhurst snapped, "Are you really as dim as you sound, young man? Haven't I already told you that this is an isolation ward? Haven't you wondered why we're wearing face masks and disposable gloves?"

Fitch glared at her, but Carlton's eyes glanced left and right, widening as he focused on Martin Balfour.

"Shit, man, what *he* got?"

"It's an infection," said Cat.

"What kind?"

"We don't know yet. That's why we're keeping these patients isolated."

Fitch was now looking around the ward too, his head movements nervous and jittery as he peered around and between the blue-clad nursing staff who had gathered around them.

"You mean we could be breathing some fucking deadly shit right now?" Carlton asked.

Before Cat could answer, Fitch shouted, "Hey, blud, check it out! There's the bitch bit Jermaine, innit?"

Fitch pointed. At the far end of the ward on the left-hand side Samantha Mellor was lying motionless on her back, her hair spread out over the pillow. As Carlton craned to look across at Patient Zero's first victim, Cat said, "Evidence seems to indicate that the infection can only be passed via the transfer of bodily fluids, but we can't be sure."

Carlton glanced back at her. "Like AIDS?"

Cat nodded.

"So that bitch gave Jermaine AIDS?" Fitch said, outraged.

This time Carlton *did* round on the younger boy. "Shut it, you fuckin' *tourist*."

Fitch cringed. Carlton turned back to Cat. "So Jermaine got infected from being bit, yeah?"

"I'm afraid so."

"Dred," said Carlton softly, shaking his head. "So where he at now? 'Cos I can't see him here."

Cat hesitated, then said, "Look, let's go outside and talk."

"Why? What you not sayin'? Something happen to Jermaine, innit? Where he at?"

Cat sighed. Sister Parkhurst said, "I'm afraid your friend is dead, young man. We tried as hard as we could to save him, but he failed to respond to treatment. If it's any consolation, his end was very peaceful. He died without regaining consciousness."

Fitch looked stricken with disbelief, his eyes darting between Sister Parkhurst and Cat, as if hoping one of them

BUSINESS
AS
USUAL

Lewisham Hospital continues to
deliver high-quality services in
state-of-the-art facilities.

OPEN

www.lewisham.nhs.uk

Lewisham Healthcare NHS

■ Pink Zone

← Suite 4   Children's ↗
         Outpatients
         –Kingfisher

← Lifts & Stairs 🛗 🚶

← The Birth Centre

← Green Zone ■

might tell him it wasn't true, that it was all a joke. Carlton's face, however, hardened like stone, his eyes narrowing, his jaw tightening. Briefly and almost unconsciously he touched his injured hip, as if he could feel the pain of his friend's passing right there, where he had been stabbed. Then he took a long, deep breath and said, "Can we see him?"

Cat glanced at Sister Parkhurst, who said, "Oh, I don't see why not. But for goodness sake don't touch him. And if you're going to stay any longer, then at least put on gloves and masks."

"I'll get them," Cat said, but before she could move there was the metallic clatter of something falling over behind the green curtains around Jermaine's bed.

Cat, along with almost everyone else in the room, jumped and turned. Her first thought was that she must have balanced a piece of equipment precariously enough to make it fall over, but then she saw the curtains around the bed billow, as if someone had flapped at them or fallen against them. She took a sudden step back – on to Mark Hardy's toes. "Oh," she said, like someone witnessing an impressive but alarming magic trick.

The curtains billowed again and a sort of slurring growl came from behind them. Sister Parkhurst looked at Cat almost indignantly. Cat looked back at her, baffled and alarmed.

Having reacted to Cat stepping on his toes with nothing more than a dismissive grunt, Mark Hardy now moved towards the curtained bed with all the purpose of a nightclub bouncer about to eject a reeling drunk. Cat felt a sudden urge to tell him not to get too close, even half-raised an arm to grab the back of his blue tunic.

Before she could, however, there was a further violent billow of curtains and the next second a figure lurched out between them. Cat gasped so loudly that the sound seemed to reverberate around the room – though perhaps that was because she was not the only one to react that way.

174

The figure, inevitably but impossibly, was Jermaine Paterson. Inevitably because there was no one else it could have been, and impossibly because Jermaine Paterson was *dead*. Marcus Blackstock had declared him dead, and Cat, who had seen her fair share of corpses, had been as sure as she could be that every single one of his life functions had ceased.

Yet here he was, flailing and grunting and definitely *not* dead. Even though he *looked* dead – his half-closed eyes were fixed and his dark skin had taken on an ash-grey lifelessness, as if all the blood had drained away from it – he clearly wasn't. Somehow he had come back from the brink of extinction. And not only that, but he seemed to have discovered a renewed burst of energy.

The first person to respond to Jermaine's unexpected resurrection was Fitch. "Jermaine!" he cried with all the giddy glee of a child welcoming a beloved father home from work. Jermaine, who had been homing drunkenly in on Mark Hardy, now paused and swung his head in Fitch's direction. Cat shuddered; the movement was oddly inhuman, as if Jermaine was something blind and almost mindless, something motivated not by thought and reason, but simply by an instinctive and remorseless aggression.

As Jermaine lurched towards him, Fitch darted across to meet the older boy. "Wass happenin', man?" he said. "What they done to you, blud?"

He threw an accusatory glance over his shoulder in Cat's direction and so didn't see Jermaine suddenly raise his hand. When he turned back the hand darted forward like a striking snake and closed over his face, Jermaine's index finger and third finger sinking deeply and unerringly into Fitch's eyes.

For a split-second there was nothing but a stunned intake of breath, a near-silence during which Cat was certain she heard the squelch of Fitch's eyeballs bursting and spilling down his cheeks. Then, as Fitch began to thrash and scream, there came a cracking, gristly, *wrenching* sound, and Jermaine, with a strength and savagery that seemed superhuman, tore Fitch's face clean off his head.

As Fitch collapsed, the room seemed to dissolve into chaos – or at least, that was how Cat would remember it afterwards. People began to run and scream. Mark Hardy and Nareed Ghazali lunged at Jermaine, clearly intending to bring him down, only to be picked up as if they were children and hurled across the room – in Mark Hardy's case so violently that he smashed head first into the desk in the middle of the ward, his neck snapping with a sound like the crack of a whip.

Having dispatched the two men, Jermaine then pounced like a tiger on a fleeing student nurse and sank his teeth into her back while she screamed and screamed. That was the last thing Cat saw before someone – she had no idea who – barged into her with such impact in their haste to escape that she stumbled sideways, slipped in the widening pool of blood from Fitch's still-twitching corpse, and banged her head on the floor hard enough to knock herself senseless.

Her period of unconsciousness – which was actually more of a nauseating swirl of disorientation that she knew she needed to claw her way up and out of but couldn't – seemed endless, but must only have lasted seconds. When light began to coalesce, like the smashing of a mirror filmed in reverse, it seemed harsh, over-bright, until she realized she was staring up at the parallel lines of strip lighting on the ceiling.

She groaned – and then the light was blotted out by a blob of darkness. It took a split-second for her eyes to adjust before she understood the blob was a face. Then the features came into focus and she realized *whose* face it was and her mouth opened to scream. But nothing emerged. Terror had paralyzed her vocal cords.

Jermaine was looming over her. Up close Cat could see that his eyes were glazed and dead and yet they seemed to glare at her, *into* her, with such avidity and hunger that she wanted to shrivel into herself, make herself disappear. She could see too that his mouth was half-open and that his teeth were coated with a combination of blood and black drool, which spilled over his lips and dripped from his chin.

She had time to hope that her death would be quick and painless – and then something swung in from the left of her vision and slammed with immense force into the side of Jermaine's head. There was a sickening impact that was partly a clang of metal and partly a crunch of bone, and a spray of blood that spattered Cat's face that she had the presence of mind to close her eyes and mouth against.

She hadn't realized Jermaine was straddling her legs, pinning her down, until he fell away from her and she felt his weight shift. Still keeping her mouth firmly shut, she swiped a hand across her eyes, then opened them and saw that the thing that had slammed into Jermaine's head was an oxygen tank, still trailing its mask, and that the person holding the oxygen tank was Carlton.

Defying the pain of the wound in his side, Carlton stepped over her, raised the oxygen tank and brought it smashing down on Jermaine's skull once again. Cat rolled away from Jermaine's still-flailing body, then found that she was rolling into a pool of Fitch's blood and scrambled to her feet. As soon as she was upright her head started to spin and she put out both hands, like a tightrope walker, to steady herself. After a second or two her head cleared and, wincing at another clanging crunch, she turned to see what was happening.

Carlton, standing astride Jermaine's body, had slammed the oxygen tank into his face. As he lifted it, Cat caught a glimpse of pulped and bloody bone, and – mostly as a reaction to what had almost just happened to her – turned and puked, her vomit spattering on the floor, and on Fitch's outstretched leg, mingling with the blood. Her stomach lurched and she puked again, hoping desperately that none of Jermaine's blood had gone into her mouth. Finally, wrung-out and enervated, she turned back to Carlton, flinching as he brought the oxygen tank down again and then again.

She averted her eyes from Jermaine's crushed head and instead looked down at his outstretched, gore-clogged hand and saw that it was still.

"Stop," she gasped, reaching out to stay Carlton's swinging attack. "No more, Carlton. He's dead."

Carlton was gasping, sweating. He looked wild-eyed, crazed. "Gotta make sure. Gotta destroy his fucking brain."

"Destroy his brain?" she exclaimed. "What *for*?"

He looked at her in disbelief. "Don't you get it? Don't you get what this infection is? What Jermaine is?"

She stared at him. "What he is? What do you mean?"

A shudder went through him. He dropped the oxygen tank, which clanged on the floor. His voice, overcome by emotion or pain, was nothing but a rasp.

"He's a fuckin' zombie, innit?"

03:57 am

"STEVE? STEVE?"

Melinda Fuller, drifting upwards on a soft cloud of medication, groped for her husband's hand. The hand that clutched hers, however, was not his; it was smaller, smoother, the fingers longer and daintier.

The voice wasn't his either. It was a woman's voice, with a soft Irish accent. "It's okay, Mel, you're doing fine."

Mel tried to open her eyes. It required a great deal of effort. It was as if her eyelids were steel shutters, which needed to be cranked apart.

Eventually, however, she managed it. For a moment a white blur swam in her vision before resolving itself into a face. It was a woman's face, thin and pale and pretty. Large grey-blue eyes. Fine hair the colour of Demerara sugar tumbling in soft curls around fine-boned cheeks, pulled into a bun at the back.

"Is it over?" Mel asked.

The face smiled. "Not yet, I'm afraid. But you're doing great."

"Too much gas and air," Mel said, her voice slurring a little. "Zonked me out."

"I think you needed it. You were in a lot of distress when you came in. Baby can pick up on that, which can make things difficult."

Everything that had happened – the police officer, the nurse, the soldiers – came back to Mel then, albeit in a dreamy, soft-edged way, its intensity dulled by medication.

"Where's Steve?"

"He's right here. He's been having a little nap too."

The girl – Maeve, Mel thought suddenly, her name's Maeve – leaned to one side so that Mel could see Steve behind her. He was sitting on a chair by the door, his upper body slumped so far forward that she could see the small but widening bald patch on the top of his head. His elbows were on his knees, his hands hanging limply between them.

"If he's not careful he'll fall and land on his face," said Mel.

"That's exactly what I told him, but he just grunted at me. He's tired out, poor lamb. So I put a cushion on the floor just in case."

She pointed and Mel craned her neck to see that there was indeed a small brown cushion on the floor in front of her husband's chair. From the way he was positioned he looked to be examining it, as if it wasn't a cushion at all but something more interesting – an unusual animal perhaps, or a meteorite.

Still woozy with medication, Mel chuckled, then winced.

"Contraction?" Maeve asked.

"Just a small one. Maybe not even that. I think I pulled a muscle in my stomach earlier."

"I think baby may be having a little rest before the final push. Probably best to lay off the gas and air from now on."

"Okay," Mel said, but she couldn't help feeling a little afraid of how distressing the memories of that evening's events might become once the heady effects of the gas and air faded away. Arriving at the Maternity Unit in acute distress, she had started gulping the nitrous oxide and oxygen mix via a black rubber face mask almost as soon as she had entered the birthing suite – had had so much of it, in fact, that she had passed out.

She had known, even as she was going under, that she would have to face reality again at some point, but she had been hoping that she would be able to defer it until after the baby was born. Indeed, she'd been hoping she could give birth without knowing much about it, had even half-hoped she might wake up to find her newborn son or daughter nuzzling at her breast.

"Right, let's give you a little examination, see how far along you are," Maeve said, planting her hands on her thighs and rising to her feet.

And it was at that moment, as if alerted by the midwife's movement, that Steve looked up.

Mel thought at first that he was simply spaced out, confused at having woken up in a strange place. He had an odd expression on his face. He looked both blank and at the same time . . . purposeful.

"Steve?" Mel said gently, uncertainly, as Maeve stepped down to Mel's business end to check how many centimetres dilated she was. Alerted by Mel's voice, Maeve half-turned, a faint smile on her face.

"Hello, Steve, back with us, are you? I was just about—"

Without warning Steve leaped up from his chair and attacked her.

His hands shot out and grabbed Maeve's head, clamping it in a vice-like grip. Then, before she could even cry out, he dipped his face towards hers and kissed her on the lips.

At least, that was what Mel thought he had done at first. Then she saw a squirt of blood between the two mouths and Maeve's body went rigid before she began to kick and thrash, her fists pounding frantically against Steve's torso. At the same time her eyes – or at least the one that Mel could see – bulged with agony and she made a hideous, high-pitched, animal sound of pain deep in her throat.

"*Steve!*" Mel screamed. "*Steve! Stop it! What are you doing?*"

Steve wrenched his head back in a way that reminded Mel of a big cat tearing a chunk of meat from an antelope, and in a swoony, dislocating moment of horror she saw that dangling from her husband's teeth was a ragged, bloody chunk of flesh.

It wasn't until Maeve reeled towards her, however, that she started to scream. The midwife's lips and a sizeable amount of the surrounding flesh had been completely torn away. She had been left with nothing but a ragged, circular hole, pouring blood, through which Mel could see her gums and teeth. Without lips Maeve looked as though she was baring those teeth in a ferocious but agonized snarl.

The door burst open and two men and a woman ran into the room. The men were wearing white doctors' coats, the woman a dark blue nurse's uniform. Before they could register what was happening, Steve leaped at them. He bit one of the men on the arm and raked hooked fingers across the cheek of another, leaving parallel lines of red scratches seeping with blood.

The nurse, whose portly frame seemed to be straining to burst out of its uniform, gaped in horror at what was happening. She looked at Mel and then at Maeve, who was now slumped against the bed, blood gushing from her mutilated face. Then, bypassing the struggling men, she ran across to Mel, raised a hand (for one crazy moment Mel thought she was about to be slapped as punishment for Steve's behaviour) and brought it down hard on the red emergency button on the wall above the bed. Immediately an alarm began to wail, its din adding to the cacophony of screams and shouts and snarls, and as it did so Mel added a scream of her own, though this time it was a scream of pain as her body was wracked by a prolonged and excruciating contraction.

04:05 am

AT FIRST TIM Marshall thought the ringing was in his head. He thought it was just another addition to the chaos raging in there. For what seemed like hours the roaring of his blood and the pounding throb of his brain had provided a backdrop to a slippery tumble of nightmarish images occupying his mind. He didn't know where the images had come from or what they might mean, but he had a sense that they were outside of him, that his mind was like a letterbox and that the images were being fed into it, crammed through the slot like pieces of mail, so fervently that he couldn't keep up with them all.

He had the odd idea too that the "slot" was the itch on the back of his neck. Somehow, in his mind, it had taken on a life of its own, widened into a pulsing gash, an extra mouth that needed constant feeding. Tim scratched at it incessantly, as if trying to scratch it out of existence, but it made no difference. It continued to suck in the darkness, to show him images of disease and death and decay, a world fallen to carnage and chaos.

The images were piecemeal, abstract, subliminal, but the message they carried was undeniable, pulsing like a black heart. Something was coming. Something that wanted him. Something that he doubted he would be able to resist.

But first he had to deal with the ringing. It penetrated deep into his mind, cutting through his fevered thoughts, offering him a lifeline. He opened his eyes to discover that he was sitting at his desk in his office, his desk lamp bent so far over that only a small pool of light leaked from beneath the bulbous hood. It was the phone next to his left hand that was ringing. He picked it up and put it to his ear.

Oddly, when he opened his mouth to speak, the name that jumped into his mind was not his own. It was one he was sure he had never heard before: *Thomas Moreby.*

Though he managed to stop himself from saying the name, his voice, halfway to speaking, caught in the back of his throat and emerged as a guttural wordless croak.

Immediately a voice said, "Hello? Dr Marshall? Is that you?"

Dr Marshall. Tim Marshall. Yes. *That* was his name. Clearing his throat, he said, "Yes, it is. Who's this?"

"It's Charmaine Jordan, Dr Marshall. On the Admissions desk."

"Ah yes. Charmaine." Tim had no idea who she was. "What can I do for you?"

"Sorry to disturb you, Dr Marshall, but there's a visitor here to see you. He says it's urgent."

Thomas Moreby, Tim thought again, and shuddered without knowing why.

Trying to keep his voice steady, he said, "Does this visitor have a name?"

"Hang on, doctor." Charmaine was gone for a moment, and then she was back. "He says he'd rather not give his name. But he says to tell you it's a personal matter. An *important* personal matter."

"I see." Tim's mind was racing. He didn't know who Thomas Moreby was, but the thought that he might be waiting

184

for Tim at the Admissions desk filled him with a strange sort of excitement. Excitement and fear.

"Tell him . . . tell him I'll be along in a few minutes."

He put the phone down without waiting for a reply. As soon as he had done so the hand that had been holding the receiver went to the back of his neck and began to scratch.

Thomas Moreby. The name was so familiar and yet Tim couldn't for the life of him conjure a face to go with it. *Could* it be him who was waiting at Admissions? And if it was, would he be able to provide Tim with answers?

But answers to what? Tim wasn't sure. He had a feeling that there were important questions hidden in his mind, important considerations to . . . well, consider. He had an itch that needed scratching, in more ways than one. Standing up, he moved out from behind his desk and across the semi-dark office, still scratching at his neck.

The light in the corridor was harsh, making him screw up his eyes. He glided towards the lift, feeling dislocated, woozy. People spoke to him as he passed, and he spoke back, but he had no idea who the people were or what was said. If this was reality then it seemed less real than the world inside his head, less present than the notion of what was to come.

He got into the lift and pressed the button for the ground floor, and as it took him down he phased out for a moment. He scratched at the itch on his neck and thought about biting into human flesh. He thought of how wonderful it would be to feel his teeth puncturing skin, to feel hot blood squirting into his mouth. When the lift pinged and he opened his eyes, he could taste blood at the back of his throat, as if the sensation was so vivid that he had partly conjured it into being. He stepped out of the lift and walked towards the Admissions area.

He had a moment – just a moment – when he felt sure that every single person in the Admissions area was dead. Not dead and motionless, however, but dead and still moving. He was not alarmed by the notion; indeed, he felt comforted by it. Dead they were all the same. He felt at one with them, and with their desire to pass on the glorious gift of death, to unite the whole of humanity.

Then the vision passed – no, not a vision, a *premonition* – and the swell of chatter rose around him. He headed for the Admissions desk, behind which sat a black woman with a round, shiny face and dreadlocks. As he did so a man, who had been leaning against the desk, pushed himself upright and turned to him. The man was tall but pudgy, his sandy hair thinning, his unshaven face sagging a little.

"Dr Tim Marshall?" he said.

Tim looked at him. He felt a stab of disappointment. Was *this* Thomas Moreby? No, surely not. He had a feeling that Moreby, whoever he was, would have a presence about him, a certain stature. This man had nothing. He was dull. Ordinary. Tim had a hard job not to sneer.

"Yes," he said. "Who are you?"

Instead of answering, the man held up a mobile phone. "Recognize this?"

Tim looked at it. "No," he said. "Should I?"

"It belongs to Gill Eaves, the nurse you've been shagging. I'm Gerry Eaves. Her husband."

He said the word "shagging" loudly enough to cause the chatter in the room to die down. Heads turned to regard the two men. Charmaine behind the Admissions desk widened her eyes, managing to look both alarmed and gleeful.

Tim scratched his neck thoughtfully. Ordinarily he would have been acutely embarrassed by the situation, but now he felt nothing but irritation. He had been dragged all the way down here for *this*?

"Then I feel sorry for you," he said, waving a hand dismissively.

The man stepped forward. "You *what*?"

"I said I feel sorry for you. For being married to such a dreary woman and yet *still* not being able to satisfy her."

Gerry Eaves' face flushed red, and then with surprising swiftness he took another step forward and punched Tim hard in the face.

Though he felt the crunch of his nose breaking and was knocked down by the punch, Tim felt no pain whatsoever. Instead, as he sprawled on the floor, he felt a kind of buzzing euphoria and a physical thrill as hot blood gushed out of his nose and over the lower part of his face. He opened his mouth and laughed, enjoying the salt-iron taste of blood trickling over his teeth and into his mouth, and then he felt energy surge through his body and leaped so nimbly to his feet that several onlookers gasped in admiration.

Gerry seemed surprised by Tim's agility too – not to mention a little ashamed at his own lack of control. Tim felt a momentary urge to leap at the larger man and bite him, but then, as though the idea had been planted in his mind, he thought of something *better*. Leaning forward, he spat a mouthful of blood into Gerry Eaves' face. And then, even as Gerry was spluttering and wiping at his eyes, he spat blood at Charmaine too.

Charmaine screamed and pushed herself back, her chair rolling on its castors.

"What you do that for?" she yelled. "I ain't done nothing!"

In his peripheral vision Tim saw a couple of security guys hurrying towards him and smiled. He would spit blood on them too. He would spit blood on as many people as possible before they took him down.

But at that moment there was a crash from the front of the building and everyone – including Tim and Gerry – looked round. The hospital's big double glass doors had swung back and a wave of blackness was pouring into the building. For a moment Tim thought that the blackness had been sent by

Thomas Moreby, that it had come for him – though whether as prize or punishment he wasn't sure. Then he realized that the blackness wasn't a single entity; it was breaking apart, shards splitting off, moving left and right, to cover the entire area.

He was almost disappointed when he registered that the shards of blackness were simply men. Men in helmets and riot gear, carrying guns. They were pointing the guns at the people in the Admissions area, most of whom were sitting around, waiting for treatment. The people were cowering and putting their hands up in front of their faces and some of them were screaming.

Tim wasn't scared, though. He felt detached from what was happening. He watched as a man marched into the building behind the black-clad men, a man who wore not riot gear, but a police uniform, complete with peaked cap.

"Ladies and gentlemen," the man bellowed, his voice echoing around the room, "please do not be alarmed. If you cooperate fully you will not be harmed. We are here to protect you. And while I am not currently at liberty to provide a reason for our presence here, what I can tell you is this: under orders of the British Government, this hospital is now in lockdown. What this means is that until further notice, and without any exceptions, no one will be allowed either in or out of the building."

04:11 am

RIGHT AFTER HE killed Jermaine, Carlton started to shake like a user without a fix. He tried to hide it – he didn't want to look like no pussy in front of the pretty nurse – but if he didn't clamp his teeth together they started to chatter and there weren't nothing he could do about it.

"You're in shock," the nurse told him – the badge on her uniform reminded him her name was Cat Harris. She put an arm around his shoulders. "Come on, let's get out of here."

It was only then that Carlton looked around and realized that, apart from the patients and the guys Jermaine had killed (including Fitch, who was lying in a pool of blood with no fucking face), he and the pretty nurse were the only two left in the room. Everyone else must have run for the doors when Jermaine started throwing guys around like they were dolls.

One of those guys, a big fucker who must have weighed a ton more than Jermaine, was lying by the big desk at the far end of the room, his head twisted so far around on his shoulders that if he drooled it would run down his back. Not that he *could* drool. He was dead, his face wearing an expression of glassy shock. The other guy who had tackled Jermaine was on his front, half-under one of the beds. Carlton couldn't tell if he was dead or not.

The sight of the guy with the broken neck made Carlton's head swim, and for a moment he thought he was going to shame himself by throwing up or passing out. He took some deep breaths, and though the smell of blood filled his nostrils, he felt his head clearing a little.

"Are you okay?" Cat Harris asked.

"I'm good," said Carlton gruffly. "Side's just hurting, thassall."

"I'll take a look at it once we get out of here. Come on, you need to sit down."

There were people in the corridor outside the ward. Some rushed up to Carlton and Cat when they came out, wanting to know how they were, whether they'd been scratched or bitten, but Cat waved them away, saying they were fine.

Soon as she got him sat down, Carlton felt all the energy draining out of him. It was like the chair he was sitting in was a giant sponge, sucking out his strength and heat. It made him so cold that he started to shake even more. The only hot part of him was the stab wound in his hip, which throbbed like coals in a fire.

Cat went off for a while and when she came back she had a blanket and a mug of tea. She put the blanket around his shoulders and told him to drink the tea. Carlton *never* drank tea, and his guts were churning like he wanted to shit or puke, but he needed the heat inside him and so he did what he was told. But the tea was good. It was sweet and soothing and he felt himself coming back to life as it trickled through him. His Mum swore by tea, said it was the British cure for everything, said it made everything a bit better, no matter how bad the situation was. Carlton had always laughed at her for that, but now, he had to admit, she might have something.

Cat Harris sat down next to him and leaned towards him as though she wanted to whisper in his ear or kiss him on the cheek. Carlton had been staring into his lap, blotting out everything around him, ignoring all the raised voices, all the people running about, but now he glanced at her. He saw she had cleaned up a little, got the blood off her face.

"What you said in there," she said quietly. "About zombies."

He gave the barest of nods.

"Were you being serious?"

He didn't answer straight away. He didn't answer because since he'd said what he'd said he hadn't really thought about it. He'd been trying not to think about anything. Been trying to keep his head empty because it was better that way. Now, though, he'd have to face the fact that he'd killed Jermaine. He'd bashed in his brains with an oxygen tank right after Jermaine had gone psycho and torn Fitch's face off like it was a fucking hockey mask.

He felt the tea bubbling like lava in his gut, and so he shut his eyes and went back to that quiet place inside himself again for a moment. When he opened his eyes Cat Harris was still waiting patiently, *her* eyes big and blue and unblinking.

Carlton tried to smile, but his face was stiff, unresponsive. "What *you* think?" he said.

She hunched her shoulders like she was cold. "I don't know. Tell me about zombies."

"Tell you what? You seen the movies. *Dawn of the Dead*, all that."

"It's not really my thing. I'm more of a rom – com kind of girl. *Notting Hill, Pretty Woman* . . ."

He rolled his eyes. "Man, that is seriously fucked up."

Her smile was tight, but not without humour. "Zombies are people who've come back from the dead, aren't they? They eat brains to . . . what?"

Carlton shrugged. "I dunno. I guess they just hungry."

191

"But *why* do they come back? And why do they come back different? Are they . . . possessed by evil spirits or something?" She rolled her eyes. "I don't know why I'm even asking these questions."

Carlton regarded her thoughtfully. He chose his next words with care. He had the sense he was picking his way through a minefield, that if he didn't pay attention to where he put his feet, something might go off. "You say Jermaine was dead, innit?"

She nodded.

"So you 100 per cent positive 'bout that?"

She hesitated. "Well, we *thought* he was dead – me and my colleagues – but we must have been mistaken. This is a new infection, or at least one we haven't come across before, one we have yet to identify."

She seemed like she was going to keep talking; Carlton raised a hand. "Yeah, but you *thought* he was dead, then he come back, and he was different. And he was *strong*. And he was crazy, killin' people and shit."

She nodded. "But that doesn't mean he's a zombie. All those things could be symptoms of the infection. What we thought was the cessation of vital signs might have been a . . . a kind of hibernation stage, a gathering of resources, which were then deployed in an outrush of energy. We know that the infection causes psychosis, which could account for Jermaine's incredible strength.

"See, physically, most of us are capable of far more than we think, but we have in-built inhibitors to stop us from harming ourselves – tearing muscles, breaking bones, that kind of thing. But when those inhibitors break down, either through mental illness or because of some extreme circumstance, we're capable of incredible feats."

"Like when women lift cars off their injured kids?" Carlton said.

"Yes, exactly," Cat said, surprised. "That's a perfect example."

Even though she bit back on over-praising him, the sombre look that Carlton gave her made her wonder whether her tone had been too condescending. She wondered whether she should apologize, but his next words made it clear he had more important things on his mind than what she thought of him.

"So if this is all true, and Jermaine ain't no zombie, what that make me?"

She frowned. "What do you mean?"

"Well, I killed him, innit? So that make me a murderer, yeah? Which mean the five-oh gonna can my ass."

"The five-oh?" She had heard him use the phrase before.

"Police, innit?"

"Oh. You mean like *Hawaii Five-0*?"

He flapped a hand in irritation. "Whatever."

She regarded him with pursed lips, as she considered what he had said. Eventually she put a hand on his.

"If it comes to it, I'll defend you, Carlton. You saved my life. I have no doubt that if you hadn't done what you did, Jermaine would have killed me."

Carlton averted his eyes. "Yeah, well," he said, and lapsed into silence. Then he stirred himself and muttered, "Y'know, there's one way to check if they zombies or not."

"What's that?"

He smiled grimly. "To merk a zombie you have to destroy the brain, innit? So if you shoot the fuckers through the heart and they keep coming, they zombies."

She looked as though she didn't know whether to laugh or look horrified. "Bit of an extreme solution."

"Yeah, well," he said again, and looked away from her, glancing almost furtively along the corridor in the direction of the isolation ward. He knew there had been a lot of hustle and bustle, of people coming and going, since he'd been sitting

193

out here, but he'd blanked it out to deal with the shit inside his head. Now he decided it was time to get up to speed, check out what was happening.

The first thing he saw were the security guards, a couple of them, standing outside the doors to the ward. Another security guard was standing beside the door at the end of the corridor, his hand curled around the metal door-pull like a doorman at a posh hotel. Carlton guessed his job was to allow entry only to hospital personnel, most likely because it would be a bad thing if ordinary people – patients and visitors – wandered in here and saw the shit that had been going down and started blabbing.

Next, there were the two hospital gurneys parked end-to-end against the wall opposite the ward doors. They had what could only be bodies lying on them, draped from head to toe in white sheets. Then there was the floor, which was covered in a mess of red footprints, as if some bloody battle had spilled out from the ward with the blacked-out windows – which, of course, it had.

Even now a hospital orderly in a face mask and latex gloves was sweeping a mop back and forth across the floor, every so often pausing to squeeze out the dripping mop head in the grilled funnel of a tin bucket. The mop head was stained pink as if it had already been used to mop up a lot of blood.

Stealing a final glance at the gurneys, Carlton turned back to Cat. "Big clean-up, huh?" he said. Then, before she could reply, he jerked his head in the direction of the gurneys. "Jermaine on one of them?"

Cat glanced beyond him. "No, his body was taken for immediate post-mortem. Those are . . ." she looked momentarily flustered ". . . his victims."

"Fitch, you mean?"

She nodded. "And the man with the broken neck. His name was Mark Hardy."

"What about them others?" Carlton asked bluntly. "Like Jermaine?"

"The infected?"

"Yeah."

"Well, they're . . . being looked after. Treated. As best we can."

Carlton stole another glance at the orderly, still mopping the floor. Almost as an aside, he muttered, "You know they gonna change like Jermaine?"

There was no reply, and at first he wondered whether his voice had been too low for Cat to hear. He slid a look in her direction and saw a tight, pinched expression on her face.

"We don't *know* that," she said defensively.

He made a dismissive sound through his teeth. "Yeah, we know it. And you know we gonna have to deal with it too."

Almost angrily she said, "So what are you suggesting?"

"I ain't spelling it out."

"I will then, shall I?" She lowered her voice to a furious whisper. "There's no way we'd consider ending the lives of patients purely on the off-chance that they'll be affected the same way that your friend was."

She broke off, took a deep breath. "Sorry."

"For what?"

"For losing my temper. You've been through enough without that."

He shrugged. "You only angry 'cos you scared."

She grunted – a laugh without humour. "You're not wrong there." Then, as if trying to reassure herself as much as him, she said, "Anyway, we won't make the same mistake twice. We know how violent the infected patients can get, so we'll keep them restrained at all times."

"Even when they dead?" said Carlton. "'Cos that's when they most dangerous."

Cat looked at him, as if that thought hadn't occurred to her. Starting to rise from her seat, she said, "I'll—"

And that was when they heard the first scream from behind the closed doors of the isolation ward.

For a split-second everyone in the corridor froze – Cat, Carlton, the security guards, the orderly mopping the floor – and then they started to move in unison. Cat and Carlton jumped to their feet, the blanket slipping from Carlton's shoulders; the orderly, still dragging his mop, backed away from the doors until the base of his spine bumped against one of the gurneys across the corridor; and the security guards with their backs to the doors turned to face them, one reaching for the handle that was closest to him . . .

Before his fingers could touch it, however, the door flew open and a student nurse, a chubby girl called Amanda Lee with maroon hair and black nail varnish, ran out. As soon as she hit the patch of wet floor her feet shot from under her and she went down with a fleshy slap that forced the breath from her in a grunting *whoosh*.

Cat had barely hunched her shoulders in a wince of sympathy when the closing door flew open again, hitting one of the security guards with such force that he was knocked on to his well-padded behind, a startled look on his face. With an agility that belied his ghastly pallor, Martin Balfour, the man with the neck wound, leaped through the gap of the closing door and pounced on the girl.

Once again Cat thought that it was like watching a lion attacking its prey. Before Amanda could move, Martin was on her back, pinning her to the floor. Dipping his head he bit into her shoulder, savagely enough that his teeth sliced straight through her tunic and into her skin, bringing forth a gush of blood that instantly caused a shockingly dark stain to bloom on the blue material.

Amanda's shriek of pain was raw and primal, the sound of

an animal in mortal terror. It was such an awful sound that Cat felt a wrench of distress in her stomach so acute it was as if all the energy had been sapped out of her. She could only stand and stare as Martin Balfour raised his head, a flap of dripping red flesh clamped between his teeth.

Focused on Martin Balfour, Cat was aware of Carlton beside her only as a peripheral blur. He remained a blur until the moment that he grabbed the mop out of the hand of the stunned orderly, flipped it around, and rammed it like a blunt-ended javelin into Martin Balfour's left eye.

Cat had no idea whether that had been Carlton's intention (and afterwards she never thought to ask him), but his aim was nevertheless true. The end of the mop went straight into the infected man's eye socket and buried itself deep in his skull.

Martin Balfour slipped backwards off Amanda's prone body like a man tumbling out of a rubber dinghy. The mop protruded harpoon-like from his eye for a second and then popped free – though it didn't fall, because Carlton, barging past her, was still holding on to the soggy end. Cat supposed the reason he was striding forwards, and all but shoving her out of the way as he did so, was so that he could finish Martin off.

However, he never got the chance. As he stepped over Amanda's flailing, bleeding body, the double-doors to the isolation ward crashed open again.

In hindsight, Cat thought she had heard a commotion coming from behind the doors – screams, thuds, clatters – before they opened, but it still sent a shock through her when they burst outwards. The way bodies immediately tumbled from the ward reminded her of oranges falling and scattering from the bottom of a torn paper bag.

First to emerge was a knot of her colleagues, four or five of them, in their blue tunics and face masks and latex gloves. They were in a panic, all but scrambling over one another, and as they emerged she saw one (she knew, by his widow's peak, that it was

Ralph Hardcastle, who had celebrated his fortieth birthday three weeks previously) trip and fall over Martin Balfour's sprawled body and get instantly trampled on by his colleagues.

Amanda was trampled on too, responding with high-pitched squeals as her workmates stumbled and stamped on her legs and back and buttocks in their eagerness to escape. What they were escaping *from* was apparent a moment later as, first, Samantha Mellor in her sexy nurse's uniform, and then Tammy Ollerenshaw in her *real* nurse's uniform, emerged from the closing doors.

Both of them were hunched over, slavering, their hands bloody. Samantha had blood around her mouth too, and quite a bit of it spattered down the front of her tight, cleavage-revealing uniform. All that remained of the straps that had been restraining the two girls was a single length of snapped leather around Tammy's right wrist.

Cat had a split-second to wonder how strong the two girls must have been to snap their thick leather bonds (bonds that had been securely buckled around their wrists, ankles and necks) as if they were cotton, and then Tammy's eyes latched on to hers and all Cat could think about was how, if she didn't move *instantly*, she would be dead.

Or, if not dead, then infected, which would be even worse. Almost before she knew what she was doing she had turned to run, intending to follow her fleeing colleagues towards the door at the end of the corridor.

She had taken no more than a step or two, however, when one of the shrouded forms lying on the metal gurney to her left abruptly sat up, the white sheet sliding away from it.

It was Fitch, his face nothing but raw, oozing meat. One of his eyes was a punctured, blood-smeared egg hanging halfway down his cheek; the other was gone, leaving nothing but an empty socket. The teeth in his lipless mouth looked as though they were bared in a simian grimace of aggression. His black clothes were part slick, part crusty with drying blood.

As Fitch sat up, the orderly who had been standing with his back pressed against the gurney jerked forward, directly into Cat's path. As he did so, Fitch's hand shot out, grabbed the orderly's hair and wrenched his head back. At the same moment Tammy Ollerenshaw leaped at Cat, her fingers hooked into claws.

As if from nowhere, the end of the mop swung round and smashed into Tammy's face. It wasn't enough to stun her, but it was enough to knock her off-balance. She stumbled and fell to one side, and then, like a cat, sprang instantly back to her feet. In the time it took her to do so, Carlton grabbed Cat's hand, shouted, "Come on!" and then the two of them set off at full speed along the corridor.

They bypassed Samantha Mellor, who was sitting astride Ralph Hardcastle's body, her short skirt riding up over her blood-smeared, stocking-clad thighs in a grotesque parody of sexual congress. Samantha was gnawing on Ralph's left fist while his right pummelled her in the side of the head. Ralph was screaming, as was the orderly in Fitch's clutches, their combined voices unnaturally and distressingly shrill. One of the security guards was down too, while Amanda, her shoulder wound leaking blood and her white, cellulite-dimpled legs bruised where her colleagues had trampled on her, was dragging herself inch by inch along the corridor by her black-painted fingernails.

Later, Cat would feel ashamed that she hadn't stopped to help the stricken girl, but at that moment her instinct for self-preservation overrode everything. Instead of responding to Amanda's bleat for help, therefore, she simply leaped over her as if she was just another obstacle.

Seconds later, with chaos raging behind them, Cat and Carlton reached the end of the corridor. Their hands were still clasped, and in his free hand Carlton was still clutching the mop. The doors here were like the ward doors, double doors which opened and closed on spring-mounted levers, the metal handles resembling capital E's with the central strut removed.

These doors were often propped open during the day, but at night, when visiting hours were over and the hustle and bustle had died down a little, they were closed to conserve heat and minimize sound. It was Cat, using her left hand (the only hand that was free between the two of them), who yanked open the door just enough for her and Carlton to slip through. Ahead of them she saw one of the security guards and those of her colleagues who had got away disappearing through the fire door on the left that led out on to the staircase. Still holding Carlton's hand she was about to follow when he tugged her back.

"Hold on."

She looked at him wildly. "What? We haven't got time."

As if to confirm this a body, presumably Tammy Ollerenshaw's, hit the double doors behind them with a crash. She and Carlton leaped against them, using their combined weight to stop them from opening.

The doors swelled apart, and Cat caught a glimpse of Tammy's ravaged, dead-eyed face through the gap, before she and Carlton managed to force them closed again. Cat didn't think they would be so lucky a second time. It was surely only because Tammy had not been expecting any resistance that they had been able to repel her attack. Once she applied her entire and prodigious strength, however, she and Carlton would no doubt be knocked back like a couple of skittles. In the brief lull before that could happen, though, Carlton released Cat's hand, then rammed the mop through the gap between the two door handles, creating a flimsy barrier.

"That won't hold for long," Cat said.

Carlton, blood-spattered, curled his lip defiantly. "I know it. Might be long enough to save our lives, though."

He grabbed her hand and dragged her towards the fire door. As they crashed through and began to descend the stairwell beyond, the screams of those who had not been so lucky faded behind them. Cat had a feeling, however, that if she *were* ever to get out of this alive, the terrible sounds made by the dying and the wounded would follow her down into her dreams for a long time to come.

04:14 am

WHEN VINCE REACHED the ground floor he saw that what he'd been told was true. Just as one of the nurses on duty in Shirley's ward had said, the Admissions area was full of heavily armed SO22 officers. And from the looks of it, they weren't letting anyone either in or out of the building.

The officers were stationed at all the exits, their guns held across their chests. They were not actually pointing their weapons at anyone, but their presence carried an unmistakable message: *Don't mess with us. We're armed and dangerous.*

Those patients waiting for treatment on the parallel rows of back-to-back seats were as silent as the officers surrounding them. Most looked as though they were wishing they'd chosen a different night on which to trip over the dog and sprain their ankle, or bash their thumb with a hammer, or have a funny turn. Most, in fact, looked as though they were wishing they'd opted to tuck themselves up at home in bed with a cup of tea and some painkillers. They surely couldn't have imagined, when they had set out earlier this evening, that they would end up being held at gunpoint in a hospital waiting room by British police officers.

Seeing the sick and the vulnerable being terrorized made Vince's blood boil. He had always hated bullies, and in fact the main reason he had become an ambulance technician in the first place was so that he could give aid and comfort to victims of intimidation and violence.

When he was twelve, his gran, who throughout his childhood had been the jolliest woman Vince knew and had always spoiled him rotten, had been beaten up by a druggie who'd forced his way into her house and stolen whatever valuables he could find – including her wedding ring, which he'd broken two of her fingers to remove. When Vince had seen her in hospital, her face so black and swollen it was unrecognizable, he'd burst into tears and had vowed there and then that when he was older he would protect the vulnerable in whatever way he could. For a while he'd considered joining the police (the irony of which was not lost on him), but in the end he had settled on becoming an ambulance driver, simply because he had liked the idea of rushing to the rescue of those in need.

He wished that he could do something for the poor souls sitting cowed and silent and casting fearful glances at the black-clad men standing menacingly around the room. Wished too that he could do something to help Shirley, who, after her panicky outburst of an hour or so ago, had now slipped back into a feverish, fitful sleep.

Her condition was a mystery; she seemed to be in the grip of some mysterious virus, although the nurse who had told Vince about the lockdown had also said they were working on the possibility that she might be suffering from food (or even some other type of) poisoning. They had taken blood samples and were running tests in an effort to get to the heart of the problem. Eventually, he supposed, they *would* come up with an appropriate course of treatment, but for the moment they were simply pumping her full of antibiotics and trying to keep her temperature down.

If he was being entirely honest, the person that Vince most wanted to help, however, was himself. His first concern when he'd heard about the lockdown had been how it would impact on his day out with Luke. He had been waiting so long and had fought so hard for this day that he was damned if he was going to let a bunch of gun-toting bully boys stop him from seeing his son. Which was why, when he stepped out of the lift on the ground floor and stomped purposefully towards the Admissions area, he aimed directly for the only people in the room who *weren't* silent.

This constituted a trio of men gathered around the Admissions desk, who were having what could only be described as a stand-up argument. On one side there was a stiff-legged police commissioner or superintendent type with a peaked cap perched above his hangdog face, and on the other there was a handsome doctor in a white coat who Vince had spoken to a time or two, and a portly, balding, fussy-looking man in a shiny grey suit and gleaming black shoes.

There was another white-coated doctor too, sitting on a nearby seat with his face in his hands. Vince wondered whether he'd become *too* argumentative and had received a rifle butt in the face for his trouble.

If so, then the little man in the grey suit had clearly taken up his mantle. With a face the colour of a ripe strawberry and eyes that were bulging out of his head as though he was being strangled, it was he who was doing most of the talking – or rather, shouting. The white-coated doctor, although he appeared to be more or less in agreement with the little man, seemed to be doing his best to stay calm and offer practical suggestions. However, the policeman, judging by his stance and general demeanour, seemed to be digging in his heels and defying both of them.

"But you still haven't adequately explained *why* you've put the hospital into lockdown, Chief Inspector Underhill," the white-coated doctor was saying as Vince approached. "Perhaps if you could explain your reasons it would help us to better understand and accept the situation."

The policeman, who the white-coated doctor had called Chief Inspector Underhill, sighed. "As I have already explained, Dr Blackstock, I am not at liberty to divulge information currently protected by the Police Special Powers Act."

"Liberty?" scoffed the man in the grey suit. "How can you stand there and talk about liberty? What about the liberty of the people here? What about the liberty of my staff to go home to their loved ones for a well-earned rest at the end of an arduous day?"

From the weary expression on the Chief Inspector's face, Vince had a feeling that the argument had been going round in circles for some considerable time. Before Underhill could reply he said loudly, "'Scuse me."

All three men turned to look at him – as did a fair number of patients. Vince saw the Chief Inspector's face harden at the sight of his green uniform with its NHS flash and London Ambulance Service badge, but before he could comment, Vince continued, "Sorry to butt in, but can someone let me out? I need to get to my ambulance."

The grey-suited man gave Underhill what could only be termed a triumphant leer, but the police officer was unmoved. "I'm afraid that's quite impossible," he said.

Vince shook his head, deciding that ignorance and bluster was the best course of action. "No, I don't think you understand, old son. I'm not a hospital employee. I work for the London Ambulance Service—" he tapped his badge with a meaty finger "—and I've got calls to make, lives to save. Without me, folk out there will die."

Underhill regarded him unblinkingly. "I'm sure there are other ambulances on the streets of London."

"Oh, I'm sure there are," Vince replied, "but the problem

is, there are never enough, and one more can make all the difference. And if just one life is saved 'coz there's an extra ambulance out there, then that's got to be worth it, hasn't it?"

The little man turned to Vince, his face sour. "Oh, it's pointless appealing to *his* better nature – believe me, we've tried and he hasn't got one. He doesn't care a fig if people die."

"On the contrary," said Underhill wearily, "as I have already explained, the lockdown has been instigated as a protective measure."

"Protection against what?" asked Vince. "Have we all got the plague or something? Or has everyone *out there* got the plague?"

There was a brief silence, during which Dr Blackstock half-smiled and raised his eyebrows as though challenging Chief Inspector Underhill to answer. Underhill, for his part, looked uncomfortable, *shifty* even, and in that moment Vince felt as though he had inadvertently hit on something.

The heavy mob were clearly here to either keep something in or something out, but what? Dr Blackstock seemed to know, or suspect, but he wasn't saying anything, presumably because this was a public area and he didn't want to cause a panic. At first, hearing about the lockdown and then seeing it in action, Vince had vaguely assumed that the S022 squad were here to arrest someone – a rioter, maybe, or some high-security criminal. Now, though, thinking about it, he was inclined to suspect that they were here not because of some*one* but some*thing*. He should have realized that this was too large an operation for the apprehension of a single person, even before he'd seen how both Blackstock and Underhill had responded to his throwaway comment about the plague (not the little man, though, which suggested that he was out of the loop – whatever the loop was).

Recovering his composure, Underhill muttered, "Now you're being ridiculous." He seemed then, with a tilt of his chin and by averting his eyes, to take a metaphorical step back from the conversation. Dismissively he continued, "Excuse me, gentlemen, but this discussion is at an end. If you wish to take this matter further, I suggest you do so through the proper channels. In the meantime I'm sure that the best thing we can all do is to discharge our duties as best we can."

And with that he turned in an almost parade ground about-face and marched away. The little man spluttered in his wake. Vince called, "Can you at least give us an idea of when this bloody lockdown'll be over and we can all go home?"

He didn't expect Underhill to reply, and he wasn't disappointed.

Raising his eyebrows, Dr Blackstock, said, "Oh well, better make the best of things, I suppose."

The little man said something about Underhill not hearing the last of this, and then the three men went their separate ways. Glancing once again at the white-coated doctor with his head in his hands, Vince wandered over to a spare seat and sat down, thinking hard.

Could he have hit the nail on the head when he had mentioned the plague? Could it be that some terrible disease had somehow been unleashed in the hospital? If so, how contagious was it? How at risk were they all? Presumably, if Underhill and his men had been willing to implement the lockdown then just *being* on the premises didn't necessarily constitute a death sentence. Which meant that all Vince had to do was keep away from any potential sources of infection and find a way to get out. After all, the hospital had many exits and Underhill's men couldn't possibly be covering them all.

He wondered whether he ought to try and get Shirley out too – and suddenly his blood ran cold. Shirley. The mysterious virus or whatever it was she had. Did that have something to do with why Underhill's lot were here? Had she caught this thing and, if so, did that mean that he was infected too?

If he *was* contagious, he needed to find out what with – and fast. He couldn't even think about escaping if there was a chance he might spread this *whatever it was* far and wide.

And, of course, until he *did* find out, there was no way – although it broke his heart to admit it – that he could risk going anywhere near Luke.

04:19 am

"HOLD UP," CARLTON said, catching hold of Cat's sleeve. "Somethin' happenin'."

Cat had been so concerned with putting distance between herself and the infected, and so engrossed in her own thoughts, that she had been blind and deaf to what was ahead of her. All she'd been able to think about during their headlong flight from the isolation ward had been finding Marcus Blackstock and telling him what had happened. She knew he would appreciate the urgency of the situation, the need to bring things back under control as quickly as possible. Knew too he'd have the authority to make it happen, or at least set wheels in motion.

Quite *how* the hospital authorities would stop the infected she had no idea, but that wasn't something she needed (or wanted) to think about. Whatever it took, the priority had to be preventing the infected from infecting others. Cat dreaded to think what would happen if Tammy Ollerenshaw and Samantha Mellor and the rest started running riot through the wards, biting all and sundry.

Desperate though she was to get to the Admissions area, Carlton's words brought her to a halt. He was right, she realized. Now that she had stopped running, and was tuning back into the world beyond her own pounding footsteps and gasping breaths, it was evident that there was some kind of commotion up ahead. The Admissions area was about thirty seconds' walk away; reaching it was a case of turning right at the end of this corridor and then passing through a wide arched opening about halfway along the next. But it was from there, or somewhere nearby, that they could hear voices raised in argument, interspersed with frightened screams.

As they moved closer, they heard a man yelling, "Get down! Get on the fucking floor *now!*" Then they heard another voice, which Cat recognized as belonging to Hilary Rooker, one of the nurses who had been part of the group that had escaped from the isolation ward and preceded herself and Carlton down the stairs. Hilary's voice was a high-pitched wail of protest: "But he hasn't *done* anything."

"Let's check it out," Carlton muttered, "but keep in close to the wall, yeah?"

She nodded and they crept forwards, Carlton moving a little stiffly because of the wound to his hip. As they turned the corner and edged towards the square arch, the sounds of conflict became louder and clearer. They heard sobbing, rapid scuffling movement, a voice, high-pitched with distress, saying, "*You can't do this!*" and another telling the speaker to shut the fuck up.

"Those are my work colleagues through there," Cat hissed, nodding at the arch. "What's happening to them?"

Carlton waved her back. "Wait here. I'll go see." He crept closer to the arch, and was flattening himself back against the wall prior to peeking around the corner of it, when a bulky figure abruptly stepped through it, almost colliding with him.

Both Carlton and the big guy – who Cat saw was wearing a dark green Ambulance Service uniform – jumped back in mutual shock, raising their hands. Carlton's hands instinctively bunched into fists, but the big man displayed open palms and said mildly, "Whoa there, young fella."

Slowly Carlton lowered his fists. The big man glanced at him and then at Cat, clearly taking in how dishevelled and blood-spattered they both were.

"You two wi' that lot who just came running in, yelling like nutters?" he asked.

He kept his voice low, as though he didn't want to be overheard, though there was so much commotion still going on in the area beyond the arch that he could probably have talked in a normal voice without attracting attention.

"Sort of," Cat said.

"Then I wouldn't go in there if I were you. What the hell happened to you lot?"

"It's a bit of a long story."

"Wass goin' on through there?" Carlton asked bluntly.

"Police," the big guy said. "That SO22 lot. Armed to the teeth. They just came bursting in apparently, shouting that the hospital was in lockdown. They're not letting anyone in or out. Their leader's a bloke called Underhill."

Carlton glanced at Cat. "This be 'coz of the zombies."

The big guy was so surprised that he forgot to keep his voice down. "Zombies?"

"They're not zombies," said Cat, flashing Carlton a disapproving look. "They're . . . well, they've been infected."

Almost eagerly he asked, "Infected how?"

Stubbornly Carlton said, "They get bit or scratched, then they die, then they come back and kill people. They fuckin' zombies, man. They *look* like zombies, they *act* like zombies."

The big guy raised his hands again. "Hang on, hang on, you're losing me 'ere. How many o' these 'infected' are we talking about? And where's this all supposed to be 'appenin'?"

"No 'suppose'," Carlton muttered. "It *is* fuckin' happenin', innit? I merked two of the fuckers myself – one of them my man, Jermaine."

There was more shouting from behind them: "Right! All of you! Get down on the floor! Do it now or I swear I'll put a bullet through each of your fucking heads!"

The big guy half-glanced over his shoulder, then leaned forward and lowered his voice to a hiss. "What say we reconvene somewhere a bit quieter and compare notes?"

"I have to let someone know what's going on." said Cat. "I have to find Dr Blackstock."

"I think they already know what's going on, love," the big guy said. "Otherwise why would they be here?"

Cat looked confused. "But how *could* they know? Why are the police treating this like a major incident when it's only just started happening?"

The big guy raised his eyebrows. "Aye, it's weird, in't it? Ever get the feeling there's summat they're not telling us?"

04:29 am

MEL DIDN'T KNOW if it was the noise that woke her or the pain. The noise made her think of school dinners – the clash of metal food trolleys, the clatter of crockery, the raised voices of hundreds of excited children, amplified beneath the high ceiling of the school hall.

It was a happy memory, one she associated with security and companionship. She would have liked to have wallowed in it, to have wrapped herself in its blanket-like warmth, but the pain wouldn't let her. It was both excruciatingly sharp and grindingly monotonous, like having hot barbed wire coiled tightly in her belly and groin. It was like the worst period pain ever. Her vagina – her 'chufty' her Mum had used to call it when Mel was little – was a throbbing mass of heat.

As she surfaced, the pain embedding itself like hooks in her consciousness and hauling her towards the unwelcome light, so the noise changed too. All at once it was no longer the happy clatter of school mealtimes, but a hard-edged cacophony, all alarm and discord. She heard screams, running feet, bangs and thuds and crashes that made her wonder how she could ever have associated it with happy childhood memories. Where was she and what had happened to her? Had she had an accident? Was she lying injured on some battlefield?

As soon as she opened her eyes and saw the white ceiling with its even whiter bands of strip lighting it all came back to her. She was in hospital! She had given birth! She was a mother!

The memory brought forth a stew of emotions, of peaks and troughs that veered between euphoria and horror, wonder and despair. She had pushed out the wailing scrap of life that was her son – *her son!* – in a shock and trauma so profound it seemed almost to have shunted her out of reality. Maybe part of that was the drugs still swilling about in her system, but mostly it was the sheer disbelief of seeing her loving, gentle husband turning crazy, violent, biting and scratching like a wild animal and having to be subdued by half-a-dozen burly security men. Even then, as he was being carried from the room, he had struggled and snarled and tried to bite his captors, his face etched with a hideous, blank-eyed rage. There had been nothing of the Steve she had known in those eyes. It was as if he had been possessed. As if, like his mother, his personality had been subsumed by something else, only in his case, instead of being nibbled away inch by inch, it had happened in one crashing, frenzied swoop.

Her heart beat so hard and so rapidly as she remembered it all that it sent fresh waves of pain through her body. She tried desperately to focus on something else, something positive – her son, her baby son, where was he?

She turned her head and saw him. He was in a transparent plastic crib by her side, his little face red, his eyes screwed into a tight scowl. But he was sleeping peacefully, his hands up by the sides of his head, his tiny fists clenched. He was dressed in a yellow baby-gro, one of the ones she and Steve had brought to the hospital, and covered up to his waist in a fluffy, cream-coloured blanket. Seeing him there, so vulnerable, so oblivious

to what was happening around him, Mel felt such a surge of love and such a desire to protect him that she almost cried out.

Then she sensed movement beyond the crib – someone standing up, moving into her peripheral vision – and she *did* cry out. All that achieved, however, was to make the someone stand up more rapidly, make them reach out towards her. Mel braced herself, ready to fight despite the pain she was in – to fight for her life, to protect her son.

But then the someone said in an urgent whisper, "Shh, shh, don't make a sound. They'll hear you."

It was a girl. A midwife. Blonde hair cut in a bob. Glasses.

Dropping her voice, Mel asked, "Who'll hear me?"

The girl's eyes flickered towards the door. "*They* will. Out there. They've all gone crazy."

Mel thought of Steve again, biting and scratching and struggling. Tearing off the lips of the other midwife with his teeth. And she thought of the girl who had attacked them in the car park, the one who had looked like a porn star playing a nurse, the one whose head had disappeared in a loud red bang.

"All of them," she said. "What do you mean, all of them?"

"The doctors, the nurses, people I've known for years . . . even the mothers . . ." The midwife's voice faded and died, and for a moment she swayed a little, her face ashen, as if she was about to pass out.

They heard a scratching at the door.

The midwife froze, but her face didn't. Mel got the impression it was lengthening as her mouth and eyes widened in terror. Both women turned their heads slowly towards the door. The scratching stopped. Despite the commotion outside, the room seemed suddenly silent.

In the quietest of whispers, the midwife said, "I think they've—"

And then with a splintering crack the door flew open.

The midwife screamed, threw herself to the floor and dived

under the bed. Mel heard her scrabbling under there like an enormous rat as she gazed in horror at her husband. Steve stood swaying in the doorway, his hands, the lower part of his face and the front of his sweatshirt bright red and smeared with clots of matter as if he had been guzzling blackberries. His pupils were pinpricks in eyes that seemed to stare without seeing, and – though he seemed oblivious to the wound – he had what looked like the handle of a scalpel sticking out of his right thigh.

For a moment Mel thought he was blind, unaware of her presence, and then their baby son – they had decided weeks ago to call him Peter – shifted slightly in his sleep. Immediately Steve's head snapped around and he took a lurching step forwards. Wincing at the pain, Mel pulled herself upright in the bed as he approached.

"Steve," she said softly, "it's me, Mel. Your wife. You recognize me, don't you?"

He halted, looked at her. His expression didn't change. He opened his mouth, as if to speak, and thick, red drool spilled out from between his lips and down the front of his sweatshirt. Then he tilted his head, seeming to focus on Peter. Mel tensed as he lurched another step closer, then another. He was standing above the crib now, staring down.

"It's your son, Steve," Mel said, her voice hoarse, throat dry. "*Our* son. We decided to call him Peter, remember? Isn't he beautiful?"

With bloody hands Steve reached into the crib and lifted Peter up. The baby wriggled slightly but didn't wake. For a moment Steve stared down at his new-born son, and Mel thought she saw a look of wonder cross his face. Then he raised Peter up to his mouth as if to kiss him.

04:55 am

NEVER IN HIS wildest dreams had Gerry Eaves expected anything like this. The evening had started badly, but since then it had only got worse.

He'd known that things weren't right between him and Gill – they worked so hard and were so tired that they hardly saw each other these days, and when they did it was invariably only to bicker about money or the kids. And he had let himself go a bit in recent years, eating and drinking too much, not doing enough (in fact, any) exercise. The knock-on effect was that his libido had suffered. In fact, he was so exhausted when he crashed into bed at night that all he wanted to do was sleep.

Thing is, he'd thought Gill was the same – too preoccupied with work and the kids to have time for anything else; too shattered, especially with all the shift-changes and overtime she had to do, to have any interest in sex. Now, though, he'd discovered that wasn't the case. On her phone he'd discovered a whole different Gill, one that he didn't know existed – or at least, one he'd once known, but who had been buried for far too long beneath the detritus of everyday life.

It saddened him to think that the old Gill was still around, but that he had somehow lost touch with her. Saddened him too that the only way she'd been able to express that side of herself was by turning to somebody else. Had he rejected her too many times? Snubbed her advances? Or was it simply that he had taken her for granted for too long, wrongly thinking that they had mutually, albeit tacitly, agreed that was just the way things were?

And was he angry too? With Gill? With this man she'd been seeing? Well, yes, of course he was, but he was surprised to find that the anger was buried deep, crushed beneath layers of shame and sadness, regret and despair. And loss too. He felt that something in their relationship had died, that it was gone forever. He felt that even if they managed to repair it there would always be hairline cracks visible. What had been done could no longer be undone.

He had never read her texts before, had never felt any need to delve into her private life (partly because he hadn't even known that she *had* a private life). He had only done it because . . . well, because he had come across her phone on the bedside table as he was getting ready for bed, and just at the moment when he had noticed it, it had made the little "ding" sound it made when a text came in, and he had picked it up, thinking that it might be important, that it might be something he would need to ring her up at work to tell her.

As it turned out the text had been nothing – just junk mail – but he had noticed that she had other texts on her phone, dozens from a bloke called Tim Marshall, and with a crawling sense of unease he had started reading them. And his fears, which had not even been formed until that moment, had all at once been horribly realized: the texts had been intimate, explicit, and they had left Gerry in no doubt as to what was going on between this man and Gill.

It had not taken him long to work out who Tim Marshall

was. He had rung the hospital – because where else could Gill be conducting an affair? – and had discovered that he was a doctor.

Not a fellow nurse, but a *doctor*. A step above. Immediately Gerry had felt inferior, had wondered how he could compete. After all, what was *he*? A haulage contractor. It was hardly the kind of profession to set female hearts afluttering. A doctor, though. A man who saved lives. There were lots of TV series where the hero was a doctor, someone dashing and heroic.

Would Tim Marshall be dashing and heroic? Gerry had to see. He had to go to the hospital, not to punch the man's lights out, but just to . . . to talk to him. To impress upon him what he was doing, what he was coming between. He and Gill had been together almost half their lives. They had two beautiful children. A history. And Gerry still loved his wife. He did. It had taken something like this to make him realize it. He loved her with all his heart and he didn't want to lose her. She was his soulmate. They were *supposed* to be together. Until death do they part.

Tim Marshall had not been dashing and heroic, but he *had* been young – it had shocked Gerry to see *how* young – and relatively good-looking. That wasn't why Gerry had punched him, though. No, it had been the man's sneery, couldn't-care-less attitude, coupled with the horrible things he had said about Gill.

There had been a moment, just a moment, of exquisite pleasure as Gerry's fist had connected and he had heard Tim Marshall's nose crunch. Then the doctor had fallen down, his face gushing blood, and instead of pleasure Gerry had felt ashamed and depressed, even a little scared of the consequences of his actions.

And then everything had turned weird. It was as if the punch had been the catalyst for a series of increasingly bizarre and violent events. First Tim Marshall had laughed and sprung to his feet like an acrobat and started spitting blood at everybody. Then the doors had crashed open and the place had flooded with men in riot gear. Then, after announcing that the hospital was in lockdown and that nobody was allowed in or out, the bloke who was leading them had had a row at the Admissions desk with several members of the hospital staff. Then, once that had settled down, a group of staff members wearing masks and gloves, their uniforms speckled and spattered with blood, had burst into the Admissions area yelling that the dead were coming back to life. Some people had freaked out, wanting to leave, and the riot police had got heavy, threatening to shoot people if they didn't shut the fuck up and sit the fuck down.

Luckily everyone had complied – Gerry dreaded to think what would have happened if they hadn't – and after a lot of shouting and gun-waving the blood-spattered nurses in the masks had been rounded up and frog-marched away.

And now, for the time being at least, everything had settled down again. Having ordered that no one was to leave the immediate area, the police had reassumed their positions around the room. And the people who'd been waiting in Admissions were sitting back down on their chairs, most of them huddled up, shell-shocked or glancing around fearfully or even, in one or two cases, looking angry and defiant.

Having wiped off the blood that Tim Marshall had spat at him, Gerry was now sitting close to the vending machine, not far from the big square arch that led deeper into the hospital. Marshall was sitting a few rows ahead of him, hunched over with his head in his hands. Gerry assumed that the doctor was cradling his broken nose, and, ashamed though he was of losing his temper and punching the man, he hoped that it fucking hurt.

Sitting a bit further down from Tim Marshall were a couple of girls dressed in sexy nurses' uniforms – figure-hugging little white numbers that showed lots of cleavage and barely covered their arses, from which they stretched out long legs clad in white fishnet stockings. Both girls were gorgeous, one white with long auburn hair, the other Asian, exotic-looking, with black hair. In fact, they were *so* gorgeous that, despite the circumstances, Gerry was finding it hard to keep his eyes off them.

See, he thought, *nothing wrong with* my *libido.* But instead of feeling defiant the thought just made him depressed. He wondered what the girls' story was. Were they strippers? Had they been to a fancy-dress party? And why were they here? Was one of them waiting for treatment? There didn't look to be anything wrong with either of them.

Then Gerry started to think about Gill. Had *she* worn her nurse's uniform when Tim Marshall had fucked her? Had *she* worn stockings and suspenders? He pressed his clenched fists against his tightly-closed eyes as if to blot out the image. When he lowered his hands and opened his eyes a moment later, the first thing he saw was that Tim Marshall was standing up.

He seemed to be doing it warily, cautiously, as if he didn't quite know where he was. He had his back to Gerry, so Gerry couldn't see his face. What Gerry *could* see, though, was that the doctor was twitching, little muscular spasms running through his hands, his shoulders, his head.

What if I've given him brain damage? Gerry thought. *What if he has some sort of seizure? What if he dies?* As Marshall turned and shuffled towards the two sexy nurses, an entire imagined future unfurled in Gerry's head. He pictured himself being convicted of murder, sent to prison, pictured his children coming to visit him, pictured them pressing their little hands to the glass barrier between themselves and their Daddy, tears running down their faces.

The two nurses glanced up as Tim Marshall lurched towards them. Then Gerry saw their faces change, their eyes and mouths widening with shock. The white girl, the one closest to Marshall, tried to scramble to her feet, but the doctor made a strange grunting sound and, to Gerry's astonishment, *leaped* upon her. Both Marshall and the girl went down in a struggling heap, the doctor snarling and gnashing like an attack dog. The other girl jumped to her feet and started screaming. Then black-clad men with assault rifles were running towards the wrestling couple, converging from all directions.

Gerry jumped to his feet to see what was going on, as did many other people in the room. Both girls were screaming now, and though Gerry couldn't quite see what was happening because there were several rows of seats in the way, he saw blood flying, spattering the seat leather. Other people were crying and yelling and making sounds of distress. Within seconds the place seemed to have crumbled into chaos again. The first of the black-clad troops arrived on the scene, running down the aisle between the seats, but as he did so, Tim Marshall sprang to his feet and leaped on him.

The doctor's speed and strength were astonishing. The SO22 man barely had time to aim his automatic weapon before Marshall was upon him. The officer had his black helmet ripped from his head and then he was screeching with agony as Marshall sank his teeth into the man's cheek. Other officers, cramming the aisle between the seats, were bellowing now, ordering Marshall down on the floor. When the doctor failed to comply, one of them stepped forward and smashed the butt of his firearm into the back of Marshall's head. There was a gout of blood and the doctor went down, the soldier he had bitten reeling backwards, his cheek hanging in a bloody flap.

Savage though the blow had been, however, Marshall didn't stay down for long. Within seconds he was back on his feet, springing at the troops closest to him. He snapped and slashed at them, his hands a whirlwind of movement. Another helmet was ripped away, another SO22 officer fell back, his face slashed to ribbons. The Asian girl was still screaming, but stopped when Marshall whirled around and raked a clawed hand across her ribs, startlingly red stripes of blood appearing on her white nurse's uniform. The SO22 troops used Marshall's momentary distraction with the girl to close in. He disappeared beneath a surging wall of black uniforms, and weapon butts rising and falling, battering him into submission.

Horrified though he was by what was happening, it suddenly occurred to Gerry that here was his chance. Everyone was screaming and shouting, focusing on the melee. If there was ever a good moment to take advantage of the confusion and slip away, then it was now. He wanted to find Gill, not to shout at her or get angry with her, but just to tell her that he loved her, that he wanted things back to the way they used to be.

Taking a quick glance around, he dropped to a crouch, then scuttled over to the vending machine. As far as he could tell, no one was looking his way, no weapon swinging round to cover him. From here it was a ten-metre dash to the arch, maybe less. He took a deep breath, then went for it. As he ducked into the arch and around the corner he heard a burst of gunfire behind him. At first he thought the bullets were meant for him, but then he realized that it was probably the only way the SO22 guys had been able to subdue Tim Marshall.

05:09 am

DESPITE THE RACKETY air conditioning, it was bloody hot in the second-floor conference room. Maybe, Sister Parkhurst thought, mopping her face with a handkerchief, it was the steadily rising tempers of those in attendance that was heating the air.

On one side of the table – metaphorically, of course – were Chief Inspector Underhill, head of the SO22 Crisis Response Team who had placed the hospital in lockdown, and Professor Déesharné, head of Research and Development for the group funded by New World Pharmaceuticals, which had set up shop on the top floor.

And on the other side was a quartet of hospital staff – the surgical director, Dr Andre De Mendonca; the site manager, Michael Rowbottom, who had already locked horns with Underhill once tonight (or rather, this morning), in the more public arena of the Admissions area; Marcus Blackstock, the on-call senior house officer and the doctor who had had most direct contact with the infected; and – representing the nursing profession – herself, who had been in the isolation ward when Martin Balfour, Samantha Mellor and Tammy

Ollerenshaw had broken free of their restraints and gone on the rampage.

Though she felt a little ashamed to admit it, Sister Parkhurst had escaped only by keeping her head while all around her were losing theirs. She had crouched down behind the bed occupied by the still-unconscious Susan Jenkins until the infected trio had gone off in pursuit of those fleeing the scene.

The seventh and final person in the room – who, along with Dr De Mendonca, had had to be roused from slumber to attend the hastily convened meeting – was the hospital's chief executive, Sir William Lennox-Wood, though Sister Parkhurst hadn't yet worked out whose side *he* was on. Although Sir William would no doubt claim that every single policy and strategy decision he made was for the good of the hospital, it couldn't be denied that he had been instrumental in granting Professor Déesharné and his team premises within the building in which to carry out their covert work.

Whether he had also been aware of Déesharné's government-granted authority to go over the heads of medical staff in procuring samples of human biological material for his research was open to debate. Not that Sir William was *prepared* to debate it, however. So far he had apologetically and rather charmingly claimed that he was unable to disclose information protected by confidentiality agreements between the hospital and their clients without first gaining permission from the Board of Directors – which, given the unsocial hour and the ad-hoc nature of the meeting, was clearly impossible.

It wasn't just Sir William who was being circumspect, however. The first twenty minutes of the discussion had yielded little in the way of progress. There had been, in Sister Parkhurst's view, nothing but a great deal of chest-beating. Meanwhile, somewhere in the building, the infected were still loose, unless the heavily armed search party that Underhill had dispatched had found them by now – though if they had, she doubted they would have done so without frightening to death half of the hospital's patients in the process.

In the last ten minutes talk had become snagged on what, in Sister Parkhurst's opinion, was a wild and tangled bramble patch of irrelevancy. Rowbottom, whose heart was more or less in the right place, but who she had always regarded as a jumped-up jobsworth, had somehow been allowed to dominate and divert the discussion to such an extent that it had now turned into a bickering match with Underhill. The squat and trollish site manager seemed more concerned by the fact that a bunch of government bully boys had moved in on his turf than by trying to establish *why* they had done so, or indeed how all parties might work together to deal with the current crisis.

To make matters worse, Sir William and Professor Déesharné had seemed more than happy to sit back and allow the debate to rumble on ad infinitum, and Dr De Mendonca looked as though he was trying hard to maintain the illusion that he was still snoozing at home in bed. Marcus Blackstock had attempted, in his polite and unruffled way, to intervene a couple of times, but even he now looked as though he was prepared to let Rowbottom run out of steam before attempting to steer things back on track.

Eventually, despite the bigwigs surrounding her, Sister Parkhurst could stand it no longer. Jumping to her feet, she slammed her hand down hard on the table.

Dr De Mendonca jumped and looked up, startled, as though he really *had* been dozing. Rowbottom, cut off in mid-flow, glared at her, and Underhill, as he had been doing for most of the meeting, glared at Rowbottom.

"Mr Rowbottom," Sister Parkhurst snapped, "do you know the story of Nero, who fiddled while Rome burned?"

Rowbottom opened his mouth to speak, but before he could say anything, she continued, "Because that's who *you* are, Mr

Rowbottom. You're Nero. And believe me, Rome is bloody burning out there."

She pointed at the door. Dr De Mendonca looked across as if he expected to see smoke seeping around the edges of the door frame.

Next to her, Marcus Blackstock said, "Hear, hear."

Rowbottom reddened. "I'm sorry, I don't see what—"

"You're going off the subject, Mr Rowbottom," Sister Parkhurst said, determined not to lose the initiative now that she had it. "You're not focusing on what's important."

"She's right, Michael," Marcus Blackstock said reasonably. "The situation is deteriorating as we speak and we should be thinking of ways to deal with it, not arguing the toss over details that hardly matter."

Rowbottom huffed. Dr De Mendonca, a short, quietly-spoken, bespectacled man with sleek black hair and a neatly trimmed beard, said, "You've been on the frontline, Marcus, which means you're more au fait with this situation than the rest of us. So what would you suggest?"

Marcus Blackstock seemed unperturbed as all eyes turned on him. "The way I see it, we should be focusing on two main areas. One, we need to contain the threat and protect the public, which is where you and your men come in, Chief Inspector—"

"Which is precisely what we *are* doing," Underhill said.

"—and two, we need to find a cure for this infection as quickly as possible – which means, Professor Déesharné, pooling our resources."

His manner was disarming, but there was a challenge in his eyes as he looked across at Déesharné. The beaky-nosed professor stared back at him impassively. "What makes you think I have anything to offer you, Dr Blackstock?"

Mildly, Marcus said, "You snapped up the body of Patient Zero for analysis almost before anyone here was even aware of

228

the nature of the infection. That suggests to me that you had prior knowledge of the condition, and yet when I questioned you about it you refused to confirm this or to disclose your findings. In addition, you seemed entirely unconcerned that the lives of patients, and possibly those caring for them, were under threat."

Rowbottom was nodding pugnaciously. Raising an eyebrow, Dr De Mendonca asked, "Is this true, Professor?"

Déesharné shrugged. "To some extent. Though Dr Blackstock's suggestion that I had prior knowledge of the infection is pure conjecture."

"Oh, come on now!" said Sister Parkhurst. "With all due respect, Professor, you pulled some pretty powerful strings to get custody of that body."

"Can you explain that, Professor Déesharné?" asked Dr De Mendonca.

Déesharné looked unperturbed. "I don't see that I have to. My work is strictly confidential."

"But surely in the spirit of mutual cooperation? Given the extraordinary circumstances?"

"The circumstances are neither here nor there."

"Poppycock!" snapped Sister Parkhurst. "You're aware of the situation out there. You're aware of how devastating this infection can be. You can't just hold your hands up and say that that's nothing to do with you, especially not when you've snatched away the one piece of evidence that might help us find a cure. You might be legally entitled to keep your findings to yourself, Professor, but you're certainly not *morally* entitled."

Déesharné looked at her calmly. "The *one* piece of evidence? Are you certain about that? What of the young boy who died just over an hour ago? Jermaine Paterson? I daresay you have pathologists rifling through his innards as we speak."

Sister Parkhurst looked as if she'd been found out. "How did you know about that?"

Déesharné rolled his eyes. "Oh, please."

"It's true that we have Jermaine Paterson's body," Marcus said quickly, "as well as various tissue samples from other sufferers of the infection. But the Sister's still right, Professor. Our investigations are only just beginning, whereas I'm guessing that your research is more advanced. Besides which, I'm frankly still baffled as to why you're being so obstructive.

"The fact is, we have a virulent infection out there that we currently don't know how to deal with. Do you honestly *want* it to spread, to become a pandemic? Because, from where I'm sitting, that's how it appears. And to be honest, the only possible reason I can think of for your behaviour is that you're under orders from your paymasters, New World Pharmaceuticals, to sit on your research, regardless of the fact that at its current rate the spread of the infection may soon reach crisis point. Now why would NWP adopt such an attitude, do you think, Professor?"

The inference was obvious – though evidently not *so* obvious to Rowbottom that he didn't feel a need to blurt it out. "Well, it's so that NWP can step in with a vaccine once everyone's desperate enough to pay through the nose for it, isn't it?" He looked pleased at his own astuteness and glared at Déesharné triumphantly. "Is that what this is, Professor? A way of getting rich by blackmailing the nation?"

Déesharné's expression had not changed, but a vein was pulsing in his left temple. "That's a ridiculous and defamatory accusation."

"You're not denying it, though, are you?" sneered Rowbottom.

Déesharné stared at him coldly. "I wouldn't give it credence by lowering myself to do so."

"So *can* you explain how you and New World Pharmaceuticals knew about the infection before it had even presented itself here in the hospital?" asked Marcus.

"Again your suggestion that I had prior knowledge is pure conjecture."

"But it's a reasonable, if not inevitable, assumption, surely?"

Déesharné sighed. "That is *your* conclusion, not mine."

"So what's *your* explanation? Why *won't* you tell us why you were so eager to procure the remains of Patient Zero?"

"We really are going round in circles here, aren't we?" said Déesharné wearily. "I refuse to subject myself to interrogation."

"Why's that, Professor?" challenged Rowbottom. "Is it because you've got something to hide?"

Déesharné rolled his eyes again. Tight-lipped, he said, "No, Mr Rowbottom. It's because, just as you did when you lambasted Chief Inspector Underhill, you seem dead set on turning this meeting into a kangaroo court."

"We're simply asking questions, Professor," said Marcus Blackstock. "We're simply trying to find solutions to a very serious problem. Perhaps I was naïve in thinking that we would achieve that by putting aside our personal interests and working together. I assumed, as medical practitioners, that our mutual overriding motivation would be the alleviation of human suffering. But it seems I was wrong."

Though Marcus' tone was, as ever, pleasant and reasonable, a simmering silence filled the room. Déesharné leaned back in his chair and folded his arms. Marcus looked at him for a moment longer, then turned to Underhill.

"Do you mind if I ask *you* a question, Chief Inspector?"

Underhill frowned, but nodded. "Not at all."

"Why did you put the hospital into lockdown?"

The officer shrugged. "I was acting on orders."

"From who?"

"My superiors."

"And who did they get *their* orders from?"

Underhill looked at Marcus as if he was being naïve. "One *follows* orders, Dr Blackstock. One doesn't *question* them."

Marcus raised his hands in acknowledgement. "All right, let me ask you something else. Were you told *why* you had to put the hospital into lockdown?"

Underhill frowned, as if he was trying to decide how much he was allowed to say. "I was told there was a situation. A possible outbreak that had to be contained at all costs."

"At *all* costs?"

He blinked slowly. "Well, naturally the preservation of life is always paramount in situations such as this."

"Naturally," said Marcus. "And you were told that what was happening at the hospital would put lives at risk, were you?"

"I was, yes."

Marcus leaned back, his chair creaking. He looked at Dr De Mendonca and then at Sir William. "So it would seem that both the Government and New World Pharmaceuticals knew about the infection before we did. And not only that, but they anticipated its appearance at this hospital and, to some extent, the effect it would have."

Sister Parkhurst looked troubled. "So are you saying that the Government or NWP, or possibly both together . . . created the infection? That this whole situation has been manipulated in some way?"

Marcus raised his hands. "I'm not saying anything. I'm simply stating the facts as I see them. As I think we *all* see them."

Sister Parkhurst looked across at Sir William, who had so far contributed little to the discussion. "Can't *you* order Professor Déesharné to share his research findings with us, Sir William? He *is* operating on hospital premises, after all."

Sir William, white haired, wiry eyebrowed and deeply tanned, smiled benignly at her. "I'm afraid not, my dear. The contract that we hold with NWP categorically states that the hospital, its employees and its representatives have no authority to interfere in the research work conducted by Professor Déesharné and his team."

Déesharné looked smug. Marcus asked, "But couldn't you at least *speak* to your NWP contacts, Sir William? Explain the situation?"

"I could try," Sir William conceded, "though I would have to put it to the Board of Directors first, which may take some time."

"Time we don't have," muttered Sister Parkhurst.

Sir William regarded her for a moment, and then flicked a finger at Marcus, in the manner of a country gentleman dispatching a waiter for an apéritif. "You say that those who get this infection turn violent?"

Marcus nodded. Although he had outlined the details of the infection right at the top of the meeting, he said, "Yes, they attack others. They seem compelled to spread the infection by scratching and biting their victims. The infected are also incredibly strong, so anyone who gets close to them is at risk."

"They're strong, but don't take that to mean they're healthy," Sister Parkhurst added. "In fact, they're desperately ill. They go downhill so rapidly after being infected – by which I mean, over the course of several hours, though it can vary from patient to patient – that in all the cases we've seen so far the sufferers reach the very point of death, to the extent that we're no longer able to detect life signs, before, somehow, finding a renewed surge of energy. After that it's as if the infection has overridden their natural inhibitors. Their strength is . . . well, incredible."

"The point of death?" said Dr De Mendonca.

Marcus nodded. "Almost beyond it. To the extent that when the first patient reached this point I actually made the mistake of declaring him dead – just before he woke up and went on a murderous rampage."

"Like some sort of resurrection, eh?" said Sir William with a chuckle.

"With all due respect, it's no laughing matter, Sir William," Sister Parkhurst said.

"No, of course not." He wafted a hand. "And you say several of these nutters are loose in the hospital?"

Sister Parkhurst frowned. "They're not nutters, Sir William, they're patients."

Exchanging a glance and a raise of the eyebrows with Sister Parkhurst, as if to say: *let it go*, Marcus said, "There are three patients currently at large that we know of, Sir William, though, of course, it's likely that they've infected others by now. Despite appearing to be on the point of death, these three were restrained with leather straps, but they broke them as easily as . . . well, as if they were made of paper."

"I have men looking for them as we speak, Sir William," said Chief Inspector Underhill.

"And what will they do when they find them?"

"Apprehend them, of course."

Sir William frowned. "And how will they do that? From what Dr Blackstock has told us, it seems that these people are incredibly strong, intent on spreading this bloody infection, and too far gone upstairs—" he tapped the side of his head "— to respond to orders. So if your chaps point guns at them and the blighters keep coming, what will they do?"

Underhill's face was set, without expression. "They will do whatever is necessary."

"Shoot 'em, you mean?"

"Which is why we need action *now*," Sister Parkhurst said, "before more people—"

She was interrupted by a knock on the door.

"Come," called Sir William before anyone could respond.

The door opened and a black-clad SO22 officer entered and stood to attention. "I'm sorry to interrupt, lady and gentlemen, but might I have a word with the Chief Inspector?"

Underhill glanced around the table. "Excuse me." He stood

up and marched across the room, preceding the SO22 officer out of the door.

As soon as he had gone, Sir William said, "It seems to me that what we need to do is round up these rogue elements without delay, and anyone else who might be infected, and keep them all together, at gunpoint if need be."

Marcus sighed. He couldn't help thinking that this meeting was like a frustrating game of snakes and ladders, in which the inability of half the participants to listen or understand sent the lot of them sliding frequently back down the snakes to square one. However, he tried to remain patient. "I agree, Sir William. But the point is, the infected don't respond to coercion, not even armed coercion. They don't have the mental faculties to recognize threat or danger. They're incredibly strong, fearless and full of rage. It's a daunting combination."

"So what are you saying, man? That the only way to stop 'em *is* to shoot 'em?"

"What I was going to suggest — what I *will* suggest to the Chief Inspector when he reappears — is that we look into arming his officers with tranquillizer guns. Something that will incapacitate the infected, but not harm them. That way we could keep them contained while we search for a cure."

Dr De Mendonca and Sir William were both nodding. "Sounds like a plan," said Sir William. "We'll put it to Underhill when he comes back. Ah, speak of the devil."

The door opened and Underhill stepped back into the room. Though his expression gave little away, Sister Parkhurst knew that something was wrong.

"What is it?" she said. "What's happened?"

Underhill looked at her. In a measured tone he said, "I'm afraid that our problem has escalated. There has been an incident in the Admissions area involving one of your doctors. A chap called Tim Marshall."

05:18 am

AS SOON AS the lift doors opened, Carlton stuck his head out and looked quickly left and right.

"Let's go."

He stepped out into the corridor, Cat and Vince behind him. All three were clutching chair legs, which they'd acquired by breaking up a seat in the Staff Room, where they had retreated to compare notes. Though what had been happening on the fourth floor of the hospital horrified Vince, he was at least grateful that the "plague", which he was worried he might be carrying, was an infection that it seemed could only be transmitted via bodily fluids. He was alarmed to discover, however, that the man he and Shirley had found earlier stumbling around the grounds of All Hallows Church was one of the three who had broken loose from the isolation ward on the fourth floor and gone on a murderous rampage, and was still – so far as Cat and Carlton were aware – at large somewhere in the building.

"If they are going round biting people, there could be millions of the fuckers by now," Carlton had said as he was handing out their makeshift weapons.

"That's a bit of an exaggeration, Carlton," Cat had replied. "Even if they have infected people, there'll be an incubation period. It takes a while before the victims start to turn aggressive."

"How long?" asked Vince.

She shrugged. "It depends on the person, but . . . an hour or so?"

"And how long since they three upstairs started chowing down?" Carlton said.

There was a moment of silence, and then Cat nodded. "All right, I take your point."

They had talked about what to do next, about ways they might get out of the hospital. Cat knew the place like the back of her hand and said she was aware of a few exits that the SO22 troops might not yet have covered. Desperate though he was to escape, however, Vince knew that he couldn't leave without Shirley. He told Cat and Carlton that she was in a ward on the third floor, just a floor down from where the infected had broken out, and that the last time he had seen her she had been asleep and feverish – and therefore vulnerable.

"Hold on, man," Carlton said suspiciously. "How you know she ain't got this thing? I mean, you and she brought one of them zombie fuckers to the hospital, innit? How you know he didn't bite her or scratch her or nothin'?"

"He didn't," Vince said, shaking his head. "I know he didn't. He was unconscious when we got to him, and still unconscious when we arrived. Besides, Shirl would've said. We're always aware of the risk of infection 'coz of HIV and that."

Carlton had looked at him with narrowed eyes, lips pursed doubtfully.

"Look," Vince said, raising his hands, "you don't have to come wi' me if you don't want to. I could go fetch her and bring her back 'ere. Or Cat could just let me know where t'best places to get out might be."

Carlton looked as though he was more than happy to agree, but Cat shook her head. "No way. We'll do this together. We're a team now."

Carlton slid her a look. "That right? Since when?"

Cat frowned. "Come on, Carlton. You know it makes sense to stick together. Safety in numbers and all that."

He looked at her a moment longer, then shrugged. "Awright, whatever."

Now, as they stepped out of the lift on the third floor, still looking around, Carlton said, "Where to?"

"This way," Vince said, pointing to the right.

He led the way along the corridor, which was strangely deserted. Or perhaps not so strangely, thought Cat, if the infected had found their way down here. However, there was no evidence that they *had* been here – no bodies, no bloodstains on the walls or floor. And the hospital *was* chronically understaffed, which, together with the curfew and the tendency these days for people to stay inside at night and batten down the hatches, meant that many of the general wards weren't the bustling hives of activity that they had once been.

When they reached the ward where Vince had left Shirley sleeping, they were surprised to find the doors not only closed but apparently locked. Curling his hands around the handles, Vince rattled them a few times and found that, although they had some give, he couldn't open them. Additionally, sheets of material had been placed over the windows so that they couldn't see in.

"This is daft," Vince said. "Where the hell have all the patients gone?"

"Maybe they still in there," Carlton suggested. "Maybe they hiding."

Cat rapped on the door. "Hello, is there anyone in there? This is Staff Nurse Cat Harris. If there's anyone there, can you please answer?"

After a moment an edge of the curtain on one of the doors was cautiously lifted aside and a face peeked out at them. Cat smiled encouragingly and waved. The curtain fell back and, thirty seconds later, one of the doors opened a foot or so.

"Come in quickly," a voice hissed.

Cat slipped through the gap, followed by Carlton and then Vince, who had to suck in his stomach to do so.

As soon as they were inside, the nurse who had allowed them entry – Vince recognized her as the same one who had told him about the lockdown earlier – closed the door again and wound a length of bandage between the handles, looping it through and around again and again before securing it.

They waited until she had finished before anyone spoke. Then Cat said, "What's going on, Suzanne? Are you all right?"

The nurse, Suzanne, nodded. She eyed the chair legs they were all carrying. "You look as though you already know what's going on. There are . . . violent patients loose in the hospital. They have some sort of infection."

Cat gave a quick nod. "Have you seen them?"

"No. Just some policemen in riot gear, who warned us to keep the doors secure and stay out of sight. Why, have *you* seen them?"

"Earlier. They were patients of mine."

The girl's eyes widened. "What's wrong with them? No one seems to know."

"They zombies," Carlton said bluntly.

Suzanne looked startled. "What?"

"Just ignore him," said Cat. "They have an infection which affects the brain, makes them aggressive."

"Are they as dangerous as the policemen told us they were?"

Cat hesitated, then nodded. "I'm afraid so. Just keep your heads down and hopefully you'll be all right."

Suddenly Vince exclaimed, "She's gone!"

Carlton and Cat turned, Cat clenching her teeth and putting her finger to her lips to remind him to be quiet.

Vince pulled an apologetic face. "Sorry," he hissed. Addressing Suzanne, he said, "The girl who was here, Shirley Teague. Where is she?"

Suzanne pulled an even more apologetic face than Vince, as if she was trying to outdo him. "Nobody knows. She must have got out of bed and wandered off when no one was looking. Then the police arrived and told us to barricade ourselves in. We went to check the toilets first, but she wasn't there."

She half-turned to her three colleagues – one man and two women – who were standing on the periphery of the hushed conversation. As if on cue they all nodded to confirm Suzanne's account.

"Bloody hell," Vince said. "We've got to find her."

"How?" said Cat. "She could be anywhere."

"Did she take her clothes with her?" Vince asked Suzanne.

"I don't know." Suzanne hurried over to the bedside cabinet next to Shirley's empty bed and pulled it open. "Yes she did."

Vince was already pulling his mobile out of his pocket and pressing buttons with his fat thumb. He put the phone to his ear and after a moment he said, "Shirl, this is Vince. Listen, love, if you get this message give us a call. And . . . be careful."

With a frown he shoved the phone back into his pocket.

Suddenly Cat blinked. "Oh my God, I've just had a thought."

"What?" said Carlton.

Looking at Suzanne, Cat said, "Has anyone been in contact with the Children's ward to tell them what's happening? Or the Maternity Unit?"

Suzanne shrugged. "I've no idea."

Hurrying over to the wall-mounted phone, Cat said, "Well, someone should, don't you think? Before it's too late."

240

05:33 am

UNDERHILL'S NEWS HAD helped to focus a few minds – not least, Sister Parkhurst noted, that of the Chief Inspector himself. It was clear that the head of the Crisis Response Team had thought his highly trained troops, with their body armour and high-powered weapons, impervious to injury. And so, when he discovered that three of his own men were among the casualties of a battle in which one of the hospital's doctors had been gunned down in front of dozens of traumatized witnesses, he had been shocked to the core.

So shocked, in fact, that it had loosened his tongue. Whereas before he had been circumspect, now he seemed positively garrulous. Sister Parkhurst could only suppose that the situation had deteriorated more rapidly than Underhill had expected, leading him to the decision that the only way they were going to survive this crisis was by sharing information.

To that end he had told them that in the wake of the battle the six people attacked by Tim Marshall had been hurriedly removed from the area and were now being detained by armed troops in a side room on the ground floor normally reserved for distraught relatives. Five of Marshall's victims, including the three SO22 officers, were suffering from scratches and bites and one – the receptionist Charmaine Jordan – was displaying symptoms of cognitive dysfunction consistent with sufferers in the early stages of the infection, after apparently ingesting blood that Marshall had spat into her face.

To Sister Parkhurst's surprise, Underhill had further disclosed that contact had now been lost with his five-strong squad of officers sent to search for the three infected patients who had broken out of the isolation ward earlier. More officers had now been dispatched to search for *them*, whereas still more were spreading out into other areas of the building, the intention being to restrict movement between the floors by posting guards at strategic junction points such as staircase entrances and lift doors.

"You'll never cover them all, you know," Sister Parkhurst said. "This place is like a rabbit warren."

"Plus what will your men do if they're suddenly confronted by a horde of infected patients intent on spreading the infection?" asked Dr De Mendonca. "Shoot them down as they did Dr Marshall?"

Underhill looked flustered. "We must contain the threat as best we can, Dr De Mendonca."

"Whatever it takes?" De Mendonca said.

Before Underhill could respond, Sir William raised a hand.

"I believe we've already been down this avenue," he said. "Time is of the essence, so let's not rake over old ground. I think Dr Blackstock may have a solution of sorts?" He swept the raised hand in a flourish, offering Marcus the floor.

"Yes," Marcus said. "Thank you, Sir William." Quickly he repeated his suggestion that Underhill's men could be issued with tranquillizer guns. In truth he expected the Chief Inspector to raise objections – such weapons would be impossible to source; his men were not trained in their use, etc – but to his credit Underhill gave a curt nod.

"Not a bad idea. I'll look into it. Can't promise anything, but it's worth a try."

"Thank you," Marcus said. "Would it be possible to do that now, do you think? With the way things are going, every minute is vital."

Underhill, who had not sat down since re-entering the room, now stood almost to attention. "Leave it to me."

He marched towards the door. As he did so, Dr De Mendonca fixed his eyes on Déesharné. "Now Professor," he said. "In the light of this latest development, don't you think it's time you put aside—"

"*Shhhh*."

Everyone turned to look at Underhill, who was standing by the door with a finger to his lips, his head cocked towards the wood.

"Someone's coming," he hissed.

"Another one of your men?" suggested Rowbottom, but Underhill waved him to silence. They all sat still and listened.

The Chief Inspector was right. Slow, dragging footsteps were approaching along the corridor outside. It was clearly not a soldier. A patient, then, thought Sister Parkhurst hopefully, one who had difficulty walking, out for a little stroll.

She was about to suggest as much, but couldn't quite force out the words. Ridiculous though she'd feel if it turned out to be nothing but an old dear with swollen ankles, she couldn't deny the fact that she was scared. She'd seen the infected in action, she knew what they were capable of and how hard they were to subdue. The thought of being bitten or scratched, of becoming one of them . . . she clenched her hands to try to stop herself from trembling.

The footsteps stopped outside the door. Underhill quickly glanced back into the room, then slowly drew a revolver and stepped back from the door.

"Who's there?" he said sharply. "Speak up."

"Idiot," breathed Professor Déesharné.

Underhill darted a scowling look at him – and then with a crash the door flew open.

It was as if it had been hit with a battering ram. It flew back with a splintering of wood and smashed into the wall. Everyone leaped to their feet in unison. "Good God!" exclaimed Sir William in the same tone of contemptuous disapproval he might have used if he had witnessed some ghastly upstart plonking themselves casually in the Captain's chair at the golf club.

A girl stood in the corridor. A nurse, in fact. She was chubby with unkempt maroon hair and a huge dark stain down the right-hand side of her uniform as if a blood-bag had burst on her shoulder. Her round face was deathly pale and her eyes were glazed, unfocused. Her plump, dimpled legs were bruised and she had lost a shoe.

Her head moved left and right, her neck seeming to creak jerkily, as if it was a mechanism that kept sticking.

"Keep back, girl," Underhill warned as she stepped into the room. Without taking his eyes off her, he said, "Is she one of them?"

"Yes," said Marcus Blackstock quietly. "I suggest we get round the other side of the table, use it as cover."

"Sod that," said Rowbottom, who was standing to the left of Underhill, and bolted for the door.

The girl, overweight and moving slowly, as if injured, had now advanced four or five steps into the room. There was a sizeable gap between her and the open door – sizeable enough for Rowbottom to have reasonably expected to be able to duck around the back of her and be out into the corridor before she even knew what was happening.

However, as he reached the point where he was closest to her – which was still over an arm's length away – she suddenly burst into life. Belying her size and her apparent injuries, she

244

leaped almost nimbly to intercept him, her arm snapping out in the direction of his head.

Sister Parkhurst didn't even realize what had happened until Rowbottom was lying on the ground, screaming. She saw the pool of blood fanning out around his head and then, turning her attention to the girl – who she recognized as Amanda Lee, the nurse who had fled from, and been subsequently attacked by, Martin Balfour – she saw her stuffing Rowbottom's ear and a chunk of his hairy, bloody scalp into her mouth.

Next to her, Dr De Mendonca said, "Oh, God," in a weak, almost girlish voice, and sat down abruptly in his seat. Sir William let loose a bellowing exclamation of abhorrence, and Underhill responded by raising his pistol and pointing it at Amanda's head.

"Stand still!" he yelled at her. "Do not move another step!"

Amanda ignored him. Still chewing, and seemingly unconcerned by the gun pointing at her face, she took another step towards him, and another.

Underhill backed up until he could back up no longer, until the base of his spine was pressing against the edge of the table. As if sensing that he was trapped, the girl suddenly growled and hurled herself at him.

Leaning back across the table, Underhill pulled the trigger of his gun. The shot was deafening; it was as if the air itself had roared and snapped. Though she had been expecting it, Sister Parkhurst still flinched as if the bullet was coming for her. Blood flew up as the round hit the girl somewhere in the region of her throat, but it failed to halt her momentum.

She hit Underhill with the force of a shark or an alligator and smashed him backwards. He flipped up and on to the table, Amanda on top of him. Even as they slid across the table-top, Amanda's hands and teeth were clawing and snapping at him. The gun flew out of his hand and hit the wall before clattering to the floor.

245

Crouched on the other side of the table, everyone suddenly scattered, peeling away left and right as Underhill and his snarling assailant slid towards them. Amanda must have opened a major artery in Underhill's neck because blood was suddenly shooting into the air like the jet of a lawn sprinkler. It hit the wall and the ceiling and spattered on the table and chairs and the pale-grey carpet.

Sister Parkhurst's heart was beating so hard she could feel it throbbing in her head like a migraine. As she tried to get around the table and head towards the door, someone barged into her from behind. It was Dr De Mendonca, whose eyes were so wild with terror that he seemed not to even register that she was there. Despite his diminutive stature he shoved his way past her, his arm flying back and hitting her across the bridge of her nose. For a moment she saw black stars; she was falling. Then she felt hands grabbing her wrists and hauling her to her feet.

"Come on, Sister, stay with me," said a voice. It was Marcus Blackstock. She concentrated on getting her feet underneath her and blinking the black stars out of her eyes.

When her vision cleared, she glanced to her right and saw Amanda still lying on top of Underhill on the table, her face buried somewhere in the region of his neck. The girl's fat, bruised legs were drawn up over his, her blue nurse's uniform riding up just enough to expose a rear view of the crotch of her black panties. It was an almost sexual pose, though grotesquely so. The slurping sounds coming from her bobbing head made Sister Parkhurst feel sick.

Another glance revealed that she, Marcus Blackstock and Professor Déesharné were the only people left standing in the room. Déesharné was on the other side of the table, stooping almost casually to pick something up off the floor. When he straightened she saw that he had Underhill's revolver in his hand. Looking grim-faced and utterly focused, he pointed the gun at the head of the feeding nurse and pulled the trigger.

The shot spanked Sister Parkhurst's ears and made her fillings ache. Amanda's body slumped on top of Underhill's as the life went out of her. Even as the young nurse's body was wracked by a last few muscular spasms, Déesharné was raising the gun again. He stepped forward, adjusting the angle, and then with no expression whatsoever he put a second bullet through the head of Chief Inspector Underhill.

05:37 am

AS THEY WAITED for the lift, Carlton wondered what the fuck he was doing. He shoulda just cut and run instead of hanging out with Florence Nightingale and Mr Fucking Goatee. If his crew could see him now they'd think he was fucking pussy. He owed these people nothin'. The nurse was pretty and she'd treated him nice and stitched him together, but he'd already saved her life, innit? He'd merked Jermaine to stop him tearing her guts out, and he'd popped that other fucker right through the eye too.

Yet here he was, all set to check up on a bunch of tinies he didn't even know or care about. This place was turning into Zombie Central and instead of looking for a way out, he and his "team", as Cat had called it, were going in deeper. It was fucked up, but Cat had said she had a "duty of care" she couldn't ignore. She'd called the tinies' ward and then the baby ward or whatever, and when no one answered she'd made up her mind she had to go there, said she had to warn them to keep out of sight until the five-oh put the zombies down.

Thing is, if she'd tole him he *had* to come with her, Carlton would've been out of there. But she didn't. She tole him he *didn't* have to come, that if he decided to go it alone she wouldn't think badly of him. Reverse psychology, innit? Carlton knew all about that. His Mum had always said he had a good heart and a good brain to go with it. She'd kept on saying he had a good heart even when he got into serious shit. Carlton had tole her to shut up a hundred times, but she never did. And if she could see him now, he knew she'd be saying it all over again: *See! I tole you! You got a good heart, boy! A good heart!*

He grimaced as if she was standing right next to him and stole a glance at the lift indicator. It was stuck on floor 6. It had been stuck on floor 6 since they'd got here.

"This lift's fucked, man," he said.

Cat followed his gaze. "Hmm. It does seem to have stalled. Maybe we should use the stairs."

"Bit risky," said Vince, glancing at the double doors leading on to the staircase, which were further down the corridor to their right. "I mean, I know it's always a hairy moment when the lift doors open, but at least in the lift you can guarantee you won't meet the infected en route."

Cat looked from the lift doors to the stairs. "So what do you think, guys? Should we—"

"Aye aye," Vince suddenly said, and nodded over her shoulder. "Looks like we might have a police escort."

Cat turned and Carlton glanced to his left. At the far end of the long corridor, beyond the main ward and various treatment rooms and offices, was a T-junction where the corridor divided left and right. From beyond that junction had appeared a couple of SO22 officers padded out in black riot gear. Though still some way off, the officers were now walking towards them.

Carlton clenched the chair leg he was holding. He didn't like the five-oh, they made him nervous. And these SO22 fuckers were meaner than most.

As if reading his thoughts, Vince said, "P'rhaps we ought to put our weapons down before they decide we're a threat and shoot us."

Warily Cat said, "Hang on. There's something not right about them."

Almost unconsciously Carlton took a few cautious steps towards the approaching officers, trying to see them more clearly. From a distance they looked bedraggled, ragged around the edges, as if they'd been in a battle. He couldn't make out details, however, not at first anyway. All he could see was that one of them was not wearing a helmet and that they were walking with their arms hanging by their sides, as if somewhere along the way they'd lost their weapons. From behind him, further back than he'd expected, he heard Vince say cautiously, "Anyone else think that p'rhaps we ought to make ourselves scarce?"

Carlton half-raised his left hand, the one that wasn't clutching the chair leg. "Yeah, man, jus' a minute."

As if responding to his voice, the SO22 officers broke into a shambling run.

It was almost as if they knew they couldn't conceal their true natures any longer. Because as soon as they started running Carlton saw what was wrong with them. The guy with no helmet had deep scratch marks, leaking blood, down the right side of his head as if he'd been clawed by a lion. And the other guy, who Carlton had thought was clenching his left fist, wasn't clenching it at all. It just looked that way because he was missing all the fingers on his hand.

"Zombies!" he shouted, and turned to run. Cat was still standing by the lift, shoulders hunched and eyes wide, as if frozen. Vince was some metres beyond her, already at the door that led out on to the staircase, reaching out to tug it open. He wrapped his meaty fingers around the metal handle, then half-turned.

"Come on, you two!"

The words were barely out of his mouth when the door burst open, smashing into him. Taken by surprise, he was knocked backwards, blood seeping from an already swelling wound on his forehead. He tottered a few steps on his heels and then, blinking dazedly, fell on to his back, his momentum flipping his legs into the air and causing him to bump his head on the vinyl floor.

Before either Cat or Carlton could respond, bodies were spilling through the door into the corridor, cutting off their route to their fallen colleague. Cat took one look at them and her face filled with horror.

"Oh no!" she said, her voice hoarse and screechy. She began jabbing frantically at the call button on the lift, as if hoping that sheer desperation could get it to respond.

Not fucking again, Carlton thought, looking at Samantha Mellor in her once sexy, now blood-spattered, white nurse's uniform. Behind Samantha, equally blood-spattered, was Tammy Ollerenshaw, her face and curly hair caked in gore. At the rear of the group, his left eye nothing but a wet, empty socket and his neck wound an oozing, black-green mass of putrescence, was Martin Balfour. All three zombies, their clown mouths dripping red and their hands gloved in blood and chunks of meat, stank like an abattoir on a hot day.

Carlton's Mum had been right. Try as he might to deny it, he did have a good brain. Looking quickly left and right, he now used it to assess their chances of survival. With zombies approaching from both sides and Vince out of reach, he knew that this was not the time to be reckless or heroic. If Vince could recover in time – and he was already scrambling to his feet – he had a possible escape route behind him, which meant that Carlton's priority was to get him and Cat out of harm's way. Glancing behind him he confirmed what he'd already registered. A little further up the corridor was a disabled toilet. It was maybe fifteen metres away, with the SO22 guys another thirty metres beyond that. Knowing they had only a couple of seconds' grace, he grabbed Cat's wrist.

"Come on!"

If she had resisted or questioned him their fractional advantage would have been lost. But she didn't. Showing complete trust, she ran with him across to the toilet door. Even though the SO22 guys were bearing down on them, she stood back so as not to crowd him as he yanked the door open. As soon as the gap was wide enough she darted inside. A split-second later he was inside too, pulling the door closed behind him and slamming the lock into place.

"What now?" she said, looking around.

Immediately something heavy thudded against the door from the other side. Cat gave a little scream – she couldn't help it – and jumped back as the door shuddered in its frame.

Carlton was already crossing to the sinks. "Check the window, see if there's a way out through there."

There was a small window on the back wall above the toilet that looked as though even a child would have trouble squeezing through. Crossing to it, Cat flipped the toilet lid down, jumped up on to it and tried the central handle, pressing the lock in the middle and flipping it clockwise.

If it had been locked it wouldn't have moved, but it wasn't locked and she was able to turn it and push the window open. After maybe six inches, though, it was halted by some sort of safety mechanism that had been built into the frame. Clearly this was a window designed for ventilation and nothing else.

"No good," she said, just as something hit the door with another shuddering crash. The door was made of thick wood and the lock was a hefty steel clasp affixed to a central locking system that could be opened from the outside if a patient shut themselves in here and got into difficulties. It should have been impervious to human assault, but the wood made a splintering crack around the lock as if it had been kicked by a horse.

"Shit," Cat hissed, her hands flying to her mouth. "Carlton, they're going to get in! We're trapped!"

Carlton was savagely kicking the porcelain sink attached to the wall as if he needed something to vent his anger on. Between kicks he gasped, "They'd've got us anyway. I've just give us a few more minutes, innit? There weren't too many options."

Cat backed against the wall, clasping her chair leg in both hands, eyes fixed on the door. "Oh God," she moaned, "I'm going to die in a toilet."

Carlton booted the sink again, concentrating on the back edge where it was fixed to the wall.

All of a sudden, with a tearing sound, it came free, a wide seam opening between sink and wall, pipes groaning under the strain.

"What are you doing?" she said, raising her voice above another splintering assault on the door. "Looking for a secret passage into Narnia?"

Ignoring her, he kept kicking at the sink, sweat standing out on his forehead and his face creasing against the jolts of pain that were lancing through his side with each kick.

Suddenly there was an even greater tearing sound and the sink fell forward, shattering into several pieces on the floor. Immediately Carlton thrust his chair leg into Cat's free hand, then darted forward and picked up a heavy, jagged-edged chunk of porcelain.

"Brilliant. Now we can't even wash our hands," Cat joked, though there was a sick, terrified look on her face.

The door crashed open. Cat screamed, expecting the infected to flood in and overwhelm them. However, only one of them entered the room, staggering slightly. It was the SO22 officer with the clawed face, the one who wasn't wearing his helmet.

Though she was terrified, Cat could see that the man, who was younger than she'd been expecting, had been handsome once. Now the right side of his tanned, strong-jawed face was hanging in bloody strips, and already the tell-tale signs of *necrotizing fasciitis* was turning the wounds putrid and blackening the flesh around them. His pale-blue eyes were like lumps of ice, the pupils so tiny they were almost indistinguishable. As soon as he stepped into the room, he uttered a groaning, gurgling sound like someone trying to speak with no tongue as he made a beeline for them.

Carlton had already raised the large piece of shattered porcelain above his head. Now he stepped forwards and smashed it into the SO22 guy's face. There was a crunch and a shocking spatter of blood and the man staggered backwards. Only a couple of steps, though. Unfazed by the fact that his nose was now splattered across his face and his bottom lip had been split open so that the skin had parted in a V, he immediately regained his balance and came at them again.

Carlton hit him once more, bringing the heavy chunk of porcelain down on top of his head this time. Though her entire body felt as though it was thrumming with terror and revulsion, Cat stepped forwards and whacked him upside the head with one chair leg and then the other.

The man stumbled, half-slipping in his own blood, remaining upright only because his back thumped against the wall and prevented him from crumpling. He was slumped over, though, his legs out in front of him in an almost-sitting position, his hands clawing at the air. The front of his skull had caved in and was an awful shape, like a piñata that had been battered with a stick, but hadn't yet shattered. The piece of porcelain that Carlton was even now raising above his head again was covered with blood and hair and splattery chunks of flesh and bone.

Eyes narrowed and lips pressed into a grim line, Carlton brought the chunk of porcelain down again. It buried itself in the man's skull, a cone of blood and brains squirting up and adhering to the white-tiled wall. Despite his hip, Carlton jumped nimbly aside as the man slid all the way down the wall, his legs shooting out in front of him. His clawing hands fell to his sides, hitting the floor with a wet slap. His fingers twitched a couple more times, then became still.

Carlton smashed the lump of porcelain down on the man's head one more time, then let go of it. Immediately he turned away, staggered over to the toilet and threw up. He flushed the mess away, waited until the cistern had filled, then flushed the toilet again, sticking his trembling hands into the toilet bowl and washing them under the gushing water, before scooping out a double handful and splashing it on to his face. He repeated this procedure once more, then turned to the toilet roll on the wall. Yanking off several yards of paper, he balled it up and dried his face.

Meanwhile, Cat, a chair leg in each hand, stepped carefully over the outstretched legs of the dead SO22 man and peered out of the open toilet door into the corridor. There was no sign of anyone out there, and no sign of blood on the floor either, aside from the few spots that had dripped from the cut on Vince's head where the door had hit him and the meagre trail that the infected SO22 officer with the severed fingers had left.

She listened for a moment, but heard nothing – no sounds of clattery pursuit, no screams of pain or desperation. She knew that at the far end of the corridor beyond the main staircase was a service lift and an emergency exit door that led out on to another narrow staircase. She guessed that Vince must have taken that route, and judging by the fact that the rest of the infected were nowhere to be seen, she guessed that they must have gone after him.

Turning around she saw Carlton dropping the wad of wet paper into the toilet bowl. He looked at her, his eyes a little wild, shreds of white paper sticking to his dark skin.

"You okay?" she asked gently.

He hesitated for a second, then gave a curt nod.

"Want me to check the wound?" She nodded at his hip.

"Nah, it's cool," he said gruffly, moving forwards and taking the chair leg that she held out to him. He glanced down at the body of the SO22 officer, then took a deep breath and stepped over the corpse's outstretched legs.

"Merked a five-oh," he muttered with a faint kind of wonder in his voice, and shook his head. "Now I's really fucked."

05:42 am

THE A&E ADMISSIONS area was in chaos.

Marcus Blackstock and Sister Parkhurst heard it before they saw it. They had been aware of a distant commotion as they clattered down the stairs after fleeing the aborted meeting, but as soon as they reached the landing on the ground floor and Marcus pushed open the door leading into the main body of the hospital, it hit them in a blast of sound.

Shouts, screams, the crash of falling equipment. And then, as though their appearance had prompted it, the flat, sharp crack of automatic gunfire – first one round, and then several more.

A couple of minutes earlier, in the corridor outside the conference room, they had made the mutual, albeit breathless, decision to return to work, resume their duties, because . . . well, because it simply *felt* like the right thing to do. Although they hadn't discussed the matter in detail, Sister Parkhurst knew that Marcus' reasons for not locking himself in a storeroom until all this was over would be pretty much the same as hers. He was a dedicated and selfless doctor, who she knew felt a huge responsibility for the welfare of those in his care. And, like her, she knew that he would much rather be on the frontline, occupying his mind doing what he did best, than staying out of sight in the hope of saving his own skin.

Despite these noble aspirations, however, they looked at each other now with almost identical expressions not only of alarm and fear, but also resignation, almost inevitability.

"This is turning into a hell of a night," he muttered.

She couldn't quite bring herself to smile at the understatement. "What shall we do?"

He glanced towards the end of the corridor from beyond which the sounds were drifting. They could still hear people screaming, shots being fired. Taking a deep breath, he said, "Just carry on, I suppose. I have a feeling there are people out there who need our help."

She nodded. But then, even though she hadn't moved, he raised a hand as if to block her way.

"But let me go first. And let's not be reckless. We might have signed the oath, but we won't be much help to anyone with bullets in our heads."

He led the way to the end of the corridor, then turned right into the next corridor, the din from the Admissions area getting louder with each step. As they got closer to the square arch, he used the wall as cover, sidling along it like an escapee in an old prison movie. Sister Parkhurst followed him as he crept to the arch and peered around the corridor. She leaned forward, holding on to his arm for balance, so that she could see what was happening too.

It had been bad enough hearing what was going on, but to see it was far worse. Sister Parkhurst had witnessed many terrible and gruesome things in her time, but the scene in the Admissions area shocked her to the core.

It reminded her of one of Hieronymus Bosch's depictions of Hell. She saw troops attacking troops, civilians fighting civilians, troops and civilians fighting each other. She saw

bodies on the floor, some lying still, some twitching feebly, some writhing in agony. And she saw blood, lots of it, pooled on the floor, spattered up the walls, streaked across furniture and equipment.

Even from her restricted viewpoint, Sister Parkhurst could see that some of the casualties had appalling injuries – an old woman slumped against the snack machine with her arm torn or shot off; a child with no face who was nonetheless still screaming as she thrashed on the floor; an SO22 officer in riot gear who kept climbing expressionlessly to his feet only then to stumble and slip on the ropes of slick blue-red intestine spilling from a series of ragged bullet wounds in his stomach.

Despite the chaos it was immediately evident what had happened. The disparate infected within the hospital, whether by design or instinct, must have flocked together to launch an attack on the living. Although they were a pretty rag-tag bunch, composed of doctors, nurses, maintenance staff, security men, SO22 officers, patients and visitors, their sheer numbers appalled her. It was clear that the situation was now well beyond crisis point – that the infection had spread throughout the hospital and was *still* spreading, far more quickly than they could possibly contain.

Although the SO22 men – those that weren't infected – were armed, they were evidently having trouble getting on top of the situation. Shot in the arm or the stomach or even the chest, the infected just kept on coming. A leg-shot would put them down, although only temporarily. They had a remorseless hunger and determination and they felt no pain.

It was a nightmarish and impossible situation and, as she watched, Sister Parkhurst saw several soldiers – caught out by their target's refusal to go down – fall victim to the infected's clawing hands and gnashing teeth. And so it was with the patients too. Many of them were old or infirm or injured, and were therefore simply no match for their voracious attackers. Others *were* fighting back, but overall it was like watching the spread of a terrible virus enacted on a human scale, like watching diseased cells overwhelming and subsuming healthy ones.

Suddenly, sensing a presence behind her, she whirled around. She was expecting to see one of the infected reaching for her with gore-clogged fingers, and so was almost relieved when the new arrival turned out to be Professor Déesharné, Underhill's revolver still clutched in his hand.

"Professor Déesharné," she gasped, but he ignored her – indeed, he strode straight past her, and Marcus too, until he was standing directly under the arch, in full view of the combatants in the Admissions area.

One of the infected lurched towards him. Calmly, Déesharné raised the revolver and shot it through the forehead. It dropped immediately, dead before it hit the floor. Stepping over it, Déesharné yelled, "Aim for their heads, you idiots! Destroy their brains!"

He demonstrated by shooting another of the infected in the head. Sister Parkhurst recognized her as one of the three hen night girls who had accompanied their friend, Samantha Mellor, to the hospital. There was something pathetic and desperately sad about seeing the girl, in her sexy nurse's uniform, crumple and hit the floor like so much dead meat. Earlier that evening she had set out in good spirits to celebrate her friend's forthcoming wedding, and now she was gone, her life cut short, her vibrancy extinguished.

As if Déesharné had revealed some great truth, or given them permission to do something previously taboo, the SO22 officers began to respond.

Soon the infected were dropping all around the room, their skulls shattered and their brains pulverized by high-velocity bullets. The combination of the carnage and the din of gunfire was so overwhelming that Sister Parkhurst (probably for the first time since her big brother had forced her to watch a *Dracula* film when she was a little girl) squeezed her eyes tightly shut and pressed her hands over her ears. When she opened her eyes again minutes later the world seemed so over-bright and hyper-real that for a few seconds she felt dizzy, as if she might pass out.

"Are you all right?" Marcus asked gently, touching her on the arm.

She felt instantly foolish. She had a reputation for being tough. Thank goodness it was only Marcus who had seen her defences crumble.

"Absolutely fine," she said, trying to sound both bluff and ironic. She glanced towards the arch, where gunfire could still be heard, albeit sporadically. "Is it over?"

Marcus grimaced. "Almost. Though I wouldn't advise you to look."

She did look, though. Much as she was dreading it, she had to. What she saw was Déesharné and the soldiers moving among the fallen and picking off survivors, locating those who had been attacked by the infected, and would in time become infected themselves, and shooting them through their heads.

A thought popped into her mind before she could stop it: *plenty of specimens for analysis now.* Then, appalled at what she was seeing, she turned away.

"It's horrible," she breathed.

Marcus looked sickened, but he nodded. "Yes it is."

"We should try to stop it."

"I tried – half-heartedly, I admit, but when you were . . . blocking it all out, I attracted Déesharné's attention and asked him if this was really necessary." He smiled shakily, as though at his own foolishness. "He sneered at me. And he said . . ." his voice faltered.

"What? What did he say?"

"He said that ruthless times call for ruthless measures. And then he smiled, as if he was actually enjoying all this, enjoying

262

my disgust of it at any rate, and he said, 'I suggest that you get on with your work, Dr Blackstock, and leave me to get on with mine'."

05:50 am

GILL WAS CALLING to him.

Gerry didn't know how he knew, but he knew all the same. Ever since sneaking away from the Admissions area he'd been feeling strange. Odd thoughts had been coming into his head, memories that weren't really memories . . .

He "remembered" lying on the hard wooden boards of a cart, wracked with unbearable pain as it rattled through cobbled streets.

He "remembered" the groans and screams of the dying around him.

He "remembered" being crushed beneath the stinking weight of the dead, unable to move, suffocating, pleading for mercy.

He "remembered" the high whine of insects, thousands of them, their fat red bodies swirling in tornado-like clouds.

And he "remembered" the man too. The man called Thomas Moreby. He "remembered" his rich clothes, his powdered wig, his burning eyes, his compelling voice. Gerry was certain that he had never met this man before; was equally certain that Moreby had been around a long time before Gerry was even born. And yet he felt there was an intimacy between them, a sense almost that Moreby was a part of him.

Gerry imagined, as he walked through the hospital, that Moreby was whispering in his ear, or perhaps inside his head. Once or twice he even turned, expecting to see the man standing at his shoulder, but of course there was never anybody there.

Another memory that kept surfacing in Gerry's mind, a real and far more recent one, was that of Tim Marshall spitting blood at him. Gerry remembered the sensation of it speckling his face, stinging his eyes, the iron tang of it on his lips. He thought he'd wiped the blood off; he *remembered* wiping the blood off. Yet as he walked he kept thinking he could feel it again, the cold prickling of it on his face, and so he kept wiping a hand across his cheeks or his forehead, and every time he did so he looked at his fingers, expecting to see red on them.

But he never did. There *was* no blood. Not a trace. At first he would feel relieved about that, and then it would occur to him that perhaps the blood was *inside* him.

Blood of my blood, he thought, wondering what he meant by that. He tried to concentrate, to find a meaning, but the harder he did so the louder became the high-pitched whine of insects, trying to drown out his thoughts.

Gill, though. *She* was still there. *She* couldn't be drowned out. Somewhere, beneath the odd notions and memories that weren't really memories, she called out to him. She wanted him; she *needed* him. He could feel her hunger. And he was going to her. She was guiding his steps. Soon they would be reunited. And once they were together again they would be together, forever . . .

. . . *let no man put asunder* . . .

. . . *'til death us do part* . . .

He had taken the lift to the basement. When the doors opened he stepped out and began walking the corridors, moving unerringly, as though he walked this route every day. He came to the Mortuary, the door of which was open. As he approached it a figure shuffled out and into his path, an old woman wearing a long white gown – a shroud – her eyes a milky bluish-grey, her jaw hanging slackly in death. Though the old woman's face was as white as her shroud, Gerry saw that her feet were black and swollen where the congealing blood, no longer pumped by a beating heart, had collected. It didn't alarm Gerry that the woman was dead and still moving. It seemed . . . *natural*.

As she shuffled towards him, he halted. Though her face was blank he knew that she was aware of his presence. A couple of metres away from him she reached out with gnarled white fingers, groping for his face. Gerry could smell the faint, deathly odour drifting from her body, the stew of spoiling innards, but he didn't flinch. She touched his face, clumsily but gently, her blackening fingernails rasping on his stubble. Then, as though recognizing a kindred spirit, her arm dropped and she shuffled on. And Gerry moved on too. Towards Gill. Towards the only woman he had ever loved.

He walked down a number of corridors and opened a door on to a service tunnel. At the end of the tunnel was another lift, and he hurried towards it, feeling the tug of Gill's hunger now, feeling that she was close.

The lift clanked and rattled as it ascended. He moved from foot to foot, his hands clenching and unclenching, like an excited child. As soon as the lift stopped he moved towards the doors, pushing his fingers into the central seam, urging them to open. The instant it did he squeezed his bulk through the widening gap and hurried to the door at the far end of the corridor. The numbers that he needed to punch into the keypad outside the door were already running through his head: *1803, 1803* . . .

He punched in the numbers. The door made a soft clicking

266

as it unlocked. Gerry pushed it open and stepped inside.

And as he had known she would be, Gill was waiting for him.

Though she was surrounded by darkness, her body was bathed in a circle of candlelight. She was naked and beautiful. In her arms she gently cradled a two-headed baby, which was suckling at her breast. Welling up around its feeding mouth, however, was not milk but blood, which trickled between the two of them and formed a small pool on the floor. Despite this Gill looked utterly content, her eyes dewy with love. When Gerry entered the room she looked up at him and smiled.

"Darling," she said, her voice clogged, husky. At first he thought it was desire that made it so, but then he realized it was something else. As her smile widened, her lips stretching wide, he saw frantic movement between them. Then, with a high, buzzing whine, a swarm of insects, so startlingly red that it looked like a rising fountain of blood, poured from her mouth and formed a slowly rotating, tornado-like spiral above her head.

05:56 am

FOR A MOMENT there Vince had thought he was a goner. The double-whammy of being whacked in the forehead with the door and then banging his bonce on the floor as he'd fallen had very nearly KO'd him. For seconds that doubtless seemed longer than they were, the strip lights lining the ceiling of the corridor had swirled and spun as he lay on his back.

It was Luke who had pulled him back from the brink – or at least Vince's determination that he would not, under any circumstances, let down his son. Through sheer willpower he'd forced the strip lights above his head to stop spinning. Then he'd propped himself up on his elbows to check what was going on.

He was just in time to see the door of the disabled toilet close behind Cat and Carlton before one of the infected SO22 officers – or "zombies", as Carlton insisted on calling them – slammed into it. It was not that Vince wished his newfound friends any harm, but it dismayed him to see the other SO22 officer, the helmeted one with no fingers on his left hand, maintain his lurching course in Vince's direction.

Furthermore, the three other "zombies", the ones who had burst out of the door leading to the main stairway, were turning towards him now, having apparently decided that he was the more accessible target. They seemed a bit bewildered, as if hampered by an inability to make quick decisions, but Vince knew that once they homed in on him they'd be as single-minded as a school of ravenous sharks.

Which meant it was time to stop laying about and look lively. Levering himself up from his elbows to his clenched fists, he bent his knees and scrambled to his feet. Immediately he felt his head starting to swim, but he scowled it away, then turned and set off down the corridor.

His first steps were dodgy – he felt heavy and uncoordinated, as though he was drunk – but after a few metres he got into the rhythm of it, pistoning his arms and lengthening his stride.

His plan – though he didn't realize he had one until he saw the EMERGENCY EXIT sign above an arrow pointing off to the left at the end of the corridor – was to head not down to the ground floor, but back to the Staff Room, which was on the first floor, the level above the Admissions area, but two floors below where Vince was now. He had an idea that if he reached it he could barricade himself in, then climb or even jump out of a window.

He knew it was pointless trying the conventional exits, because they'd be guarded by SO22 troops, but he couldn't imagine that every metre of the building's exterior would be under scrutiny. Course, there might be patrols wandering about, but he'd just have to take potluck. He realized that as plans went, it wasn't particularly foolproof or well-conceived, but under the circumstances it was the best he could do.

Weren't zombies supposed to shuffle along like they had their legs in plaster? If so, he wished someone would tell *this* lot that. As he turned left at the end of the corridor he could hear them behind him, grunting and snarling as they jostled for position, their feet thumping the floor. They might not be all that coordinated, but they were bloody fast, especially when they had the scent of blood in their nostrils.

Vince could feel the adrenaline surging through him, the electric tingling of fear in his nerve ends. He hadn't felt like this since he'd been chased by a load of Chelsea skinheads through Leeds city centre when he was sixteen.

Halfway along this latest corridor, which was mercifully empty, another EMERGENCY EXIT sign was suspended below the ceiling, the arrow pointing to a set of fire doors whose upper panels had been glazed in reinforced glass. Vince reached them maybe ten metres in front of his pursuers and crashed through, moving so fast despite his bulk that he was across the short landing and halfway down the first narrow stone staircase before the door had even started swinging shut behind him.

Down he plunged, right hand skimming over the plastic-coated rail as a precaution against tripping and falling. He took the bottom three steps of the first flight in one leap and used his momentum to swing around the corridor on to the next.

As he did so, his pursuers spilled through the door above and hurled themselves down the stairs after him – literally in one case, as Martin Balfour, his empty eye socket bleeding a black, viscous substance, pitched forward like a diver from a diving board, his face smashing into the edge of a stone step with a sickening crunch and his momentum flipping his body completely up and over so that he ended up slamming down on his back.

Although he winced at the impact between Martin Balfour's face and the step, Vince couldn't help feeling an almost primal glee at the man's downfall. But then, as he reached the bottom of the stairs and rounded the second-floor landing, he saw to his horror that Balfour, his nose crushed and his shattered and dislodged lower jaw swinging in what now amounted to little more than a hammock of skin, was climbing to his feet on the landing above as though nothing had happened. Clearly the accident had smashed Balfour's ankle too, because he now lurched drunkenly as he walked, his foot turned inward at an odd angle.

Tearing his eyes away and continuing his descent, Vince didn't know what was the most horrible – the extent of the man's injuries or the fact that he appeared to feel no pain from them.

Maintaining his lead over his pursuers down the next flight of stairs and the one after that, Vince reached the first-floor landing. He burst through the fire door, hesitated for less than a second to get his bearings, then wheeled to his right. The sign above the right-hand turn ahead read WARDS 1–5/ ACCIDENT AND EMERGENCY. Vince knew that the Staff Room lay not far down that corridor on the left, almost opposite the lift doors.

He put on an extra spurt of speed in the hope of shaking off his pursuers by ducking down the right-hand turning before they emerged from the fire door behind him. However, it was not to be. He was still five metres shy of the turning when the fire door thumped open and the infected spilled out of it.

Reaching the turning, Vince grabbed the corner of the wall and swung himself into the right-angled corridor without slowing. When he saw what was ahead of him, he faltered. Twenty metres away, standing side-on in the middle of the corridor, was a corpulent middle-aged man in blue pyjamas. His feet were bare and a long plastic drip tube dangled out of the bottom of his pyjama top and trailed on the ground behind him. Vince was about to call out a warning, tell the man to get out of sight, when he slowly turned and Vince saw that the left side of his pyjama top was torn and saturated with blood.

Seeing Vince, the man snarled and jerked to life, marching down the corridor towards him.

"Fuck's sake," Vince muttered, looking around for a weapon. It was only now that it occurred to him he was no longer holding the chair leg, that he must have dropped it upstairs in the dazed few moments after the door had smashed into his face.

On his right, parked next to a door, was a tall, wheeled equipment trolley, on each of whose metal shelves were stacked various items of monitoring equipment. Though it looked heavy and cumbersome, it also looked as though it would do a lot of damage if it hit you at speed.

Darting forwards, Vince grabbed it and, with a roar of aggression, dragged it around in front of him. Then, pushing the trolley ahead of him, he began to run along the corridor.

The man, his teeth bared and his gaze fixed intently on Vince, seemed oblivious to the fact that there was a large, heavy object bearing down on him. He altered neither his speed nor his direction, but simply kept on coming, as though the trolley, its castors squealing, wasn't even there. Vince clenched his teeth as he and the man rapidly closed the distance between them. Then, when they were no more than five metres apart, Vince gave an almighty shove and let the trolley go. It smashed into the man and knocked him flying against the wall, then tipped over, crashing on top of him. The din was tremendous and Vince could only imagine what damage the trolley had done to the man's body. However, he didn't wait around to check, but took to his heels, jumping over the corner of the upended trolley, whose wheels were still spinning.

Glancing back he saw that his pursuers had now turned the corner into the corridor and were lurching after him, the slight delay having allowed them to close the gap to less than ten metres.

The door to the Staff Room was now only a few metres ahead on his left. Vince ran up to it, grabbed the handle and hauled it open. Jumping inside he pulled the door shut behind him, hoping that the infected were too stupid to remember how door handles worked.

Then he ran across to the nearest items of furniture – metal-framed chairs with orange plastic seat covers and low wooden tables strewn with newspapers, magazines and coffee mugs – and began to pick them up and hurl them towards the door, the chairs first and then the tables. The items *on* the tables slid to the floor, some of the mugs breaking and tea and coffee dregs spilling over the carpet tiles.

There was no finesse involved in this, no strategy, no time to think about creating the most effective barrier. Vince's aim was simply to buy himself a little time by placing obstacles between him and his pursuers.

That done – though still upending chairs and tables in his wake – he crossed the room to the little kitchenette. Above the sink were two large windows, one of which was open a few inches to let in some air. As he scrambled on to the metal draining board, knocking aside yet more mugs, which fell to the floor and smashed, there was a crash behind him and the door flew back on its hinges as though it had been blown open with dynamite.

"Give me a fucking break!" Vince snarled as the infected tumbled into the room, almost clawing each other aside in their eagerness to get at him. The sexy nurse, who really wasn't so sexy any more, tripped over one of the upended chairs and went sprawling. Martin Balfour, his one good eye peering out from a face that was a shattered red ruin, trampled over her as if he didn't even know she was there, lurching lopsidedly on his broken ankle. The other two, the real nurse with the curly, blood-clotted hair and the SO22 guy with the missing fingers, forged ahead through the tangle of tables and chairs as though wading into an oncoming tide.

Although Vince's obstacle course was slowing them down, it wasn't by much; he had bought himself no more than three or four extra seconds. It was tough turning his back on the infected, but he knew that if he had any chance of getting out of this he had to concentrate, assess his options.

Not that there were many options *to* assess. Pushing open the window that was already ajar, he realized that he was higher up than he had thought. This might be the first floor, but there was a whole other floor below this one, which meant that he was faced with a drop of around ten metres, maybe more. At least directly beneath him, between the building and a concrete walkway that traversed the outside of the hospital, was a foliage border mostly comprising bushes and small trees.

The briefest of glances informed him that there were no SO22 officers in sight, no military patrols that would most likely shoot first and ask questions later if they saw him. But even if there had been, Vince would have gone for it. Better to be dead, he thought, than infected.

Then there was no more time to think. He could tell from the sounds behind him that the infected, chairs and tables clattering and squealing in front of them, were almost upon him. Sitting on the ledge, he swung his legs out in front of him and took one more glance at the ground, horribly far below. Then he shouted, *"Fuck!"* – and jumped.

06:03 am

"WHY'S IT SO fucking quiet?" Carlton asked.

Cat glanced at him. Carlton was jittery and his eyes looked
. . . the only word that sprang to her mind was *haunted*. But
she supposed that for a seventeen-year-old kid, who'd been
stabbed in the hip and who had battered to death at least two
people tonight – one of them a police officer and one of them
his friend – he was holding up pretty well.

"Government cutbacks," she said and answered his scowl
with a smile to show she was only half-joking. "Well, it *is*
true we're horribly understaffed. But I think the real reason
is that people have got wind of what's happening and are
lying low."

"Who you think infected they soljas then?" he asked.

"The patients who escaped from the isolation ward?" she
suggested. "Or the people *they* infected. Isn't that the obvious
explanation?"

He slid her a shrewd, sidelong glance. "Obvious or just best
case scenario?"

"What do you mean?"

He sighed. "They zombies prob'ly infected loads by now.

275

They infect guys, who infect other guys, and on like that. What if the whole fucking building is fucking zombieland?"

She shook her head. "We'd know if it had spread *that* far, wouldn't we? The infected would be wandering about all over the place." She tried to look convinced by her argument. "But they're not. Which suggests to me that the SO22 guys have wiped them out or rounded them up, and that in general people have battened down the hatches, that we're just dealing with isolated cases." She paused a moment, then added, "Maybe the infected only attack you when they can see you – like with those soldiers, and with us and Vince a while ago. So hopefully, if people keep out of sight, they'll be safe."

Morosely he said, "If that true then what the fuck *we* doin'?"

Since their encounter with the infected on floor three she had been asking that same question. She was getting married in six weeks, for God's sake! No one could possibly have blamed her if she'd wanted to keep a low profile. But she said firmly, "We're checking up on those more vulnerable than ourselves. I'd never be able to live with myself if I didn't at least warn them what was coming."

He shook his head. "You is too fucking good, y'know that? Like a fucking guardian angel or whatever."

She smiled. "So what does that make you? An angel-in-waiting?"

He pulled a face. "Allow it. I's just with you 'cos you know the way out, innit?"

"Oh, is that it?" she said, still smiling.

Maternity was on floor five, the Children's ward on the floor above. Emerging from the disabled toilet after killing the infected SO22 officer, they had moved across to the door leading on to the stairwell, listened for a moment, then cautiously pulled it open. Hearing nothing, they had crept up the stairs, wielding their chair legs like cavemen on a buffalo hunt. There had been a couple of weird echoes floating either up or down the stairs, which had made them freeze, their heads cocked to listen, but on neither occasion had they been able to identify the sounds or tell where they had come from.

Now they were standing beside the door to floor five, Carlton with one hand on the handle. Cat had already told him that Maternity was a sealed unit, accessible only via a keypad for staff and a door buzzer for visitors. Gone were the days when anyone could stroll into a Maternity ward clutching a bunch of flowers for a new mother. Which could only be a good thing, because it made it less likely that the infected would have found a way in.

"Set?" he said, glancing back at her.

She nodded. "Go for it."

He clenched his teeth, then pushed the door open. His eyes darted this way and that as an ever-expanding slice of the corridor beyond was revealed.

But Cat was right. This part of the corridor, which actually served as little more than a vestibule to the Maternity Unit, was quiet and deserted. The door leading into the Unit itself was ten metres to their right. Slipping in front of Carlton, Cat crossed to it and peered through the reinforced glass panel in the upper portion of the door.

All she could make out was a sort of ante-room containing a row of padded seats against the wall and an empty corner desk on which sat a vase of flowers, a *Buffy the Vampire Slayer* mug and a computer surrounded by stacks of paperwork. On the right-hand wall was a big cork board on which were pinned dozens of thank you cards and baby photos. Opposite that was the entrance to a corridor that Cat knew led to the birthing rooms, the postnatal wards, the incubator section and various offices, toilets and storerooms.

"No one around," Carlton muttered, peering over her shoulder.

"Maybe they're all keeping out of sight."

She pushed her thumb down on the buzzer above the keypad beside the door. When she received no response, she thought for a moment, then lowered her hand, extending a finger towards the keypad.

Before she could punch in the first digit, Carlton grabbed her wrist. She looked at him in surprise.

"Just 'coz it look quiet, don't think everythin's okay," he said.

She nodded her understanding and he released her wrist. Quickly she punched in the four-digit code and leaned her weight against the door.

Though they had hoped to enter quietly, the door made a hearty *clunk* as it opened. They paused on the threshold. From down the corridor to their left they heard the rustle of movement. Over the past hour or so, Cat had almost got used to Carlton's and her own battle-worn state, but now, looking at her companion with his blood-spattered clothes and wild eyes, his chair leg clutched in his hand, she grimaced.

"We're going to scare them to death," she said.

He raised his eyebrows. "This was *your* idea."

"I know, I know. Let's just . . . try to look as friendly as we can."

Closing the door behind them, they padded across the room, heading for the corridor entrance on their left. Cat felt an urge to quietly call out a greeting, but remembering Carlton's warning she stayed silent. Planting what she hoped was a warm smile on her face, she walked up to the opening and peered around the corner.

She froze, the smile dying on her lips.

The walls and floor of the corridor were smeared and spattered with blood. Some of it was in the form of handprints as though children had been running riot with red paint. The only person Cat could see in the corridor was a dark-haired woman in a pale-blue hospital gown who had her back to

them. The woman's feet were bare and her head was tipped to one side as if she was listening. Blood gloved her hands and dripped from her dangling fingers.

Shocked, Cat stepped back, bumping into Carlton. Taken by surprise he grunted as the pain in his hip flared. It was only a small sound, but it was enough.

The woman in the corridor seemed to tense, then turned slowly towards them. As she did so Cat couldn't help but gasp. The woman was heavily pregnant and the front of her gown, from her waist to her thighs, was stained a deep, dark red. Worse, though, was that dangling upside-down between her legs, its skin purple-blue, its arms above its head, was a new-born baby.

"Shit," Carlton said, his voice a groan of revulsion. The woman, who must have been infected at the very moment of giving birth, opened her mouth and hissed. Suddenly, as though the sound was some kind of signal, doors along the corridor began to open and more of the infected started to emerge – nurses and doctors, heavily-pregnant women and their expectant partners.

"We're too late," Cat groaned, backing away. "We're already too late."

Jostling for position, the infected – many of them blood-stained, many with bites or scratches or missing chunks of their bodies – began to turn towards them. Then, like an approaching wave made of teeth and claws and glaring eyes, they surged forward.

"Run!" Carlton yelled, grabbing Cat's wrist again and wrenching her arm so hard that she was almost yanked off her feet. As one, they wheeled towards the exit door.

As one, they ran.

06:15 am

IT WAS PAIN that pulled Vince down into black, spinning unconsciousness, and pain that brought him back up again.

Once he'd started falling he'd been alarmed at how abruptly gravity took over. As when he'd jumped off walls as a kid, pretending to be a superhero, he'd expected to retain some modicum of control. He hoped he'd land and roll like a parachutist, the impact travelling up through his body like a wave of energy, dispersing as it went.

But he was three times heavier now than he'd been when he was ten, and the instant he began to fall it was as if a great invisible hand had closed around his ankles and yanked him down. The ground hurtled towards him at an alarming rate and before he could even *begin* to prepare himself, he was slamming into it feet first.

He heard a sharp crack an instant before unbelievable agony tore up through his body. Like an internal explosion, it seemed to shred everything in its path – his ability to move, his ability to make a sound, his ability to think.

Then it swept through his head, enveloping his brain in a great black mushroom cloud and he passed out.

For however long he was under – seconds? Minutes? Hours? – he was gone, as good as dead: no sensations, no dreams, no nothing. Then abruptly, like a switch had been turned on, he was back again, and it was like being born anew, in agony and terror, everything harsh and jagged, everything inside him pulsing and racing.

Painpainpain. It crammed every molecule of him, it filled him both physically and mentally, it possessed him body and soul. He couldn't move because of it, he couldn't think around it. It was absolute and it was unendurable and it was endless.

He lay there, terrified of dying and at the same time wishing he *would* die. The pain swamped his ability to remember where he was, what had happened, where he was supposed to be heading.

And then . . . a stray thought rose in his mind, like an air bubble rising to the surface of a fetid, black pool. The thought, a single word, rose and burst with a tiny, almost insignificant pop . . .

Luke.

And then suddenly, as though that one tiny bubble was a forerunner, a pioneer, other bubbles began to rise, one after the other, each one a memory – *pop! pop! pop!*

Luke. His son. He was going to see his son. He'd fallen – no, jumped. Yes. He'd jumped to escape the infected. He'd hit the ground and he'd . . . he'd . . . The memory caused a fresh wave of pain to sweep through him. He felt his head spinning, unconsciousness tugging at him again. He clenched his teeth, battled against it. *What* had he done? Did he dare to look?

Infinitesimally slowly, each tiny movement bringing fresh, jagged waves of pain, he levered himself up on to his elbows. The world tilted, righted itself. He was lying among bushes and small trees, his body concealed by foliage. Distantly he heard screams, a brief firecracker-like burst of gunfire. He was on his back. He raised his head, looked down the length of his body.

It took every ounce of willpower not to pass out again.

His right leg was broken. Quite spectacularly broken. The limb below his shin was bent outwards at a grotesque angle and a jagged spike of bone was sticking out through the torn material of his trousers, which were drenched in blood.

His left leg looked okay and when he tried to move his ankle he saw his booted foot twitch in response. So at least that one seemed fine, which meant that if he could get help he might be able to move about with the aid of crutches.

Not that that seemed even remotely possible at the moment. Just raising his head had almost made him pass out again. And even if he *did* somehow manage to stand, how the hell would he get away if more of the infected turned up?

He slumped back, the rich, mulchy smell of soil filling his nostrils. As his best mate Danny was fond of saying, "Son, you are F-U-K-T, fucked." Wincing and sweating and shuddering with pain, he prised his mobile out of his pocket and brought up the Contacts menu. The effort caused his head to swim. He blinked at the screen, trying to focus, then thumbed a button.

The ringing of the telephone at the other end sounded impossibly distant. It rang and rang, the idiot chirrup of an insect in his head. When a voice finally said, "Hello?" it sounded tinny, and as groggy as Vince himself was now starting again to feel. He felt *so* groggy, in fact, that he couldn't for the life of him now remember who he had called.

"Who's this?" he said.

The voice at the other end was wary. "This is Diane Masterton. Who's that?" Then all at once she seemed to realize. "Vince, is it you?"

"Diane?" All at once his voice didn't seem to work properly. It sounded slurred, indistinct; his thoughts too felt as though they were sinking into sludge.

Summoning up every ounce of willpower he said, "Need help. Get help."

She fired two questions at him in quick succession. "Do you know what time it is?" And then: "Are you *drunk*?"

"No," he mumbled, hoping she could hear what he was saying. "Not drunk. Hurt." He tried to articulate what had happened to him, but the words wouldn't come. He might as well have tried pulling handfuls of snakes out of sacks and tying them into bows.

Then she was talking again, filling his head with sounds that were like thorns, jagged and sharp and unpleasant. He couldn't grasp the meaning of them, though he got the gist: she wasn't happy. She wasn't happy about the call and she wasn't happy about the prospect of handing her son over to him later that day.

"Luke," he said, clinging to the driftwood of his son's name. "Tell Luke I love him, tell him I'll see him soon, tell him . . ."

Whether he spoke the words or just thought them he wasn't sure. Not that it really mattered. She had already rung off.

06:31 am

"WAIT . . . CARLTON, PLEASE . . ."

Once they were safely back in the corridor and the door to the Maternity Unit had closed behind them, Cat stopped and slumped over, her hands on her knees.

Carlton, who had moved a few paces ahead, stopped and turned, throwing a nervous glance at the door, through the glass of which he could see the infected milling, glaring out at them, could see the wood shuddering as the first of them thumped their hands against it.

"No time to wait," he said. "They fuckers be out in a minute. If they don't work out how to open that door, they just smash it down."

"I know," gasped Cat. "It's just . . ." she drew in a sharp breath that sounded like a sob ". . . it's horrible. All those mothers and their babies . . ."

Carlton hesitated, then stepped up and put his arm around her. "Yeah, I know," he said gruffly, "it's fucked up. But we gotta go, Cat. We don't, we be like them. Believe it."

She sniffed, nodded, and then, still clutching their chair legs, they moved towards the door leading to the stairwell.

They were three or four metres from it when it opened and a bare-footed boy wearing *SpongeBob SquarePants* pyjamas stepped into the corridor in front of them.

He was maybe nine years old and had clearly been suffering from some form of cancer. He was pale and thin and chemotherapy had caused his hair and eyebrows to fall out. A strip of flesh had been torn from his scalp and he had a number of small bite wounds, presumably made by a smaller child, on his left cheek and chin. Blood from the wounds had run down his neck and soaked into the collar of his pyjamas.

A look of weary distress crossed Carlton's face. "Ah, fuck, man," he moaned, "you gotta be fuckin' kiddin' me."

Cat knew exactly what he was thinking. The boy's eyes had that familiar flat and hungry look, and as soon as he had seen Cat and Carlton his lips had curled back from his small white teeth. They both knew there would be no reasoning with him, no way he would let them pass unmolested. Which meant, abhorrent though it was, the only way they would get past him would be to put him down.

She glanced at Carlton. "You okay?"

He shook his head. "Nah, man."

The words were barely out of his mouth when, with a screech, the boy attacked.

Cat reacted instinctively. Stepping forward, she swung the chair leg and hit the kid as hard as she could in the side of the head. The sound of wood connecting with his skull made her think of a cricket bat impacting with a ball, as a batsman whacks it for six.

Blood sprayed out of the kid's mouth and he fell, twitching. His skull was dented where Cat had hit him, a sight that made her feel light-headed with horror at what she had become capable of. One thing she knew she *wasn't* capable of, however, was pressing home her advantage and finishing the boy off –

and neither, it seemed, was Carlton. Grabbing her free hand, he shouted, "Come on!"

They leaped over the sprawled body of the boy, Carlton reaching out and yanking open the door on to the stairwell. As soon as the gap was wide enough, Cat let go of his hand and slipped through ahead of him – then realized her mistake.

She should have guessed that the boy would not be alone. There were more children on the stairwell, both above and below her.

On the lower flight she could see an Asian boy of about seven with his arm in a cast and his torn pyjamas wet with blood where he had been bitten and scratched. On the upper were a girl of four or so with blonde pigtails and a nasogastric tube taped to her cheek, an older girl with dark hair, a bruised face and blood around her mouth, and a chubby boy of around twelve with a gauze eyepatch and a Batman dressing gown, whose pyjama legs were saturated with blood from the wounds on his stomach and mangled left thigh.

There were a couple of adults behind the children on the upper flight too – a nurse so soaked in blood that her shoes squelched with it, and a Polish man called Piotr who Cat knew worked in the Mortuary. She had only spoken to him once or twice, but he had struck her as a rather sweet and lonely guy.

As soon as she stepped on to the landing, all six of the infected turned her way and headed towards her. It was as if she was a powerful magnet and the infected were metal filings drawn towards her. Swinging the chair leg in front of her to repel attackers, Cat lurched backwards, almost into Carlton's arms.

He stepped up beside her and swung his own chair leg into the face of the nearest of the infected – the dark-haired girl who had leaped down the last four steps of the upper flight and come stumbling towards them. As Carlton's chair leg connected, her nose cracked and blood gushed down and into her open mouth.

The girl reeled away, colliding with the chubby boy who was lumbering in her wake. Cat and Carlton took advantage of the momentary confusion by scrambling back through the door into the corridor and pulling it shut behind them.

To their left, the boy with the SpongeBob pyjamas was sitting upright, his head swivelling to regard them, like a ventriloquist doll come to life. Beyond him the door to the Maternity Unit was cracking and bulging as the infected threw their combined weight against it.

"Fuck!" Carlton yelled, looking around wildly.

Cat pointed to their right. "This way! There's an emergency exit at the end of the corridor."

They began to run, but had taken no more than a few steps when there came a rapid series of ear-shattering bangs in the stairwell behind them. It sounded as if someone had thrown a lit match into a box full of fireworks and cranked the volume up to maximum.

Cat screamed, both she and Carlton bending double as they ran, as if they expected the ceiling to fall in on them. For one crazy second Cat thought of terrorists, thought the building was under attack. "What's happening?" she yelled above the din.

"Them solja boys, innit! They merking the zombies!" Carlton yelled back.

The door to the stairwell crashed open behind them. Cat glanced back to see the kid with the SpongeBob pyjamas clambering to his feet and several of the infected – the chubby boy, the nurse, the Asian boy and Piotr the Mortuary attendant – spilling into the corridor.

Suddenly Carlton grabbed her arm, yanking her sideways. "This way!"

Still running in a crouch, she almost fell, then righted herself. "What are you doing?"

"Saving your life!" he shouted, dragging her across to a door on the right of the corridor. Awkwardly, using the hand that was holding the club, he pushed the handle down, then threw his weight against the door, forcing it open. The room beyond was a medical storage cupboard, no more than two or three metres wide (most of which was taken up by shelving, which lined both walls with a narrow aisle between them) and five metres deep. Carlton dragged Cat inside and slammed the door behind them. Still clinging to the handle, he turned and whispered, "Don't say nothin'."

His eyes were wild and his forehead gleamed with sweat. In that moment he looked fervent, almost maniacal. She wanted to ask him why he had diverted them into a dead end, but the expression on his face encouraged her to stay silent. Not that she needed to ask her question as it turned out. A moment later she had her answer.

She heard the infected advancing along the corridor towards their hiding place. Crouching down, she drew in her shoulders, expecting the door to be wrenched open at any second. But it didn't happen. The infected were still – as far as she could tell – several metres away when she heard the stairwell door crash open again.

She had a momentary impression of heavy thudding footsteps and then that exploding firework din started up once more, drowning everything else out. It was even louder and more sustained this time; it sounded as if the very fabric of the building was being torn apart.

Cringing with shock, Cat tucked in her head and dropped the chair leg so she could press her hands over her ears. She half-expected the walls to start cracking around her, for the floor to split and tilt and tip her into an abyss of falling masonry.

The noise went on for so long that – despite having blocked her ears – she felt sure that her brain would eventually rupture with it. And even when the din did finally stop she wasn't entirely sure that it had, because her head remained filled with crashing, throbbing echoes that felt as if they might ricochet around her skull forever.

It wasn't until Carlton touched her arm that she eventually raised her head. She was almost surprised to find that they were still in the same place and that the room was still intact around them. Crouching in front of her, he said something, but although she saw his lips move she couldn't hear a word.

She pointed at one of her thrumming ears and shook her head, and said (though to her it sounded like a wordless rumble), "Sorry, I can't hear you."

He winced as though she'd spoken too loudly and tried again. *You* he mouthed, pointing at her; then he made a circle out of the thumb and forefinger of his right hand and deliberately mouthed *Okay?*

She nodded and pointed at her ears again. "Just deaf."

He nodded back. *Me too.*

As if by mutual agreement, they sat side by side, their backs to the door, waiting for the throbbing in their ears to subside. Cat rested her head against the wood. It was dim and cool in the storeroom. Probably for the first time tonight she realized how utterly exhausted she was.

She closed her eyes and immediately felt her mind swirling down towards sleep. The throbbing in her ears was like being enveloped within the beating of a giant heart. It was soporific, comforting, strangely womb-like.

"Hey."

She opened her eyes. Carlton was looking at her. Though his voice was a little muffled, she realized she could hear him.

"What?"

"You back, yeah?"

She frowned, puzzled. "I never went away."

He snorted, grinned. "Yeah, right. You was asleep, innit?"

"I was not!"

"You so was. You was even snoring."

She was going to deny it again and then she smiled. "Was I?"

"For real."

She shook her head. "I didn't even know I'd nodded off." He shifted position beside her and she noticed him wince. "How's the hip? A bit sore?"

He shrugged. "It's awright."

"You want me to check it for you?"

He looked reluctant, embarrassed even, but she nudged his arm gently with her elbow. "Come on," she said. "I am a nurse, you know. Might as well while we've got a moment."

He conceded with a shrug and gingerly pulled up his jacket and the hospital gown that he was still wearing underneath. She shuffled round on her knees so that she was facing him and examined the wound. Though a little blood had seeped out, the dressing was still in place.

As she carefully probed around the wound, checking with her fingers that there were no unnaturally swollen or tender areas, no potentially worrisome fluid build-ups, he said, "So how long you been a nurse?"

She shrugged. "Since I left school. Six years or so." She glanced at him. "What do *you* want to do?"

He shrugged. "Dunno. Go to college maybe."

"To study what?"

He looked embarrassed. "Somethin' useful."

"What do you call useful?"

He shrugged. "Electronics. Engineerin' maybe."

"Do you like building things?"

"I like *designin'* tings. Solvin' problems. Figurin' out how to make tings work."

She nodded approvingly. "You must be cleverer than me."

He made a cluck sound with his tongue against the back of his teeth. "Dunno 'bout that. You pretty smart."

She smiled and carefully pulled his gown and jacket back

over his wound. "Well, that seems to be fine – which is pretty surprising, considering what we've been through tonight."

He narrowed his eyes. "So you gettin' married?"

She nodded, drew a deep breath. "That's the plan."

"When?"

"Six weeks."

"What your boy called?"

She tried to answer, but a sudden stab of emotion caused her throat to close up. Swallowing, she tried again. "Ed. He's called Ed."

"He cool?" Carlton asked.

She nodded. "*I* think so."

He held up his hands. "Don't mean nothin' by this, but . . . he must be cool to be marryin' you. He a lucky guy."

"Thank you," she said quietly.

He shrugged, as if it was of no consequence, and tilted his head to emphasize the fact that he was listening. "Quiet out there now. I reckon they solja boys merked them zombies, innit?"

Slowly Cat rose to her feet, brushed dirt off her knees and picked up her chair leg.

"I guess we'd better go then."

He stood up too. He hesitated, as if debating whether to put his thoughts into words, then said, "Out there . . ."

"I know," she said, putting a hand on his arm. "It's not going to be pretty. But we'll be okay."

He nodded, drew a shuddering breath. "I know it. So where we goin' now? We gettin' out?"

"Yes," she said firmly and tightened her grip on her chair leg. "We're getting out."

06:47 am

WITH A SURGE of panic, Vince woke up.

He had the sense that he'd forgotten something vital – but what? Felt sure he should be somewhere – but where? For a second or two his desperate need to remember was all that occupied his mind . . . and then it was as though another layer of sleep had been ripped away, and suddenly the physical world crashed in again.

The pain. That was the first thing. The unendurable pain that he was having to endure nonetheless. He clenched his entire body, dug his fingers into the soft earth, as the pain rushed up through him, wave after awful wave. He screwed up his face, wanting to cry out, but the pain was so all-encompassing that it paralyzed his vocal cords, immobilized him like snake venom. He was aware of his surroundings only on some abstract level: the waving greenery around him, the brightening sky above, the dew soaked grass on which he lay, the damp chill of it seeping into his bones, making him shudder not only with agony but cold also.

Vince hadn't cried since he was . . . what? Ten? Eleven? Maybe the last time had been at his gran's funeral. She'd died two years after being beaten up by the junkie who'd forced his way into her home, having never fully recovered from her ordeal, since when Vince had always thought of her as a woman who had been in love with life, but who had ultimately had her heart, her spirit, broken by it.

So yes, maybe that had been the last time he'd cried. And maybe that had been the *first* time he'd realized that life could be cruel and unfair and sometimes unalterable. All of that came back to him now as despair washed over him and he shocked himself by beginning to weep. He felt a sense of shame as he did so – as the sobs wracked his body and the tears ran out of his eyes. He thought of what Shirley would say, what Diane would say, what *Luke* would say, if they could see him now.

But that didn't stop the tears. They ran down the sides of his face, dripped into the dewy grass and damp earth on which his body lay. Above him the dawn sky blurred. He had never felt so desolate. As he blubbed he whispered, "I'm sorry, Luke. I'm so sorry."

There was a rustling in the bushes somewhere to his left. Instantly Vince drew in a breath and held it, stemming the tears mid-flow. Although humiliation hadn't been able to stop them, it seemed that fear could. It was not because he was afraid of dying, that wasn't it. No, it was because he was afraid of becoming one of *them*. One of the infected. The infection was a terrible thing, an evil thing, and he would rather die than become another link in its chain, a vehicle for terror and destruction and death.

The rustling came closer. It was too haphazard, too localized, to be wind whispering through the foliage. Maybe it was a stray cat or dog – or even a hedgehog or fox. Even a SO22 guy in riot gear would be good right now.

Closer still. Whoever or whatever this was it must be almost upon him. He closed his eyes in the child-like belief that it would somehow protect him, prevent him from being seen. A shadow fell across his face, darkening the insides of his eyelids.

"Vince?"

The voice was a hoarse whisper, and so unexpected that his eyes popped open. A face loomed over him, hair hanging down on either side of it in sweaty coils like snakes or tentacles. The light from the paling sky threw the features into shadow for a moment, and then his eyes adjusted.

"Shirley?" His own voice was less than a croak. "Is it really you? Am I dreaming?"

Her lips curled upwards and she grunted a laugh, but she looked ill and exhausted – pasty skin, bloodless lips, hollow eyes. And there was something around her head, a jittering like static, like a million tiny scratches on old film.

"No," she said, "you're not dreaming. It *is* me." She dropped on to her knees beside him. "Was a bugger to find you."

"How did you even know I was here?" Vince croaked.

She gave him the look she always gave him in the ambulance when he said something she thought was stupid. "Phoned me, didn't you?"

"Did I?"

She shook her head pityingly. "What are you like? Don't you remember?"

"No."

Sighing again, she said, "Told me you'd jumped out of a window and were lying in a bush, said you'd bust yourself up pretty bad." She glanced down at his leg. "You weren't bloody joking, were you?"

He followed her gaze, then quickly glanced away. "It's not looking good, is it?"

"Do you want me to be honest or reassuring?"

He thought about it. "Reassuring."

"It's nothing but a flesh wound. You'll soon be right as rain." She put a hand on his cheek, bent over and kissed his forehead. As she did so, Vince heard a very faint but high-pitched buzzing sound. Where she had kissed him it prickled slightly, like an insect bite. He closed his eyes.

06:58 am

"HERE YOU ARE. I thought we'd lost you."

Marcus Blackstock looked up. He was sitting on a bed in one of the A&E treatment bays, the curtains pulled around him, cradling a plastic cup of black coffee from the machine in the corridor. He smiled wearily at Sister Parkhurst, who had poked her head through a gap in the curtains.

"No such luck."

"Slacking off, are we?" she teased.

He chuckled. "Taking a five-minute break. A *well-deserved* five-minute break, I might add. It's been quite a night."

"Mind if I join you? My feet are killing me."

"Be my guest."

There was plenty of room on the bed, but he shuffled along a little. When she sat down he held up his half-full cup. "Fancy a sip of noxious black sludge?"

She made an "ooh" face, as if he'd offered her a selection of the finest Belgian chocolates. "I'm sorely tempted, but I'm trying to give it up."

"Your loss," he said, raising the cup to his mouth and taking a sip. Then he shuddered. "Or perhaps not."

Since the battle in the Admissions area, the SO22 officers had set up an exclusion zone within the hospital. To protect patients and aid medical personnel in their effort to find a cure for the infection, this encompassed the Admissions area itself, the A&E treatment area and Professor Déesharné's R&D unit on the sixth floor. The exits and entrances to all of these areas were heavily guarded by officers who had orders to shoot dead any suspected sufferers of what (to Marcus' annoyance) was now widely and rapidly becoming known as the "Zombie Plague".

Additionally, several four-man units were currently and systematically patrolling the stairwells and hospital corridors in the immediate vicinity with the intention of putting down any further resistance. Marcus had tried once again to argue that the infected were victims who should be tranquillized, not destroyed like rabid animals, but after the death of Underhill and the heavy casualties sustained in the Admissions area battle, his protests had fallen on deaf ears.

His only victory had been a concession by the SO22 team's new acting commanding officer, a Chief Inspector Cook, that those sufferers currently sedated and under restraint were — for the time being at least — to be spared so that the hospital's medical team could continue to treat them in the hope of making a breakthrough. This amounted to two patients who had not been involved in the earlier breakout from the isolation ward: Staff Nurse Susan Jenkins and the woman who had bitten her in the first place, Anna Carstairs.

While Marcus had been arguing with the military, Sister Parkhurst (working around armed riot police, who had been stalking the corridors, poking their noses suspiciously into every nook and cranny) had been attempting to rally her shell-shocked troops. With the infection contained, at least for the time being, she had encouraged her depleted staff to get back to work attending to those patients in the Admissions area who had survived the earlier carnage. As well as dealing with a succession of gashes, sprains, dislocations and broken bones, she and her team had found themselves having to cope with, and treat, many patients suffering from the effects of shock and trauma.

There had been a great many tears shed over the past hour or so – and not all of them from the patients. It had been a trying time, both physically and emotionally, and Sister Parkhurst was exhausted.

"How did Susan's surgery go?" she asked. "Have you spoken to Mr Masters?"

Robert Masters was the on-call consultant whose surgical opinion had been sought on Susan Jenkins' worsening condition. Mr Masters had recommended, at the very least, a surgical debridement – the removal of dead tissue and other cellular debris from around the infected area. The last time Sister Parkhurst had seen Susan, she had been heavily sedated and on her way to theatre.

Marcus nodded. "Yes, about ten minutes ago. Susan's out and recovering in ICU. She's still unconscious, of course."

"And?" said Sister Parkhurst, placing her hands together in her lap as though mentally bracing herself. "I can tell from your tone of voice that it didn't go according to plan."

Marcus sighed. "Susan's arm was in a right state, as you know. During skin prep the Betadine-soaked gauze used to clean the area just . . . well, it took the skin off right up to the elbow. Robert said the muscle beneath was so necrotic that he decided there and then to perform a glenohumeral amputation."

Sister Parkhurst looked horrified. "He took her arm off at the shoulder?"

Marcus nodded.

"Oh my God, the poor girl." She blinked and huffed out a lungful of air, like a boxer trying to shake off a particularly fierce punch. Then she said, "I must go to her. She'll need a friendly face there when she wakes up."

Marcus nodded again, though vaguely this time. "I'll come up when I can. I'm a little concerned that she's there with . . ."

"With what?"

He grimaced and looked away. "Well, I was going to say *normal* patients. Is that awful of me?"

She smiled sympathetically. "Based on what we've seen tonight, no. But don't worry, I'll keep an eye on her. And besides, now she's had the surgery she'll probably be fine."

"Yes," he said, still keeping his eyes averted, "she probably will."

She frowned. "I take it you're not convinced?"

He was silent for a moment, and then he slowly raised his head. She was shocked at how haggard he looked, at the genuine fear in his eyes.

"Do you want my honest opinion?" he asked.

Her voice hushed, she said, "Of course."

"I don't think this is over," he said. "Not by a long chalk. In fact . . ." He paused, swallowed. "I think this is only the beginning."

07:09 am

SHIRLEY SEEMED TO be gone for such a long time that after a while Vince began to wonder whether she had ever been there at all. Perhaps he had dreamed her. Perhaps she had been nothing but a figment of his imagination.

Then again, maybe she hadn't been gone as long as he thought; maybe it had only been minutes. Time seemed unstable, elastic to him now, as did what he had always thought of as the real world. It was as if the pain of his shattered leg had opened doors to other realms of consciousness, as if, paradoxically, it had both imprisoned him and set him free.

He had seen this many times before, of course. He was aware of how an injury such as his could bring on fever and delirium. But being inside it, experiencing it, was different. It seemed far more . . . *meaningful* somehow.

Shirley had taken something out of his pocket, hadn't she? He vaguely remembered her holding something up that flashed and caught the light, that tinkled softly.

Keys. Yes, that was it. The keys to their ambulance. She'd told him that she'd be back soon, that she was going to get him out of here, take him to Luke. He'd wanted to tell her to be careful, but what she was supposed to be careful *of* he couldn't remember. It was something obvious, something to do with the hospital, but it had slipped his mind, melted away. He knew it was something to do with why he was here, with his leg, with the pain, but when he tried to concentrate, to remember, all he heard was a high-pitched buzzing in his head.

It was like there were insects in there, insects that had burrowed into his mind and were now busily eating his thoughts and replacing them with new ones. His forehead where Shirley had kissed him itched and itched. Was that where the insects had got in?

He heard a sound. A deep, throaty rumble. He imagined the earth splitting open, clouds of insects swarming out with the dead climbing after them. A new regime. A new world. His forehead itched and itched.

Then the sound came closer, became clearer. It was an engine. It seemed to be right beside him, though he couldn't see anything but waving grass, and above it the sky, fresh and bright, the sun rising on the first day of May.

Rustling in the undergrowth, coming closer. A shadow falling over him. And here was Shirley. Real or a dream? Perhaps she was both.

"Come on then," she said in her soft Welsh accent. "Let's be having you."

She crouched beside him, slid her arms underneath his body.

"No," he said, thinking of the pain, of how it would explode inside him, rush into every crevice of his being, if he didn't remain still. "No . . . please, Shirley . . ."

"Shhh," she soothed, like a mother to a baby. "Shhh, it'll be okay. Trust me."

And it was. It *was* okay. She lifted him as if he weighed almost nothing at all, as if he was a husk. And though the bones shifted and ground inside his leg – he could *hear* them, scraping together – he felt nothing. Nothing but the itch in his forehead where she had kissed him.

She carried him out of the undergrowth and across to the ambulance. It was like a dream, like he was floating. The world spun slowly around him, a kaleidoscope of colours and shapes with no meaning. He saw the hospital, all grey smooth stone and black windows in the early morning daylight, and he heard the cracks and bangs of not-so-distant gunfire, and suddenly he remembered. He remembered it all.

Gently she placed him in the passenger seat of the ambulance, pulled his seatbelt around his belly, clicked it into place. Looking down the length of his body he saw the shattered bone sticking out of his leg, blood trickling from the wound, running into the footwell and pooling on the rubber mat beneath his feet.

But he felt nothing. Nothing but the itch in his forehead. He was protected by her kiss.

"The police," he said, feeling a need to warn her. His voice seemed to come from very far away. "They'll stop us. They won't let us leave."

"The police have got enough to deal with," she said, smiling as if she'd made a joke.

She put the ambulance into gear and released the brake. The sound of the engine rose from a rumble to a growl as she pressed her foot down on the accelerator and they began to ease forwards. Vince felt as though he was looking at the world through a haze, a protective screen, but he was still aware that theirs was the only moving vehicle in the vicinity. How could they *not* be a target? A big, white, moving target? Why were men in helmets and riot gear not converging on them from all sides, pointing their guns at them, yelling at them to stop?

It was only when they skirted the perimeter of the car park and were approaching the main gates that he realized why. The police were under attack. There were several of their big, black TSG wagons parked nose-to-tail on the road outside the hospital entrance, and people were swarming towards them, climbing all over them, like ants converging on dropped fruit.

The SO22 men, in their black body armour, were fighting a rearguard action, shooting into the crowd. Some of the attackers, their flesh shredded with bullets, blood flying out of them in spatters and arcs, were collapsing to the ground, but even that didn't deter the rest of them in their remorseless advance. And as Vince watched he saw that even those who had been shot were getting up again and dragging themselves back into the fray. And all at once he realized.

"Those people," he said, "they're infected."

Shirley nodded happily. "Yes."

Vince looked at them in wonder. "But where are they coming from?"

"Everywhere," Shirley said.

The ambulance crept up to the entrance and on to the road. Vince watched as the infected advanced upon them and swarmed around them, filtering to the left or the right so as not to impede their progress. They were like a shoal of fish, he thought, moving and acting as one.

"Why don't they attack us?"

Shirley looked at him. When she smiled he heard that high-pitched, insectile buzzing again. Was it coming from her or was it in his own head?

"Why would they attack their own?"

07:16 am

EMERGING FROM THE store cupboard – and trying to avert their eyes from the sprawled corpses of the infected, many of them children, whose shattered heads were leaking blood and brains all over the vinyl flooring – Cat and Carlton quickly found themselves embroiled in a deadly and inverted game of snakes and ladders.

The aim of the game was simple: to descend six floors to the hospital basement, where Cat had assured Carlton they may be able to exit the hospital via the Medical Museum. The tricky part, though, was that en route they had to avoid both the infected and the trigger-happy SO22 patrols that were hunting them.

At first, descending the building via the stairwell, the game seemed easy. They made it from the fifth floor to the third without incident, and it was only when they were between floors two and three that they heard the echoing clump of booted feet from below that they knew could only be the sound of an ascending SO22 patrol. Halting, they glanced at each other, and then, without a word, scooted back up to the landing above and crossed to the

double doors leading on to the third-floor corridor.

Their intention was to find a cubby-hole in which to lie low until the patrol had passed, but peering through the reinforced glass panels of the double doors to check that the coast was clear, they received a shock. The doors of the ward they had visited earlier – the one from which Cat had tried in vain to call the Children's ward and the Maternity Unit – had been smashed open and the left-hand one was lying in splintered segments on the floor.

Far more distressing, however, was that some of the occupants of the ward were now milling aimlessly in the corridor, their bodies variously wounded and blood-stained. Suzanne, the nurse who had let them in, was among them, standing motionless, her eyes half-closed and her head cocked to one side as if she was listening for something. Cat was horrified to see that she had a large chunk of her scalp and left cheek missing, as well as other lacerations to her arms and body.

With the third floor out of commission, Cat and Carlton were forced to backtrack yet further, to the floor above – the one which had latterly been home to the now-abandoned isolation ward. Although this corridor, viewed through the glass panel of the stairwell door, still showed signs of the battle that had taken place there – blood up the walls and spattered across the floor, furniture and equipment upended – the area itself now appeared quiet and deserted.

Slipping through the door, they took a quick look left and right and then, on Cat's instructions, hurried across the landing.

"Fucking déjà vu, innit?" Carlton said, opening the door on yet another storeroom. Once they were inside and had closed the door behind them, he hissed, "Okay, listen, this the plan. They soljas gonna merk all them zombies on the floor below, then they gonna come up here and check this place out. If they find us they either gonna merk us, depending on how jumpy they are, or arrest us, so soon as we hear them shooting down below we out of here. We don't think about it, we just run down them stairs and past the door before they done shootin'. If we get below them we be safe, 'cos they be on their way up. Yeah?"

Cat looked frightened, but she nodded.

"Awright," he said. "Be ready."

When the time came, they *were* ready. As soon as the gunfire started on the floor below, as Carlton had predicted it would, they were out of the storeroom and racing across the corridor to the stairwell door. Tearing it open, they raced down the stairs, Carlton in the lead, taking the stone steps two and three at a time, his chair leg, in case of unexpected encounters, held out in front of him.

When they reached the third-floor landing, they ducked beneath the glass panels in the door through which they had peered a few minutes earlier, and from behind which now came a barrage of gunfire so loud that it made Cat's teeth throb. As they scuttled past the door and headed for the descending staircase beyond it, Cat's heart ached for Suzanne, who had a boyfriend called Nige, and a cat called Mr Spinks, and the tattoo of a dolphin on her right shoulder to commemorate the time she had swum with them in Florida – and who was now almost certainly dead.

An ache, however, was all that Cat allowed herself. Taking a deep breath, she forced the door shut on the mother lode of grief and horror that she knew was building inside her, and that – assuming she ever got out of this – would no doubt erupt from her in due course.

Continuing to descend, they managed to reach the flight of stairs above the first-floor landing when one of the double doors on to the stairwell there clattered open and two of the infected – one of whom Cat recognized as Anna Carstairs' boyfriend, Peter James – lurched into view. Instantly Carlton grabbed Cat and hauled her back up the stairs to the second-floor landing, both of them moving as quietly as possible.

308

Checking through the glass panels in the door that the second-floor corridor was clear, they slipped through the opening and closed the door quietly behind them. Carlton motioned to Cat to push her chair leg through the metal handles to prevent the doors being opened from the stairwell side, and then they crouched down with their ears to the wood, their heads out of sight beneath the glass windows.

"Think they heard us?" Cat whispered.

Carlton shrugged. "We soon find out."

The two infected, moving slowly, thumped and shuffled up the stairs and across the second-floor landing. They shuffled right up to the doors behind which Cat and Carlton were crouching – and then passed by.

"Maybe they're drawn to the gunfire," Cat whispered when they had gone. "You know, noise equals victims?"

Carlton gave a slow, mean grin. "If that true, they gonna get one fuck of a surprise."

When they were sure that the infected had moved on, they slipped back out on to the stairwell and continued their descent. Creeping down the flight of stairs that led to the first-floor landing, they could see, through the glass panels of the stairwell doors, bulky dark shapes moving to and fro in the corridor beyond. Motioning to Cat that she keep tight in to the banister and stay low to avoid detection, Carlton scuttled across to her.

"Five-oh, innit?" he whispered. "Don't let 'em see you."

"How can we avoid it?" Cat whispered. "We've got to go right past them."

"They got their backs to us. If we lucky and quiet they might not turn round."

As it turned out, they *were* lucky and quiet. Crouching low, they were able to sneak past the door without being detected.

The floor below was unlike the rest. For one thing there were no more stairs – they culminated in what amounted to a three-sided concrete box. And for another the door was different here. Instead of a pair of heavy-duty wooden doors with reinforced glass panels, there was what looked like a metal bulkhead emblazoned with a sign that read: NO UNAUTHORIZED PERSONNEL BEYOND THIS POINT.

On the wall beside the door was an intercom and an entry keypad. Carlton glanced worriedly at Cat. "You know the code for that?"

"I do," said Cat, already reaching out. It was probably a security risk, but the code was identical for all such doors within the hospital: 1803. She punched it in and there was a sort of hydraulic sigh. "In we go."

Tentatively Carlton pushed the door open a foot or so and peered around it. Standing behind him, Cat saw his tensed shoulders relax a little.

"All clear," he whispered.

She stepped through after him and Carlton pushed the door closed, holding on to the handle to prevent it from booming shut. They were at the end of a long corridor, which eventually branched off to the left. It had clinical white walls inset with doors at regular intervals, and grey vinyl flooring. Strip-lights obliterated the very possibility of shadows, giving the place a slightly unreal, two-dimensional look.

"Where we going?" he asked.

"Straight ahead. There's like an emergency exit door beyond the Mortuary with a metal bar across it."

He raised his eyebrows. "The Mortuary?"

She gave a wry smile. "This *is* a hospital, you know. We have to keep the dead somewhere."

He considered this. "There goan be any of 'em down here?"

"Possibly. Though when we saw the children on the stairs there was a man with them, remember?"

He shrugged.

"His name was Piotr. He works down here. So I guess he could have been infected here and then let the rest of them out. Because that's what they'd do, isn't it? Go looking for victims?" She sounded almost plaintive, as though she needed him to agree with her.

Carlton shrugged. "Guess so." Then he frowned. "Hey, you okay?"

Cat had come to a sudden stop, as though she felt faint, and put out a hand to the wall to steady herself. "Oh God," she said.

He frowned. "Wassup?"

"I've just realized – I've accepted all this, haven't I? I've accepted that it isn't simply an infection, but that there are people actually coming back from the dead." She laughed, but it was a sick, slightly desperate sound. "It's ridiculous . . . impossible . . ."

"Believe it," Carlton said quietly. "Fucking zombie apocalypse, innit?"

She looked at him almost angrily. "But it *can't* be happening!"

He looked indifferent in the face of her indignation. "If you say so."

"But it can't! I'm getting married in six weeks!"

This time he simply shrugged.

"Oh God," she said again, and slumped against the wall. She was quiet for a moment, and then she seemed to recover, to rally herself. She pushed herself upright, took a deep breath. "Sorry," she said. "It all got a bit much for me for a second there. I'm okay now."

He hesitated, then put a hand on her shoulder. "You all right, blud," he assured her. "You doing fine."

They began walking again. Cat glanced sidelong at Carlton. "So . . . 'blud'?" she said. "Does that mean I'm your mate now?"

He looked momentarily embarrassed, then abruptly he

311

grinned, and suddenly he seemed much younger, boyish almost. "Sure," he said. "You my bro, innit?"

They walked on in silence for a few seconds. They were approaching the place where the corridor branched off to the left when all at once Carlton stopped.

Cat didn't need to ask why. They both heard the sounds of running feet somewhere beyond the bend of the corridor ahead – running feet that were getting closer.

They didn't hesitate. Cat crossed to the nearest door – it bore a small metal plaque reading DR N. D. JOYCE – and tried the handle. It opened.

"In here," she hissed.

They entered the room, a fairly nondescript office, and Cat pulled the door closed behind them. Before she could close it fully, however, Carlton put a hand on it.

"Wait, I wanna see."

She looked at him with alarm. "It's too much of a risk."

"It only be open a tiny bit. I wanna know what's down here with us."

She frowned, but stepped back. Gripping the handle, Carlton pulled the door back against the toe of his trainer, leaving it open the merest crack – just enough to see a sliver of the corridor ahead. They waited, hardly daring to breathe, as the pounding footsteps came closer, accompanied now by rapid, panicked breathing. Cat, standing behind Carlton, gripped the chair leg in her right hand and tightly clenched her left. Her body was rigid.

Carlton was staring so intently at the narrow strip of corridor between the edge of the door and the frame that it seemed to pulse with light. When a dark shape flashed across it he almost jerked back, as if someone had jumped out at him, but he held his ground, and was still doing so a moment later when a second dark shape flashed by in pursuit of the first.

As the two sets of running footsteps faded he quietly pulled the door shut and turned to Cat.

"Well?" she hissed, eyes wide, impatient with curiosity. "What did you see?"

"Soljas," Carlton said.

"Soldiers? You mean SO22 men?"

He nodded.

"What were they doing?"

"One was chasing the other."

"You mean one was infected?"

"Must be. He had . . ." He scowled in an effort to express himself, raising his left hand. "I dunno . . . like, *stuff* around his head."

"Stuff?"

"Yeah. Like insects maybe."

"You mean, flies or something?"

"Yeah, maybe. It was fuckin' weird."

Cat digested this. The Mortuary was one of the most scrupulously clean and clinical places in the hospital. What would flies be doing down here?

But she didn't have time to think about it. She pushed at Carlton's arm. "Come on. We should leave before they come back."

He nodded and, although the footsteps had faded now, eased the door open and peered tentatively through the gap, checking that the coast was clear. Seeing that it was, he pushed the door wider and the two of them slipped out of the office and began to hurry along the corridor, glancing back nervously over their shoulders.

A moment later, from somewhere behind them, they heard shouting, which, although too faint and distant to make out the words, contained an unmistakable note of panic. Then there was silence. They looked at each other.

"How's the hip?" asked Cat.

Carlton shrugged. "Awright."

"Think you can run?"

"Believe it."

They began to jog along the corridor, alert for any signs of movement ahead, glancing at each door they passed for fear it might suddenly burst open. Cat didn't think the infected had much in the way of guile, but they did seem to have an instinct for those who had not yet succumbed. It was as if they could sense them, and in so doing feel an overwhelming need to convert them.

They were approaching the Mortuary, jogging side by side, when Cat stretched out a hand. "Hold on."

She slowed to a walk, as did Carlton. "Wassup?" he asked.

"The Mortuary door. It's ajar." She gestured at a large metal door on the right-hand side of the corridor ahead. The keypad on the wall beside it, like the one outside the basement door at the bottom of the stairwell, suggested that here was an area with fairly rigid security restrictions.

But the door was part-way open. It made Carlton think of the door of a bank vault, discovered in the morning after the thieves had fled.

"I got it," he said. He ran across and pushed it shut. In his eagerness to do so, the heavy door swung away from him and closed with a crash, the booming echoes of which seemed to reverberate endlessly.

As the door slammed, Cat raised herself up on her tiptoes and clenched her teeth, as if by doing so she might somehow contain the noise. Carlton turned sheepishly.

"Ouch."

Cat glanced back along the corridor. "Come on, let's go."

They began to jog again, glancing behind them more frequently now. The corridor, after running straight for a while, bent off to the right a few metres ahead.

"Nearly there," she said encouragingly, and then she rounded the bend and came to an abrupt halt.

Carlton halted too, his body flinching back and his arms jerking up as if he had turned a corner to find himself about to step off the edge of a precipice. Together they stared at the scene in the corridor ahead, trying to take it in.

There was a body in a hospital shroud lying on its front, its head shattered into unrecognizable mush, like a melon that has been hit with a mallet. There was spatter up the white wall that looked less like blood and more like old, half-congealed engine oil, and there was a stubby black machine gun on the floor close to the body.

Cat was still trying to work out what had happened when Carlton gave a delighted cry and ran across to the gun. Throwing aside his chair leg, he picked it up almost reverently and examined it.

"What are you doing?" Cat asked nervously.

Carlton looked at her in surprise. "Wassit look like? I'm takin' this, innit?"

"But it isn't yours."

Carlton looked at her as if she had said something unbelievably stupid and nodded down at the corpse. "It ain't his either."

"What I mean is, you can't just take it."

He nodded stubbornly. "Watch me. We got better chance've gettin' out with this than with lumps of fuckin' wood."

"But if the police see you with that, they'll shoot you. They'll think you stole it."

He shrugged. "I tell 'em I found it."

"They'll most likely kill you before you get the chance."

He waved away her concerns. "We nearly out now, innit? This just see us the rest of the way. Once we safe, I'll fuckin' dump it."

"Will you, though?"

315

"Word."

Cat still looked uncertain, but she was now glancing at the corpse and the spatter on the wall. "I wonder why it was just left here."

"Easy, innit? That zombie five-oh musta dropped it after this guy attack him." He pointed at the corpse. "Then the other five-oh merk this guy, then get chased by his friend."

Cat looked doubtful. "That doesn't sound right."

"Why's 'at?"

"Because the infection doesn't act that quickly. And even if it did, why didn't the other SO22 man use his gun?"

"Maybe he don't wanna shoot his friend."

Cat was thinking hard. "Perhaps those insects you saw had something to do with why the SO22 man turned so quickly. Perhaps this is a whole new aspect of the infection that we haven't encountered yet. And perhaps it wasn't the infected man who dropped his gun. What if—"

"*Fuck!*"

Cat saw a look of horror cross Carlton's face, heard him swear, saw the gun in his hand jerk up. At the same time, behind her, she heard running footsteps, already horribly close. Instinctively she threw herself forwards and down, and then the world exploded above her.

Clamping her hands over her ears, she drew up her knees, tucked her chin in and squeezed her eyes shut. Almost as soon as the shooting had started, however, it stopped. Jerking her hands from her ears she looked up and saw Carlton, his eyes wide and his mouth half-open, the gun drooping in his hand. He looked like a school kid whose science experiment had had a far more devastating effect than he'd anticipated.

Scrambling into a kneeling position, she jerked her head around to see what he was staring at.

Two SO22 officers were lying on their backs in the corridor. One had his knees bent, his legs tucked beneath him, and the other had his arms stretched above his head. They both still wore their bullet-riddled helmets, though their faces beneath were raw, shredded meat embedded with chunks of shattered visor. They were lying in a slowly widening pool of blood.

Cat looked away, sickened, then back at Carlton. "Are you okay?"

The gun was now dangling from Carlton's hand, its muzzle pointing at the floor, as if all at once he was finding it incredibly heavy. He nodded, though judging by the look on his face she wasn't sure whether he had even heard her question.

"I couldn't help it," he muttered. "Was either them or us."

She approached him cautiously. "I know," she said, her voice gentle. She reached him and put a hand on the arm from which the gun dangled. "Do you want to put that down?"

His eyes flickered from the bodies and focused on her face, and she saw him come back into himself. "No," he said.

She was silent for a moment, then nodded, realizing she couldn't argue with him. The gun had saved her life – both their lives. She hated it, hated the fact that they needed it, but she couldn't deny that without it they would be dead.

She picked up her chair leg, which she had dropped as she had flung herself forwards, and then without another word they turned and trudged away. A minute later they reached the service door she had described to Carlton, and passed through it into a run-down corridor with scuffed walls and missing roof panels.

The strip lighting was dimmer here, more primitive. At each end of the corridor a lift faced its twin, their steel doors tarnished and dented. Cat led the way wearily to the one at the far end and pressed the call button. She and Carlton waited in silence as it clanked down towards them.

As the lift doors opened Carlton raised his weapon almost wearily, but the lift was empty. They stepped inside and Cat

317

pressed the topmost of only two buttons on the interior panel, and then closed her eyes as the doors juddered closed and the lift hauled itself upwards.

Desperate though she was to get home, she found herself wishing that she could prolong this journey a little longer, if only to grab enough of a snooze to dispel some of the fatigue that was settling in her bones. But barely had the desire formed in her mind when the lift stopped with a bump and the doors creaked open.

Another corridor, this one shorter and more run-down than the last. The light was even weaker here, some of the bulbs in the dusty strip-lights having expired. The crumbling remains of polystyrene ceiling panels lay scattered across the floor, the gaps where they had once been exposing a grimy network of pipes and wiring, the hospital's secret innards. At the end of the corridor was another door with yet another entry keypad on the wall beside it.

"That it?" said Carlton.

"That's it," she confirmed. "Our way out."

She hoped she was right. If not, she'd . . . well, she didn't know what she'd do. She felt exhausted, like a runner coming to the end of a marathon. She felt almost as if she had paced herself for this distance and no more, and that if she was to now find out that this wasn't the end, after all, she would probably collapse in a sobbing, quivering heap. The only thing that might prevent her from doing that, the only thing that might keep driving her on, was the thought of Ed waiting at home, and of her wedding in six weeks' time.

Reaching the door she was struck by a sudden thought. She halted abruptly, then turned and gripped Carlton's arm.

"If I invited you to my wedding, would you come?" she asked.

He looked startled. "Why you want *me* there?"

She barked a laugh that sounded slightly hysterical. "After

all we've been through, do you even need to ask?"

A number of expressions chased themselves across his face – wonder, disbelief, confusion. For a moment he seemed lost for words, and then he mumbled, "What do I wear?"

She laughed again. "You wear whatever you like. I don't care *what* you wear. *Would* you come?"

Suddenly he reproduced that boyish grin. "Awright. You want me there, I be there."

"Good." She leaned forward and hugged him briefly, surprising him again.

Without any further discussion she turned and punched the entry code into the keypad. The door to the Medical Museum clicked and she pushed it open.

Raising the gun, Carlton stepped ahead of her, edging over the threshold, narrowing his eyes in an effort to make out the vague, blocky shapes he could see in the gloom. He had taken no more than a single step into the Museum itself when something large hurled itself out of the darkness and hit him side on.

Standing at Carlton's shoulder, Cat thought at first that he'd been hit by a swinging punch bag that had been propelled towards him at great speed. It crashed into him with such force that he was knocked off his feet, his gun flying out of his hand and clattering off into the darkness. As he disappeared from view, she yelled and sprang in after him, clutching her chair leg in both hands and swinging it in front of her.

Her head snapped to the left, where she could hear Carlton groaning in pain and make out what she was pretty sure was him struggling feebly in the shadows. She was about to call out, to ask whether he was okay, when, to his right, she saw the thing that had hit him shift and slide upright.

A thrill of horror went through her. It was not a punch bag then. It was something alive. A man? Although it was hard to make out in the darkness, she got the impression that the figure – if it *was* a figure – was tall and bulky. She saw it move in Carlton's direction.

"Carlton!" she yelled. "Look out!" Not entirely sure what she was doing, she ran forward, swinging the chair leg in a wide arc and hitting the bulky shape as hard as she could.

The chair leg connected with something solid, but also with a bit of give in it – something like a large sack packed with a dense substance such as sand or flour. If it had been a man it would have grunted or groaned, she thought, but then she realized: not if it was one of the infected. They didn't seem to feel pain. They just kept on coming.

"Carlton!" she screamed again, but her adrenaline-fuelled heart was now pounding so hard in her ears that she couldn't even hear whether he was still moaning.

Once more she swung the chair leg, aiming higher this time, and was rewarded with a satisfying bony clunk that jarred her elbows. Even as she drew her arm back in readiness for a third blow, her mind was filled with racing thoughts: How long would it take to smash someone's skull in with a chair leg? How far away was the gun? How many of the infected were in here with them? How badly hurt was Carlton?

Then something flew out of the darkness and hit her full in the face, causing a starburst of pain and light to ignite her senses. Tottering backwards, she tried desperately to stay on her feet, but her limbs refused to cooperate.

As she went down she gripped the chair leg tighter, determined not to lose it. She didn't lose it, but holding on to the weapon meant that she couldn't use her arms to cushion her fall and the impact of her back slamming against the floor knocked the breath out of her.

She was frantic to leap back to her feet, to defend herself and Carlton, but for long seconds she could only lie there, wheezing, feeling the first flutterings of panic at her inability to get air into her lungs. Sparks danced at the edge of her vision as if her oxygen-starved brain cells were fizzing and dying. For a horrible moment she thought she was going to pass out.

Then her lungs seemed to inflate and she whooped in air. The action only caused pain to flare in her back, however. She sensed movement to her right, something wriggling with a frenzied and somehow obscene need across the floor towards her. It was making a hideous sound as it came, a kind of squelching scrape, and it was the thought of this thing, whatever it was, touching her skin that got her up and moving.

Gritting her teeth against the pain in her back, she pushed herself into a sitting position and pedalled her legs, scrambling away from the crawling thing that she could see only as a pale blob in the darkness.

But then she heard something else to her left, the sound of something weightier dragging itself across the floor. Her head snapped around. What *was* that? Although it was barely discernible in the gloom, it put her immediately in mind of tripe.

And then, all at once, the room seemed *alive* with movement. It seemed to be converging from all directions, a kind of maggoty scuffling, closing in on her. With shudders of revulsion rippling through her body, she jumped to her feet, hissing at the pain in her back. She raised her chair leg, ready to bring it down.

Then something loomed out of the darkness to her right and snatched the lump of wood from her hand.

She gave a cry of shock and stumbled to her left. "Get back!" she screamed. "Get away from me!"

The shape reared over her, huge and bear-like.

A voice tore through the darkness. "Cat, get down!"

It was Carlton. Instantly, despite the crawling things around her, she dropped. A split-second later the gun cracked and chattered, lighting the room in jitters and sparks. The periods of illumination were as rapid as blinks, but what they revealed were like flashes from a nightmare.

321

All around Cat, slithering and crawling and dragging themselves along the floor, were some of the Museum's grislier exhibits, things she had last seen lined up on shelves in specimen jars.

There was an aborted foetus, hideously deformed; a severed hand sprouting far too many fingers; a coiling mass of interconnected tissue that she thought might once have been the uterus of a sheep or cow; a pair of hairless Siamese twin puppies, joined at the belly; a pulsating lung, black and barnacled with tumours; a rat born not with legs but with boneless strands of pink flesh that branched off into quivering masses of root-like tendrils.

All had been inert for decades, but all were now alive again, animated by something that Cat had come to realize was far more than a mere infection.

But what was it exactly? A force? An energy? Voracious, murderous even, but at the same time miraculous, able to imbue even the long-dead with vigorous new life. But why? To what purpose? Was it sentient? Was it here to conquer? Or was it merely a mindless parasite, propagating and multiplying for its own sake?

These questions flashed through her mind even as she was leaping to her feet with a scream on her lips, even as she was hunching in her shoulders and crossing her arms across her chest, her body instinctively recoiling from the prospect of making contact with one of the vile, crawling things around her.

Where was the looming figure that had snatched the chair leg from her hand? Had Carlton shot it or was it still at large somewhere, getting ready to pounce?

"Carlton!" she yelled again, her head jerking left and right, her eyes trying to look everywhere at once.

"Here," he shouted from across the room. "Wait up."

There was a click and a sudden, soundless explosion of light. Cat cried out and bent double like a woman in a sandstorm.

She squeezed her eyes shut, but felt as if the light had already flooded her body and that by closing her eyes she had merely trapped it inside.

Blindness brought panic; she imagined the crawling things, unaffected by the light, coming closer. She began to kick out with little yips of disgust, desperate to keep them away from her but horrified at the thought of connecting with one of them, of feeling its pulpy, weighty softness against her shoe.

Her eyes took an age to adjust – or so it seemed. In reality it was probably no more than ten seconds, fifteen at the most. As the glare subsided she blinked rapidly, tears forming from the sting of light and blurring her vision all over again. She swiped the tears away, and gradually the room around her began to acquire shape and definition.

"Cat," Carlton called. She swung in the direction of his voice. And there he was, hazy at first but a bold statement all the same, dressed all in black, like an exclamation mark. He was standing by the door, beside the light switch he had found and pressed. It was possible that the light flooding the Museum might announce their presence to any passing SO22 patrols but, compared to knowing who and where the enemy were, Cat thought that was a worthwhile risk.

"Carlton," she said. "Are you okay?"

He nodded abruptly. "You need to move."

He was looking not at her, but at the floor around her. She looked down to see that the closest of the creeping monstrosities – the many-fingered hand – was now no more than a metre from her foot. In the harsh light the specimens looked even more hideous than they had when she had glimpsed them in the darkness. They were entirely bloodless and mostly hairless, their flesh uniformly damp and white, albeit with a yellowish tinge. Many of them left wet, slug-like trails as they dragged themselves across the floor.

Shuddering with revulsion she leaped out of the circle

and over the hand. Immediately the specimens halted their advance, then began slowly and clumsily to readjust, to turn, as if homing in on a signal.

The rat raised its blind, hairless head and seemed to sniff the air. The fingers of the over-endowed hand scuttled crabwise to its left, hauling the rest of its "body" round to face in the other direction.

Cat ran up to Carlton, who nodded at her. "Are you all right?" she gasped. "How's the wound?"

As she asked the question she looked down and saw a wet, glistening patch slowly spreading across the left hip area of his black jacket. It was on his jeans too, creeping down from his waistband towards his pocket.

"You're bleeding!" she exclaimed.

He shrugged it off. "I be awright. You can patch me later." He nodded ahead. "Right now we need to get out of here."

She turned. The Medical Museum was spread out ahead of them, aisles and corridors leading through a maze of exhibits, some of which, Cat knew, were like three-sided theatre sets with open fronts. Some housed the more traditional display cases and information boards; others were reconstructions of various rooms – a Victorian operating theatre, a rookery-like hovel, a First World War hospital ward.

Before they could negotiate the route to the glass-fronted entrance, however, they had to cross the line of resurrected medical specimens, which, having altered their course, were once more creeping towards them.

Although, in truth, the specimens amounted to little more than pathetic scraps of life that it would be simple to outpace and outmanoeuvre, there was nevertheless something about their dogged persistence that horrified Cat. In a way they were like manifestations of the ferocity of the infection itself, like a sobering reminder that unless the threat was eradicated, it would continue to hunt and spread, tirelessly and voraciously.

At least Carlton had stopped one more carrier of the infection from spreading it further, though as that had meant killing another human host it hardly felt like a victory.

The same man who, Cat guessed, had slammed into Carlton and snatched the chair leg from her hand was lying motionless on the ground, the upper half of his skull missing and a mess of blood and brains strewn across the floor above him like the contents of a smashed jar.

The man was tall and bulky, and it gave Cat a pang to see how ordinary he was, with his shapeless blue sweater and M&S jeans and scuffed Timberland boots. She wondered who he had been, how he had come to be in the Museum, how he had been infected. She supposed she would never know; maybe no one would. And that, as much as anything, sickened her.

They walked forwards, stepping over the advancing line of medical specimens casually, almost disdainfully. Cat stayed tight to Carlton, holding on to his arm, not because he needed the support, despite his leaking wound, but simply because, having come this far together, she wanted to do all she could to ensure that it stayed that way.

They didn't rush. They took it slowly, carefully, looking around every corner, peering into every potential hiding place.

They moved past the display area where the specimen jars had been kept, Cat noting the smashed glass, the chemical smell of preserving solution.

They edged past a Victorian operating theatre, cautiously eyeing the bewhiskered mannequins in leather aprons crowding around a restrained man having his left leg sawn off below the knee, his mouth open in a frozen scream.

They passed a Victorian hovel with – curiously – a nurse's uniform complete with underwear and shoes strewn across the filthy bed. The ragged woman sitting in there startled Cat for a moment before she realized that it too was a mannequin, even if its glittering eyes *were* disturbingly life-like.

The closer they got to the Museum entrance – and what Cat prayed would be their exit from the hospital – the more nervous she became. Now that they were close to salvation she was terrified that something would go wrong, that some final threat would rise up from nowhere and overwhelm them.

She gripped Carlton's arm, her eyes darting every which way. She felt horribly exposed in the brightly lit Museum, imagined the glare of it shining out through the windows, far brighter than the pearly dawn light around it, attracting the infected like moths to a flame.

All at once she heard something. A tiny sound coming from a passageway to their left.

She gripped Carlton's arm tighter. "Did you hear that?"

He frowned. "Yeah, maybe."

They halted, listened. After a moment the sound came again.

And then a woman stepped out of the passageway, directly into their path.

She was around forty, and she was naked, her belly and breasts starting to sag a little. Or at least, her right breast, heavy and darkly nippled, was sagging. The left had been reduced to slashed and bloody ribbons of fatty flesh.

"Whoa," Carlton said softly, raising the gun another inch or two, pointing it at her head.

"I know her," Cat hissed. "Her name's Gill Eaves. She's a nurse."

"*Was* a nurse," corrected Carlton. "She a fucking zombie now."

If Gill Eaves had run at them, attacked them, it would have been easy, or at least easier. With their lives in imminent danger it would have been natural to do whatever they needed to do to defend themselves. But she didn't run at them. She simply stood there, her eyes staring and unfocused, as if she was in a trance. And so Carlton and Cat stood there too, waiting for her to make her move. They waited for ten seconds, maybe more.

And then Gill Eaves yawned.

That was what it looked like, at first. Her mouth opened wide . . . but then it continued to open, her lips stretching and stretching.

"What the fuck she doin'?" Carlton muttered.

"I don't—" Cat said and then the words dried in her throat.

Something was coming out of Gill Eaves' mouth. No, not just something – *lots* of somethings. Insects. Thousands of them. An entire swarm. They were turning the air black – no, *red* – above the woman's head.

Carlton fired the gun, and suddenly it wasn't only insects that were turning the air red.

"*Go!*" Cat yelled, remembering the SO22 men in the basement corridor and her theory about why one of them had succumbed so quickly to the infection. "*Fucking run!*"

Carlton needed no further prompting. Even before Gill Eaves' body had collapsed like a suit of empty clothes, the two of them were racing down the nearest right-hand corridor, past a display case of surgical instruments, an exhibit tracking the development of childbirth techniques.

They kept their heads low and Carlton clutched his side with his left hand as he ran. Cat had no idea if the insects were behind them, or if they had even given chase. She only knew that if they succumbed to them – if they breathed them in, or were bitten by them, or whatever it took – then all was lost.

She thought of Ed; she thought of her wedding. They were her talismans; they would keep her from harm. They gave her the extra energy she needed too, the impetus to survive. She and Carlton turned left, heading back towards the Museum's glass-fronted entrance. She scanned the air ahead. No insects.

Carlton stumbled, crying out at the pain in his side. Cat grabbed his arm to keep him on his feet. His sleeve, where he had pressed it to his side, was wet and sticky with blood. "*Come on!*" she screamed at him. "*We can make it! Give me the gun!*"

He handed it over without protest. It was lighter than she had expected, almost like a toy. Holding it in both hands, her left hand curled around the stubby grip beneath the muzzle, she pointed it at the entranceway and pulled the trigger.

The gun jerked in her hands like something alive. The entranceway dissolved in a cascade of shattering glass. It was like a vast wave crashing down on to a beach, spray kicking up from it. Cat closed her eyes as she felt the spray on her skin, like flecks of cool water at first, which almost immediately began to itch and sting. If she got out of this she would spend the rest of the day picking tiny shards of glass out of her face with tweezers, but she didn't care. For the first time in what seemed like forever she could feel a cool breeze in her hair, could see their way out gaping ahead of them.

"*Okay?*" she yelled at Carlton, and at that moment, turning to him, she saw the cloud of red insects, hovering close to the ceiling, around ten metres behind them.

He nodded.

"*Come on!*" she screamed.

She grabbed his hand and together, their feet crunching across a sea of broken glass, they ran for their lives.

07:33 am

HER FIRST THOUGHT was that there was a fire, that she needed to grab Luke and get out. It was only when she surfaced, flailing and breathless with panic, that she realized there wasn't an alarm in the house, or at least not one that sounded like the old fire bell at school.

Scrambling into a sitting position, kicking off the duvet, Diane grabbed her mobile from her bedside table and held it up to her face. She blinked at the time beneath the date on the home screen until the numerals shrank into focus. 07:33 am. Her alarm had been set for 08:00.

So who was ringing the bloody doorbell so early? It better not be the postman, not after she'd made her feelings more than plain the last time he'd woken her up. But if it wasn't the postman, then who could it be? Whoever it was, he (and she was sure it was a he; only a man would be so bloody thoughtless) wasn't just *ringing* the doorbell, he was fucking *leaning* on it, for Christ's sake! She had a good mind to open the window and chuck something at him. What she wouldn't give for some boiling oil right now. Or even a cup of piss.

For a second she actually contemplated peeing in a mug, but that would have meant going downstairs and fetching one. Instead she settled for propelling herself out of bed and stalking to the window.

Glancing quickly down at the grey vest-top she was wearing to ensure that her nipples weren't standing to attention (she wanted to give the bell-ringer a bollocking, not an early-morning thrill), she yanked the curtain aside with one hand and shielded her eyes against the sudden glare of daylight with the other.

And there she froze, her stomach instantly contracting into a hard, tight knot of fury. Parked outside her house, like a great white wall across the end of her drive, was an ambulance.

"You are fucking kidding me," she hissed, so viciously that flecks of saliva speckled the window pane. This was typical of Vince. Having been offered a yard, he was duly grabbing a mile. He *always* took advantage, *always* took things to extremes. It was precisely this tendency of his that had caused Diane to dig in her heels where the upbringing of Luke was concerned.

Anyone talking to Vince would no doubt be convinced that she had been a prize bitch about the situation, but she had known from bitter experience that as soon as Vince got access to their son he would see their shared responsibility as a competition, as a popularity contest with Luke as the judge.

She knew Vince would use his time with Luke to fill the boy's head with lies about her, would shower their son with presents and treats in an effort to win him over. But would Vince actually give a thought to Luke's welfare while he was doing this? Would it occur to him what a confusing and de-stabilizing effect it might have on his son's happiness? No, he wouldn't, because he was stupid and stubborn and self-centred. He was not a *bad* man, she knew that, but he was a thoughtless one.

And this . . . this was just like him. He was supposed to turn up at 10:00 am, but here he was, two-and-a-half hours early, having no doubt not even considered the fact that Luke might still be in bed, that he might not be ready, that he might not have had his breakfast.

To all intents and purposes, this was an outrageous and wholly unacceptable violation of their agreement, but she knew precisely how Vince would respond to that. He would look aggrieved and indignant, would try to make her feel she was being uptight and unreasonable, that she was intent on spoiling his and Luke's fun.

"I just wanted to surprise him," he'd say – she could *see* him saying it. "I just wanted to give him a ride in the ambulance, get the day off to an exciting start, give him a thrill."

Then he'd look at Luke and say, "You want a ride in an ambulance, don't you, son?"

And Luke would probably say yes, and then Vince would look at her as if she was the villain of the piece.

The doorbell rang and rang, grating through her head, causing the knot in her belly to tighten and tighten. She turned away from the window. This wasn't a simple bollocking from on high. This was a discussion she and Vince needed to have face-to-face.

Grabbing her dressing gown, she marched out on to the landing – and there was Luke, shuffling out of his bedroom, rubbing the sleep out of his eyes.

"What's that noise, Mummy?" he asked.

Though she was angry her voice immediately became gentle. "It's nothing, sweetheart. Just someone at the door. I'm going to tell them to go away."

"Is it time to wake up?"

"Not quite yet. Go back to bed for a little while."

She watched as he turned and dutifully shuffled back into his room. Then, her face setting hard again, she stomped downstairs.

She could see Vince through the upper panel of the front

door – could see his dark bulk, like a storm cloud pressing against the patterned glass. She wanted to scream at him to *stop pressing the fucking doorbell!* But she didn't want to upset Luke. So she bit back on the words, and with sharp, jerky movements that were full of rage, she unlocked the door, tore off the security chain, and yanked the door open.

He all but tumbled into the house. Would have done, if he hadn't been mostly leaning against the wall beside the door rather than against the door itself. He was hunched over, his head hanging down so that she couldn't see his face. From what she *could* see of him – the top of his head, his hunched shoulders – he looked filthy, dishevelled, as if he had spent the night sleeping in a hedge. And . . . she wrinkled her nose. He smelled bad.

"What the fuck do you think you're doing?" she snapped at him – or rather, at the top of his sweaty, matted head.

He groaned in reply, mumbled something unintelligible.

She looked at him in outrage and astonishment. "I don't believe this! Are you fucking *drunk*?"

She came to a decision there and then. There was no way, no *fucking way*, she was going to allow this man to look after her son. They could fight another long, bitter battle through the courts, if that was what it took, but it simply wasn't going to happen. Not now, not ever.

He was mumbling something. She bent lower to hear him.

"Want Luke. Come for Luke . . ."

"You must be fucking kidding," she said. "Now please piss off before I call the police."

He reached out a hand (the fingernails of which, she noticed, were caked with dirt), grabbed hold of the doorframe and hauled himself upright.

She gasped. There was a swollen lump, crusted with blood, on his forehead and his skin was grey, ashen. It was his eyes, though . . . they were the worst. They were blank, empty, as if there was nothing behind them.

He shifted, straightening up further, and she realized there was something wrong with his leg. She looked down, and immediately felt faintness wash over her. Oh God, his leg was crooked, badly broken. His trousers and his shoe were soaked in blood, and she could see . . . Jesus, she could see a jagged spar of bone poking out through a tear in the fabric.

"Oh, Christ, Vince," she said, the anger draining from her voice. "What the hell happened to you?"

He snarled. His voice was thick, clogged, as if his throat was full of dirt.

"Want . . . Luke!"

And then, with shocking speed, he lunged at her.

08:00 am

"THERE!" CARLTON SHOUTED, pointing. They were outside the Museum now, running across the empty parking lot in front of the building. He was partly dragging his left leg and grimacing at the pain in his hip.

To their right, beyond the southern edge of the car park, was Albacore Crescent, while directly ahead, across fifty metres of asphalt, was a waist-high wall with a gate in the middle of it. From 10:00 am, when the Museum was open, the gate was pulled back to allow visitors access into the car park from Lewisham High Street, but at this time of the morning it was closed and locked.

It wasn't the gate that Carlton was referring to, though; nor was it the pub across the road, where Cat and her friends sometimes went for an after-shift drink. No, it was the car parked in a resident's bay in front of the pub, a silver Audi Quattro. Cat assumed he intended it to be their getaway car. Not that she had ever broken into a car before, or would know how to start one without a key. She only hoped that *he* did.

When they reached the wall, she dropped the gun on to the pavement on the other side, then scrambled up and over, scuffing her shin on the top of it as she did so, but ignoring the discomfort.

Then she turned back to help Carlton, who was struggling a little. She grabbed his jacket and dragged him after her, ignoring his grunts of pain. As she did so, she looked up.

The swarm was flecking the white morning sky above the shattered glass entrance of the Museum like red static. Between there and the wall over which, with her help, Carlton was now gracelessly scrambling was a trail of blood, the quantity of which alarmed her. She knew that if she didn't stop Carlton's bleeding and patch his wound up pretty soon he was going to be in serious trouble.

First, though, they had to get away, which meant making it across the road to the car before the swarm did. However, as Carlton fell on to the pavement and tried, immediately though weakly, to rise, Cat became aware that the pursuing insects and Carlton's blood loss might not be their only problems.

She was aware of a commotion to her left, of movement glimpsed in her peripheral vision. As she bent to retrieve the gun, she glanced along the length of Lewisham High Street, which ran parallel with the front of the hospital, and saw, some distance away, the dark, bobbing heads of a milling crowd.

Immediately she felt wary, felt a sense of unease coiling in her stomach. It was not that the sight of people out on the streets of Lewisham was unusual. It was a highly populated area, and at this time of the morning it was only to be expected that it would be getting busy.

No, it was more the fact that the behaviour of the crowd was a bit odd, or at least different from the usual bustle of pre-work commuters. Rather than scurrying in all directions, intent on their own agendas, they appeared more . . . condensed somehow, more single-minded.

Like a swarm.

Yes, she thought suddenly, that was it! The crowd gave the

impression not that it was composed of individuals, but that it was acting as a single entity. It was as if the people that comprised it were under strict orders, or at the very least had been drawn together by some common purpose.

But what purpose? Were they about to set off on a march of some kind? Was it a protest against the Coalition Government cuts, or the New Festival of Britain? Or could it be as she had feared?

Could it be that they were all infected?

The notion that the infection had spilled out beyond the confines of the hospital, that it was not just loose but apparently *rife* in the wider world, was terrifying. Clutching the gun with one hand, grabbing Carlton's arm with the other, Cat hauled her companion to his feet and dragged him, staggering, across the road.

When they reached the car she let go of his arm, leaving him to slump with a groan against the bodywork, while she tried the door.

"It's locked," she said, her panic making her indignant. Out of the corner of her eye she could see a few dark shapes peeling off from the crowd further down the High Street, heading in their direction.

"Use the gun," he gasped, and then, when she pointed it at the car, he shook his head. "Don't shoot it . . . Use the butt . . . Break the window."

She flipped the gun around, drew it back with both hands, then rammed it against the window. She was surprised at how easily and almost soundlessly the window broke, the glass crumpling rather than smashing and dissolving into cubes. She reached in, unlocked the door and yanked it open.

Without hesitation, Carlton ducked inside, scrambling across from the driver's side into the passenger's side, leaving a slither of blood behind him on the leather upholstery.

"You drive," he muttered, "I'm fucked, blud."

336

"But I don't know how to start it without a key," she protested, her voice shrill and scratchy.

He was leaning forward in the passenger seat, peeling off his blood-soaked jacket, to reveal the even more blood-soaked hospital gown beneath.

"Jus' get in . . . I start it . . . You drive."

She threw herself into the car, irrespective of the blood and the glass on the driver's seat. Swapping the gun from her right to her left hand, she pulled the door closed behind her.

"Y'got somethin' sharp? Knife or scissors or—"

"I've got scissors," she said, producing a small pair from the breast pocket of her tunic.

He nodded, smiling faintly. He looked as though he was struggling to stay conscious. "Sweet." He thrust his jacket at her. "Block the window with this t'keep they fuckin' flies out . . . I get this bitch started."

She took the sticky, sodden jacket from him and did as he asked, bundling it up and stuffing it into the hole in the glass as best she could. Carlton leaned across her – at first she thought he had passed out – opened out the scissors and jammed the end of one of the blades into the ignition. He jiggled it around for a moment, and then the car coughed and roared into life.

"You're a genius!" she exclaimed.

He eased himself back into his seat, face creased in pain, his left hand, now covered in blood, clamped to his side.

"Yeah, right," he said. "Let's jus' fuckin' move."

Cat glanced into the rear-view mirror and saw dark shapes advancing rapidly on the car. Then, facing front again, she saw a fat red insect – not a fly, but something that looked like a very large flea – alight on the windscreen directly in front of her face. For a split-second she had the bizarre and unsettling impression that the flea was peering in at her, assessing her. Then, as more of the insects began to settle, she gave a clenched-teeth snarl and flicked up the lever that operated the windscreen wipers.

Immediately the wipers scythed through the thickening coating of insects, reducing them to red smears. With a sense of savage satisfaction she pressed a button on the end of the wiper lever, causing jetting arcs of screen wash to cascade across the windscreen, which, combined with the wipers, made quick work of clearing the insect debris away.

By now the car was already moving, Cat having placed the gun in the central well between the two front seats so that her left hand was free to work the gears. Within seconds, as they picked up speed, the advancing infected began to dwindle into the distance behind them and the hovering cloud of insects, unable to keep up, swirled away.

Cat took a left into Davenport Road, intending to work her way home via the back streets. She wondered what she would find en route, how widespread the infection was. She couldn't believe that only eight hours ago the world had seemed normal and now it was hovering on the brink of . . . of what?

"Carlton?" she said, keeping her eyes on the road, fearful of what might suddenly lurch out in front of them.

There was no reply. She spoke his name again.

Suddenly fearful, she glanced at him, half-expecting to see him slumped motionless beside her, his mouth open, his eyes glazed in death.

But no. He was just sleeping. She could see his chest moving as he breathed, could see him grimacing with pain each time the car hit a bump in the road.

"Hey, Carlton, we got away," she said, her voice suddenly shaky. "We bloody well made it."

But then she fell silent. Had they *really* got away? Or was the night she and Carlton had just survived simply the first of many? Was the human race now at war, and if so, against what? What was this force that reanimated the dead and used them as soldiers?

A zombie war. The prospect was terrifying. Cat couldn't

imagine what it would be like to live in a world like that.

She thought of her wedding in six weeks' time. She thought of Ed.

And she wondered what would be waiting for her when she got home.

08:09 am

"OI, AL, POINT that phone over here. Come on, hurry up. And don't make it so fucking obvious. The pigs'll have it off you if they see you filming."

"They can't do that."

"You just watch 'em, mate. Fucking fascist state we're living in now. Not that we ever weren't. It's just that now the Man don't care whether the people know it or not . . . Is it on?"

"Yeah, it's filming. Just get on with it."

"All right, don't throw an eppy. You're the director. Aren't you s'posed to say 'action' or whatever?"

"Action."

"Right. Okay . . . Hello, all you people out there in YouTube land or whatever. I'm Dean, and behind the camera is my mate, Al, and we're Anarchy TV in the UK. We're here to tell you the truth, and let you know what's *really* going on behind the new Iron Curtain."

"Keep your voice down, mate. That copper's looking over here."

". . . Sorry, folks, I'm gonna have to whisper a bit. It's . . . er . . . I dunno, fucking early o'clock on . . . what day is it, Al?"

340

"May 1st."

"Oh, yeah, cool. Fucking Mayday. There should be some, like, Morris dancers and shit . . . So anyway, yeah, it's May 1st, and it's, like, eight o'clock in the morning or something, and we're here at All Hallows Church in Blackheath. This is, like, a dead old church, and the fascists have decided to knock it down so they can build a tramline for their fucking New Festival or some shit like that.

"So we're here, right, with loads of other people to stop 'em doing it. This is people power, man. This is the country fighting back against the fascists. 'Cos this is, like, *London*. This is *our* London, and *our* England, and we're not gonna be pushed around by no fucking fascist Nazis.

"Point your phone over there, Al. Let the viewers see how many people are out here today, how many *true* Londoners care about this country and about our heritage and all that . . .

"There, you see. That is people power, man. That is fucking people power. The people have spoken and they will not be silenced. My great-granddad fought in the war, against Hitler and all that, so we could be free, and we could say what we like. And no fascists are gonna stop us doing that. We are British, and we are proud."

"Okay, it's really kicking off here now, man. I don't mind saying it's getting fucking scary. Me and Al are ducked down behind a car, and there's, like, people running around all over the place. It's going mental. We're not sure what happened—"

"It was them red things. Them insects or whatever."

"Yeah, some people were saying that there were these red insects coming up out of the old graves they've been digging up or whatever, and they've been biting people and giving them rabies or some shit, and sending them mental."

"People started biting other people—"

"Yeah, all right, Al. Shut the fuck up, yeah? I'm the fucking presenter and you're the director. You do your job and I'll do mine, all right?"

"All right. I was just saying . . ."

"Yeah, well, don't. Let's just stick to what we're good at, yeah? So . . . er . . . where was I?"

"The red insects."

"Oh, yeah. So people were saying there were these red insects—"

"Coming up out of the plague pit—"

"Fuck's sake, Al! What did I say just now? *I'm* doing this. So why—? *Shit! Shit!* What was that? Was that shooting? Are the pigs *shooting* at people? I don't believe this! The fucking pigs are *shooting* people! This is fucking uncool. Can you hear that? Can you hear that screaming? This is so-called British *democracy*. The world out there needs to know about this. They need to—"

"Fuck that, Dean. Let's just get out of here."

"Okay, okay. Right, everyone out there. We're heading out. Later, guys."

"It's just me. Al's gone. He's . . . he's fucking gone, man. I don't know where he is. He got . . . there was this woman . . . this old woman. And she attacked us. And . . . and she fucking bit Al. She *bit* him right in the face. She went for him like a wild dog, and she took half his fucking cheek off. Blood everywhere, man . . .

"We were in, like, this doorway, just taking shelter from all the fucking . . . *mayhem*, and she came along, and we thought she was, like, in shock or something. So Al stood up to talk to her, see if she was all right. And next thing . . . it was *brutal*, man. I've never seen nothing like that before.

"And then Al tried to run, and the old woman went after him. And she was . . . she was *snarling*. And her eyes . . . fuck, I've never seen anyone look so . . . so *crazy*. She was just batshit

342

crazy, man. And . . . and Al ran off and I don't know where he is. But then I saw he'd dropped his phone in the road, so I picked it up. So now I'm like . . . I need to get home . . . I'm just gonna try and get home. There's, like, shooting and screaming and people running around, but . . . I can't stay here. It's like Beirut, man . . .

"So I'm gonna get home. And when I get back, I'll . . . I'll speak to you then, yeah? 'Coz maybe Al'll be back by then, and we can, like, tell you what happened and stuff. So . . . er . . . yeah, this is . . . this is Dean from Anarchy TV in the UK. Signing off for now . . . Speak to you all later . . ."

ACKNOWLEDGEMENTS

Many thanks to Duncan Proudfoot (as always), Nicola Chalton, Max Burnell, Joe Roberts, Clive Hebard, Michael Marshall Smith, Peter Crowther, Paul Finch, Christopher Fowler, Paul McAuley, Lisa Morton, John Llewellyn Probert, John Jarrold, (the real) University Hospital Lewisham and, for those who know, Nigel Kneale. Special thanks, of course, to Mark Morris for kicking off the zombie apocalypse with style and sexy nurses. Dedicated with love to the memory of Dorothy Lumley. —SJ

First and foremost I would like to thank Stephen Jones for allowing me into his apocalyptic, zombie-infested world and letting me play with all his cool toys (I hope I didn't break anything). Many thanks also to the contributors of both *Zombie Apocalypse!* and *Zombie Apocalypse! Fightback* for making "research" into it such a fun and entertaining process, and in particular to John Llewellyn Probert and Paul Finch, who not only created characters and timelines which I was able to use as a solid basis for my novel, but also provided me with additional medical/police-related pointers along the way. For further medical insights – particularly in relation to the practices and procedures of nurses, paramedics and the ambulance services – I'm hugely grateful to all those medical personnel who responded to my desperate plea for help on Facebook: Emma Fleming, Leland Rhodes, Dean Hempstead, Sam Skevington and Nigel Daniel. If I've left anyone out, many apologies – but I'm shunting the blame on to an anonymous member of a certain communication company's technical team, who, while "fixing" my misbehaving email account via remote access in November 2013, somehow managed to entirely delete my previous six months' worth of emails (even now I imagine them wandering the remote hills of cyberspace like a flock of lost sheep, bleating mournfully). —MM

Mark Morris is the author of over twenty-five novels, including *Toady, Stitch, The Immaculate, The Secret of Anatomy, Fiddleback, The Deluge* and four books in the popular *Doctor Who* franchise, two short-story collections (*Close to the Bone* and *Long Shadows, Nightmare Light*) and several novellas. His short fiction, articles and reviews have appeared in a wide variety of anthologies and magazines, and he is editor of both *Cinema Macabre*, a book of horror movie essays by genre luminaries for which he won the 2007 British Fantasy Award, and its follow-up *Cinema Futura*. His script work includes audio dramas for Big Finish Productions' *Doctor Who* and *Jago & Litefoot* titles, and also for Bafflegab's *Hammer Chillers* series. Recently published work includes an updated novelization of the 1971 Hammer movie *Vampire Circus* and a short novel entitled *It Sustains* for Earthling Publications. Upcoming is a new, as yet unnamed, short-story collection from ChiZine Publications, a novel entitled *The Black* from PS Publishing, and *The Wolves of London*, Book One of the *Obsidian Heart* trilogy, from Titan Books.

Stephen Jones is the winner of three World Fantasy Awards, four Horror Writers Association Bram Stoker Awards and three International Horror Guild Awards, as well as being a multiple recipient of the British Fantasy Award and a Hugo Award nominee. He is also the recipient of the HWA Lifetime Achievement Award. A former television producer/director and genre movie publicist and consultant (the first three *Hellraiser* movies, *Nightbreed, Split Second,* etc.), he has written and edited more than 125 books, including the *Fearie Tales: Stories of the Grimm and Gruesome, A Book of Horrors, Curious Warnings: The Great Ghost Stories of M.R. James, Psycho-Mania!* and *The Mammoth Book of Best New Horror* and *Zombie Apocalypse!* series. You can visit his website at www.stephenjoneseditor.com.